CW01636285

This is a work of fiction. Names, characters, places, and incidents are either the product of the author's imagination or used fictitiously. Any resemblance to actual persons, living or dead, events, or locales is entirely coincidental.

Cover Art by: Getcovers.com

Edited By:

Natalie Liddell - n.liddellbooks@gmail.com

R. A. HATTON

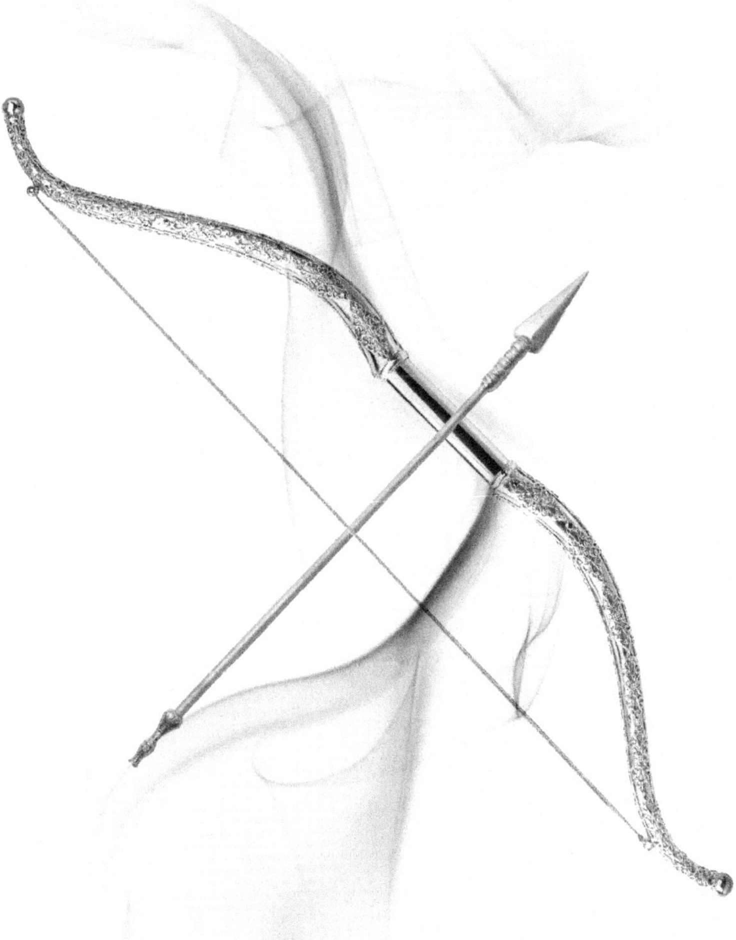

INCANDESCENT

Prologue

The End Of A Rebellion

I felt sick; my stomach twisting in knots as I signalled for my armed guardswomen to fan out within the perimeter, taking my protective position beneath the queen's balcony. My hands were shaking as I wrapped my fingers around the base of my bow, willing its magic to give me the strength I needed to see through the events of the day.

The turnout was impressive, barely a space left in the bleachers as it seemed the whole kingdom had come to The Coliseum. The large dome's circumference dominated the centre of our city. The arena was often a hive of festivities and celebratory ceremonies where elves could compete and show off their abilities. On the rarest of occasions, it was also used for more sinister purposes, such as public lashings and executions.

"Behold, the traitor of the people," Queen Callidice called. The crowd began to heckle and hiss as the guards dragged Truda out to stand in the centre of The Coliseum. They had dressed her in fine leathers, her hair slick and tied back into her usual neat ponytail. Truda held her chin high, her face as stern and intimidating as she would want them all to perceive her. Only her pale complexion and the slight stumble in her step revealed any sign of the injuries she had suffered.

Not so long ago, the same crowd disrespectfully jeering her, would have saluted and cheered harmonious gratitude for our general. Now, the kingdom believed Truda to be a traitor, holding her responsible for the death of our previous monarch, and joining the rebels.

Imelda kicked at the back of Truda's knees, forcing her to kneel, and for a moment, I closed my eyes, unable to watch their attempts to render her humbled.

"Now we cut off her head," Queen Callidice bellowed, feeding off the excitement of her audience. At the queen's command, Imelda's blade swung down and touched Truda's neck in a mock strike, slow enough for us to imagine the moment her head would be removed. I contemplated looking away, questioning whether I could truly watch the moment her life ended; A sight that would likely haunt me for years to come.

Truda would not suffer; I ensured as much by visiting her in the dungeons in the middle of the night and giving her a potion that would lessen the pain to the point of feeling nothing at all. Truda had confessed her truth to me then, elaborate stories of triumph and deceptions, and at the heart of it, a confession of a forbidden love. With a human no less. She admitted to me all the heinous crimes she had committed to free and protect him, choosing the morality of a mortal man over her duty as general.

Above me, Queen Callidice chuckled in delight as the dark mage, Freyja, muttered something in her ear. They wanted this to happen. Long before she was found to be guilty of any crimes, I knew how much they hated Truda, and would have found a way to eliminate her sooner if they could.

The number of years Truda had served this kingdom, the lives she had saved and the personal sacrifices she had made, meant nothing to them. Now she was only surrounded by those who were envious of the power she had held for so long.

I looked up to scowl at their disrespectful snickering, only to be distracted.

Black clouds were rapidly advancing above us, a torrent of heavy droplets falling from the sky. A bright light lit up the arena, followed by a deep rumble that could be felt from beneath our feet.

The walls of The Coliseum began to crack, and the crowd dispersed, desperate to find a safe exit for escape. With a thundering blast, the black gate flew from its hinges, landing in a haze of billowing dust.

A bolt of lightning scorched the ground at Imelda's feet as an elf I did not recognise entered the arena, her arms motioning as her fingers pointed skyward. Imelda stumbled away from Truda in alarm.

Instinctively, worried for her safety, I ran to Truda's aid, but another reached her first. A human, donned in a mismatch of armoured leather, scooped Truda into his arms and cradled her tightly to his chest.

I froze at the sight of them.

"Kill Truda and the intruders at once," shouted Freyja. Her conniving pet raven flew from her shoulders, its sharp talons exposed as it swooped down menacingly.

"You will not touch them," a melodic voice called, and I looked towards the strange elf as she swung her arm again, wielding lightning before our eyes and aiming it directly at the descending black raven. The bolt fried the bird to a crisp within seconds. His body fell to the ground with a heavy thud, without a single feather remaining on his scrawny body.

Freyja screamed in rage. She aimed her staff at the newcomer, wielding a flaming orb to form at her command and fired it toward the elven beauty who had killed her pet bird. With another delicate rotation of her wrist, the regal stranger created a wall of water from the downpour and effortlessly extinguished the ball of fire meant to cause her harm.

I watched, completely stunned, my gaze transfixed on the elf wielding the power of the skies. There was something inherently familiar about her. Long champagne hair cascaded down to her hips, her facial features playing on my memory. If it were not for her glazed white eyes, I would have sworn I had met her before.

"Who are you?" Queen Callidice demanded, mirroring my own curiosity, but none acknowledged her. The blonde elf strode forward gracefully, crouching as she spoke with Truda. Several mismatched armoured humans and elves were now entering the Coliseum in haste, joining the rest of Truda's newly formed party of protectors.

These must be the rebel factions, those Truda had tried to convince me were inherently good, fighting against the city with an even greater cause than those who would fight against them.

"I said, who are YOU!" Queen Callidice screamed again; her frustration evident. At the shrill of her voice, the blonde elf stood and turned towards them. As she approached the balcony, my focus was transfixed upon her as my mind reeled.

"My name is Fortuna. I am the first daughter of Queen Cassandra, born in the city of Kven and rejected by the Mages Temple."

My mouth fell open. She was Queen Cassandra's daughter! That was why I had felt a keen pull of recognition the moment I set my sight upon her.

"That cannot be, there is no way she would have survived," Freyja exclaimed in shock, and I looked at her with disdain. We all recalled the day the palace had announced Queen Cassandra was in mourning over the loss of a new-born. I had been just an elfling myself when the news of the princess's death broke across the city, though the details of her passing were never specified.

Was it possible we had been lied to?

"And I suppose you would know, as it was you who cast me out," Fortuna announced, and I could hear the audible gasps and murmurings from the guardswomen beside me.

"She was an abomination, blind, weak, and pathetic. I had to get rid of her. I was saving the city from future failures." The dark mage seethed back, and I faltered, unable to hide the anguish from my face. I was Head of the Royal Guard; it was my duty and honour to protect the true heir to the throne of Nysa. By this false monarch and black mage, we had all been deceived.

Truda had been telling me the truth all along, she spoke of the lost princess, but I had been so angry of her other confessions, I scarcely wanted to believe anything she had said.

"Guards, kill the imposters, I command it now!" shouted Freyja, and immediately I raised my hand, silently commanding my guardswomen to do otherwise. Standing before us now, was the true queen of our kingdom, this magical elf who possessed the gifts of our ancestors, and it was the royal guards' life purpose to protect her. Slowly I stepped out from beneath the balcony, raising my magical bow and taking aim towards Freyja.

"You do not command us mage," I said, as the beginnings of a gold arrow formed at my fingertips, ready to fly.

1

Nine Years Later

We were a dying species.

That was the topic of conversation none would raise at this morning's council meeting. Instead, we spoke of the sparseness of our fields and housing shortages for all unsheltered humans. No one wanted to admit we were now paying the gravest of consequences for our actions. The decisive battle between the city's armies and the woodland rebels had forever shaped our fate, beginning a new and uncertain future for our people. As with any turn of new proclamation, abandoning the old ways came with its price. Releasing the human breeders from their bonds incapacitated our ability to manipulate the natural order.

We could no longer create life.

Some sought a cure, while others advocated for a

revolution. Believing that forcing humans back into servitude was the only way to take control of our future.

All the while the rest of us contemplated our life's purpose, now our time in this kingdom was temporary, it seemed one unspoken question was more prevalent than all others.

How would we be remembered?

"Acqueline!" General Maiya barked. When silence lingered, I looked up to everyone watching me from across the table. Quickly I swallowed and straightened in my chair.

"Apologies general." I hid my nervousness for the verbal onslaught I would likely receive. Often, I am plagued by recurring thoughts of self-doubt, distracting myself while the council continued their debates on greater matters. I felt like the imposter, undeserving of a seat as an advisor at this table.

It was ironic my wavering concentration only gave her more cause to doubt my abilities, but I could not help negatively comparing myself to them. Especially to the new general whose narrowed eyes currently glared through me.

"I need more warriors; you are to present the summons to your guard," General Maiya commanded, her expression stern.

"More warriors?" I asked, immediately wincing as General Maiya raised an eyebrow.

This would be the third time in the last few moons General Maiya had made such demands, reducing the royal guard to less than a dozen. My guardswomen were worn out, deprived of sleep and rest, fulfilling duty on willpower alone. I feared the consequences of our responsibilities spread so thin.

"The rebellion is over, General Maiya, what war are you fighting exactly?" Truda challenged. A flutter of nerves flooded through me at her intervention. It was at moments like this I was reminded I was not the only elf who recognised my inadequacies. Though her intentions were honourable, Truda only reinforced my show of weakness, as I did not have the courage to protest General Maiya's orders myself.

"A good general does not wait for a war to fall on our front gates before we are better prepared for it," General Maiya replied, her impatience evident. Truda's eyes narrowed, and I could not tell if she was sensing Maiya's enigmatic disposition or concentrating on the insult hidden within her reply.

"Acqueline needs her guard. As much as you your warriors, it seems nonsensical to replenish one's numbers by depleting another's," Truda argued.

"I implore the council to trust in this command." General Maiya gave us all a challenging glower.

"Trust goes both ways," Erik added.

Up until the end of the rebellion, humans had been kept as slaves, they were our workers, our servants, and our breeders. Erik had once been appointed as Truda's breeder, it was only due to her stubbornness and duplicity that he was alive and well today.

Truda had saved his life, by almost forsaking her own.

"Maiya wouldn't ask without good reason," Cobal interjected, to calm tempers. The second human to have been granted a respectable seat at the council table. A much older human, his hair was a peppered grey, creases across nearly all the surfaces of his deeply tanned skin, and eyes the colour of clouds on a rainy afternoon.

"She would, if only to delight in the aggravation she causes," Truda accused.

"You think me to be so petty?" replied General Maiya, her plated vambrace clinking against her chest piece as she crossed her arms and leant back in her chair.

"The city has no enemies," Truda argued again, becoming frustrated at the general's unflinching disposition, her deep voice elevated and echoed throughout the high-ceilinged room. "Not unless you worry over those exiled to the woodland?"

"I am not the one who should be concerned about them."

"What do you mean by that?" Truda snapped.

General Maiya remained silent, looking upon Truda with uncharacteristic calmness, while the latter glared venomously in return, her knuckles turning white, gripping the table's edge.

Those exiled to the woodland beyond the catacombs had been condemned traitors after their betrayal to the crown and the numerous assassination attempts against our previous general. Though Truda had since passed on her title and duty over to Maiya, it was no secret the woodland elves still held a grudge against the one that had encouraged and orchestrated their exile. All of them found a common enemy in Truda.

At that moment, watching General Maiya bait Truda into mania, I feared what my friend would do if I did not intervene, and decided this, for now, was a battle not worth fighting. I could manage with the loss of another guardswoman. Even if it meant more time patrolling the palace myself.

"I will meet with my guard and request further reassignments," I replied softly with my chin tilted upward. Confident General Maiya would not relent until she had what she wanted, whether other members of the council displayed their unhappiness at her demands, or not.

"Good," she said triumphantly, concluding the discussion.

Truda turned away from me, her frustration visible. She would have me resist, to demand further explanation or refuse the order altogether, but I was not like her. I did not have it in me to openly challenge or confront authority. One wrong move would have me demoted from this table, and then I would be nothing more than a palace guard; A rank barely respectable enough to be recorded in our ancestor's history books.

Erik reached to caress Truda's shoulder and tentatively whispered in her ear as his hand lightly travelled down her arm. I watched as Truda reached up, and placed her palm over his, their foreheads touching for the briefest of moments with a look of silent reassurance passing between them.

With Erik by her side, she had become more patient, and not so brashly opinionated as she once was. There were times when it would not be so easy to diffuse her anger, when blood would have been spilt to end such altercations. It was one of the reasons why she had excelled in her authoritative position for so long.

It was only as I heard the screech of the wooden chairs sliding across the marble floor that I realised the council meeting was over. General Maiya left first without announcement, and Truda stormed out of the throne room shortly after, with an angry purpose in her stride as Erik followed closely behind.

In her absence, I noticed there were small, curved indents where Truda's fingers had pressed into the wood. It was proof Erik's presence at the table to keep her calm, was a good thing.

"Acqueline." A deep voice spoke softly, and I turned my head to find Cobal looking at me thoughtfully. "Are you alright?"

The first time we met, I did not know how to address or interpret his kindness and consideration. An elderly human who had once been a Guan; a slave raised in a kingdom as the inferior species, he should have hated us. Yet, despite all he must have lived through, he still showed compassion for all Kven's people.

Elves and humans alike.

At some point over the years in his company, I had become used to him lingering at the end of council meetings, if only to ask about my well-being. For many moons, I would reply as I believed I should, even when it was clear he could see through my automated replies. Slowly, I began to speak more openly and appreciated having him as a confidant. It was nice to have someone I was not intimidated by to talk to.

"Why the sudden need to build her army?" I whispered,

leaning towards him.

"Maiya knows what she's doing, you can trust her." Cobal stood and moved over to the vacant seat beside me.

"But it is my forces she is targeting. Does she not understand the importance of my duty?"

When General Maiya had been newly appointed, I had pledged my support and service, but she had only sneered at my gesture, disregarding the offer, and addressing me as nothing more than a commoner sitting amongst the privileged. Now she revelled in reducing my guard to inconsequential numbers, proving how nugatory and pointless my appointment to the palace was. "She despises me," I added and Cobal chuckled.

"That's just how Maiya is, she doesn't treat you any different to anybody else."

"She is kind to you," I said, airing my observations.

"Believe me, she wasn't always. I've known Maiya for a long time." His face softened as he laced his fingers together on the table. "In my many years, I've come to know elves who are monstrous, and humans willed to be subserviently obedient, but Maiya taught me we're not what they bred us to be. In the end, we get to choose."

I was bred to be a warrior.

Raised to be ruthless, merciless, and trained to wield my weapon upon our enemy without a moment's hesitation. I depict all the desired qualities of an elf; strength, skill, and beauty. Perfections that unlike most, ran only skin deep. Beneath the armoured shell, I was softened, empathetic, and as Truda often reminded me, far too amiable. Amongst my peers, my organs quaked against those inadequacies. I could scribe a list as long as my quiver of all the warriors that would do my job better than I.

In truth, I was a poor representation of what nature intended, and General Maiya knew it.

"How fares Shanon?" Cobal asked, changing the subject.

If there were one elf I would have willingly given over to General Maiya's army, it would have been Shanon. Shockingly though, those two did not get on either. Cobal's interest in the young elf's well-being was motivated by the fact he had been the one to have aided in her creation. He had been a long-term breeding slave and had likely participated in the conception of several elves and humans in his prime. Why he had taken a particular interest in Shanon's wellbeing, I could not say.

"I am sure she is delighting in tormenting someone's patience by now."

"Already? Surely it's too early?" Cobal asked, his eyebrow raised in jest.

"She would take that as a challenge," I replied, rolling my eyes.

Leaving the Throne Room, I headed straight for the gardens to attend a duty I favoured above all others, to watch over the royal family.

Mages in the city of Kven possessed extensive botanical knowledge and were able to imbue objects with special abilities, a diminished version of our ancestors. According to old transcripts, they had been so powerful, mages had once commanded the earth and skies. Queen Fortuna was the first elf in centuries to show us a true glimpse of what we had once been.

It took many of us by surprise watching her wield her magic, as she transformed what had once been a stone courtyard, into a wonderous utopia, full of lush greenery and exuberant flower beds. Where the stone had cracked, grass had grown, and the marble parted to make way for a stream to run through as plants sprouted and turned into magnificent trees within a matter of moments. Flowers of all kinds and colours, decorated every corner. Butterflies danced above the blossoms as the sun beamed down making the stream glisten and sparkle in the light.

I smiled as I saw Queen Fortuna and her consort sitting on a blanket beside the bank. Their son, Prince Felyx, paddled in the shallow water. I began to approach them before I heard a familiar yelp. I turned to find Yuki, Queen Fortuna's white fox, staring up at me expectantly with one eye. His other was covered in a small leather eye patch, a faint hairline scar ran down from behind it to his snout. I smiled and bent to one knee, my hand reaching into the crevice of my pocket.

"If I steal any more of these from the raven keeper, you will get me into trouble," I told him, flicking the dried vertebrae in the air and watching in amusement as he quickly twirled before catching it between his teeth, munching on the shell greedily. The crunching sound that followed caused my nose to crinkle.

"Disgusting," I muttered, but held my smile. Leaving Yuki with his treat, I walked over to present myself to the queen.

"Good morning your majesty." I held a closed fist above my heart. "Phoenyx, how are you both this morning?"

The queen's consort looked up, offering a polite nod of his head, before standing and walking over to where his son sat playing beside the stream.

"Acqueline," Queen Fortuna replied with a smile. "How was the council meeting?"

"Nothing of importance to relay," I replied, keeping my tone light, feigning indifference.

"That's good." Queen Fortuna bit her lip tentatively. "And no one asked of my absence?"

After her coronation, the queen had sat on the dais every morning while the council convened over city matters, but when Prince Felyx was born her attendance began to dwindle, until suddenly she stopped coming altogether.

I shook my head. "General Maiya has everything in hand," I said before retreating, worried if I lingered too long, she would soon notice my expression betraying my internal struggle.

I walked to my favourite spot in the gardens, standing beneath the largest oak, in full pink blossom, shading me from the sun's rays as I watched over the royal family.

Queen Fortuna, still so young, her innocence on display.

Scarcely would she walk anywhere without being wrapped in the arms of her human consort. Even now, as Prince Felyx and little Yuki play hide and seek in the garden brush, our queen lay on the ground with her head in her consort's lap. He picked up a book that sat in the grass beside them, beginning to read to her while his fingers ran through her silky blonde hair.

Suddenly, Prince Felyx rushed out of the water toward his parents, and his father began to laugh. As the boy launched into his arms, Queen Fortuna shrieked delightfully, droplets of water falling to her face from the prince's sodden hair and clothes. A look of overwhelming delight and love passed between the three of them.

A strange feeling pulled at my chest.

I heard someone approaching but was too caught up in watching the joyful interaction with the royal family to turn my attention.

"You spend too much time in the gardens." General Maiya came to stand beside me beneath the large blossoming tree, her hand resting on the hilt of her broad sword.

I kept my gaze on the royal family.

"Does it not warm your heart to watch them?" I asked, taking the opportunity to invite a friendly conversation.

"Are you envious?" I frowned at her deflection but answered all the same.

"Is it enviable to bask in the warmth of the sun, or to find joy in the laughter of elflings?" I returned and when she did not reply I glanced over at her. Her attention was on the royal family, her eyes following young Prince Felyx. The last human to have been born after the manumission and with it, the end of the breeding regime. A human boy, born from an elf without the aid of a magical brew, an anomaly not even the mages could explain.

"The prince is to begin training, I have assigned you to the task," General Maiya commanded.

"Would Truda not be better suited?" I replied carefully, attempting to keep my tone neutral. It was not that I was appalled by the notion of teaching the prince how to fight, but as my dutiful days seemed to extend, the moments of respite becoming fewer and farther between, I did not know how I would find the time.

"If you do not think yourself capable," General Maiya remarked slowly, leaving her sentence unfinished. A sinking feeling swooped in my gut, recognising the hidden threat behind her reply.

"Of course." I smiled, turning to face her. "I will train him with great diligence. If he is to rule one day, he will need to have a warrior's skill." Her eyes narrowed and the strangest of looks I could not identify crossed her features as she watched Prince Felyx play. Perhaps she, like many others, believed a human would never sit on the throne, regardless of the bloodline in which he was born.

General Maiya turned as if to leave but paused for a moment, her attention turning back to me.

"I expect regular updates on his progress." I bowed my head, a closed fist placed respectfully over my breastplate. "I have yet to see any new recruits Acqueline, I assume you are capable of fulfilling two commands at once?" Then without care to address herself to the royal family, she left.

2

The Sanctum

I was running, the ice-cold rain assaulting my skin like a thousand needles. The city streets were barren and full of shadow; all torchlight vanquished by the heavy downpour. My heart was a thundering drum beneath my breast as I hurled my body forward, desperately parting the tendrils of my wet hair that had stuck to my face. My thighs ached with the burn as I broke into a run.

I halted at the crossroad breathing heavily, looking between two paths. I wanted to scream, to cry out, but words were trapped in my throat, unable to escape. There was an ache that pulled at my heart, as though it wanted to be wrenched out of my body, and my skin flushed warm despite the chilling storm ransacking our city.

I felt it, the heaviness, as my eyes blurred with unshed tears.

My heart continued to hammer, pounding against bone so loud it pulsed in my ears. Lightning forked across the black veil and the booms of thunder swiftly followed.

I shot awake, my brow covered in sweat as I realised a fist was pounding in frantic thumps against my chamber door, echoing the sounds of the thunderstorm in my dream. Quickly, I clambered out of bed and opened my door to find my guardswoman, Lyzaria, standing on the threshold. She immediately bowed her head and saluted before speaking.

"My apologies, Acqueline, but there is a quarrel at the gate." I took in her flustered demeanour. Lyzaria had been in service of the palace guard for almost as long as I. Setting the highest example in symbolic proportions for an elf that represented us best, she was quiet, composed, and athletic. Highly skilled in hand-to-hand, she possessed stealth-like qualities I had not seen in any other elf amongst the guard. She took pride in her appearance, never a lock of her ash blonde hair out of place or piece of armour without its shine, but when I looked at her waist, I frowned, noticing the absence of one of her sheathed daggers.

"Quarrel?" I asked, automatically reaching for my breastplate and bow.

"Yes, Brenith needs help," she replied, her hazel eyes wide with worry.

"Elves from the market?" I hastily fastened the buckles on my armour while thinking of earlier complaints at the council meeting. Without human slaves to propagate and harvest our fields, certain essential grains were becoming harder to obtain.

"They are not elven," she replied, and my eyes widened.

"I will deal with it, follow my lead." I tried to fathom what could have caused such a stir in humans to have them act so aggressively. She nodded and immediately fell in step behind me as I charged down the dimly lit corridor.

When we reached the gate, I saw Brenith, her lance extended, thwarting the advances of a dozen humans trying to get past her. I quickly stepped forward to address them, Lyzaria following closely behind.

Suddenly I halted, almost causing my guardswoman to stumble into my back.

My body froze as my breath caught, recognition and dread assaulting me all at once.

He stood tall above the others, his face illuminated by the glow of torchlight. For a moment I hoped my eyes were deceiving me, that they were fabricating an unbidden memory. Surely, I was mistaken, this was just another ordinary human, insignificant and unimportant, but as I slowly drew closer, there was no denying it was him.

Brenith pushed forward, placing a palm against the gate to prevent it from opening further as a muscular arm stretched through the steel bars, reaching for her spear. Acting immediately, I raised my bow, taking a deep breath as the wisps of gold materialised on command, its light glow reflecting against my pale fingertips. Taking aim, I released and watched as the magical arrow landed on the ground before their feet, startling the humans enough they jumped back in surprise.

"That was a warning," I bellowed as fiercely as my voice would carry. "Step back before you learn how good my aim truly is." The lead human raised his head and our eyes locked. Of all the humans still dwelling in the kingdom that could cause trouble, why did it have to be him?

"We demand justice," he said forcefully, his tone thick with furious intent. It was obvious from his stance he was the instigator of this party, his bulky form dominating the presence of the others as he stood in front of them. His hair was the same fallow colour as the hide clothing he wore, his sleeves were rolled up to his elbows showcasing the prominent veins spanning his forearms, only mildly covered with the tattered bits of fabric wrapped around his wrists. On his shoulder, he wore a training vambrace of hardened leather, the top end curved upward to shield half of his neck. He stared at me unblinking, his menacing eyes piercing, his brow knitted with anger.

"For what?" I asked, lowering my bow slightly, but keeping a tight grip. His eyes narrowed, and when he inhaled, I saw the muscles on his large chest expand. At first, he did not reply, just stared at me; his gaze so intense I had to briefly look away.

"You will answer our questions." Brenith bellowed and I raised a hand to prompt her silence. The human watched my actions carefully, an all but brief understanding passing between us. With a nod to one of his companions, he took a step to the side gesturing for them to come forward. Two more men approached, supporting another human, seemingly injured as he struggled to remain standing.

I stepped forward, curious, and my guards tensed beside me as I examined the man more closely. There were cuts on his bare forearms, blood dripping down his feet from injuries I could not see beneath his lower coverings. Slowly and carefully, I placed my hand under his chin, raising it. His face was hideously bruised, his eyes violaceous and swollen. His nose curved unnaturally with blood cresting at the ingress of his nostrils. Patches of his thick short black hair were missing as though ripped from his scalp.

"What happened?" I asked.

"Isn't that obvious?" Their leader replied, impatiently crossing his arms.

"If it were, I would not have asked." I met his hardened gaze, ignoring the anxious glances between his companions. After a moment I turned away, feeling flustered, returning my focus to the injured human.

"This man needs a healer," I pronounced, unable to take my eyes away from his wounds. "The rest can be addressed with the council on the morrow." I removed my hand slowly, watching the human's head lull and droop. I turned behind me to face my guard. "Lyzaria." She nodded and stepped past me, but the leader took a protective step in front, the other two men affirming their hold.

"We'll not let you take him anywhere without us," he stated, stepping forward far too close for me to ignore the difference between our sizes. I straightened and craned my neck to look up at him.

"What is your name?" I asked calmly, and his eyes briefly flickered in surprise, before studying me.

"Addox," he said, after a moment.

Addox I repeated silently in my head, my heart thrumming fast. Thousands of times I had wondered what name he may have been given, testing the taste of every single one I could think of to see if any of them suited him. None of them did.

"This human needs a healer and if you instruct the rest of your following to go home, you can accompany him," I added, instantly feeling nervous at the thought of inviting him inside.

He hesitated, looking between his men and me.

"She means to deceive us," another human commented.

"What guarantee do we have of his safety?" Addox asked, drawing my attention back to him.

"I vow no harm shall come to him, or you." I took a step back, desperate to create some space between us. Addox still studied me, his gaze travelling as he looked down my armoured body. I felt a flush of heat flow through me again and my breath quickened.

Finally, with a nod to his men, Addox lifted the barely conscious man by his limp arm, supporting his weight by wrapping it across his own shoulder. Lyzaria mirrored his movements on the other side.

"Take him straight to the healer," I instructed her, and then turned my attention back to Addox, hoping the colour in my cheeks had remained a normal shade. "Do not give me cause to regret my cordiality," I warned.

"No promises," he muttered under his breath as he and Lyzaria walked past me, heading to the healer's chambers inside the palace. I watched him leave, feeling bereft from our brief interaction. After he and Lyzaria fell from sight, I waited for a moment longer, ensuring the human party did not loiter nearby before speaking with Brenith.

"I fear what may have happened if you had not arrived," she said, re-securing the threshold, her relief evident at finding no visible damage to the arched double doors or gates.

"They would not have gotten far," I replied, noticing one of Lyzaria's knives discarded to the shadows as I quickly collected it. While examining the blade, I recalled that Brenith should not have been left at her post alone and I had not instructed Lyzaria to stand in someone's stead.

"Who was supposed to be on duty with you tonight?" I asked, feeling as though I already knew the answer and dreading her reply.

"Shanon." I closed my eyes, exhaling a huge breath as I clenched my fists. I almost refrained from asking my next question knowing the answer would most definitely anger me.

"Do you know where she is?" I opened my eyes to look directly at my guardswoman as she answered.

"The Sanctum."

What had started as an enigmatic and degenerate form of

entertainment, birthed by the lack of regular championships held in the Coliseum, The Sanctum had become a delight for those who sought untamed violence.

We all knew of the elusive fighting haunt; the location was no longer a secret thanks to its growing popularity. The matter had been raised by the council several times, but it was not considered enough of a concern to act.

I knew my second was in regular attendance, another of her indiscretions I had forced myself to overlook. When I had told Cobal Shanon was likely exhausting someone's patience, this had been in no way an exaggeration. Shanon always had a fire simmering from within, but after the death of her twin, she had been unable to fully curb the rage that burnt through her. One slight push was all it took for her to forget sense and reason. Only the force behind her fists relieved her of any tension.

I had tried to take her under my wing, giving her the title of my understudy, hoping that giving her purpose would help calm her mind. It seemed she only agreed to appease me. I should have raised it to the council many moons ago that Shanon was not fit for service, but I was more concerned about what would happen if she did not have the discipline of the royal guard to distract and occupy her.

Usually, I would be furious at the thought of drudging through the city in search of my disobedient guardswoman, however, right now, I found myself thankful for the distraction taking me away from the palace and the humans now residing within.

He had changed much over the years, his body much larger and firmer than I remembered, and I had been embarrassed to find my reaction to him unchanged. I did not like that he seemed so full of fury; his muscles flexing, his posture closed and defensive, ready for conflict at any moment.

After the manumission of humans, I had thought of him more than I would ever admit. I had wondered if he still lived, but without knowing his name there had been no easy way to ascertain the truth.

I suppose, now, I have my answer.

With the dim light of the city's torches, I briskly walked through the streets whilst trying to compose my thoughts, nodding in greeting to the few figures I passed. Many elves slowed and gestured the salute of respect, while a few humans avoided eye contact, their heads bowed down low. Though no longer slaves, it seemed some customs were not easy to adopt, and I felt compelled to overlook the discretions of those who had been bred to fear us.

I approached the forge, smoke still streaming from the top of the chimney, evidence of today's smelting. The building was not so colossal in size compared to many, but unlike other establishments, it consisted of a large underground space that had been excavated for storage. One of General Maiya's first orders had been to move all the weapons into one of the old prisons, in fear that those who did not agree with the new proclamations would arm themselves and fight back. Only those she trusted the most had direct access to its facility and contents.

I pounded against the heavy wooden entrance and shortly after, it creaked open, an elven face peering just beyond the door.

"Fighter or Patron?" she gruffly asked, and my brow furrowed.

"Neither," I replied honestly, and when she looked at me confused, I realised for a moment, it may be possible she would refuse me entry. I should have thought better of my answer. "This will be my first attendance. Must I choose without having seen what your establishment has to offer?" I asked and she smirked, finding amusement in my reply. With a singular nod, she opened the door, gesturing for me to come inside.

"An elf of your rank will have nothing to prove, I am certain, but perhaps you will enjoy the entertainment."

I nodded in silence, my focus honing in on the chorus of faint shouts coming from below. Like cheers in the coliseum, albeit denser, the sound was enveloping, rather than echoing. The elf gestured to the stone stairway leading down and I began to descend. The sound of my heavy footfalls was drowned by the chants and screams coming from below.

The room, seeming much smaller than the building's exterior, was packed full of elves. The air felt thick and hot, the taste of copper and sweat lining the inside of my mouth with every breath. I pushed my way through the crowd, gaining a few disinterested looks as I went. Nobody seemed to care who I was, which only gave me more cause for concern.

Usually, the presence of a higher-ranked elf would caution even a crowd of this size, which enlightened me to believe this was not the first time a figure of great importance had been in their presence.

As I reached the edges of the mass, I saw two stocky elves engaged in hand-to-hand combat, both bruised and bloodied as they swung their fists at each other. The crowd circled around them, determining the size of their battleground. Finding discomfort in their expressions, I watched how they relished in it. The closeness in the brutality, the sound of bare clenched knuckles thumping against each other, the ground reverberating as the crowd stomped their heavy boots against the chalk-covered stone.

I looked away from the two battling and scanned the room for a familiar face. It did not take me long to find one.

She, I noticed, was not absorbed in the current violent spectacle, but was having a heated conversation with a human. He wore no protective gear, his dress plain though well put together, under his arm he clutched an odd wrap of parchments. I did not recall seeing him before, and at this distance, with so many raised voices and arms thrusting toward the ceiling in cheer, I was unable to determine the subject of their conversation.

I retreated from the edge of the ring to find an easier route through. An overwhelming roar of triumph echoed, and I was suddenly thrust against the wall by the crowd. I kept my hands firmly pressed against the stone as I regained my balance, and the elf who pushed me looked back absentmindedly for a moment before recognition hit her and her eyes widened. She extended a hand in aid, and I shook my head, refusing her assistance.

I hastened my steps to reach the other side of the room and charged the moment I saw Shanon. She did not even baulk as she caught my approach, instead, she cast the human holding the bound papers aside to better anticipate my confrontation.

"You should not be here," she stated, her voice raised over the noise of the rabble.

"You took the words right out of my mouth!" I shouted back, taking extra care to pronounce my sentence slowly over the din.

"I am where I must be," she argued, and I shook my head in anger.

"You neglected your duty and there was unrest at the palace."

"It could not have been anything too serious, you would be preoccupied otherwise." She sneered.

"I handled the situation in your stead."

"Then all is well."

"No, it is not," I said incredulously, but Shanon was not listening. She looked past me, as another round of events had begun. The human with the papers tapped her shoulder and whispered in her ear. She nodded and then turned to face me.

"I am fighting next, feel free to stay and watch." She rubbed the back of her knuckles together. I held her gaze for a moment, perplexed.

"Shanon!" I said, my tone full of dismay, as I waited for

her to see reason. I silently pleaded for her not to put me in a position where I may have to take action that would have dire consequences for us both. She shrugged, not an ounce of care or remorse, as she turned and walked away.

Frustrated, I headed back toward the exit when another figure I knew caught my attention. Immediately I recognised the two silver buns of curled hair, pinned above two prominently pointed ears, her dyed red leathers, and whips still hitched at her waist.

Peril, a previous council member, sauntered through the crowd. On either side of her, were two hardened warriors, pushing anyone aside that would prevent them from passing. Trailing behind was a tawney human in torn clothing.

"Please," he begged, his arms outstretching to get their attention. At first, they seemed to all ignore him, until finally, Peril turned to address him, her warriors assessing him with dispassion.

"He is too scrawny to be of use," one of the warriors beside her snarked.

"I can embroider and clean, I'm sure I could stitch wounds if shown how." His eyes were wide and full of pleading. Peril smirked as he submitted himself at her feet.

"All right, pet, let us find you bathed and fed. Then we shall discuss how you can pay back such kindness," she said menacingly, and I shuddered at the thought of what that could mean. The human let out a huge sigh of relief, nodding tersely as one of the warriors pulled him to his feet, all of them retreating down the corridor.

Peril had relinquished her seat on the council after she had been stripped of her title. With the end of the rebellion and the manumission of the slaves, we no longer had the need for a Master of Guans. It had been years since I had seen her, and I had found myself wondering once or twice how she had spent her days. It seemed she had found a new purpose to occupy her time.

Peril scanned the room, and I ducked out of sight, not wanting to raise any questions by alerting her to my presence. Quickly I strode toward the exit, suddenly feeling unnerved and keen to get back to the palace as soon as possible.

Standing on watch outside of the healer's chambers, Lyzaria looked tired. Her face was taut and her posture slack.

When was the last time I had given her rest from duty?

I could not deny I had been relying on her heavily of late, with Shanon's constant neglect of duty and General Maiya depleting our forces. I watched her chest rising with irregular breaths as she kept her focus forward, her exhaustion evident.

On the opposite side of the corridor, Addox stood tall with his arms crossed and his eyes open, alert, and sharp. His short, light brown hair wildly curled in all directions and coarse stubble now covering a jaw I had remembered to be smooth. He was taller than I recalled, and broader, too. I suppose it had been several years since I had last seen him, more than enough time for one's appearance to change immensely.

Taking a deep sigh, I straightened myself and aligned my shoulders to feign confidence as I strode forward. Lyzaria saluted when she saw me approach. Addox's gaze shifted, watching me stand between them.

"Has he risen?" I asked Lyzaria, gesturing toward the healer's chamber, she shook her head in response.

"It may be some time yet."

Bravely, I turned to Addox. "You should return home, we can send for you when he wakes."

"No," he said adamantly. "I'm not leaving him alone." He turned his attention towards the door.

Nervously I glanced toward Lyzaria.

"Your companion is in safe hands, my guardswomen will watch over him until he is recovered," I informed Addox, but he did not reply. Instead, his eyes flicked to mine, causing me to catch my breath.

Get it together Acqueline.

I exhaled heavily.

"The Sanctum will be dealt with," I added, feeling the need to fill the silence, in an attempt to seem unaffected by his disinterest. He raised an eyebrow confused at my comment.

"What's that got to do with anything?"

"What do you mean?" I mumbled, suddenly very aware of his scrutiny upon me.

"Why would this have anything to do with that place?" he asked again, taking a small step forward, and instinctively I stepped backwards.

“I just thought…I mean, how did he…” I began, but Addox stepped forward again, his eyes narrowing.

“He was attacked by elves and left for dead.”

“Why would they do that?”

“Because they can.”

“You saw this attack?” I asked, looking to meet his anguished expression.

“I found him after.”

“Then how do you know they were elven?”

“You honestly think a human would do this to another human?” he asked, frowning deeply in dismay. “We don’t find sport in violence like your kind do. We fight because we must.”

“Listen, I understand you are angry...” I began, but Addox cut me off for the second time.

“I really don’t think you do,” he snapped. I flinched, surprised by the hatred and hidden accusation behind his words.

I stepped back again, eager to create as much space between us as possible.

“It is late, I shall convene with the council at first light.”

“You do that,” he muttered dismissively and turned away from me.

“Should I send for another to relieve you?” I asked Lyzaria, hoping she did not think less of me for momentarily showing cowardice in front of her.

“You need not rush. I am content to stay, and heedful of another stationed in my stead who may be…” She glanced over at Addox, “less patient,” she finished, and Addox grunted. She was referring to Shanon. Not that my second was presently available for duty anyway.

“I will send someone as soon as I can,” I said, and Lyzaria nodded gratefully, holding a closed hand to her chest.

My loyal guardswoman, the epitome of what it means to be a protector of the palace and all its inhabitants. Remaining neutral, and fulfilled at the opportunity to prioritise duty over anything else. These are qualities I had desperately hoped I would possess, believing it would satisfy and fill my heart with joy, there was no greater honour to be had.

The lie I told myself to hide from my truth.

I took a final fleeting glance towards Addox, noticing him get more comfortable in his position against the wall, ignoring Lyzaria and me completely.

“I shall retire then,” I announced awkwardly, and slowly retreated down the corridor. It may have been my imagination, but as I turned the corner, I could have sworn I caught him watching me leave.

3

Footprints

The water soaked the bottom half of my leg, the splashback from the puddles seeping through the coverings beneath my boots. Running, my face mixed with the streaks of the rain and the tears that had escaped the well of my eyes. There was an ache that pulled at my heart, my breathing ragged and desperate. I paused at the familiar crossroads, unable to determine which path I should take.

I opened my mouth to scream, but no sound left my lips as the intense anguish enveloped me. I clenched my fists in frustration, only to realise there was something between my fingertips. I looked down to see a singular piece of paper, ink bleeding through the sodden parchment, rendering the words unreadable. Lightning forked across the black veil again and the booms of thunder swiftly followed with a strange rhythm.

I woke and immediately looked down at my hands, the feeling of the saturated parchment still lingering between my fingers. I sat up, swinging my legs over the side of the bed, enjoying the cold marble floor beneath my bare feet. I swept my hair to one side of my neck, my skin feeling hot and streaked with sweat.

Mornings were getting heavier; the eagerness I held in my youth of getting up and adorning my armour was gradually waning. In the past, I would have looked proudly and frequently at my mirrored reflection. Now, I felt as though my armour was merely a metal casing, holding nothing substantial beneath it.

My chambers, adjacent to the palace east tower, were furnished humbly, bearing only the essentials.

I grew up with much more humble beginnings than most of the warriors I knew, a modest life with two loving mothers and no household Guans. It made it easier to adopt a life with little attachments. Aside from the ceremonial custom-crafted armour and the magically imbued red-winged bow, my chambers were much like my family home.

Devoid of luxuries and sentiments.

As I approached my armour stand, I stiffened. I noticed my door was slightly ajar. I had been certain I had closed it on my return, but then, I was so overwhelmed with yesterday's events, perhaps I had just forgotten. Barefoot, I tiptoed and peered down the empty corridor and closed the door, giving myself the privacy to don my armour.

I dressed swiftly and without ceremony. I was a half

measure compared to my peers, shorter, with a dainty, childlike appearance. My eyes were a dusty brown and my hair the same shade. Even the point of my ears were less prominent than most.

I pressed my palm across my face, feeling completely overwhelmed as I thought of all I needed to address today.

The council needed to put an end to The Sanctum.

They needed to be notified of the attack and the injured human.

I had to confess of Shanon's disobedience and neglect of her duty.

Where would I even begin? How could I articulate the importance of each matter? There was only one whom I could turn to for advice in times like this. Though not much older, Truda had been a mentor for much of my life and was the elf I would often seek when I felt confused or needed guidance. I only hoped she could counsel me on what to do now.

I made my way down the cobblestone paths, past the closed market square, and beyond. The streets were empty, the evening torches still lit from the night before. The glow of the flames matched the rising colour of the dawn; at least I still found the freshness of a cool spring morning pleasant.

In the past, Truda and I would often rise early to spar together in the Training House, a routine I frequented less and less the more our duties distracted us from one another.

Truda spent much of her time training humans these days, which was why, despite the earliness of the hour, I knew I would still likely find her there.

As I turned the corner, my steps slowed, noting a cloaked figure approaching the Training House. She wore full leathers, sandals and a cloak covering most of her torso. Her long blonde locks parted in two plaits falling down either of her shoulders.

The hairs prickled on the surface of my skin.

What was she doing here?

Was she looking for me? I squashed the idea the moment I had it; far too much time had passed for her to seek me out now. I took a moment while her back was turned to focus on my breathing and compose my sudden nerves. Quieting my steps, I hoped I could slip past unnoticed.

"Quin?" she asked, with a slight gleeful surprise in her tone. I paused, turning to face my once-best friend, Lelane. My stomach twisted in knots the moment my auburn eyes met her fervent green. She blinked a few times in rapid succession, both of us a little startled and clearly speechless.

"It has been many years," she said politely, with a sort of fondness I did not expect from her. I felt unbalanced, avoiding eye contact as I strode past her towards the large double doors of the Training House.

"Have you nothing to say to me at all, not even a pleasant greeting?" she called, her tone laced with a hurt that was all too familiar.

I hesitated, wanting to turn around and speak, but as

images of her trembling lips and tears came to me unbidden, I was completely lost for what to say. Instead, I strode up the steps, pulled open the doors and rushed inside the Training House, letting them slam shut behind me.

I winced, as I pictured what she must think.

Why could I not greet her pleasantly as I would any other and then go about my business? How long will it take for me to move past this and not reimagine the scene a dozen times with all the responses I should have made?

I glanced back at the door, with the brief imagining it would open; that she would enter to seek me out. Thankfully the door remained closed, and I let out a sigh of relief and walked further into the Training House. Immediately I squealed and shielded my eyes at the sight of Truda's uncovered breasts, and Erik on his knees before her.

"Acqueline! Did you not think to knock?" Truda exclaimed, standing unashamedly half-naked in front of me.

"This is a public house!" I argued, squeezing my eyelids shut behind my palms, desperate for as many protective layers as possible. "I should go," I quickly added, spinning on my heels.

"No, it is fine, just give us a moment to dress," Truda said, and I could hear the distinct sounds of buckles refastening and leather rebinding. "I am surprised to see you rise so early for training." She sounded mildly irritated.

"That is not why I came."

"I see." I bit my lip to hide back a groan at how awkward I felt at that moment. "We are presentable, you can turn around now." With great hesitancy I parted my fingers and peered through with one open eye, finding Truda and Erik standing fully clothed.

"Sorry, we weren't expecting company," Erik said, his cheeks reddened, having the grace to show embarrassment.

"I noticed, and if circumstances were different, I would be inclined to leave you to your privacy, but I am afraid I come with disturbing news."

"The queen?" Truda asked in a rush.

"Is fine," I replied quickly, "But, there was a disturbance. Last night a human was brought to the palace, half dead and on the verge of unconsciousness."

"What?" Truda snapped.

"He was in the company of a dozen humans, all enraged and demanding immediate justice. My guard barely managed to prevent them from barging through." I still hoped I had not made another monumental error by allowing Addox inside.

"Who attacked him?" Erik asked, his face marred with concern.

"We do not know, but it is possible the perpetrators were elven," I answered, thinking of how Addox had challenged my assumptions otherwise. "We took the injured to the healer's chambers. Another human by the name of Addox accompanied him." At the mention of his name, Truda's gaze quickly shot to Erik's, a slight frown on her features, piquing my interest. "What should I do?"

"We should keep this between us for now," Truda said sternly, her voice lowering slightly.

"What of General Maiya?" I asked. "It is our responsibility to report such incidents to her." Truda stepped forward and placed a tentative hand on my shoulder.

"And what do you think she will do with this information?" she asked, her tone indignant. "You are under enough scrutiny as it is, we should not draw any further attention to your weaknesses." I flinched, instantly feeling a pang of anguish at her words. I knew Truda did not mean to insult, she was just imparting the truth, but her reaffirmations of my inadequacies stung all the same.

"Besides," Truda continued, "Maiya still gives no explanation as to why she keeps reassigning your guard to her ranks and I think it is time we consider whether she is to be trusted at all."

"Then, what do we do about the humans?" I asked. "Addox will not leave until his companion shows signs of recovery and if they stay, General Maiya is bound to notice."

"I can talk to him," Erik offered.

"It would be better for all if the injured human and Addox were moved to Tobias's House," Truda added, her comment directed towards Erik, and in return he gave her an affirming nod.

"You need not worry, Acqueline, trust Erik and me to handle this situation."

We returned to the healers' chambers in haste, neither of

us striking up conversation with one another as Erik and I approached the healer's chambers. I was grateful to not find Lyzaria present, assuming she had finally taken my heed and retired to get some much needed rest. Brenith stood on guard in her stead, offering a salute as we approached. I felt my breath catch and the hair on my arms prickle as Addox came into view, his gaze intense as we strode towards him. It was not until Erik cleared his throat that I realised I had stopped walking and had frozen in front of Addox, the pair of us just staring at each other.

"I will give you a moment to talk," I said, gesturing for Erik to step forward. Addox studied me a moment further and I moved away to give them privacy.

"How long have you been on duty?" I asked Brenith.

"Since the early hours, Lyzaria had already retired by the time I got here… I confess, it is a dull duty in comparison to yesterday."

"Let us hope that continues," I replied, glancing over my shoulder towards Addox, who was now in a rather heated discussion with Erik.

"He should be moved to Tobias's House. He will be safe and cared for there," I overheard Erik say.

"You didn't see him Erik, he was near dead when we found him," Addox replied, his husky tone barely above a whisper.

"Then, the sooner we get him transported the better."

"He won't make the journey. I'm not leaving his side until he wakes, and we find out who's responsible."

"You should ask the healer," I suggested, drawing both

of their attention towards me, Addox scowling at my eavesdropping. "She can determine whether he is safe to be transported."

"That's a good idea," Erik said, glancing toward the chamber door.

"She is not there," Brenith advised, suddenly interrupting the conversation.

"What do you mean?" I asked, all of us looking towards her.

"I passed her on my way here, she said she was heading to the Mages Temple to gather more healing supplies."

"But I heard movement inside the chambers," Addox said.

"If he were awake, would he not have called out for someone?" Erik asked.

Suddenly, Addox rushed for the door, barging through. The three of us followed closely behind. Immediately my attention was drawn to the distinguished wet footprints on the stone floor that led to the open bay window. They were evenly spaced as though not hurried, demonstrating the calmness in which the impressions were left.

Small footprints laid in red.

Erik and Addox's attention were drawn to the pale body lying still on the small cot bed. A trail of blood still flowing steadily from his lacerated throat. A puddle spread across the floor, undisturbed aside from the footprints. The perpetrator had watched the human bleed out, waiting for a pool thick enough to submerge their feet, purposely leaving their mark as though it were a game.

"You promised he'd be safe!" Addox snarled, his expression thunderous. Charging forward, he clutched the top of my chest piece and thrust me back against the wall with force. "Made a vow no harm would come to him." He seethed, lifting me from the ground, showing his strength, his grip tight against my armour. Behind us, I caught sight of Brenith raising her spear at Addox and I instantly displayed my flat palm, silently instructing her to stand down.

"I never meant for this…" I started, but Addox cut me off, baring his teeth.

"You lie!" he snapped. His face now so close to mine I could feel his hot breath against my skin.

"Addox, Acqueline wouldn't have ordered this, it's her life's duty to protect people," Erik interjected.

"Elves, Erik, the royal guard protects elves." He slowly released his grip on me, his fingers uncurling from the ridged edge of my breastplate, stepping back. "They don't care what happens to humans, we are worthless creatures in their eyes."

"It's not like that anymore," Erik argued.

"Isn't it?" Addox said, pointing toward the lifeless body. "We're at their mercy. It's always going to be like this."

"Where're you going?" Erik asked as Addox began to back away, his nostrils flaring as he took a final glance at the lifeless body lying on the cot.

"To do what you won't." His eyes briefly flicked towards mine.

"Addox, wait!" Erik called, but he did not listen, his fists clenched as he shoved his way past Brenith. Erik reached out to grab him, but his fingers grazed against his tunic.

"Let him go," I said calmly, pressing my palm gently against Erik's chest.

"He should be apprehended, punished for his insolence," Brenith mumbled, and I ignored her, instead, stepping closer to the deceased. His eyes open, his face already sunken and gaunt.

Elves did not value human life the same way they did their own, at least not for the most part. When an elf was born, we would name them after our mothers, or a legendary warrior written in old scriptures. When we died, there would be a day of mourning, their vessel given an honorific place of rest. Stories were written by scribes or temple acolytes and stored in the great library, leaving them readily available for any to research the origins of their ancestry.

Human births were recorded only for logistical purposes, noting the details of their bloodline when arranging breeders. We did not want an elf to become pregnant by a human that may have been birthed by their grandmother.

When a human died, there were no stories.

No elflings or humans are named after them.

Their bodies were cremated in the last clothes they wore and wholeheartedly forgotten about.

Addox had been right to be angry. He had been born into a cruel kingdom, where one species considered themselves superior. We determined the rules and cultivated the culture to revere one kind over the other, singularly to our own benefit. There would not be many elves mourning the loss of one human, no matter how he died.

"Truda won't like this, I thought this senseless violence was behind us," Erik said solemnly, raising the furs to cover the human's upper body.

As the fabric covered the human's lifeless eyes, I realised someone was making a show of power. They trespassed into the guarded palace, murdered him, and left the body purposely to be discovered as though they were taunting us.

"What should be done with him?" I asked, not ready to air suspicions, nor discuss implications.

"We have a small garden beside Tobias's House, I'll bury him there," Erik replied.

When Truda had lost her first human servant during the rebellion war, she honoured his memory by naming a building after him. Tobias's House. With dozens of chambers and a dining hall large enough to feed double the number of humans living there, a refuge and sanctuary for all humans.

"Did you know him?" I asked, and immediately regretted my question, as though I would so naively presume all humans would know each other.

"Our paths crossed once when he was a boy. I knew his master."

"What is going on here?" the healer said sternly, slowly re-entering her chambers. "I left clear instructions for the human to not be disturbed."

"He's dead," Erik replied.

"How…" she began, immediately stunned into silence at the grim sight of the deceased.

"Clean and dress him," I instructed the healer, then turning to Brenith, I added, "Help Erik to deliver him to his place of rest, I will fulfil the rest of your duty for today."

After another long day of duty without rest, I approached my chambers, too exhausted to contemplate doing anything but sleeping once I arrived. As I turned the corner, Shanon came into view, and I greeted her weakly but made no pause to stop.

"Are you not going to ask me how my fight went?" she asked as I walked past.

"I imagine you would not bring it up if the outcome was not what you wanted."

"There certainly is some truth in that," she replied, falling in step beside me. "Heard about the dead human." I gave her a sideways glance, frustrated she did not show an ounce of compassion or even bother to give me so much as an apology for her misgivings or interest in the duty she had neglected. "Wish I had seen it, sounded gruesome."

"Cobal has been asking after you," I said, ignoring her contempt. Shanon rolled her eyes, feigning defiance. "He would be displeased with your participation in The Sanctum."

"It is none of his business."

But it is mine, I thought, though I remained quiet. I wanted to tell her how unacceptable it was for her to abandon her duty to participate in the barbaric fights. I could have used her help last night. The palace was my responsibility, and I had once again demonstrated a lack of control over everything that happened within it.

"Wonder why someone wanted him dead," she said, persistent in her own inquisition.

I had not really considered the reason why someone would go to such great lengths, assuming it was down to the prejudice most humans expected.

"Perhaps he knew the identity of the persons who beat him?" I suggested, the only reason that came to mind. A killing would be the simplest solution to cover up a crime committed.

Shanon shrugged. "I bet that was not the reason he was killed."

"I am more concerned over the safety of the royal family," I replied. "As you should be."

"Queen Fortuna can take care of herself, she does not need us."

"That is not for you to decide," I said, my patience growing thin.

"Does she know about the dead human?"

"No," I quickly replied, pausing in my stride, and turning to face Shanon. "I think it is best that she does not learn of it for now, I do not want to worry her."

"Not that she would do anything anyway," Shanon scoffed. "She is too preoccupied playing happy families to care about the broken kingdom she inherited."

"You should not be so thoughtlessly cruel, you know she

was not prepared for this," I said in Queen Fortuna's defence.

"Neither was Maiya, but she seems more than settled in her new role."

"That is entirely different. General Maiya is…"

"A hellion?"

"No, that is not what I—"

"A tyrant, and most definitely arrogant," she teased, and I sighed in irritation.

"Experienced," I replied after taking a long breath. "She is already a respectable leader."

"I do not see how orchestrating a rebellion earns respect." She referred to the fact General Maiya had indeed, for over two decades, coveted a myriad of rebellious elves. Shanon had her own burdens to bear when it came to the rebellion, her actions causing the most grievous of consequences. By giving up secrets she had been entrusted with, the events that followed resulted in her twin sister being killed, a truth I would never use against her in fear of the hurt it would cause.

"General Maiya fought to protect her people, you could not ask for a greater sacrifice from any leader."

"She incited war, while others worked for peace."

"There are many who would disagree with you," I replied, choosing my words carefully.

"Let them, it does not change where Maiya came from nor what she did, and we would be foolish to forget that," she replied sardonically.

"General Maiya makes her commands with the interests of the people at heart."

"Which people would that be?"

"That is enough, Shanon," I said, running a hand down my face and becoming too weary to listen to her any longer. "You should return to your post."

"Fine. This conversation was becoming tiresome anyway," she replied, disgruntled, and I immediately felt guilty for my rudeness.

"Shanon, wait!" I called. She swivelled, giving me a brattish look. "You should give Cobal a chance, he cares for you," I told her, thinking if I could not get through to her, perhaps her father could.

"Sure, whatever," she said and walked out of sight, leaving me alone in the quiet.

I would have to deal with Shanon sooner rather than later. It had been many years since she lost her sister and the hate and vengeance continued to twist in her gut. She sought more dangerous challenges elsewhere and had lost her discipline and practised mind. I kept meaning to confront her about it, but I had been avoiding broaching the subject, and over the years her attitude had only gotten worse.

As I finally headed toward my bedchamber, the darkness and silence lingering, I felt a sudden sense of unease. Instinctively I looked behind, expecting to see someone there, but found nothing other than unmoving shadows and flickering torchlight.

Still, the hair prickled on my skin, my instincts certain I was not alone.

"Hello?" I called, my voice echoing through the corridor,

but there was no response, everything was seemingly as it should be. Ignoring the shudder that ran through me, my grip instinctively tightened on my sheathed dagger and just as I stepped forward, a hand clamped firmly over my mouth, a large body pressing into me from behind.

"Finally, you're alone," a gruff male voice whispered into my ear.

With a thrust of my elbow into his gut, I wrenched myself from his tight grip, spinning around to come face to face with Addox. He leapt forward to grab me again and I vaulted back out of his reach.

"You're fast," he coughed, one hand cradling his side where I had winded him.

"How did you get in here?" I raised one hand defensively.

"Maybe I never left?" He countered, something flickering in his eyes.

"You are stalking me?"

"You're not what I expected," he said, not denying anything.

"I have no expectations at all when it comes to humans." I kept my voice stony. "You all look the same to me."

"Is that right?" He crossed his arms defiantly, as though he was not standing in the middle of the palace corridor, openly challenging a royal guard.

"Yes, so go back to where you came from before I have you detained," I replied, swallowing past my sudden dry throat. He tilted his head, smirking as he watched me carefully, and I felt that familiar tremor run through me.

"You're a bad liar, little elf," he said with conviction.

"What do you want?" I was desperate to change the subject. His gaze turned serious, and he took an intimidating step forward, reminding me of our size difference. I gripped the hilt of my blade.

"Outside the healer's chambers, you brought up The Sanctum," Addox said, his tone firm as he added, "why?"

"I thought your companion had been fighting," I replied honestly.

"Humans are not bred for battle."

"Then why wear armour?" I noted he was still donned in hardened leathers and vambrace.

"Would you rather I be wearing something else? Chains and a loin cloth perhaps?" he retorted and my mouth fell open.

"No. That is not what I was—" I mumbled, but he cut my sentence short.

"What did you see in The Sanctum?"

"Why should I tell you anything?" I kept my focus locked on him, sensing that if I glanced away, even for a moment, he would advance on me.

Before he could reply, the sound of heavy boots reverberated down the corridor.

"Acqueline! You must come quick, the queen is distressed, she is destroying her chambers!" Lyzaria shouted in panic. I was about to ask her what she meant when the stone trembled beneath my feet, the whole palace seeming to vibrate. I turned to Addox, but he was gone; returned to the shadow. Deciding not to waste time and dwell on where he had gone, I sprinted behind Lyzaria, not stopping for breath as I headed towards the queen's tower.

4

Propositions

Her bedchamber door was already ajar and immediately I saw our young queen cradling her knees while her consort stroked her back trying to soothe her.

"She just woke up screaming, I didn't know what to do," Phoenyx said, his clothes dishevelled as he knelt on the rumpled furs, I could see the desperation in his eyes. The room was a mess, with broken ceramics and books shredded and strewn about as though a storm had erupted.

"Your majesty?" I stepped tentatively inside her chambers.

"Acqueline," she sniffled, looking up, her cheeks streaked with tears. "I'm so sorry."

"Are you okay? Would you like me to send for someone?" I asked, approaching her bedside.

She shook her head.

"Then at least let me summon chamomile leaves to aid your sleep," I offered, glancing to Lyzaria, who nodded before retreating. "Can you tell me what happened?"

"I was dreaming, and then I saw them," she said, her chin resting on her knees. Seeming so small and vulnerable in that moment, she reminded me how wrong Shanon had been to presume Queen Fortuna had no need for our protection.

"Who?" I straightened a fallen chair from the floor and took a seat near the bed.

"My sister and the dark mage. They were executing everyone I loved, just as they had threatened they would," she whimpered, her lip trembling and Phoenyx leaned in to hold her tighter.

"It was just a nightmare, your majesty. None of that was real."

"But I murdered them." She cried, fresh tears welling in her eyes. "I used my power and watched as they were crushed to death in the rubble."

"You didn't murder anyone, you saved us," the queen's consort said.

"Phoenyx is right. You only used your magic to protect those you care about."

"I am a danger to this kingdom."

At her declaration, I stood, striding the small distance, and perched at the edge of her bed.

"You are a gift, your majesty. I will not have you thinking otherwise."

After a moment Queen Fortuna gave me a small smile,

her hand reaching out to hold mine.

"I'm glad you are the one to train Felyx," she said, changing the subject.

"It is a pleasure and a joy," I replied, bowing my head.

"I know Maiya disagrees, but I told her I wouldn't see him train with anyone else."

I straightened, trying to hide my embittered struggle. Though it came as no surprise, it still hurt that General Maiya had spoken of my incompetence. I wondered who she would have deemed worthy in my stead. "He has a soft heart like his mother," she continued, her tone full of apathy. "Anyone else would treat him too harshly, I think."

"I only want what is best for him," I said softly, feeling honoured. At least the queen has faith in my abilities.

"If something happens to me, will you protect him, forever and always?" she asked with such earnestness I found myself surprised.

"Your majesty, nothing is going to happen to you," I said, worried over the desperation in her tone.

"But if it did, do you vow to watch over him?" Her hand gripped me tightly.

"I will protect him with my life," I said, meaning every word.

"Thank you Acqueline, you don't know how much it means to me to hear that." She seemed to relax slightly. "Promise you won't share my night terrors with anyone," she pleaded, and I vowed to keep her secret safe.

When Lyzaria returned, placing the pot of leaves on a

small table, the queen's consort rose and began brewing the tea. I discreetly gestured for my guardswoman to follow me outside.

"We must be more vigilant in our patrols. Secure every door and window that is not in frequent use." If both a murderer and Addox could so easily slip past our defences, then I had more cause than ever to worry over the safety of the royal family. I could not deny this visit had left me shaken.

"Of course, it shall be done."

Prince Felyx was excited and full of energy when I collected him and Yuki from the gardens, talking animatedly as the young boy questioned our training plans with unending curiosity.

"Will I get armour?" he asked.

"Padding," I corrected, hoping I could find protective leathers that would fit a human of his age. "Training with armour comes much later when you are well-practised."

"I want green armour as bright as a flower stem. So, everybody will know it's me, even from very far away."

"It is not such a good idea to make yourself so easily identifiable," I replied and Prince Felyx looked up with a puzzled expression.

"Why not?"

"What if you are on the battlefield? An enemy will know exactly who to target and end a war before it ever truly began."

"Maiya has gold armour and Truda's is blue," he points out. "And they fight battles."

Yes, but they are seasoned elven warriors and wear their colours as an invitation for those who would dare to think themselves a worthy opponent. Of course, I do not mention this to the prince in fear I would knock his confidence.

"A prince is much more valuable than a general," I said instead. "I would challenge you to consider what example you would set to those who would look to you for leadership.

The rest of our journey was silent as the prince stared ahead; his light brows furrowed, and he bit his lip in concentration. Yuki weaved in and out of his legs, attempting to gain his attention.

As we approached the Training House, I noticed a familiar figure lurking nearby. It was Lelane, she was here again.

This time I did not pause, continuing forward directly into her path. At first, she paid me no heed. Her body leaning, oblivious of my approach, she was distracted by her inquisitive search beside the structure.

When she noticed me, her expression saddened in recognition, and she turned away abruptly.

"I was just leaving," she said as she began to back away, raising her closed fist to her chest respectfully.

"Wait," I said, clearing my throat. Pausing, she straightened and met my gaze, "Prince Felyx, go on ahead, I will join you in a moment." He followed my direction without question, Yuki bounding inside after him.

"I apologise for how I acted before. I had not expected

to see you here," I admitted. Her expression turned passive, making it difficult to determine if she thought my comment to be sincere.

"It has been a long time," she replied, looking down at her hands as she spoke.

"That it has."

"You look well."

"As do you." Neither of us were able to hold eye contact for more than a few mere moments. Perhaps if I had acted appropriately the other day, this secondary greeting would have seemed less awkward.

After another bout of silence, and conscious of leaving Prince Felyx alone for too long, I moved to suggest I needed to leave. "I must go, I have business inside." Lelane looked towards the Training House.

"Of course, some things never change," she mumbled. I inhaled a sharp breath, as a feeling I thought I had long forgotten washed over me — a time when those words from her had caused great pain.

I walked past her, but as I began to ascend the stairs to the Training House entrance, I felt suddenly angry. Insulted she would speak to me this way after my sincerity, I spun on my heels and quickly marched back down the steps.

"I cannot believe you just said that." She paused, utterly surprised by my outburst.

"Would you rather I ignore you then, as you did me?"

"You asked me to stay away!" I did not like the tone either of us were taking with each other, but it seemed we were helpless against the accusatory anguish.

"And you kept that promise," she replied, resolute.

"Was losing my best friend not punishment enough? Did you come here to add insult to injury?" Stunned, her mouth parted as she exhaled an exasperated breath.

"Quin, I would never," she said, her features torn.

Quin.

I closed my eyes at the memory of that nickname and calmed immediately, reflecting on the ridiculousness of our current situation.

"I am sorry, it has been a trying day." A simple sentence that would offer the perfect cover for an array of impractical emotions.

"No, this was my fault," she replied with sincerity, no longer any trace of malice in her voice. "I knew there might have been a chance I would see you here and still I found myself unprepared for what to say." I nodded in agreement.

"What brings you here?" I asked, keeping my voice soft.

"I am looking for someone."

"Behind the Training House?"

"Sometimes," she muttered.

"Can I help?"

She shook her head. "I do not mean to keep you from your duties. It was good to see you, Quin."

I frowned as I watched her disappear out of sight, wishing I had said something more to keep the conversation going. Could things be different between us now we were no longer the same as we were?

It would be nice to have Lelane in my life again, a thought I supposed would be foolish to hope. With a heavy sigh, I turned and headed inside the Training House.

"Close one, Your Majesty," I teased, as Prince Felyx and I played a game of chase as a training warm-up. Both his arms outstretched, he lunged at me again and I laughed, dodging his advances easily. Yuki yelped playfully as he watched intently, crouching with his tail in the air as though he were preparing to pounce.

"Stay!" I commanded, pointing my finger at the white fox. He ignored me until I hovered my hand over my left pocket and immediately, he lowered. His singular eye was keenly focused on my next move. I shook my head in amusement and retrieved a dried insect, tossing it over to him.

When Truda arrived, she greeted us eagerly and promised to spar with the prince after he had learned how to wield a blade well enough. He seemed delighted at the thought.

I led Prince Felyx over to the weapon rack and gestured towards the stand of wooden swords. He frowned and pointed towards the steel blades, and I heard a chorus of chuckles from behind me.

As more warriors arrived, many began to gather, curious to watch the beginning of the young prince's training. Although Prince Felyx seemed to like the attention, I worried about what they thought of him, the boy without pointedly prominent ears; instead rounded like an ordinary human's.

There were still many who would gaze at him with scrutiny; the first royal to be born human. He would have much to prove as he grew. I retrieved one of the smaller carved wooden replica swords and extended it to him, hilt end first.

"Show me you can expertly wield this, and we shall further explore the racks of weaponry." He nodded and gripped the handle firmly with both hands.

Suddenly the Training House doors burst open, and a group of rowdy humans entered, one of which I instantly recognised. Donned in the same leathers as before, Addox strode through the building with swaggering confidence in his step, his companions by his side. Addox scanned the room, his gaze instantly catching mine and I noticed the corner of his mouth lift slightly in amusement at my stunned reaction.

"Acqueline?" Prince Felyx asked, and I turned, smiling brightly at him. Selecting a wooden replica of my own to train with, I pretended to ignore the presence of the humans and instructed Prince Felyx to mirror my movements. I stretched my arm and delicately rotated my wrist. At first, he seemed to struggle to hold the sword one-handed, little creases forming at the bridge of his nose in concentration. Once he fell into a rhythm, he beamed, speeding up as he swung the sword back and forth, becoming comfortable with the weight.

From my peripheral, I watched as Addox and the others joined Truda at the other end of the courtyard. For a moment, I wondered what he was doing here, until suddenly the humans spread out into a formation before Truda. They were part of her elite, the faction of humans she had been training since the end of the rebellion, and Addox was one of them.

"This is easy, I'm ready for a real sword now," Felyx chimed.

"I am ready," I corrected, still glancing cautiously behind me. Addox had his back to me, focusing only on Truda's instruction. "There is much more for you to learn about sword fighting," I added.

"I can do it," he exclaimed.

"Then come little prince and show me what you are capable of." I chuckled, displaying my sword defensively at him. We sparred a little, with Prince Felyx lunging haphazardly as I deflected his strikes, keeping my attention only on him as I delighted in the distraction he provided.

The boy was eager to absorb any knowledge I would impart to him, and I found that revelation was addictive. After a long while, I let him stop for a moment of rest, reminding myself he was still so very young. Approaching his seventh year of life, his features still plump and rounded, we all pondered what he would look like fully grown.

"You are good with him," Truda said, causing me to flinch in surprise as she suddenly appeared by my side.

"You sound surprised," I replied, nervously, both our gazes looking toward Prince Felyx as he refilled his water decanter.

"Not at all, his enjoyment of your instruction is enlightening." I raised an eyebrow towards her.

"He is more eager than my last student."

"So, I see," Truda replied, pointing at the young prince who was now twirling whilst enthusiastically waving the wooden sword, forcing Yuki to leap out of the way to avoid getting struck. "You should let my students demonstrate their skills to the prince, it may inspire him," Truda suggested, gesturing to the humans sparring against each other. My heart rate increased as I searched for one face in particular, my breath catching suddenly when our eyes locked.

Swiftly, I looked away.

"You still train the humans?" I said, feeling his eyes boring into me from behind.

"Of course, where they are lacking in strength, I have taught them to be cunning. Where they are flawed, I have directed them to reproach defensively and to be observant. To allow their opponent to underestimate them but not rely on that advantage." I nodded, unable to prevent myself from glancing over again, thankful to find his attention now drawn to another.

"And Erik?" I turned to face Truda.

She smiled endearingly at my question.

"His heart belongs to the infrastructure of the city, he works tirelessly to maintain its beauty, he is not a warrior."

"I hear Tobias's house is finished, Cobal speaks highly of it."

"Then he should say so to Erik directly, he would appreciate the praise for his accomplishments."

"And what of yours?" I resisted the temptation to glance at Addox again. "Do you still have plans to present the human elite to General Maiya?" I asked, but Truda had stopped paying attention to me, instead, she scowled.

"Get out!" she bellowed angrily, a furious look stretching across her features. The Training House fell silent, all eyes turning to watch Truda stride forward with her finger pointing towards the entrance. "You are not welcome here," she roared.

I stepped to the side to follow her gaze, catching only a glimpse of long wisps of blonde hair from a figure no taller than Prince Felyx, swiftly retreating. Truda's eyes were wild and furious, her hands clenched as she stared at the space where the trespasser had been standing.

"Gotcha!" Prince Felyx cried joyfully as I felt a light whack across the back of my leg. The action made me jump, and I turned to find a gleeful prince aiming the point of the small oak sword at me.

Truda walked away in silence, disappearing into a back storage room. I watched, confused as she left, until my focus was drawn to Addox, my heart thrumming loudly as his dark eyes studied me.

"So, you did," I said, putting on a fake reassuring smile, turning my attention back to the prince.

"Can I have a real sword now?"

"Not today my prince, you still have much to learn." He pouted. "We should return to the palace." He nodded silently, his disappointment evident from his expression. "Although," I added, "I may need your help since you have severed one of my limbs." Prince Felyx laughed proudly.

"You could hop?"

I chuckled. "Back to the palace? I am not sure it can be done."

"I could do it!" he exclaimed.

"That my prince, you will have to prove," I said playfully. At that, he enthusiastically took off, hopping on one leg, and forgetting I am the one with the supposed compromising injury.

As we left the Training House, Yuki caught sight of a moving shadow, his hackles rising, and he bared his teeth, growling down the dark cast alley.

"Wait here," I instructed Prince Felyx, speaking softly as I crept towards the dark shadows cast by the looming buildings. I was almost startled when a human stepped out from the darkness. His feet bare, his trousers long and torn at the ankles, he was wearing a cropped tunic which revealed a smooth toned stomach.

"Have you need of something?" His voice was gentle and soft, only just above a whisper.

"No, I…" I tried to look past him but saw nothing. "I thought I saw something."

"If you're lonely, I can provide comfort," he said, his hand reaching for me. I flinched back, and my eyes widened. Quickly I withdrew from the alley, feeling awkward at the human's advances.

"What was it?" Prince Felyx asked, curious and trying to peer past me.

"Nothing." I ushered him forward. My hands pressed

lightly against his shoulder to encourage him to hasten away.

"I thought about what I would do," he said as we strode forward.

"Do about what?" I asked, still distracted, and focusing on creating as much distance from the alley as possible.

"If I had green armour." I looked down at him. "If there was a battle, I'd just have someone else wear it," he continued. "Then, I could trick the enemy and we would win."

I smiled. "A diversion. That is clever."

As we began to walk away, a pebble landed suddenly at our feet. I glanced back but saw nothing.

5

Lost And Bound

I could already hear raised voices as I approached the large, domed, double doors and quickly slipped inside, taking my seat at the grand table.

"You cannot seriously expect me to consider this," General Maiya bellowed, her expression hard as her mood seemed less tolerable than usual. Truda's nostrils flared and her jaw flexed in response.

"If our general means to deny the request of my human elite joining her ranks, then it is within the council's right to demand an explanation," Truda said, anticipating resistance. Long had she advocated that the humans fight alongside the city's elven forces. As it seemed, elves did not like the thought of humans being ranked in equal reverence as them.

"You think me a fool." General Maiya slowly rose from

her chair. "You would have me arm the same humans who threatened the queen's guard?"

"A misunderstanding that was quickly rectified," Truda urged.

"As was the human's death, I am sure."

"A death? Who died?" Cobal interjected, troubled by the news.

"Would you like to inform Councillor Cobal, or shall I?" General Maiya asked firmly.

"We were going to tell you," Erik said, trying to intercede, but she ignored him.

"A human was found injured in the streets by Truda's noviciates, and instead of seeking out their instructor, they thought to incur their wrath upon the palace guard." Cobal scanned the room, searching our eyes for justification of why we would hide such important matters. I looked away, immediately feeling guilty for keeping it from him.

"What happened?" he asked.

"He was given shelter and care from the palace healer," Truda said on my behalf.

"Why didn't you tell us this before?" Cobal's question was directed at me. I could see the hurt in his eyes. After all his efforts to gain my respect and trust, I had just demonstrated how little that meant.

"Truda knew the truth would sway my judgement regarding her elite, this incident only further proves my point. Training the humans is dangerous," General Maiya declared.

"We fought for their freedom Maiya, they should have equal respect and rights as us," Truda argued.

"And look at what they would do with this freedom, you are giving them the means to fight back against the race that enslaved them. Humans should no longer be permitted to learn how to fight."

"You'd deny them the chance to defend themselves?" Erik asked.

"If he had trained with my elite, the human may still be alive," Truda added.

"We should find out what happened," Cobal said, attempting to settle the tension in the room.

"Leave it with me." Truda stood, as if to have the final word on the matter.

"To learn of more secrets to hide from the council, I think not," General Maiya replied.

"You're the one who has more reason to find the humans at fault," Erik accused.

"His death must be investigated," Truda added.

"Agreed, but not by you," General Maiya snapped again.

"What about Acqueline?" Cobal asked. "It was her guards they threatened, seems only right she'd be given the task."

"Fine," General Maiya relented, turning to me. "You will inform the council the moment you have news."

Hesitatingly, I nodded in agreement.

"Father wants me to learn how to scribe and etch, but I have told him my hands are not grown for such things," Prince Felyx said as we strode towards the Training House, Yuki bounding in front.

"Is that so?" I replied, and he grinned.

"These are warrior's hands." He held up each of his palms and spread his fingers as if to demonstrate their size. "I want to be the greatest in the kingdom."

"If you follow my instructions, one day you will be," I replied, unable to hide the smirk that appeared on my face.

"Do you think so?" he asked hesitantly. I looked down at his wide eyes.

"Of course. But, only if you practise fervently."

"Even though I am only human?" I frowned, considering perhaps the young prince was more observant of our divide than I had given him credit for. "They look at me differently, don't they?" Immediately my heart ached for him. Despite being elven, I had felt inadequate for most of my life, believing myself to be inferior, and abnormal compared to most. I recognised in him the familiar streak of doubt I had grown up with.

I bent down to one knee, silently shooing Yuki away as he advanced on my pocket. "Prince Felyx, you are very special." I reached for his hand and clasped it in mine. "If they look at you strangely, it is only because you are miracle born, one of a kind."

"I am?"

"Yes. Do not let any others make you believe otherwise."

"I like training with you, you're nice and a good teacher," he said, returning my smile.

"You bestow such compliments on me, my prince." I stood, urging him to continue to walk alongside me. Much of my time was gladly spent training the future king and ensuring the safety of his family, but I did not think the council understood my responsibilities. How did they expect me now to find the time to investigate a human death?

I thought about how I would even start, recalling the human's injuries. The healer reported there was no trace of blood beneath his fingernails, nor any swollen skin on his knuckles to indicate he had fought back. Addox said he had found him alone after the initial attack, and as much as I abhorred the idea of asking anything of him, it did seem he was my most likely source to finding the truth of what happened. I faltered for a moment, smoothing down the fabric of my leathers and running my hands through loose strands of my hair, letting them curl and drop over my shoulders.

As we entered, I noticed a few humans practising hand-to-hand combat in one corner of the large open space, but Addox was not amongst them. After a session full of Prince Felyx fulfilling my various instructions, I approached Truda in the hope she would know of Addox's whereabouts.

"You have not seen him?" I asked, my tone chagrin.

"Not for a few days," Truda replied, seemingly unconcerned.

"I was hoping to speak to him about the human who died."

"This task should not have been appointed to you. It goes against every grain of your current duty, as you spend far too much time outside of the palace as it is," Truda snapped.

"That's not her fault, Truda," said Erik, who had been silently focused on the repair of a weapon rack until now.

"Maiya did this on purpose. Anything to remind me I am no longer in charge of the council. I should be the one to investigate the human death." Truda's jaw ticked. "But of course, Erik is right, I should not blame you. My apologies for my outburst, Acqueline. You know I am always here to advise if you need me."

"Thank you." I felt comforted by her now relaxed tone and warm smile. I tried not to be offended, as I did not doubt in my mind Truda would ascertain the truth much faster than I, just as she would have been a better instructor for the prince.

"Addox said he found the human after he was attacked, I was hoping from there I would find a clue as to what truly happened," I admitted.

"I saw him at Tobias's house this morning, might still be there now," Erik suggested. "Just be careful, Acqueline," he continued. "Addox has had it tougher than most."

"Do not find yourself alone with him or provoke his anger," Truda added.

"Understood," I said, slightly worried, and I wondered if I should share the details of his behaviour in the palace. "Thank you for your help," I replied instead.

It was only after stepping away from Truda and Erik

that I realised I could no longer hear the training grunts of Prince Felyx, my heart rate increasing as I scanned the room for him.

He was missing.

"Where is he Yuki?" I asked, causing the curled little fox to abruptly awaken and jump to his feet. "Prince Felyx!" I called, keeping my tone short and sharp as the occupants of the Training House turned to me in unison, shrugging to show they had not seen him. My pulse quickened as I vaulted the steps, hauling open the Training House doors and taking my search to the streets as a fluffy white body squeezed past me.

I glanced down our common route of the sandstone path but as far as my elven eyes could see, there was no trace of him. Panicked, I was about to sprint off when Yuki yelped towards the edge of the shadowed alley where the mysterious pebble had appeared from earlier. With a wave of relief, I heard his light animated voice talking excitedly nearby. I spotted him on the edge of the shadowed alley, seemingly too distracted to hear my approach. I grabbed his arm and spun the prince to face me.

"You should not have left without informing me!" I said, my voice high and my cheeks flustered in anger, but he did not look upset by my scolding, instead his eyebrows inclined towards themselves as though he himself was quite aggrieved.

"She won't speak," he whined, his attention returning towards the darkness, and I tried to look beyond him but could see nothing.

Behind me little Yuki growled.

"Who?" I asked, curious and wary, still annoyed he would take such a risk to run off.

"She's been watching us," he said, but even as I narrowed my eyes to focus, I could not make out anything in the dim light. Recalling the human who had propositioned me in this area days ago, I felt the urge to usher Felyx away.

"Come, your mother will be waiting." I reached for his hand.

"I'll be back tomorrow," he called, leaning away from me, and seeming disheartened when the shadows did not answer. As we headed to the palace, I noticed Yuki frequently glance behind us protectively.

After dropping Prince Felyx off at the palace, I decided to get the next part of my day over with as soon as possible.

As much as I was dreading facing Addox again, it would increase my chances of ensuring the protection of the royal family and preventing further harm to humans.

I had a singular destination in mind; Tobias's house.

I knew I had reached my destination when I saw a group of humans working in the front curtilage. A young man swept the sandstone path, as another sheared a small bushel of greenery. Two muscular men pulled heavy crates from a stationary cart.

"Castor, where do you want the supplies?" a familiar

female voice shouted. Shanon appeared at the open doorway a moment later, taking a coffer from the extended arms of one of the humans. She noticed me immediately, silently raising an eyebrow as I approached. Both of us were clearly surprised to see each other.

"I am not on duty," she remarked.

"I am not here to scold you, Shanon," I replied as she held my inquisitive gaze. A second human piled another crate onto her already full arms.

"Make yourself useful then," she said dryly, before turning and disappearing into the building. I pulled a large chest from the cart and followed her inside. The interior was densely populated with humans of various ages busily preoccupied, talking and moving around one another.

I noticed a pale and malnourished young boy tucked into an alcove beneath the stairs, clutching something small in his hands. As I tried to identify what it was he held, he folded into himself more, crossing his arms and hugging the object closer to his chest.

"The meds are needed on the second floor," a young man called, striding quickly down the wide staircase. I continued to hold the crate firmly against my breastplate, feeling awkward as I was unsure of what I was supposed to do with it.

"Acqueline, right?" He leapt down the last four steps. I nodded, surprised to be greeted with such a warm demeanour. "I'm Castor, pleased to meet you." He stepped forward and took the chest from me, smiling warmly.

Of course, Truda's old house Guan. I recognised him now, though he had grown much since I last had seen him. When in Truda's service he was a timid and sinewy boy, barely over ten years. He was now broader and taller than me, his sandy hair a dishevelled mess atop his head with hazel eyes as friendly and inviting as his smile. He was one of the first slaves to be freed, and if I recall correctly, adopted by council member Cobal, Shanon's birth father.

"Naill has the medicinal lotions and fresh bandages," Shanon said, gesturing to a human behind her, seeming agitated at my presence.

"It was great to meet you, Acqueline," Castor said, and gestured to Shanon, "be easy on her, okay, I know she's annoying—" Shanon smacked him lightly across the head.

"Be gone, boy," she snapped as Castor smiled cheekily, shaking his head as though this was a playful familiarity.

Shanon eyed me suspiciously.

"Why do you need medical supplies?" I asked, my voice quiet.

"Humans are fragile, and quite demanding. Many seek the safety and nourishment that is provided here, including healing aid."

"Is that why you come? To help them?" I glanced around at the figures skirting past us. All humans. Shanon and I were the only elves.

"You sound surprised." She crossed her arms. "My visits are not frequent, and my presence is not entirely appreciated." I felt it too, the shift in atmosphere, the way the humans avoided eye contact.

We are a reminder of cruel things, intruders in a safe sanctuary.

"So, now we have established why I am here…" she said suggestively.

"I have questions for a human named Addox, do you know where I can find him?"

"Is he in trouble?" Castor interrupted, peering around the doorway.

"What have I told you about eavesdropping?" Shanon barked, her body stiffening. I raised my hand to silence her, and she let out a slight growl at the gesture.

"We were desperate, and he only wanted to help," Castor blurted.

"What did he do?" I asked.

"Be quiet!" Shanon snapped at Castor, and I stared at her confused. "Go, you are needed elsewhere." He hesitated for a moment, but Shanon's heated glare convinced him to retreat.

"Whatever this is about, leave Castor out of it," she gritted out in a low tone. Surprised at her defensiveness, I took stock of the vast number of crates now stacked high in the entranceway.

"Where did these supplies come from?" I asked, thinking of what Castor had said.

"If you are looking for Addox, you will likely find him in The Sanctum, he is becoming a regular," she drawled, ignoring my question.

"Which you would know because you are still attending

the fights," I accused, crossing my arms.

She shrugged.

"Shanon, how you choose to spend your free time is up to you, but I can no longer ignore your flippant attitude towards your responsibilities," I said, holding my stern tone. "If I catch you abandoning your duty again, I will inform the council and you will be disbanded from the royal guard."

"You said you had not come to scold me." She smirked, fearless of my threat.

"What can I say," I remarked as I began to turn to leave. "I underestimated your skill of infuriating me to distraction."

I headed straight towards The Sanctum, still frustrated after my encounter with Shanon.

"Back again so soon?" the elf at the heavy door commented rhetorically, and I replied with silence.

This place had the familiarity of the way things were before the end of the rebellion, and I did not like it. The heady roars and competitive thrills made my stomach churn. I prefer the eery quiet of the palace to the barbaric festivities of mock battle.

I took my time descending the crumbling stone stairs, noticing two humans huddled closely together at the bottom, staring nervously at the crowd. I walked past them, ignoring their wary eyes as I headed towards the packed area; bodies clambering in front of each other to get a prime view of the fight.

I weaved my way through, searching for Addox's familiar form, but I could not see clearly through the dense crowd.

In the centre of the room were two elves in the midst of unarmed combat, both barefoot as they circled each other anticipating the perfect moment to attack. One was larger in form than the other, her size a potential advantage. The smaller elf caused the other to lose footing and climbed on top of her the moment she fell forward to the stone floor, grasping her ponytail to lift her face. The larger elf thrust her head back quickly in retaliation, her skull cracking the bridge of her opponent's nose, causing her to scream. She quickly vaulted from the floor to her feet, clenching her fists ready to strike.

Cradling one hand over her bleeding nose, the smaller elf grabbed someone from the crowd and shoved them in front of her, the spectator receiving the hardened punch in her stead. The room erupted in howls of displeasure, and another elf jumped into the fray.

Before long, it seemed the whole audience had become involved, and I quickly found myself smothered between bodies trying to grab at each other. I ducked, frantically searching for a route to escape but someone was pushed towards me, and I stumbled back, falling to my hands and knees. I tried to crawl away, but my path forward was blocked, and I cradled my head in fear of getting trampled.

A firm grip tugged at my arm and pulled me free of the crowd, fingertips pressing firmly into my skin. Without pause, I was pushed inside a small storage room, the door slamming shut behind me.

I stumbled and adjusted to stand straight, finding Addox blocking my way out.

"Addox," I breathed, immediately feeling uneasy in the dim light, Truda and Erik's words of warning rang through my ears.

'Do not find yourself alone with him or provoke his anger'.

"You're nervous." He narrowed his eyes.

"No," I quickly replied, as something heavy thumped against the door, causing me to flinch. Addox crossed his arms and raised an eyebrow.

I straightened again and cleared my throat, remembering why I had come.

"I have been looking for you, I did not expect to find you here."

"Well, I asked this little elf her reasons for accusing a human of being involved with The Sanctum, but she didn't want to provide answers."

"You ambushed me in the middle of the night," I snapped.

"Tonight, I also saved you from being stomped to death. You're welcome, by the way." I watched his mouth move as he talked, the way he leaned his balance casually to the right, his thumb brushing over his bottom lip.

"Look, I did not come here to argue," I replied, feeling intimidated and losing confidence with every word I spoke. "The council have charged me with finding those responsible for the human's death. It would help my investigation immensely if you could share the exact location he was found." My palms were sweating, and I felt as though the walls were closing in around me.

"Okay," he said after a long pause.

"Okay, what?"

"I'll help you."

"Just like that?" I asked sceptically.

"Isn't that what you want?" I blinked, my breathing halting as my mouth felt dry.

"Yes, but I thought—" I started to say, still confused by the ease of gaining his cooperation, but Addox cut me off.

"Meet me tomorrow at dawn in the market square. I'll show you where I found him." Before I had time to respond, he turned and left, leaving me alone in the small supply room wondering what had just happened.

When I felt as though my heart rate had returned to normal, I crept towards the door and almost tripped on an overturned barrel. I pressed my cheek against the wood and listened to find out what was happening beyond. I could hear the crowd cheering and chanting, but all seemed to have returned to normal compared to the previous outbreak of chaos. I left the room hastily, acting as inconspicuous as I could.

6

Allies And Enemies

"This is where you found him?" I asked, looking around the shadowed alley beside the marketplace. The streets were quiet, with only a few passers-by towing carts to prepare for early morning trade. "There is nothing here."

"I could've told you as much, but that wasn't what you asked."

"I was hoping for at least a modicum of evidence." I raised a hand to my forehead as I took in the surroundings that were absent of any wrongdoings. There was no blood, torn fabric, or discarded weapon. "Was anyone else here when you found him?"

Addox shook his head.

Then I had wasted my morning.

"I will have to convene with the council," I said.

"That's it?" he replied, blocking my path. "You've no clever clue, or someone else to question?"

"There is nothing here to lead to suspicion," I countered, trying to walk past him but he blocked my path again.

"I thought you'd have some special skill or intuition."

"Well, I do not." I turned to walk in the opposite direction, finished with this conversation.

"Then why give this assignment to you?" He followed close behind me as I quickened my pace, eager to escape his judgement. "Surely this isn't the queen's best." I spun to face him, unable to remove the anguish and hurt from my expression.

"I did not mean for your companion to die. I would have helped him further if I could," I said in earnest, raising my chin, attempting to bury my emotional display of weakness.

His brow furrowed and for a moment his eyes softened. "I didn't mean…" he started, stepping towards me, but I shook my head.

"Thank you for your assistance. Goodbye, Addox." I quickly retreated to flee the alley. As I checked behind to make sure he was not following, someone walked directly into my path, and we collided. A basket of green apples flew into the air, rolling down the cobbled paved path.

"Quin!" Lelane exclaimed, reaching to steady me, just as an apple caught under my boot, tipping me forward. I instinctively grabbed her for balance but instead caused both of us to topple over.

"Lelane, I am so sorry." I scrambled on my hands and

knees to gather the scattered fruit. We both reached for the same apple and as our hands brushed, she sharply inhaled and pulled away.

"I did not expect to bump into you again so soon," she said.

"And probably not quite so literally," I said awkwardly, as I stood and extended my hand to Lelane to help her to her feet. "I apologise again if I startled you."

"I am fine. This reminds me of the time you spooked that horse straight into a cart full of apples." I smiled at the memory. Our mothers had all but dragged us by the point of our ears back to clean up the mess we had created.

"Just another reason for me to despise horses."

"And apples," she mused, and I grinned back.

I took a small step closer, taking in her appearance. Half her hair was plaited over one shoulder, the rest of her locks draped loosely down her neck. She wore similar attire as before, brown leather with a fur-covered cloak, her bright celadon eyes above rosy cheeks and lips. She had always been breathtakingly beautiful, and I remembered being envious of that in our youth.

A large shadow suddenly formed over us, causing Lelane to look up.

"Oh, hello," she said politely as I let out a frustrated groan, causing Lelane to flick her gaze back towards me.

"Are you sure you are okay? Do you need any assistance?" I asked, ignoring Addox, and she briefly shook her head, adjusting the basket on her forearm.

"It was good to see you, Quin."

"You too," I said, watching as she walked away.

"Who's that?" Addox asked, stepping beside me, and crossing his arms.

"No one." A heaviness filled my chest as I walked in the opposite direction to Lelane.

"Seemed like you knew each other well."

Ignoring him, I bit my tongue, and I quickened my steps in the hope of forcing him to fall behind, but he shadowed my side, not taking the hint at all.

"She called you Quin, is that another nickname, little elf?" he asked, and when I still did not reply he added, "I'm getting the sense you don't want to talk about her."

"Perhaps I do not want to discuss that which is none of your business," I said, feeling irritated at his inquisition. "Why are you following me?"

"Because we've got work to do." I paused, turning to look at him.

"We? There is no we. You told me what you knew, and now I must report my findings to the council."

"And then what?"

"They shall decide what to do and provide further instruction."

"What about The Sanctum?"

"What about it?"

"You think it's related, and you're a councillor, too, right? Shouldn't you do something about it?" he asked, incredulously persistent, and I loathed how close he was to the glaringly obvious. I may sit on the council, but I do not hold the same level of authority as my peers.

"The council as a collective will decide what to do," I said neutrally, watching as anger filled his expression, distaste in his eyes.

"So, you'll do nothing," Again, I remained silent, unable to meet his disappointed gaze. "Fine, I didn't need your help, anyway," he muttered, before turning and angrily striding in the other direction.

Feeling uneasy over my last conversation with Addox, I could not shake the thought I was withholding important information from the council about The Sanctum. Although I had frustrations with Shanon neglecting her duty in favour of attending the fight, the haunting vision of the young human begging at Peril's feet troubled me deeply, reminding me of the old ways. I knew I could trust Truda, so I told her everything I had witnessed between the human and Peril.

"I immediately sensed someone of high rank was in attendance, but I had never imagined Peril would be behind orchestrating such a place," I told Truda.

"She refused to return to her seat as council member the day Queen Fortuna was crowned and she lost her title as Slave Master, it does not surprise me she would seek a modicum of control elsewhere."

I had known Peril quite well when she was part of the council and had thought highly of her. Though, she was very fond of the power she maintained over the lives of humans; responsible for their placement and disposal.

"Do you think it is something to worry over?" I asked.

"Peril is a pragmatist and believes in the old ways. I for one would like to know what she is doing with these humans."

"Should I say something to the council?"

"You were instructed to investigate the human's death, and from what you have told me, you have little by the way of answers."

"Then, what should I do?"

"Question Peril. At least that is what I would do if I were in your position."

I agreed, even though I felt unsure about how to take the next steps.

"I can accompany you if you like," she added, as though hearing my thoughts. "Just to back you up, of course." Truda had barely waited for my acceptance of her offering as she had readied herself, and before I knew it, she was accompanying me as we walked through the city side by side.

There was a sense of her haste that I felt unsure of, but I could not deny it felt good to walk beside Truda once again, an elf that emanated power. A disposition that came naturally to her, it was in her blood.

Being in her presence felt like it somehow elevated my importance, even without her previous title of general. Her every step taken with entitlement, figures would scurry out of her path, and she made eye contact with no one.

"Shanon has been fighting at The Sanctum," I said,

suddenly conscious that Truda may see my understudy during our visit.

"I am surprised you allow her such freedoms." She cocked an eyebrow disapprovingly.

"She has no care for her duty and often neglects her responsibilities, regardless of what I say."

"I see," she replied, and I felt the judgment in those simple words. Truda had once been such a positive influence on the twins' lives growing up and they admired her, regularly seeking praise and guidance.

Since the death of Shanor, Truda had distanced herself from the remaining twin, leaving Shanon solely in the care of those much less equipped to deal with a strong-willed elf who disliked following orders.

"In truth, I do not know what else to do," I admitted.

"I am sure she is merely seeking a way to test her skill," Truda said dismissively. "Give her time, her temper will calm."

I nodded, forcing a polite smile.

"Have you been to The Sanctum before?" I asked her as we approached our destination, and she emitted a low, arrogant, "humph."

"I hear the reigning champion is unbeatable. Though I cannot deny I found myself a little tempted by that invitation, I have no intention of tainting my honour for the sake of strengthening my ego," she said.

"That must have been difficult," I replied playfully, and Truda gave a boastful grin.

"I was very, very tempted." Truda snickered.

I did not doubt she would have beaten whoever held the current title; she was probably the only elf in the entire kingdom who did not need to prove such nonsense. None would dare challenge her abilities.

"But we are still council members, and we have a reputation to uphold," I remarked with a deep sigh, readying myself as Truda raised her fist to pound against the heavy door.

As before, the door creaked open, and a shadowed face appeared through the darkness. Truda glanced towards me, prompting me to speak. I cleared my throat, raising my chin high.

"We have come to speak with Peril," I demanded. The elf's eyes narrowed, her sharpened gaze switching between Truda and me from the small open frame.

"She is busy. No visitors today," she rasped sharply and prepared to slam the door in our faces, but Truda quickly wedged her boot in the opening and forced her way through.

The elf stumbled back unguarded, crying out in surprise.

"By order of the council, I command you summon Peril to us now," Truda bellowed, stunning the elf before she scurried away.

Moments later a silhouette began to ascend the stone stairway with little urgency and a familiar human approached us clutching a leather-bound book of loose parchments. I had seen him talking with Shanon days before. His solemn features were as plain and inexpressive as his attire.

"Where is Peril?" Truda demanded, irritated by her lack

of immediate presence.

“She welcomes you and instructs me to bring you to her lounge.”

“We are not here for pleasantries. This is a serious matter.” I attempted to replicate the intimidating tone Truda had emitted, but the human did not seem threatened by either of us.

“I’m sure she’ll relish in the details. Come, this way.”

Both Truda and I exchanged looks of bewilderment as without further remark, the human casually turned and walked back the way he came.

We followed him, the air seeming thicker the further we descended, and an array of unpleasantness assaulted my senses all at once. The makeshift arena was empty apart from two humans, one lighting torches while the other mopped dark, dry blood from the stone floor.

Our escort led us deeper through the underground structure than I had ventured before and as we reached an uncomfortably tight corridor, he opened a red door and gestured for us to walk inside.

We entered a lavish room with low lighting, and the smell of incense wafting all around. Peril sat at the centre on a burgundy chaise longue with opulent ornamental legs, surrounded by luxurious chairs. Behind Peril, stood a well-armed elf who must have been her personal guard.

“Thank you, Sole,” Peril crooned as she made eye contact with us. “What a very unexpected and pleasant surprise.”

“You may not think so when you hear what we have to

say," Truda snapped.

"I see. Then please, do sit and tell me what has brought you both to my Sanctum."

I began to take a seat in a chair close to Peril but stopped when I realised Truda had not moved. The human, Sole, moved past us and positioned himself by Peril's side, bending over to whisper something in her ear. The corner of her mouth lifted, and she raised her hand to stroke his jaw, his fingers clenching at the touch, but Peril did not seem to notice. "Such wonderful allies, are they not?" she asked, her attention returning to us as Sole moved away.

"It seems he is more your servant than ally," Truda remarked.

"There must always be a chain of command, Truda, you of all elves can appreciate that."

"We have come to ask questions," I said, but Peril continued to challengingly stare at Truda. "A human was murdered," I continued, "What do you know about it."

"Nothing," Peril replied, giving me a pleasant yet misplaced smile as she lifted her head.

"I find that unlikely," Truda said.

"Perhaps you should question the palace guard, surely someone would have seen something," she suggested nonchalantly.

"We did not say he was killed in the palace," I pointed out, but Peril merely shrugged, as though the slip-up had been unimportant.

"Word travels fast."

"You said you did not know anything," Truda countered, clearly sceptical.

"Of value," she corrected, "I may no longer be on the council, but my little ravens are everywhere. They bring me whispers from all over the kingdom."

"Your ravens?" I asked, knowing she did not refer to real birds.

"I still have many friends, Acqueline, they keep me informed."

"What of the humans you keep here?" Truda asked, glancing between Sole and Peril.

"They come of their own free will, because of what I can offer them."

"Which is, what exactly?" Truda crossed her arms.

"In exchange for food, shelter and security, the humans pledge their skills to the service of this Sanctum and its patrons."

I silently watched the exchange between them. Now and again, my gaze would flicker to Sole, who stood by Peril's side. He stared beyond us, as though the conversation did not affect him at all, but I noticed the tremble he tried to hide in his hands.

"What kind of services?" I asked, sensing Sole's discomfort.

"Fighting, labour, fornication. Whatever skill they possess, I utilise."

"You are exploiting them," Truda accused.

"I am only fulfilling the needs the council have neglected. Those poor creatures in Tobias's house, weak, and malnourished, their place lost in this kingdom. In the Sanctum, they are safe, their purpose redefined."

It was difficult to deny that Sole looked healthy compared to the other humans I had seen. His clothes, though plain, were of a good quality and he looked cared for.

"Humans are not your playthings, Peril," Truda snapped.

"How is breeder twenty-three? Well-kept at home I assume?"

"You should be careful with your next choice of words."

"I meant no offence, what you choose to do with your human is your business, just as this, is mine."

"The council does not agree. I command that you permanently close the doors to The Sanctum."

"You have no evidence of any wrongdoing, Truda, and since you are no longer the general, I shall assume you do not have the authority to stop me," she challenged. She was right of course; Peril is all too familiar with how the council would usually deal with such matters.

"This is the only polite warning you shall get," Truda said, maintaining the lie.

"Then I look forward to your next visit," Peril said, waving her hand to dismiss us.

7

Missing Raven

"Did you know Shanon volunteers in Tobias's House?" I asked Cobal while we waited for General Maiya to arrive. Erik and Truda were engrossed in their own private conversation at the other side of the council table.

He nodded. "She avoids me when I visit. Castor says she's a great help, and despite his best efforts, he can't seem to get rid of her."

"In truth, I was shocked to find her there."

"Why?"

"She is aloof when it comes to her duty, behaving as though completely detached from feeling," I replied, venting my frustration. "To find her in Tobias's house, helping and protecting the humans residing there, has confused my opinion of her." Cobal frowned, his forehead creasing as his features fell into despair. "I forget myself. I should not have told you that," I admitted.

"It's okay. I've made it known that I care. She's my blood and I only want happiness for her."

"I want that, too, but perhaps I am not the mentor she needs."

"You're wrong, she needs your kindness and patience Acqueline. She's angry right now, but when that fades, she will need someone like you beside her."

"I wish she would give you a chance." I felt sorry for him, so compassionate.

"I'm a patient man. I know she blames me for what happened to her sister."

"Shanor's death was not by your hand," I replied, recalling the tale Truda had told of the rebellion's final battle. Neither Cobal nor I were present that day, but we had been told of Shanor's fight to protect the humans. Shanon had witnessed the archer fire the arrowhead that pierced her sister's throat, powerless to prevent her death.

The echo of heavy boots stomping from the hall suddenly muted all our private conversations. The throne doors thrust open, slamming against the wall, and vibrating on their hinges.

"For two decades, with the constant threat of battle and death, I led the elves in the woodland!" General Maiya bellowed as she stormed into the room. She pounded her fist on the table, leaning leeringly over us. "And yet, I found more peace in exile. Never had I faced so much difficulty, as I have in the short years leading this council."

"Then perhaps you should relinquish your duty," Truda calmly suggested, causing General Maiya to glare at her, nostrils flaring.

"Or you should be stripped of yours," she snapped back.

The room fell silent.

"Where is he?" General Maiya demanded, addressing us all.

"Who?" Cobal asked as we exchanged a puzzled look.

"The human from The Sanctum," General Maiya roared. "Not only did you openly interrogate a well-respected elder, but you also kidnapped a human in her care!"

"Maiya, explain what's going on?" Cobal said, attempting to calm her down.

"Peril has claimed that her assistant has been stolen from the Sanctum," she said as she leaned across the table, palms pressed flat. "This happened after two members of this council questioned her involvement in the death of a human. I have promised Peril I will find who was responsible and return the human to her."

General Maiya was referring to Sole, I realised.

"She doesn't care about him. Humans are her pets, treats them like slaves," said Erik, now standing.

"The human was killed for a reason, Maiya," Truda added, her voice eerily calm.

"The investigation was not assigned to you!" General Maiya growled.

"Acqueline asked for assistance, as is her right," Truda

snapped back.

"Did you take him?" Cobal asked, and I turned to watch Truda's reaction to his question.

"Of course not."

"It seems I cannot trust my own council. You are both removed from the investigation and forbidden from entering The Sanctum." General Maiya glared between Truda and me.

I remained silent, only puzzling over who could have taken Sole and why. If it was not Truda, who else would be so motivated to take Sole from the clutches of the Sanctum, and for what possible purpose?

"Fine, I didn't need your help anyway."

Addox had been in the Sanctum and had likely witnessed the same things we had. He had warned me he was going to take matters into his own hands, it was entirely possible he would go to this length, and I felt my stomach drop. I should have aired my suspicion to the council, but the thought of Addox being brought under General Maiya's judgement caused a feeling of dread to wash over me.

I shook my head. I had no time to dwell on the behaviour of humans, if he wanted to go rogue and kidnap Sole that was his prerogative, and if it got him in trouble, that was also no concern of mine. I had much more important responsibilities to worry over.

The moment the meeting ended, I fled from the hall, ignoring the unsettling feeling in the pit of my stomach.

The storm raged on, the wind and rain howling against my ears. My eyes frantically searched for anyone who could help, but the streets were barren.

Reaching a crossroad, I checked left and right, torn between which route to take. I looked down to the parchment in my hand, desperately unfolding it to read the words but the black ink blurred and smeared into nothing more than blotches on the page.

A flash of lightning flickered across the sky, followed by a thundering clap so loud I flinched as a storm, stronger than I had ever known, assaulted the city. I could barely hear my scream over the din of the rainfall.

I heard a clicking sound and my eyes shot open. I could see nothing from my bed; the room pitch black, no light from a torch or candle. I heard footsteps from my right, causing me to immediately jerk into a seated position and I noticed the large silhouette of a person blocking my chamber entrance.

The image of the slain human appeared in my mind, and without hesitation I reached across to my nightstand, feeling for my dagger. Clasping the weapon, I rolled off my bed and launched myself forward.

The figure tried to evade but I was too fast, alert as adrenaline pumped into my bloodstream. We both toppled to the floor, and I landed on top as I held the blade below the intruder's chin.

"Relax, little elf, it's just me," a deep voice rumbled, and I instantly knew it was Addox. I drew back, lowering my blade as I stood up to give him space to do the same.

It is then I realised the state of my undress.

As the nights grew warmer, I had found it a necessity to wear only my cotton undergarment at night, a decision I regretted at this moment.

Quickly I spun and grabbed the furs from my bed, pulling them high to cover myself.

"How did you get in here?" I coughed.

"Much too easily." He eyed me up and down as I tried to cover myself.

"Leave before my guards find you," I threatened. Addox quirked a smile, crossing his arms as he leaned against the wall in casual indifference.

"You plan on stabbing me, little elf?" He gestured toward my hand clenched tightly around the small blade. He took a single step forward just as I retreated. "You can't seriously expect me to believe you're afraid of me," he added.

"Why should I not be fearful, it is you that would sneak into my bedchambers."

"I didn't come to fight. Just to talk," he said, his arms open.

"Did you kidnap Sole?" I asked, and he raised an eyebrow in surprise.

"Yes." My mouth dropped opened, shocked he would be so honest.

"Where is he?"

"Safe and away from The Sanctum's clutches," he told me as he examined my personal effects laid out on my clothing chest. "You don't have a lot of stuff," he added, casually moving around my chambers.

"What do you plan on doing with him?" I asked, feeling uncomfortable at his perusal of my personal space. Addox turned and smirked.

"Sole says more men will die if The Sanctum isn't stopped, and he wants his freedom back. I promised to negotiate on his behalf."

"He is willing to talk to the council?" I asked, hopeful.

"Uh-huh. If you can ensure he will be protected."

"We can," I blurted, excited at my chance to present this new evidence to General Maiya.

Addox nodded, both of us transfixed in silence as we watched each other, unsure of what to do next.

"I have duty at dawn," I said softly.

"I got what I came for. I'll leave you to your rest, little elf."

"You could at least address me by my given name, which is Acqueline, by the way."

"Think I prefer little elf, or Quin," he replied, a small smirk appearing on his lips again as he started to leave. "You were having a nightmare when I got here, weren't you?" he asked, but I did not answer. "I wonder, what is so terrible it would torment an elf's dreams?"

Then he stepped out, leaving me alone in my chambers.

Another human had been found dead.

His body was discarded in the street and once reported to the guards, the corpse was immediately transported to the healer's chambers in the palace. This time, I accompanied Lyzaria on watch until General Maiya arrived, her face stern with impatience. The remaining three council members came shortly after, waiting for the examination to be completed and the cause of death to be announced.

"What is taking so long?" Truda muttered impatiently, pacing in circles.

"Do we know who he is yet?" Erik asked and I shook my head.

"This is the second human to be killed in a matter of days, our inaction can no longer be afforded," Truda snapped, directing her comment at General Maiya. "Peril should be brought in for interrogation."

"We should not act so hastily," Cobal said, and Truda drenched him with a look of disdain. I shrank back, taking a position opposite Lyzaria while General Maiya waited in silence for the healer's door to open.

The healer finally emerged, gesturing for us to follow her inside.

"A clean cut to the throat, he died by blood loss," the healer said, pointing to a high tunic that had been cut away, revealing a deep swollen gash at the base of his neck.

"There were no other injuries?" General Maiya asked the healer.

"Aside from some minor marks on his wrists, there are no other distinguishing wounds on the body."

"So, he was bound but not beaten," Erik added.

"The first human was assaulted so the two incidents may

not be related," General Maiya said.

"That's what we call dead people now, incidents?" Erik asked angrily.

"Of course, this is related!" Truda bellowed. "Maiya, someone is killing humans."

I ignored them and moved to examine the body in greater detail, feeling the blood drain from my face instantly as I recognised his features.

"His name was Sole," I said numbly. The others stopped their bickering and turned to me.

"Peril's missing human?" Cobal asked and I nodded, glancing over to Truda for her to reaffirm, but her attention was focused on General Maiya. I silently pleaded for her to take notice, to look past her grievances and recognise I was desperate for her guidance.

Addox had apprehended Sole, and now Sole was dead. I had foolishly allowed myself to be manipulated by his taunts and distractions, even now, as I withheld this information from those who trust me.

"Peril will be aggrieved to learn of this," General Maiya said.

"More likely she is the one responsible," Truda added.

"How can you both bicker at a time like this?" I asked, incredulous, my voice high-pitched. All eyes looked towards me, stunned by my sudden outburst. "Do you not see? Queen Fortuna trusts in our ability to run this city and protect all its inhabitants." My heart pounded as I met all of their eyes. "We are failing her."

"Acqueline is right," Cobal interjected. "Perhaps we should tell Fortuna what is happening."

"No," General Maiya snapped. "She is still but a child, this should not be burdened upon her."

"Then what will you do?" Truda demanded.

"I will order more patrols throughout the city, and perhaps we should enforce prohibitions," General Maiya replied. "A curfew for the human's protection."

"What kind of curfew?" Erik asked, his brow furrowed.

"No human be allowed to walk the streets after dark unaccompanied." General Maiya glanced towards Erik and Cobal, and said, "Including the both of you."

"You would punish the humans for a crime they did not commit?" Truda questioned.

"We do this for their safety. The restrictions can be lifted once we know the city is safe."

"If you think that's best," Cobal said humbly.

"Inform the raven keeper to send out this new proclamation to every home in the kingdom," General Maiya bellowed loud enough for every guard in the palace to hear.

The rain assaulted every windowpane, the wind howling and whistling down the corridor. Just the thought of being outside in the horrendous weather made me want to retreat to the sanctity of my bedchamber furs all the faster. I was exhausted after taking on my guardswomen's duties to allow them respite and had been awake for a whole night and day worried over the human deaths.

General Maiya had done as she proclaimed, commanding the Raven Keeper to send a message to every home within the kingdom, notifying all that humans were forbidden from travelling the streets alone after the sun had set. For some reason, I found myself partly troubled that Addox would ignore that order, and the other part worried he would not. I did not like the way thoughts of him unnerved me, or that he was occupying my thoughts at all.

As I wearily returned to my bedchamber, I opened the heavy door and stepped inside, only to halt on the threshold, stunned to find it already occupied. Addox was sitting at the end of my bed, his head hanging low and resting against the palms of his hands.

"You should not be here, it is dark out," I whispered, instantly thinking of General Maiya's curfew. He looked up, his expression dismayed, and I felt completely immobilised.

"I don't know why I came," Addox replied, while I stood watching him. It was dark, the only light coming from the glow of the pale moon, which etched the sadness on his face. Carefully I closed the door behind me, slowly stepping further into the room. "I had a brother," Addox began, breaking the silence and I paused to listen to him speak. "We worked the fields together as boys. I was a quick hand, filling my pockets with extra food when I could, and he was always on the lookout. We protected each other, shared clothing, and rations."

His words shaky and wavering, I continued to listen and watch him.

"I was seventeen when they separated us. He was twelve."

"Where is he now?" I asked softly, although I suspected I already knew the answer.

"Dead. One moon after the manumission they found him locked in a cupboard, nothing but skin and bone. He'd been mistreated for years before his master left him to slowly starve to death. She didn't want him to be free."

"I am so sorry," I whispered.

"They killed Sole."

"Who did?" I asked, but Addox did not seem to hear me as he continued speaking solemnly.

"I had him safe in Tobias's house, but something spooked him into running and they'd killed him before I could find him." He stood to face me, his expression crestfallen. "That's twice I've failed to protect someone who trusted me."

"Neither of their deaths were your fault."

"I didn't ask for your pity." He stepped forward, crowding me. "I know this doesn't matter to you."

"Of course, it does," I said, my voice quiet and sullen as I moved towards him.

"I promised I wouldn't let what happened to my brother happen to anyone else," he said and I felt his warm breath at the tip of my ear, I closed my eyes.

"Addox," I breathed, feeling him slowly press his chest against mine. I sensed him edging closer, our foreheads lightly touching. I did not know what was happening, why I was drawn to him this way, why my body felt so unbelievably alive whenever he was near.

"Why can't I leave you alone?" he said aloud, mirroring my thoughts, his brow frowning as he rested against me, our chests rising and falling heavily in unison.

My body was trembling as I slowly lifted my head, our lips a hair's width apart, but suddenly Addox pulled back, shoving past me and slamming my bedchamber door closed behind him.

8

Haunted Past

"They're all staring," Prince Felyx commented, twitching nervously as he noticed a crowd gathering around us.

"Pay them no heed," I said reassuringly, thankful Addox was not amongst the group of spectators. With a glance behind him, Prince Felyx refocused his attention to the target at the far side of the room and pulled the string taut, holding it until he was confident in his shot. When he released, the arrow flew straight into the centre of the target, sitting beside the previous three. The muttering behind us increased.

Continuing to ignore them, I handed Prince Felyx more arrows. Investing in the prince's training kept my mind from obsessing over the events with Addox the night before.

Specifically, on the almost kiss we had shared.

"Now the other two," I instructed, and immediately he

took a fresh aim, both arrows landing swiftly in the centre of the target with each shot as intended. It seemed the little prince may one day even rival me in his skill with ranged weaponry. I smiled at the thought, wondering what Truda would say, as memories of when she and I first met resurfaced.

She had stopped to briefly observe me practising with my poorly crafted bow and self-made arrows. Back then I harboured no ambiguous ambition or dreams of earning a prestigious title. When the fiercest of elves, donned in full plate armour, peered down at me with envious intrigue and challenged me, it would be an understatement to say I was intimidated. I could still taste the fear, as bile found its way up my throat. Despite losing our archery match, she invited me to spar with her, changing the course of my destiny. Soon after, I passed the trials to join the royal guard. Despite how accomplished we both became, to this day, Truda never could beat me in archery.

Perhaps Prince Felyx would.

He performed well under pressure for someone so young, and his mother was the most magical being in the kingdom.

Excited, I grabbed my bow, and knelt beside him. "Do you know what this is?"

"A bow." He raised an eye and quirked his lip.

"Yes, it is." I chuckled, "But this is a very special, imbued, red wing bow, gifted by the Mages Temple." His eyes widened with intrigue as I continued. "It produces arrows on command, allowing the bearer to not need a quiver." I extended it closer, allowing him to graze his hand along the engraved wood, fingertips pausing over the orange gem recessed at its centre.

"Master it, and I shall gift it to you," I stated boldly, handing it over to him. What a sight for this crowd to witness; A human prince able to wield magic as expertly as any experienced elf. I wanted them to see the gift that he truly was to our kingdom.

Gingerly, he took it from me, barely able to balance the huge wingspan within his grasp. Still, eager to see if he could summon its magic as I had described, he raised the bow. The whispers started anew as the crowd waited to see what would happen next. Prince Felyx's strong gaze never left the centre of the bowstring as he tried to summon an arrow with all his might, but nothing happened.

No golden arrow appeared.

Seemingly unimpressed with this new development, the fickle crowd began to disperse and depart from the Training House and my heart sank. It mattered not that his skill with a bow would far outmatch my own, they wanted no less than extraordinary, and I had just given them reason to doubt him.

I sent the prince to refill our waterskins while I gathered arrows from the targets, pulling the flint heads from the splintered wood. Despite my determination to do otherwise, I still found myself glancing over my shoulder towards the humans, hoping to see Addox. I had wanted to provide him comfort last night after he shared his story, feeling sorrowful of all the anguish he must have endured, and that was a dangerous thing to desire.

When all was quiet around me, I realised Prince Felyx had not returned, and Yuki was also missing. Straightening, I sighed in frustration, having a good idea of where they had run off to again.

I rushed to the alley opposite the Training House and immediately saw a white fluffy tail swishing impatiently at the threshold between the open street and the dark passageway. I could hear the prince as I approached. "Keep your feet still," he said, followed by a slight swatting sound. Reaching him, I was about to begin my barrage of scolding when I glimpsed another small figure, half hidden in the shadow, facing Prince Felyx with a wooden sword clutched in their hands.

"What is going on here?" I asked, not nearly sounding as authoritative as I intended. Startled, the elfling dropped the wooden weapon.

"She wants to train," Prince Felyx blurted, "look, see," he rushed out, pointing between his weapon and the discarded sword. My eyebrows raised as I glanced between the pair, my attention lingering on the girl lurking in the shadows. When our eyes met, she stalked back, as though wary of me.

"Don't go." Prince Felyx raised his free hand, palm flat towards her and she paused.

"You have nothing to fear from me," I said sincerely, keeping my tone gentle. I lowered myself onto one knee and rested a hand on Prince Felyx's shoulder, hoping to demonstrate his comfortableness, and therefore encourage hers. It worked, and she took a timid step towards us both. When she stepped closer, I saw her completely.

Two of the largest and brightest of blues met my gaze, her unkempt blonde hair was darkened by sand and dirt. Her clothes were torn and unclean, her boots scuffed and splitting at the heel. I thought her features were familiar, though I could not place where from. A similar age to Felyx, her skin was a healthy olive colour, her eyes turning a slight shade darker as she peered at me curiously.

"This is who you saw the other day?" I asked Prince Felyx and he nodded.

"She followed us but won't come inside the Training House, can she train with us?" Prince Felyx asked as he stood up straight, resolute in his idea.

"That will not be possible, my prince, yours is a special kind of training. She will have to find a mentor of her own." Immediately, his brow furrowed in disappointment.

"I can be her mentor."

"One day, prince, you will be a mentor to a great number of people, but until then, you are my student, and you must start listening to all I say," I told him, in a sterner tone. "Come, your mother will be expecting us."

"See you soon, okay," he said with a promise to the girl now stepping backward, her face expressionless as she slowly retreated, until all that remained was the shadow.

In General Maiya's absence, this morning's council meeting was brief. I waited behind for the rest of the council members to leave, allowing the opportunity to address Cobal alone. It had been weeks since General Maiya had prohibited Truda and me from continuing our investigation into the human deaths. It had not escaped my notice that Cobal still lingered after meetings hoping to talk to me, but I found myself consumed with guilt for hiding our visit to The Sanctum from him, amongst other things. Only now, did I finally have the courage to speak with him alone again.

"I have been meaning to apologise," I said the moment we were alone.

"There's no need, Acqueline, I know you questioned Peril for the right reasons."

"Still, you should not have found out like that, you have been nothing but kind to me."

"You're too hard on yourself, Acqueline, it's fine, honestly." He quirked a smile.

"After everything that happened to you, how can you be so understanding towards us?" I asked, thinking of Addox and his hatred towards our kind.

I watched as Cobal stood from his chair, shuffled over, and sat beside me.

"She'd be about Maiya's age now, though you would've been far too young to remember Lilith."

"Shanon's mother?"

"The most incredible elf I've ever met. She was compassionate, thoughtful, and so very beautiful," he said adoringly.

"Is she the reason why you have no disdain towards us?"

I asked and he nodded.

"They called Lilith a human sympathiser, because of how she was outspokenly appalled by the way humans were captivated and forced into submission. She believed we were capable of so much more."

"What happened to her?" My tone gentle and solemn.

"After the twins were born, I'd been reassigned to another elf for conception and Lilith fought to free me. It was forbidden to grow attached to humans, especially breeders," he said as he lowered the collar on his tunic, revealing the top of an old, branded mark. My eyes widened at the top of the circular numbered indent, and I instantly thought of Addox, grimacing at the thought of the scars he had likely collected over the years. "They sentenced her to death," he finished, his head dropping low.

"I am sorry."

"We can't change the past, Acqueline. None of us would be here if not for the old ways."

"It should have never been like that, we should have used our abilities to protect humans, not enslave them."

"Lilith once said something similar. She would have loved to see the future we're trying to build." Cobal replied, taking a stand.

I stood also, following him out.

"How is it you hold no animosity towards us, after everything you lost?" I asked him tentatively. Cobal paused, turning to address me.

"I made a promise, to never lose my compassion, even in

the face of a kingdom full of hatred. What we do in our lives is what defines us in the end, and I'm going to be damned sure to make good use of mine," he added with a wrinkled smile. "For her."

"She would be proud of you," I said, returning a sweet smile, and Cobal let out a soft sigh.

"I sure hope so," he replied, picking up the pace again. "Now if you'll excuse me there is a sick little boy I promised to visit at Tobias's House."

"Is he alright?"

"Nothing one of Castor's hot stews can't fix." He smiled, before turning and leaving the hall.

As I headed to the south tower to relieve Brenith of guard duty, Truda swiftly appeared by my side, grabbing my arm, and pulling me towards her.

"Walk with me," she said in a low tone. Sensing I had no choice in the matter, I followed her. "This is not the first time General Maiya has left the city."

"What do you mean?" I asked, confused as she quickened her pace, her steps echoing within each archway we passed.

"She led a small myriad of warriors beyond the grasslands. They were not seen for three days."

"How do you know of this?"

"One of my elite assists in the stables. He saddled and armoured the steeds himself. More disturbingly though, he said General Maiya returned alone."

"What happened to the other warriors?"

"I was about to ask you the same question." She gave me

a pointed look and I raised my palms.

"You think General Maiya would clue me in on her plans?" I asked, my eyebrows raised.

"The number of secrets kept from the council is mounting."

"I am sure there is a logical explanation," I replied sharply, hoping to immediately diffuse her trail of thought. Truda paused and turned to me.

"You should make arrangements to have her followed."

"Tru." I groaned.

"What if I am right? If Maiya is found not to be trustworthy, she could be dangerous," she challenged.

"General Maiya is too perceptive. She will know if she is being followed."

"Then choose your spy wisely." She elongated her words in a low, resonant tone.

"What if we do not like what is discovered?"

"Then I will deal with her myself." She rested her hand on the hilt of her sword.

"I understand," I replied, as a wave of conflicting emotions ran through me. The last thing I wanted to enable was a two-women war. It was no secret the pair hated each other and perhaps it was their heavy likeness that drove them apart. With evenly matched fighting skill, beauty, and unbelievable arrogance, by all accounts, they should be kindred spirits.

"How is your human elite?" I asked nervously, hoping she might talk about Addox's absence.

"They continue to show promise. If only Maiya would take the time to assess them in person, she would see merit in my accomplishments," Truda replied, not mentioning anything about Addox or showing concern for his disappearance. I still had not seen him since he stormed from my bedchambers, I simply nodded, afraid that if I enquired further, she would question my curiosity.

"Tell me the moment you have news," Truda said, ignoring my fleeting apprehension. As I watched her stride away, I considered the task ahead, already knowing who I would assign it to.

"You sent for me?" Lyzaria asked, cautiously entering my small chambers.

"Please," I said, gesturing for her to sit. Closing the door tentatively, she walked inside and sat in the wooden chair in the opposite corner.

"You are my most loyal of guards, Lyzaria, always setting the highest of examples," I said, hoping to ease her concerns about my unusual summoning to my private quarters.

"It is an honour to serve you and the royal family," she said, saluting.

I favoured Lyzaria above all my guard, not only for her loyalty but also her discretion. She reminds me of how I had once been, steadfast and assured before my insecurities caught up with me. This would not be the first time I would ask the elf to spy on my behalf.

Before the rebellion ended, Truda had believed Counsellor

Freyja, the ambassador to the mage's temple, was planning something deceitful. She had ordered the elder be followed. No one knew who I had assigned to this task, not even Truda.

"I would rather not ask this of you," I started, regretful we would resort to this once again to protect the city. Lyzaria stared at me with trepidation. "I have a task for you."

"A task?"

"I want you to follow General Maiya. Find out why she depletes my ranks, learn who she confides in and discover her secrets."

"Is there something specific I should look out for?" Lyzaria asked, her posture relaxing as she accepted the request unflinchingly.

"I know little, except she has been extending her attention beyond the city walls. We need to learn why." Standing, Lyzaria nodded. "Any information you can retrieve will be useful, but it is essential you are not seen," I added.

"I understand."

"Do not share the details of this duty, or your discovery with anyone but me."

"On my life, I swear," she said, saluting before leaving me alone in regretful silence.

9

Into The Light

The young prince had gained a second shadow.

In the days that followed, I had become used to seeing her small form make brief appearances whenever Prince Felyx and I left the palace. Little pebbles would periodically fall at our feet and Prince Felyx would collect each that was tossed our way.

Curious, I had wanted to ask Prince Felyx what he had planned to do with the stones, but each time we reached the Training House, he would rush to the alley opposite and place them in a neat pile at its entrance. Without comment or question, I watched him, marvelling as he encouraged this silent communication with her.

As we walked from the palace gate, I noticed a small bundle of soft leather tucked under his armpit.

"What is that you clutch so tightly?" I asked.

"A gift." I looked down at him.

"For whom?" He did not answer me, merely smiling with the smallest of blushes spreading across his cheeks. "Can I see it?" Prince Felyx nodded and removed the bundle, unrolling it steadily to reveal a small wooden slingshot.

"I carved it myself," he told me, and I raised my eyebrow in surprise. It was quite small, but I could see the intricacies of its detail, with vines and flowers carved into its base, the bottom whittled into a bulbous shape. Prince Felyx turned it upside down to show me the detail he had carved into the wood.

"Is that Yuki?" I asked, recognising the pointy ears, and narrowed snout, with hairline strokes depicting whiskers. Felyx nodded eagerly and then rewrapped the sling.

"Do you think she'll like it?" he suddenly asked, his voice quiet and full of uncertainty.

"A gift handcrafted by the prince?" I said with absurdity at the lack of his confidence. He fidgeted where he stood, and I found myself once again kneeling before him so our eyes were level. "If it was made with the desire to capture her attention, I think we both know you have already done that," I told him, tucking a strand of his blonde locks behind his pointed ear.

I noticed movement in the darkness beside a house and smiled. "I think she will adore it," I added as I stood and gestured to the shadows behind us.

I watched, amused as he rushed over to greet her, and I

kept my distance a few paces back as I followed. Bursting with unconcealed excitement, he extended the parcel to her. She took it from the prince's outstretched fingers and sat cross-legged on the paved floor, carefully peeling away the layers of the leather parcel. When the sling came into view, she gave a puzzled expression before looking up to notice Prince Felyx crouching beside her.

"This is so you can aim better," he told her, and I witnessed the smallest smile appear on her lips. She held the sling as she abandoned the wrapping, taking a pretend aim. Felyx reached inside his pocket and pulled out a small bundle of smooth pebbles, "I kept these for you, they're the perfect size." Tentatively she held out her palm and allowed the prince to drop the handful of stones into it. He stepped back, gleefully watching how she stared at the clutched items, as though they were the most precious of gifts.

As we walked to the Training House, I noticed Prince Felyx's smile growing bigger and brighter at every pebble that was flung into our path.

The next day, as the prince and I left the Palace gate, I noticed the girl once again dart out of sight beside a building, the slingshot swinging as she moved. A thought flittered across my mind, and I approached her hiding place with Prince Felyx close on my heels.

"Would you like to walk alongside us on this beautiful

afternoon?" I asked softly to the darkness, aware she would most certainly hear me. The small girl took a timid step from the shadow, peering past me to catch sight of Prince Felyx.

Knowing she was tempted, I smiled and twitched my fingers into a curve, suggestively enticing her to follow. I began a languid pace towards our usual route and Prince Felyx looked up at me, a glimmer of hopeful glee in his eyes. I winked to inform him to trust in my plan.

Chancing a glance over my shoulder, I caught sight of her hiding behind a pillar before carefully stepping out behind us. Prince Felyx's steps slowed until he was situated promptly by her side.

He broke the silence by beginning an animated one-sided conversation.

"I was going to be a sword master, because all the toughest warriors have swords," he said, chattering continuously. "But it's only fun if someone else has one, too." He pulled his arms back, pretending to aim. "I like bows more because you can play fun games with them. Once when Acqueline wasn't looking, I shot an arrow straight in the air to see how far it would go before earth magic pulled it back down."

Stopping abruptly, he pointed to the sandstone path. "Because that's what keeps us on the ground, earth magic that is, and I know cause my mother controls it, but maybe feathers are stronger than magic. Ravens don't get pulled down and they fly. Arrows do too, which is why I think they're the best. What's your favourite weapon?" he asked, finally taking a large breath.

I found myself absorbed and eager to hear if she would respond. When she remained wordless, Prince Felyx did not allow the silence to linger, instead, he provided answers to his own questions.

As we approached the Training House, it took me a moment to realise a familiar figure was standing just outside the entrance, this time without a cloak to hide her distinguishing features. When she turned and saw us, her mouth dropped open in surprise.

"Lera?" Lelane called as she approached and I watched the little elf take a small step behind Felyx, seeming to use him as a shield. As the girl crept from behind the prince, Lelane placed her palms on the girl's cheeks. "You need to stop doing this, I was worried about you," she said wistfully.

"She is your daughter," I mumbled. As I watched them side by side, the similarities became apparent; her beautiful blonde locks had been inherited from her mother.

Avoiding my gaze, Lelane pulled at Lera's ruffled clothing, swiping away dried dirt with her flattened palm. Her fingers ran through the girl's hair, attempting to tame it. "I am sorry if she caused trouble," she said when she had finished fussing.

"Not at all," I said hurriedly.

Lelane looked at Lera sternly, "running away will only make things worse for us both," she quietly huffed.

Feeling my stomach sink, I took a step forward and offered my hand to Lelane as she straightened.

"She will not disturb you again," she said.

"She did not, well, aside from some stone throwing," I mumbled with an awkward short laugh, Lelane raised an eyebrow. Clearing my throat, I lifted my shoulders. "Lelane. Allow me to introduce Prince Felyx," I said, and she reacted with immediate cordialness. Her head bowed, she closed her fist over her heart and gave the most courteous of salutes.

"A pleasure, your highness."

"Prince Felyx, this is Lelane, we…" I paused, searching for the words, unsure of how best to describe what we meant to each other. How does one summarise, in a short sentence, the history we shared? If I once considered her a friend, can I still describe her as such?

"We grew up together," Lelane finished for me, with a brief tentative smile. Prince Felyx politely waved and then drew his attention back to Lera.

"The prince and I enjoyed her company." I gestured towards the silent Lera. "Perhaps you would both like to join us for our walk back to the palace?"

"Have you not just arrived?" Lelane asked, looking confused.

"Ah, yes, well," I looked around and my hand rubbed the back of my neck as I tried to muster up something to say. I glanced at the prince, my eyes creasing, "Prince Felyx was just telling me how he felt unwell… so… I thought to skip training today."

Both Lera and Lelane looked at Felyx, and my face crinkled in worriment.

To my surprise, Felyx made a little moan and placed his

hand on his stomach.

Lelane quickly hurried over and crouched in front of him. "Are you in pain?"

"I think I've eaten too much; my tummy feels too big," replied my little accomplice, and I had no mind to correct his common tongue.

"Then perhaps a walk would do you some good," she told him reassuringly as Prince Felyx shot me a subtle wink.

I bit my lip to hide my smile.

It was official, I was the worst mentor ever. Not only did I encourage childish behaviours that may undermine his royal appearance, but now I openly invited him to deceive others. Still, as Lelane fell in step beside me, the children leading as we strolled, I found I suddenly had no care to feel regretful.

Summer was by far my favourite season. The mornings were fresher, and the sweet smells of the blossoming fruit trees wafted through the breeze, the sun warming the dusty city as it stirred. I appreciated these details even more, thanks to the company I kept.

I had asked Lelane if she and Lera would accompany the prince, Yuki, and me on our short walks to and from the Training House, and in the days that followed, we fell into a delightful routine.

It felt incredible to have someone to smile with again, joking and laughing over silly things that did not involve council meetings, training, or strategy. Lelane was a low-born healer and had no interest in palace matters. Addox had still not made himself known after our almost kiss, and I surmised that was a good thing. I hoped he would keep his distance, allowing me to move on from the temporary distractions and bring myself back to the relevant.

"Thank you," Lelane said suddenly, following our latest menial conversation.

"What for?"

"I am sure you have noticed that Lera is quiet."

"It does not seem to bother the prince," I said, pointing towards the pair, Prince Felyx delighting in scrutinising a pebble out loud, before taking aim and encouraging Lera to predict its trajectory.

"I am grateful to him, also."

"Is she mute?" I asked softly.

Lelane shook her head. "She is very selective of who she interacts with. I rarely hear her words."

"What made her that way?" I asked, but Lelane did not answer.

Anxious that I had upset her, I quickly changed the subject. "I am grateful for this, a second chance. Things were not left on good terms between us, and I have been regretful of that since. I want us to be friends again."

"I would like that," she replied, and I beamed.

"So, what I have missed in the last ten years?" I mused, and she chuckled lightly. I wanted to know everything she had experienced in her life after I had joined the royal guard.

"I do not think our short walk will allow me the time." We laughed as the children walked on ahead of us, Yuki's fluffy white tale swaying as he strolled behind them.

"Tell me about your home," I said.

"Lera and I live in the centre of the city, not far from the marketplace. It is small but comfortable. And you? What is it like living in the palace?" she asked.

"The queen's garden is wondrous, alive, with many sights and sounds native to the city," I said, animatedly. Spending time with Lelane was an escape from the weight of my responsibilities, even if only for a short time.

"And what is the queen like?" she asked, seeming uplifted.

"As precious and beautiful as the garden she reimagined. Her heart is full of kindness and love."

"Then Prince Felyx does her proud, mirroring his mother's likeness," she replied, and I nodded, agreeing with her completely. "She should spend more time with her people, we would like to know her better," she followed.

"Queen Fortuna is still very young, and nothing like her mother. She never intended to take over as ruler and is overwhelmed with it all."

"Then she is lucky to have such a supportive and caring councillor," Lelane replied pleasantly as she slightly leaned towards me, her fingers brushing over my hand. "Quin, are you free of duty this evening?" she asked nervously.

"Why do you ask?" I moved my hand away, unable to hide the surprise in my tone.

"Lera and I were wondering…" she began but stopped

as the child looked back at her with a confused expression. Lelane cleared her throat, "I want to invite you to supper with us."

She was inviting me to her dwelling, surrounded by her interests and habits, an insight to her life I had no right to be curious about and considering our past, I did not want to give her the wrong impression.

"I am afraid my nights of late are consumed with duty, just as my days are," I replied in earnest, instantly reminded of the pressure sitting on my shoulders.

"I take that as a rejection," she replied, a hint of embarrassment in her tone.

"No," I uttered quickly, "I am humbled and grateful you would invite me, but it is unlikely I will find the time."

Thanks to General Maiya, The royal guard has slowly been reduced to a meagre party of nine, two of whom were constantly watching over the royal family. As I was either training Prince Felyx or attending council meetings, we had too few guards to patrol the palace in its entirety. With hundreds of doors and windows, surrounded by a city of aggrieved habitants, the cold-blooded killing of two humans had shown that some would exploit this vulnerability.

"I understand," she said, pulling away slightly in disappointment. "Perhaps if you are relieved early?" she asked, smiling hopefully.

"Perhaps," I replied, but I knew the probability would be slim. Things were in motion that I needed to focus on.

"Well, I am making vegetable stew this evening. If you

have the time, here is my address." She passed me her details and directions that were written on a torn parchment. I stared at the paper for far too long, feeling the grain between my fingertips as I thought back to my recurring dream.

"Quin?"

I shook my head and offered a smile, and we exchanged brief goodbyes, as Prince Felyx and I headed to another training session inside the large wooden structure.

After returning the prince to the royal family, I continued with my mundane duties. There had been no word from Lyzaria on her secret mission, and I had not seen Addox for what felt like an age. I found myself recalling the day of pleasantries with Lelane, someone who liked me for who I was, not what they wanted me to be, and her invitation ran through my mind.

As I retired for rest, I could not help but wonder, what would it hurt to spend one evening away, in the company of a friend? Resolute in the idea, I shot up from my bed and reached for my cloak, setting off to make my way out the palace.

As I followed the directions scribbled on the material Lelane had given me earlier, I realised entering this part of the city in my guard's attire was not the smartest of ideas.

This thought had crossed my mind for what felt like the millionth time before I reached her home, the dwelling harder to find than I had imagined. She lived amongst densely compacted buildings surrounding the market, her residence midway down a dank, shadowed alley. This place was devoid of sunlight and greenery, a stark departure from the fields surrounding our city, where we had spent most of our time growing up. A heavy, damp smell caused me to cough lightly as I approached her front door.

I checked to see if anyone had noticed my presence, my silver and black armour likely an odd sight so far from the palace, but none seemed to care.

Taking a breath and adjusting myself, I did not understand why I felt so nervous. Perhaps I liked having something in my life that was familiar and safe. Lelane was separate from my duty, my conflictions with Addox and the complications that accompany my position. With her, I was just Quin.

I knocked on the front door, and when I heard faint footfalls approaching, my lips curved as the door creaked open. However, my heart plummeted, and my smile dropped at the person standing before me.

"Yes?" snapped an angry, muscular elf, crossing her arms and blocking the entranceway. "What do you want?"

I instantly noticed the quality of her attire, which indicated a higher rank than one would expect for someone living in these parts of the city. Her intricately embroidered armless tunic revealed her entire neckline, her soft leather trousers matching her finely crafted boots.

Flustered, I opened my mouth to speak but lacked confidence in how to reply. Perhaps I had the wrong address.

The thought of General Maiya finding out I had been in this part of the city caused a physical shudder to run through me. Realising I had remained in awkward silence, I was about to make my excuses and leave, when another came to the door.

"Quin?" Lelane gasped in desperate surprise, her eyes pleading with me. Helpless to interpret her wordless communication, I responded with a wry smile, choosing to ignore the other elf in our presence.

"Is your offer still open?" I asked her.

"What offer?" The other hulking form asked angrily as she glared at Lelane, who returned the sweetest of smiles.

"I invited Quin to supper with me," she answered, a slight tremor in her voice.

"You invited a royal guard?"

"Yes," Lelane replied as she reached for my arm, ushering me inside as if desperate to get me off the street.

"Acqueline," I said, extending my arm in greeting to the largely muscled elf, though tension lingered in the air as we stood in the hallway of the small house. The elf gave me a quick look up and down, assessing my composure, and a small smirk fell upon her lips.

"Terra," she replied, clasping my hand in a purposeful clenching grip, and squeezing my fingers slightly too hard. Lelane offered to make some tea and headed to the kitchenette as I entered the open plan sitting room. The house did not seem sizable enough for a family; everything was compact, with furniture cramped within damp, plainly decorated walls. A small table, adorned with a brown cloth, sat in the centre of the room, with two rickety chairs at either end. The legs screeched against the wooden floor as Terra dragged one backward and she gestured for me to sit. I complied, and silence filled the room as she stared at me.

"Your home is lovely," I said cordially to Lelane as she sheepishly placed the pot of tea at the centre of the table.

"This is an old Guan residence. Slaves to the manor next door, not really fitting for a family, is it?" Terra questioned, her arms remaining crossed, and I took another glance around the room.

"A home is what you make it," Lelane said as she poured two cups of tea for the both of us, but left Terra's cup empty. Terra glared at her venomously while she poured her own drink.

"My chambers are much humbler than this," I replied, hoping to change the atmosphere.

"Right, no unnecessary possessions," Terra said in a tone I disliked, seeming far more menacing than simple jest or tease.

"Have you eaten?" Lelane asked me sweetly, and I shook my head. "I will warm up some leftover stew," she replied, reaching over, and placing her hand over mine lightly. Terra did not miss a moment as she watched with furious scrutiny.

"So," Terra said loudly, suggesting I had something to say to her.

"So?" I replied, taking a small sip of my tea.

"You know who I am?"

"No, I cannot say that I do."

"I am the unbeaten champion of The Sanctum," she

declared, an arrogance about her as she spoke.

"Some consider that a great achievement," I replied, keeping my tone neutral.

"It is, which means I can crush any opponent, inside and outside of the ring." She leaned towards me menacingly. Suddenly, she slammed her fist on the table in front of her, causing the crockery to shake violently, with steaming liquid spilling over the sides. My heart pounded, but I was thankful I had not flinched, as my hand instinctively reached for a dagger hidden within my boot.

"Terra please!" Lelane protested.

"I am just trying to wrap my mind around why a member of the royal guard would be bothering my family," she said with flippant possessiveness.

"Lelane and I have been friends for years," I replied, my composure returning.

"Funny, I do not recall her ever mentioning you," Terra said, leaning back and resting an arm on the back of her chair.

"Where is Lera?" I asked.

"Upstairs, sleeping," Lelane replied, and I chanced a glance towards the stairs, wondering if the elfling was lingering in the shadow there. I found it difficult to believe she would remain asleep with all the commotion going on beneath her bed. Lelane busied herself in the kitchenette, while Terra continued to assess me judgmentally as I finished my tea.

"As interesting as this evening has been, my presence is needed elsewhere," Terra suddenly announced, rising from her chair. Looming over me, she paused, causing me to crane my neck to peer up at her. "I had wondered how it was possible for that Guan to die under the protection of the royal guard," she said, her voice low and full of cynicism. Then, bending down lower to whisper in my ear she added, "now I know."

With a canned laugh and ignoring my flustered composure, she strode over to Lelane, placing a hand under her chin and forcing their eyes to meet.

"Think about my offer, hmmm. You know I can protect and provide for you both," she whispered intimately. Lelane gave her a small, timid nod.

"I hope we do not meet again soon," Terra directed to me, casting another affronted gaze before heading out the front door and slamming it shut behind her.

"Well, that was unpleasant," I said, taken aback at the situation and still feeling the uncomfortableness from it.

"I am so sorry, I did not know she was going to be here."

"Are you in some sort of trouble, Lelane?" I asked, recalling how blatantly Terra had tried to intimidate me whilst making her territorial claims obvious. Lelane shook her head vehemently.

"No, I have tried to make it clear it is long over between Terra and I, but she does not like my decision." The pairing of elves was a serious and common affair, the bond between two developing into a permanent lifetime partnership. Break-ups did occur, but rarely. This was largely because of the unflinching loyalty and unrelenting stubbornness of our people. “Please, Quin. I want you to stay,” she whispered.

I closed my eyes as I inhaled a deep breath. I knew the responsible thing to do now would be to leave. I could not afford to get mixed up in this. Things with Lelane were supposed to be simple, an easy friendship that would only cost the little time I was able to give, now I worry there is more going on here than she is divulging.

When I opened my eyes, Lelane was watching me, nervously twitching her hands whilst waiting for my decision. She looked far removed from the confident and playful elfling I would wrestle and chase all those years ago, now she looked vulnerable.

I walked to her and pulled her close to me, wrapping my arms around her and letting her head rest on my shoulder as she nestled into my embrace. Neither of us tried to move for a long while, as our bodies remembered what it felt like to be held, to find comfort in one another. When Lelane sniffled and gradually stepped back, I reluctantly released her.

“Now about this vegetable stew…” I said, causing Lelane to smile and exhale in relief, nodding as she wiped away a tear.

10

The Ratite

I knew something was wrong before I stepped foot in the palace. As I returned from Lelane's house, far later than I had planned, guards were running past me frantically.

"What happened?" I asked Brenith as I raced towards her.

"An explosion in the queen's tower," she replied, panic filling her features. "They say the queen woke hysterical, her scream shattering all the glass in her chambers."

"Was anyone injured?"

"Her Majesty is unscathed. Her consort Pheonyx sustained minor cuts, but he is more concerned with the queen."

I ran towards the queen's tower, through the throne room and vaulted up the stone stairs. My pace slowed as I reached the hall, and I barely avoided the large crack running jaggedly down the centre of the corridor. As I approached the queen's chambers, General Maiya emerged, her scowl evident, intensifying as I got closer.

"Where have you been?" She seethed.

"Helping a friend," I replied truthfully, knowing a lie would not help me now.

"Queen Fortuna says this has happened before. She loses control of her magic when she has bad dreams. Did you know this?" Her tone was full of malice.

"Yes, I was there the first time this happened."

"Yet you failed to inform me!" General Maiya screamed.

"You are not always available," I countered bravely.

"Tonight, neither were you, Acqueline."

"I was not on duty," I replied, knowing the futility of arguing with her.

"You are not a blacksmith, or a cultivator who requires daylight to work. You are Head of the Royal Guard, there is no respite from your duty. The only time I would find it acceptable for you to leave these walls is when training Prince Felyx. Am I understood?"

"Yes," I replied, my expression blank. "I will request Erik to coordinate the repairs tomorrow," I followed, desperate for our interaction to be over. I felt like an elfling being scolded.

"It is only by the queen's request that I do not disband you from your post where you stand." She stepped forward, towering over me, her jaw tensing, "If anything happens to her on your watch, Acqueline, I will shame you so publicly your name will be hated for generations to come." I flinched. It did not seem to matter to her that I was tired for lack of sleep, or that I cared more deeply about my duty than any other elf I knew. I was still not worthy of the position in her eyes.

"My arrows will pierce the hearts of any who would hurt the royal family," I declared, holding my head high.

"You are a ratite. A raven born without wings and underserving of the reverence the queen gives," she grumbled; her teeth clenched. "You do not belong with this flock." Then with a scoff, she left, leaving me to regain my composure before entering the queen's chambers.

After checking on the royal family and being assured they were safe and in need of rest, I stood alone at the edge of the raven's tower, deciding to take a moment to watch the sun rise. I felt strung out, exhausted after the day's events, but I knew I would be unable to sleep. My thoughts were shrouded with worry over the queen as General Maiya's words played on repeat.

As I leaned over the edge, peering down at the sheer drop beneath my feet, the wind caught in my hair, and I pictured myself as the flightless black bird she said I was.

Her flock spread their wings, flying freely towards the horizon as I slowly plummeted to my doom.

I would never throw away my life so wistfully. When the ancestors demand my blood, it will be in the service of those I have sworn to protect. What other cause would be worthy to sacrifice oneself?

That was a royal guard's purpose after all, the sole reason we were not permitted to have families or attachments.

With all I had to contend with, I felt isolated. There was no-one I could truly console or draw strength from. It was the loneliest I had ever felt in my entire existence.

"Messy way to go," a deep voice said from behind me, and I jolted. My foot slipped and I drew a sharp breath as my body began to fall forward. A strong arm wrapped around my waist, pulling me back from the tower's edge and holding me steady.

"You startled me!" I snapped, turning to Addox as I pushed him away lightly. My voice sounded hoarse, as I choked on my words. As I wiped the streaks from my face, I realised I had been crying.

"You're welcome," Addox replied, stepping back, and leaning against the arched stone frame.

"For what? Almost killing me!" I exclaimed, trying to steady my erratic heartbeat from the scare of almost plummeting to my death.

"You're crying."

"How shocking it must be to learn elves are capable of emotions," I said, seeing no point in denying the fact.

"I wouldn't have pushed you."

"How ambiguously candid of you."

"Simple-minded, remember?" He tapped his index finger to his temple. "Best use small words I'd understand."

"You disappeared," I said, hating the way that sounded

like I had been crying over his absence.

"Had some things to take care of."

"Where did you go?"

"Were you worried about me, little elf?" He teased, and instantly I felt regretful for being concerned over his absence these past few weeks.

"What do you want, Addox?" I asked, becoming impatient.

"I thought you ought to know that Sole told me things before he died. Shared his secrets."

"What kind of secrets?"

"The kind that got him killed." I stayed silent, mirroring his posture against the wall whilst waiting for him to explain. "Sole said The Sanctum is a cover-up, a lure to entice competitive folk. They use humans to grant elves their desires, in exchange for loyalty. They make bargains with humans too, bad ones."

"Why would humans agree to them?"

"Cos they're desperate, cold, and starving. When times get tough who do you think suffers the most?"

"The last harvest yielded more than enough to sustain us for months."

"Elves keep almost everything for themselves, so we must work harder for our meals. What choice do humans have but to make back-alley bargains with monsters?"

"If we are monsters, then why did you almost kiss me?" I blurted, instantly regretting it, but Addox only smirked.

"Do you wish I had?"

"No," I snapped, looking away, feeling the warmth in

my cheeks as blood rushed to my face.

"Perhaps you'd prefer a kiss from your companion? I've noticed you've been spending lots of time together lately."

"Have you been following me?" I asked accusingly.

"Hardly, I was on my way to the Training House and saw you together." He shrugged, his gaze slowly shifting from the floor to meet mine. "You looked friendly," he added, his common twang emphasising the pronunciation of the latter.

"It is late, Addox, and I have an early patrol. Can you reserve your taunting for another night?" I said, my voice weary from worry and exhaustion.

"You, okay?"

"I am fine," I replied, slowly turning from him as I walked back to the edge of the raven's tower. "Thank you for the information, I will pass it on to the council," I finished, expecting him to leave as I sat down and daringly dangled my legs over the side. At this height, I could see miniature orbs of light moving around below, with patterns forming as the populous held torches, while navigating the city in darkness. After a beat of silence, Addox came and sat down beside me, resting his arm on a raised knee.

"Wanna talk about it?"

"About what?" I asked, my focus on the sheer drop below.

"Whatever has you looking at the ground like it's an invitation."

I looked over at him and frowned, "I was not going to jump."

"Then what are you doing?" he asked, dangling his leg

over the edge next to mine.

"You would not understand."

"Try me anyway," he said, and I sighed deeply.

"Sometimes, I like to sit up here and allow myself to imagine a different life," I replied, returning my focus to the constellation of flickering, golden dots moving about below. "Mine is dictated by ambitions that are not my own. My path is steered by who they would want me to be, and not who I truly am," I admitted, looking at him.

"Sounds lonely."

"Such is the life of a royal guard," I replied. "Our lives belong to those whom we serve."

"Yeah, I know what that's like," he said, reminding me of the life he had been born into, and the services he would have fulfilled against his will. The only real difference between us was I had chosen to become a royal guard, whereas Addox had been born into enslavement.

"I suppose you do."

"What's this imaginary life like?" he asked, his palm gripping the edge, far too close beside mine.

"A peaceful and humble life, without armour and arrows. One where I could teach elflings childish games instead of swordplay, and spend my nights gazing up at the stars," I said dreamily, before my brow crinkled, remembering whose company I kept.

"What about you?" I asked, clearing my throat.

"I'm not sure," he said quickly, "I've always wanted to travel and see the land, build my own house in the shade of a tree. It wouldn't be very big or likely well built, but it would be mine." I looked over to Addox, curious about his openness.

"So why not do those things?" I asked, "no one is stopping you."

"Why don't you?"

"It is not so easy," I said, my voice raised, feeling frustrated at his deflection. "I have responsibilities and people who rely on me."

"Then I guess we're both stuck dreaming."

We sat in silence after that, looking over the edge, both enchanted by the scattered glow of tiny flames, glittering like starlight. It was difficult to ignore how I felt in his presence, the differences he brought in this imaginary future caused my stomach to flutter, and dare to dream.

"I did not say that!" I exclaimed.

"Yes, you did! I had to bite my lip to prevent myself from laughing!" Lelane chuckled.

"Well, I cannot be held accountable for the guards' gullibility." I laughed.

We had spent our entire journey reminiscing of the mischief we had managed in our youth, and how we used to delight in wasting the guards' time, creating a multitude of false scenarios and distractions. We would deceive them with elaborate stories and hoaxes, and they were all too eager to investigate, leaving us to the true mischief, sneaking into places or stealing rare fruits for ourselves. It is an irony that was not lost upon me now I was a guard and would be aggrieved to have my time wasted in such a way.

As we approached the Training House, I noticed Truda and Erik coming from the opposite direction and raised my hand in greeting. The gesture was not reciprocated as Truda glared at Lelane venomously, her attention drawn down until she set her sights upon Lera.

"This was a mistake," Lelane said suddenly, her voice shaking, taking a few steps back towards her daughter and reaching for her hand. "Sorry, Quin, we should not have come."

"Wait, Lelane?" I asked, but she ignored me, offering a quick submissive salute before dragging Lera away. Dumbfounded, I watched them leave as Prince Felyx moved forward as though he wanted to follow them.

"Did we do something wrong?" he asked, his voice quiet.

"No," I said, feeling suddenly angry. What was Truda's problem? Why did she think that was an appropriate way to behave? To make an intimidating stance so brazenly, especially towards someone as kind and thoughtful as Lelane. I marched to the Training House, Prince Felyx trailing closely behind me with Yuki at his side. Truda and Erik entered, and we followed behind.

"Prince Felyx, go and set up the ring targets," I instructed, as I stormed towards Truda.

Her eyes bore into mine on approach.

"Acqueline, wait," Erik implored, cautioning me, but I ignored him.

"No, Erik, it is fine, let her continue," Truda said, looking me up and down with such distaste that I almost felt the physical impact of it.

"Are you going to explain to me what your problem is?" I asked, surprised at the anger in my tone echoing through the courtyard. However, I could not shake the look of worry that had marred Lelane's features a moment ago from my mind.

"That family know to keep their distance from me," she said, her contempt evident.

"What could Lelane possibly have done to you?"

"Are you truly so clueless?" she asked, unamused. Truda took a deep breath, while Erik shifted uncomfortably beside her. "Did you take a good look at her daughter?" she asked, unflinching.

I frowned. Of all the things she could have said, what did Lera have to do with any of this? Why would the elfling's presence offend Truda?

I pictured Lera, how young and small she was, her clothes often dirty and torn. The blonde locks she inherited from her mother, and the piercing blues she inherited from… I looked at Erik, the same eyes, crystal, and haunted.

"She is…"

"One of the last elves to be born, a child Erik was forced to create," Truda reaffirmed, and I felt the blood drain from my face, my mind a frantic whirl of anguish and confusion.

Lera was Guan made; I knew that, yet I had not made the

connection. Before humans were decreed free from servitude, we were all created the same way. Prince Felyx was the exception, a miracle born from love between a human and an elf rather than controlled procreation. Still, a flicker of guilt ran through me at the thought of how Erik would have been forced, and Lelane equally having to endure it.

"Lera did not choose how to be born into this world," I snapped, and Truda's face froze in astonishment, unaccustomed to me answering back.

"Actions speak louder than words, Acqueline, her mother knew exactly what torment she was inflicting." Her arrogance made me furious. It was unfair to judge someone for their past actions, especially when they were merely following our customs. Yes, Truda had decided to break the rules, to fight against her people to protect something she wanted, but many innocents died at the hand of her sword long before she met Erik. An adversary to many, she should not be so quick to condemn others.

"So, your past actions do not make you a villain, but they do her?" I asked.

"I never touched a human against his will," she said, and I glanced at Erik, his head bowed, not wanting to take part in Truda's accusations of his victimisation. "Perhaps Lelane had been thrilled by it, spreading her legs, and wrapping them around the innocent like manacles."

I felt the rage rise from my stomach, my hands clenching as my breath shook. Truda's perfect face sneered down at me, proud of her opinions. Before I had a chance to regain control, I swung my fist, landing a punch on her jaw with a loud 'crack', the vibration of the impact reverberating down my arm.

She stumbled back, her hand cupping the side of her face.

Immediately, I dropped my arms, the limbs heavy at my side. My fingers uncurled as my mouth opened wide, stunned at what I had just done.

"You behave as though you are so above everybody else, completely disregarding those whose lives you so unmercifully took before you had a change of heart," I said, sounding much braver than I felt. Truda turned away and as Erik reached for her, I was immediately overcome with guilt. "You are the last elf in this kingdom qualified to pass judgment on others," I added to affirm my point, though my words did not have the same bitter bite to them as my first. Truda remained silent as Erik put his arm around her, and as they headed to the exit, I returned to Prince Felyx.

While we trained, I purposely kept my focus on the young royal's progress, trying to ignore the tears I wanted to shed from the hurt I had inflicted on my best friend.

For the remaining week, I did nothing that could incur General Maiya's wrath. I had yet to receive word from Lyzaria regarding General Maiya's movements, and Truda and I had not spoken since the incident. I remained silent at meetings, avoiding eye contact with everyone.

Sometimes I thought of Addox, secretly hoping I would see him again soon, however, just like Lelane, it seemed he too had concluded it would be better to keep his distance.

Prince Felyx, still so young and hopeful, looked everywhere for signs of Lera's presence on our journeys through the city. He checked beside buildings, tracing every shadow for movement and still collecting pebbles as he would any other day. When we arrived at the Training House, he left a small formation of smooth stones at the entrance of the alleyway. It was only when we left later that morning, he noticed them untouched, and the realisation finally sunk in.

We were not going to be seeing them again.

As a result, Prince Felyx was utterly miserable and barely willing to communicate. He held no interest in playing with Yuki, ignoring the yelps and cold nose nudges the little white fox made in attempt to beckon his attention. I gave him the space he needed to grieve his lost friendship, despite the reminders that witnessing his agony brought forth. With my own friendships in tatters, I could relate to his anguish.

After a few days, his misery mirroring my own, I found I could no longer stand it. On our next walk through the city, I dropped to one knee in front of him.

"My prince, it pains me to see you this way, I would give anything to hear your insistent conversation again," I said in the hope of gaining a smile, it did not work.

"I don't understand," he said, his face lowering. "I thought we were friends."

My heart broke at his words.

"I am sure you are friends," I said gently.

"Then why?" he whined, his voice choking.

"Not all things can be so easily explained," I told him truthfully, not eager to dive into the politics of the situation.

"It's not fair."

"Life is full of choices and sacrifices, my prince. It hurts now, but some things happen for good reason."

"And the other things?"

"We have to learn to let go," I told him, thinking of my own situation.

With a sniffle, he nodded.

"Let us skip training again today. Tomorrow you can wield your first blade of steel." I squeezed his shoulder reassuringly. Catching me off guard, Prince Felyx wiped away the tears that had welled in his eyes and leaned into me, his head resting on my shoulder, his arms snaking around my waist. Stunned, my limbs hanging uselessly by my sides, I froze.

"I don't want things to change." Feeling the hurt behind his words, I lifted my arms and embraced him in return.

"Do not despair, my prince, all is not lost," I said, while stroking his long blond hair. "You still have Yuki and I to keep you company, and as time goes by you will make new friends." Standing straight, he wiped his nose with the back of his hand and stroked the white fox's head with the other.

I was woken abruptly at dawn by the sound of thumping

against my bedchamber door. Instantly alert, I rose to find Brenith waiting.

"The prince is gone," she blurted.

"What?" I replied, a sudden flood of panic running through me. "What do you mean 'gone'?"

"The queen cannot find him. There are no signs of forced entry. The white fox remained asleep, suggesting the prince snuck out. General Maiya summons you to the gardens." I hurriedly dressed in my armour and rushed to the throne room, finding an anguished Queen Fortuna wrapped in the arms of her consort. In front of them, General Maiya paced back and forth. She scowled at me the moment I entered, her heavy boots charging across the monumental room in an echoing, pounding procession.

"The prince is missing." she bit out, slowly.

"I have just been informed."

"Perhaps you misunderstand my affront, Acqueline. I mean to ask, why, is the prince missing?" I was not surprised at her suggestive accusation. As I opened my mouth to reply, she raised her hand. "On second thought, I do not care for your excuses."

I pursed my lips into a thin line, accepting her aggressive criticism. She was right, I was his guard and mentor. His sudden irresponsible behaviour reflected badly on our training. I was the one tasked with ensuring the safety of the royal family, of course she would blame me for his disappearance.

"I will find him," I said with confidence.

"I'll help," the queen's consort quickly added.

"You will stay with our queen," General Maiya instructed.

"He's my son!"

"It's okay, Phoenyx. Acqueline and Yuki will find him together," Queen Fortuna said, wiping the wet streaks from her cheeks.

"Yes, they will," General Maiya said. Taking a step closer, she added, "Do not give me further reason to doubt leaving the prince in your charge." Before I had time to salute, she turned abruptly and left. I remained frozen in place, trying not to get angry at her words. Prince Felyx was in my care, and I should take responsibility. Recalling his recent sultry moods, I knew exactly why Felyx had run away, all I needed to do was figure out where he went.

I looked up towards the Queen and her consort, "Rest assured, we will find him," I said with a salute and Yuki instantly rushed to my heel.

"I have need of you," I said briskly, as I approached Shanon. Deciding to ignore the fact she looked like she had just returned from brawling.

"Surprised you did not seek out Lyzaria," she snarked.

"She is busy," I snapped as Yuki emitted a low, impatient grumble.

Shanon looked at the fox, and then at me. "What has happened?"

I told my second about the events that had transpired in the week prior with the prince, avoiding specific details. Instead, I concentrated on the unlikely friendship with Lera and how her sudden absence had affected him.

"You think he ran away to find her?"

"I cannot think of any other reason he would flee," I told her honestly.

"Perhaps he detests your training." I glared at her, and she smirked. "Well, he cannot just be walking through the city openly, someone would have reported seeing him by now," Shanon said, quite rightly. "Could this creature pick up his scent?" she asked, pointing at Yuki, his eye patch twitching with the movements of his nose.

"Only one way to find out."

11

Runaway

When I thought of where Lera liked to linger, I imagined her dirty and dishevelled from roaming in the shadows. I led Shanon and Yuki to the place where we first noticed Lera, the alley beside the Training House. It was currently absent of any sign of her or Prince Felyx, but Yuki instantly shot his snout to the floor, puffing dust in the air as he sniffed the area.

We followed the fox through the alley, discovering that its exit opened onto another wide sandstone path that forked in different directions. Prince Felyx could be anywhere in the city, a settlement full of desperate people, envious of the life a young prince would lead. My heart plummeted at that.

Shanon was being uncharacteristically quiet as she glanced around at the shadowed nothingness, shrugging nonchalantly.

"The council should show concern over the neglect of our streets, this pavement is filthy," she proclaimed. I rolled my eyes, regretful I had not spent more time seeking any other guardswoman to assist me in her stead.

Yuki suddenly squealed and started violently scratching the floor, spraying dirt and dust under his stomach, and matting his white fur.

"I think he agrees," Shanon chuckled, and I shot her a disapproving look.

The fox's digging intensified, and I noticed a metallic object form from under his claws, buried under the sand. I thought of Lera, her clothes and skin far dirtier than the pavement alone could offer.

"Good boy, Yuki!" I shouted, tossing him an insect vertebra, as he stepped back to reveal a grated hatch, concealing the opening of a drain.

"You cannot be serious," Shanon said, peering over my shoulder.

"Lera was always filth-ridden, her clothes frayed and torn. She also relished avoiding people. It is very possible she could have used the drains to get about."

"But the prince?"

"Is very observant, it is possible he came to the same conclusion."

"You give the boy far too much credit."

Ignoring her, I leaned forward and clutched the metal bars, finding the hatch loose and easily removable. As I lifted the grate, Yuki growled loudly and instantly dove headfirst into the dark hole.

"Well, that settles it," I said, and began removing the layers of my armour.

"You are not going in there?" I ignored her as I peeled off the final layer of my thick leather tunic, removing my bow and heavy leather boots.

"I can fit," I told her, finding no joy in the idea of squeezing my tiny frame in the dark hole.

"You do not know where it leads."

"It is either this, or we return to the palace and tell General Maiya to begin a city-wide search, for the prince, and now also the queen's fox," I told her. Shanon grimaced and began to gather my things.

"Follow me if you can," I called above as I descended into the tunnel, trying to ignore the damp dirt that clung to my clothes. She grunted in response.

I began to crawl, and I could hear the muffled sounds of the city echoing around me. I headed for the fractured light source in the distance. My thigh caught on something sharp, and it tore through fabric and skin, causing me to wince, but it did not slow my efforts. When I approached the next juncture, there were three options. I called for Shanon through a vent above my head. She had remained in the street above and as a shadow blocked the sun's thin rays, her face came partially into view.

"Having fun?" she asked, as I glanced at the tunnel's options. "Perhaps even facing Maiya is less perilous than this?"

"I can keep going," I told her. "There are three routes ahead."

"Too bad there is only one of you." I let out a huff, annoyed at her lack of assistance. I rested on my elbows and peered between the separate tunnels. "Made a decision yet?"

"Give me a moment," I called above.

"The longer you wait, the more Maiya's anger will build. I know I have other things I would rather be doing."

"Shanon! Will you please give me a moment to…" My words trailed off as I leant further forward into the central tunnel, something catching my eye. A tuft of bright white fur.

"I know which way he went," I said, hoping Yuki's strong nose was leading us towards the prince. I pushed on, pleasantly surprised when the air seemed to clear, and I was not frequented with the disposal of liquids in the tunnels. Shanon followed from above, my voice prompting her as I traversed the network of shallow passages with Yuki's fluff guiding me. When I reached a dead end, I coughed up at a barred opening. Sensing my desperation for fresh air, Shanon promptly moved a loosened crate from the hatch, lifting the grate and pulling me up.

"You smell awful," she said, her nose scrunched, turning from me. I tried to brush away the dirt that had gathered in the crevices of my clothes and considered it might be simpler to just discard the garments, rather than having them cleaned when I returned to my chambers.

"I shall not be volunteering myself to do that again any

time soon." I took my items from her, begrudgingly layering my armour over my dirty clothes.

"Do you recognise where we are?" Shanon asked as she looked around. We were beside a farm that Lelane and I used to play near as elfling's, and a vision of us laughing and running through the grassy fields came to mind. I nodded.

"So, now what?"

"We search," I told her. Admiring the green landscape that was so incredibly different, yet in the same token, so familiar. Yuki was nowhere in sight, but I had a strange feeling he was nearby. "You should search the farmer's fields, then make your way to the palace to see if he has returned home."

"What will you do?" I looked over towards the fruit and rice farms, taking in a deep breath.

"I am familiar with these parts, where elflings may go to play. I will search there."

"And if he is not found?"

"Then, you will soon come to understand why I would rather crawl in sewage than face the wrath of General Maiya."

I passed the occasional human working the fields, imagining two familiar childlike silhouettes running beside me, throwing fruit, and chasing each other. "Catch me, Quin!" The memory of Lelane exclaimed. We were young and innocent, before that fateful night when our friendship would never be the same again. My choices had changed everything, and we had been pulled apart for over a decade.

The shrill of real young laughter pulled me from my reverie. The sound so rarely heard anymore; it carried a surge of emotional weight across the landscape towards me. I spun on my heels, following the noise.

Sure enough, without a care in the world, Prince Felyx was running along the base of a tree, while a slightly smaller blonde was perched on a thick branch, halfway up, shrouded by the crown of leaves. Yuki sat meters away, his fur stained brown across his entire body, desperately in need of a wash.

"That one!" Felyx exclaimed excitedly as he pointed up high. Lera silently reloaded her sling and aimed. After a moment's pause she released, and I watched a jagged pebble slice through the stem, causing fruit to fall freely. The prince leapt forward in haste, his arms outstretched, successfully catching the fruit.

I allowed his chuckles to fade before I revealed myself. Yuki looked up at me dopily, his face covered in grime. Making my presence known to the elflings, I clapped slowly and loudly. Startled, they both spun around nervously, their eyes wide when they saw me.

"Impressive," I said, taking leisurely strides towards them. Lera lifted her arm and started aiming her sling at my chest, I raised my eyebrows at her bold behaviour.

"Are we in trouble?" Prince Felyx asked nervously, hiding the fruit behind his back.

"Most definitely," I said in an authoritative tone. Prince

Felyx flinched and lowered his head.

"I'm sorry."

"And you?" I said, looking sternly at Lera. "Have you no fear for the consequences of your actions?" Unmoving, she held her fierce gaze, her bottom lip puckering in moody determination as she closed one eye and held her aim at my chest. Yuki's throat started to rumble behind me.

"Put that thing away, before I take umbrage and break the gift the prince so gracefully gave you." An empty threat, as I would do no such thing, but my warning gave her pause enough she opened her eyes and lowered the weapon. "Go home, Lera, I must speak to the prince alone," I enunciated slowly, crossing my arms, and looking down at Prince Felyx.

He made a nervous keening noise, before glancing at Lera and giving her a tight nod. I kept my eyes trained on him, as I waited patiently for the blonde wisps of hair to disappear.

I should have been furious; his actions had caused me embarrassment and undermined my authority. I knew any other in my stead would have heavily scolded him, punishing him through vigorous and repetitive training. He would remember the ache in his body before he thought to run away again.

After all, is that not what the likes of Truda or Maiya would do in my situation? We stood in silence as I watched Prince Felyx's body shift awkwardly from side to side.

"There will be no punishment," I said, finally. Prince Felyx looked up in confusion.

"There won't?" he asked, his voice timid.

"Do you understand what you did was wrong?"

He nodded.

"Which is why, there shall be none," I confirmed, getting down to one knee. "My prince, my duty as your mentor is to guide you to the realisation of your mistake and advise you to do better. I have about as much desire to punish you, as you have to receive punishment."

"I don't want Lera to be punished either."

"That is for her mother to decide," I said, thinking the elfling would benefit from some discipline, considering she did not show any sign of regret for raising her weapon at me.

"I shouldn't have run away."

"It was irresponsible to put yourself at risk." I tried to avoid thinking about what could have happened if he had been found by the wrong person. "And look at the state of poor Yuki, he stinks!" I followed, which drew a slight smile from the prince.

"I just miss her," he said, and my heart instantly warmed for him, "I knew you wouldn't let me go," he whined, and I placed my hand under his chin to lift his head.

"I missed them too," I replied softly.

"Really?"

"Yes, and if I had known of your intentions, I may have offered my help. So next time, ask, understand?"

"Okay." He looked over to where Lera had recently stood, likely contemplating when he might see her again.

"What if I could guarantee you more time with Lera?" I asked curiously, an idea suddenly springing to mind. Prince

Felyx's face lit up with immediate enthusiasm. "You must promise me you will never again do anything this foolish," I said, adamant my days of trawling through sewage tunnels would forever remain in my past.

"I won't ever run away again!" He beamed.

"Then let me take you home, we all need a bath, and afterwards I can work towards giving you reason to remain faithful to that promise."

When I returned Prince Felyx to the relief of his parents, I was thankful General Maiya was not present to provide me with further reprimanding, and headed to my bedchambers.

After a well-needed wash and change of clothes, I ventured back through the city towards Lelane's house, intent on presenting my proposal. Although my plan was primarily constructed with Prince Felyx in mind, if executed correctly, it would also grant me the opportunity to spend more time with Lelane. Though I worried after the incident with Truda, she would want nothing to do with me, I felt an unsettling in my stomach from the pressures of fulfilling my promise to Prince Felyx and Lelane's potential rejection.

Would Prince Felyx's disappointment cause him to resent me? When his training regressed, would I be dismissed? Who would replace me as his trainer? These intrusive questions fed my anxiety as my boots moved of their own accord.

I stopped in front of Lelane's house and noticed damage

to its already dilapidated exterior. There was a crack in the small window, and the front door was uneven on its hinges. As I prepared to knock, the door swiftly opened and Lelane tumbled out hurriedly, wiping away streaks of tears from her cheeks. She collided straight into my chest, and I had to grasp her to prevent her from falling. Her lips parted as our eyes locked, and her hand gripped my forearms as she automatically pulled herself closer, as though she was relieved to see me.

"Are you okay?" I asked, and she locked her arms around my waist in response and pressed her body tightly against mine, with her face resting in the crook of my neck. Immediately I cradled her, offering soothing sounds as I stroked her hair, and she began to cry. She trembled in my arms, upset, but by what or who, I did not know.

Seeming to remember herself and our exposed presence at her front door, she pulled back, glancing around nervously as she wiped at her eyes.

"What happened?" I asked, standing in the doorway.

"Nothing," she said in a broken voice, "I am just happy to see you."

"You seem distressed." She shook her head and fronted a smile.

"I was hoping you would find me, I am so sorry for what happened the other day. I would never put you in that position."

"What position?"

"It was why I thought it best to stay away entirely, I have

no desire to make trouble for you, Quin, and my life has become somewhat complicated and I—" Was she blaming herself for Truda's brutish behaviour?

"I punched Truda," I blurted, cutting her off. Lelane's face paled.

"You did what!?"

"I felt it was deserved, though I wished I had handled it better. I confronted Truda for how she acted towards you, and her responses only angered me further."

"So, you hit her?" I nodded. "I cannot believe you did that."

"Neither can I," I said, releasing a huge breath. "She did not retaliate; I think even she was too shocked."

The bottled nervousness finally seeped out of me; I felt a powerful surge running through my veins for confessing what I had done in her defence. On reflection, I was still surprised Truda did not challenge me to a fight. She had unsheathed her sword for far less in the past.

"Why?" I knew she was referring to my violent outburst.

"Because you are my friend, and it felt like the right thing to do," I said, and she looked at me completely dumbfounded. "Can we go inside for a moment?"

"Okay," she replied, still slightly bewildered. She stepped aside to allow me to enter, this time she did not offer me a beverage or supper, Lelane merely stood in the sitting room, waiting for me to speak.

"I came to talk about Lera, specifically regarding how I would like her to become Prince Felyx's sparring partner."

"Quin," she replied, her tone regretful. "Lera cannot go back to the Training House."

"She will not need to; I have arranged for equipment to be transported to the palace. She will train with the prince there."

"Lera is not like other elflings."

"I had noticed," I replied, but Lelane shook her head.

"Despite my protests, Terra often takes her to The Sanctum. She says I am neglecting my duty to her training, that I am being too lenient." I frowned as I recalled the stench of blood and sweat in that forsaken place. I remember the cover-up Addox claimed The Sanctum is being used for. It is no place for an elfling so young to attend. "I fear what it is doing to her, sometimes when I look into her eyes, she seems…unfeeling." I stepped forward, placing a comforting arm on her shoulder.

"All the more reason for her to train with me, Lelane. I have witnessed her confidence, her voraciousness. She is also curious, and as you may have already noticed, quite fond of Prince Felyx. I believe they can bring out the best in each other."

"You truly believe so?" she asked, a glimmer of hope in her eyes.

"I do. Besides, I have a sneaky suspicion it will be difficult to keep them separated regardless." She smiled.

"I know Lera has missed him."

"Which shows she is not as immune to feelings as you believe." I squeezed her shoulder lightly. "You could come too," I suggested. "To support her training and further build the bond between you." Lelane smiled.

"I do wish we could become close again," she replied, looking at me intently as she said so.

"You will not regret it, Lelane, I promise," I said, hoping I could deliver on all the declarations I had made that day.

12

Distractions

I looked around the large hall and marvelled at my handy work. In the space of a mere few hours, and with the help of Brenith, I had transformed the abandoned banquet hall, full of dust sheet-covered furniture, into a fully-fledged training room. It was complete with balance beams, leather mats, wooden dummies, freestanding archery targets and a fully stocked weapons rack. Tomorrow would be the first day I would train Prince Felyx and Lera together, and I was more than excited at the prospect.

After assessing the room once more and deciding to reposition the wooden dummies, I was ready to turn in for the night. No doubt I would need much rest to keep up with the trainee's energy levels. When I saw a shadowed figure lurking behind me, I knew it was him before he had the chance to announce his presence.

"A little risky is it not? Frequently stalking a member of the queen's council, especially now the human curfew is in effect," I said without turning.

"You gonna lock me up?" he asked, his voice playful.

"I should."

Wearing all black, he removed the hood that was hiding his features, revealing his curly dark hair.

"But you won't," he said with confidence, standing next to me with an annoying grin on his face. "What's all this?" He gestured to the apparatus in the room.

"For the prince," I told him. "We are to continue his combat studies here."

"What's wrong with the Training House?" He walked around and inspected the equipment.

"His new training companion is not permitted to enter."

"The elf from the marketplace's kid?" I nodded, how did he know that? "Will your friend be attending too?"

"Perhaps," I replied, glancing at him through narrowing eyes.

"Will you teach them hand to hand?"

"Of course," I said incredulously at his questioning. Addox took a step onto the leather mats at the centre of the room, removing his heavy surcoat and revealing an armless tunic, and his rippling muscles hidden underneath.

"Show me."

"What?" I asked, my eyes wide.

"Teach me what you would them."

"You are one of Truda's elites, I doubt there is anything new you could learn from me." I took a step back, hesitant at the thought of once again being so close to him.

"Probably not, but I'm game if you are?"

"No," I said, my voice clear as I held eye contact.

"Why not? No one's here." He spread his arms wide. He was right, it was late, and I knew the whereabouts of my guards, none were close by, and the royal family were likely in a deep slumber.

"I do not have the time."

"Sounds like you're just making excuses. Afraid I'll hurt you little elf?" he taunted, full of egotistical assurance.

"You seem very confident."

"Don't tell me the thought hadn't crossed your mind, too." He uncrossed his arms, his stance wide as he raised his chin. "Come on, think you can take me?" He was baiting me, and I knew better than to feed into it, but for some reason, the thought of wiping that smirk off his face made my pulse race.

I barred the doors to the hall to avoid any unexpected visitors from entering and I exhaled a deep breath, turning to find Addox staring at me intently. Watching him back, I slowly removed my chest piece and armguards, carefully placing them on the floor in the corner of the room. I slipped my boots from my feet, placing them down neatly and walked towards him on the mat. I stood opposite him, stretching my limbs in preparation.

"What're you doing?" he asked, his tone humorous. I ignored him, focusing only on the rhythm of my rising chest.

Resting my palms together, I closed my eyes as I calmed my mind, imagining it was not Addox standing before me, but an ordinary foe, an elven challenger who would compromise my position if I did not put them in their place.

I opened my eyes and nodded briefly. It was time I taught this human a lesson.

"Let us see what you have learnt," I replied, my voice calm and measured.

Addox bounced on his heels, then quickly lunged at me, reaching for my throat. I swerved, deflecting his arm, spinning as I grabbed his wrist with my free hand and yanked it hard behind his back. Immediately he grunted and I released him, calmly stepping backwards. He looked surprised, stretching his arm as if to check it was still attached to his body. Keeping a defensive stance, I watched him carefully as he began to circle me.

He launched at me again, and this time, I ducked under his arms, staying low as I turned and thrust my elbow into his chest. Taking the hit, he tried to wrap his hands around my neck, but I pushed him up, rotating my body away from him, and pulling his arm straight while applying pressure on his elbow. The shock of pain brought him immediately to his knees.

"I didn't expect you to be so strong," he grunted.

"A mistake often made," I replied serenely in his ear, my grip on his arm firm and unyielding. I had spent a lifetime dealing with others' perceptions of my abilities based on my size. It was one of the many reasons I had trained rigorously until I became worthy of their recognition. "Did you think I had acquired command of the royal guard by skill of my bow alone?"

Addox pushed up from the floor with all his strength, forcing me to release him and skip backwards. The muscles in his forearms flexed as he righted himself, his chest rose as he inhaled deep breaths.

"Good, then I don't have to hold anything back." He stared at me defiantly, removing his hardened vambrace from his shoulders, throwing it to the floor and rotating his neck.

"Try not to hurt me," I mimicked sweetly, locking my eyes with his.

With a low growl, he charged, swinging his right arm to grab me, then his left. Taking measured steps and tilting my body, I easily avoided both attempts. I raised my bare foot and kicked him hard in the chest in retaliation. He stumbled back, cradling his centre with a stunned look in his previously focused eyes, as though he could not quite believe what was happening. Seemingly more determined, he came at me again, his nostrils flaring as he charged with full force, a loud battle cry erupting from his lips.

I held my position and waited until the absolute last moment, before feeling my weight slowly shift beneath my heel. I jumped forward, wrapping my legs around his waist as my arm tugged around his neck, spinning under his weight, and throwing him over onto his back. I held a crouched position directly over him.

"How?" He coughed, looking up at me from the floor,

his breathing ragged.

“Practise and discipline,” I replied, unable to hold back my smile from his dazed expression.

“I got you all wrong, didn’t I?” he said suddenly, his demeanour changing. I frowned, not understanding what he meant, when he reached up and brushed a lock of hair from my face. My heart racing both from the exhilaration of our fight and the tentative interaction between us now.

“You’ve got power, but you don’t use it,” he said, getting up off the floor.

“I do not incite unnecessary violence.” I hoped that would bring an end to the conversation. I had already taken things too far with this man, I could not compromise myself again. Slowly I backed away from him, heading towards the heavy doors.

“Quin, wait!” Addox cried, reaching for my arm. I shrugged him off.

“Do not address me by that name,” I snapped, irritated he had used the name reserved only for Lelane, and that I had behaved so foolishly around him again. What was I thinking sparring with a human? Allowing him to bait me into a challenge. I had nothing to prove. He followed closely and jumped in front of me to block my path.

“Why are you so angry?”

“I suppose it must take the fun out of your taunting, to know I was never threatened by you,” I replied, shrugging past him and donning my boots and armour. When I was dressed, he was right there, invading my space.

"Why are you being like this?" he asked, his face leaning down towards mine.

I tried again to shrug him away, gently, but Addox gripped my arms, guiding me reluctantly back until I was flush against the wall.

"Leave it be," I pleaded, feeling shame wash over me as his gaze intensified. He shook his head.

"You're not going anywhere." He placed his palms at either side of my head. "So, you might as well tell me what's got you so spooked all of a sudden, now we both know it isn't cos you're afraid of me."

I looked away, my eyes glittering as I held back my frustration.

"I'll find out one way or the other, might as well just—"

"I wanted you to kiss me!" I blurted, cutting him off. His arms dropped, and he stepped away from me. I continued to ensure he understood the danger I posed to him. "You invade my thoughts, make me feel things I have never known before," I told him. "I am depraved and full of longing for things I should never hope to have. Do you understand now?"

"Yes," he replied, his throat bobbing.

"You must stay away from me, Addox," I finished. Angry I could not rein in my emotions like my peers. I had become the damaged, sentimental disappointment my mother always insisted I was destined to be. I pressed a hand over my face, trying to hide the true depth of my shame from him.

I lunged for the door, but gasped as Addox suddenly yanked me back, pulling me from my thoughts. He spun me into his arms, cradling my face, and fiercely brought his lips to mine.

I melded into him, pressing myself against his solid form as he hungrily devoured me. His lips were soft and warm, his tongue forcing me to open to him as he delved deep, his fingers running up my neck and into the back of my hair. I reached my arms up around his neck, arching against him. I felt dizzy and delirious, several sensations assaulting every nerve in my body all at once. He bent slightly to lift my legs, wrapping them around his waist, his fierce kisses relentless, and I gasped as I felt something hard against my thigh.

"Addox," I gasped, as he continued to kiss me.

"I know." His voice was guttural and anguished all at the same time, as his fingers dug into my flesh. It was wrong and perfect all at the same time, and I never wanted the kiss to end.

Then suddenly, remembering myself and the vow I took, I pushed him away and vaulted out of the banquet hall, leaving a bewildered and breathless Addox in my wake.

As expected, Prince Felyx was beyond ecstatic with the set-up in the palace banquet hall, beginning the day with animated inquisitions.

"Will you teach her archery?"

"I have yet to decide," I replied as we made our way to the palace gate.

“I propose sword fighting, she’d like that,” he said excitedly, mimicking the movements he had learned, waving his arms around haphazardly.

“Are you saying that just to prevent her from surpassing your skill with a bow?” I asked, chuckling.

“No,” he replied, blushing, and here I had thought our prince did not have a competitive bone in his body.

“It would only be fair for me to test all her abilities. That way I can fairly derive…” The remainder of my sentence escaped as an inaudible gasp. Prince Felyx froze beside me, our attention drawn to the sight ahead.

Dressed in finely matching training leathers adorned with armless embroidered bodices, armguards, and polished calf-covering boots, stood Lelane and Lera. Their blonde hair, twisted into symmetrical singular plaits, hung over one shoulder, almost rendering them unrecognisable. With an extra skip in his step, Prince Felyx rushed forward to greet Lera, her lip curling upward on one side at his reaction. Lelane bounced on her heels lightly, tucking away a strand of hair that had fallen across her face.

“Is my attire appropriate?” she asked innocently as I looked her over, amazed at the outfit she had chosen. “We wanted to ensure we were presentable for the palace.”

I glanced down at Lera, stunned at how far removed she was from the dirt-covered street stray that had been stalking us from the shadows. She was pretty, like her mother, her bright blue eyes seemed more enhanced against her clean hair and skin.

“You both look incredible.” I extended my elbow as an invitation to escort them inside. Lelane laced her arm through mine, her face beaming. “Everything is set up and ready, this way.” The elflings ran on ahead, while my friend fell into step beside me as I guided her through the palace. Lelane’s mouth dropped in dazed wonder as she absorbed her surroundings, marvelling at the opulence of the tapestries and fabrics draping the walls and window frames. When we reached the training hall, she was in awe of the assemblage of equipment.

“This is amazing!” she exclaimed, taking note of the archery targets, training dummies and obstacles.

“Is the queen okay with this?” she asked, clearly referring to us training together.

“She encouraged it. Prince Felyx has been quite vocal in his desire to see Lera, and this creates a beneficial opportunity.”

“This one’s mine.” Prince Felyx beamed as he pulled Lera to a wooden figure in the corner of the room. Lera cocked her head, smirked, and then strode forward confidently, punching the dummy in its centre. Debris spilt from the canvas onto the floor, straw tearing the material at its sides.

“Lera!” Lelane shouted, aghast at her disrespectful behaviour. She ignored her mother’s outburst and pulled at the threads now barely holding the object together.

“Let me handle this,” I said to Lelane before approaching. Lera quirked a challenging grin, waiting to see what I would do. “Are you going to give me trouble, Lera?” I asked calmly. “Because I had promised Prince Felyx a sparring partner, and I would hate to go back on my word." Prince Felyx's worry-stricken face quickly shot to me, something pleading in his features. With a roll of her eyes, Lera flippantly let go of the dummy and moved away.

"I thought you would see things my way," I commented before directing the elfling and prince to the first weapon stand.

"Prince Felyx, would you like to demonstrate to Lera how accomplished you are with a bow?" I asked and the prince bit his lip, looking at the ground.

"Okay."

"Lelane, would you mind helping me move the targets away from the windows?" The likelihood he would miss and crack one of the windows was slim, but the image of General Maiya's enraged face cautioned me not to take any chances. Lelane bent to lift the wooden frame, only for her face to contort in pain as the target slipped with a thud to the floor. She cradled her wrist with her other hand.

"What happened? Are you hurt?" I stepped to her and reached for her wrist. Wincing, she tried to pull away, but I held firm.

"I am fine, Quin, it is nothing," she said desperately as I unwound the lace to her cuffed bracer. I was immediately silenced when her marred skin was revealed, an array of small, mixed-coloured bruises adorning her wrist. She shrugged out of my grasp, refastening the bindings on her sleeve and decided to stand opposite the elflings, ignoring my worry-stricken expression.

The bruises I had just seen, did they occur by an accident? Or had someone hurt her?

My blood boiled at the thought.

I took a watchful position as Prince Felyx and Lera each practised a turn against the elevated straw-stuffed bag dangling from the wooden cross beams.

"Keep your feet firmly planted, Prince Felyx, this exercise is for your arms, not your legs," I called. He acknowledged my instruction, before continuing his practised assault, displaying the same rigorous energy as before.

"Lera, observe his positioning." I attempted to keep them focused on the task at hand, yet my mind lingered on the fingerprint bruises lining Lelane's wrist. My mind was plagued with an onslaught of scenarios; rough hands gripping her tightly, her knees buckling in submission, her cries of pain, begging for release. Lelane had remained wordless since I had seen the bruises, her focus drawn to the children while they trained. It was only for the sake of their presence that I had not immediately demanded an explanation. I suspected I knew who had hurt her, and I would not let Lelane out of my sight until I learned the truth of the matter.

When our session was finished, I waved for my guard.

"Brenith, return the prince to his chambers for bathing. I will escort our guests home." She saluted and gestured for the young royal to follow her.

"Bye, Lera, I'll see you tomorrow." Prince Felyx waved.

"I will," I corrected him, feeling too irritable to let the mispronunciation go unchallenged.

As we silently ventured through the city, I considered how I would separate the daughter from the mother. The burning need to find out who had inflicted those bruises consumed me, and I remembered how distressed Lelane had seemed the day I had asked for Lera to train with the prince.

The centre of the city was busier than usual, the market bustling with trade and supply. The crowds parted respectfully at our approach, as Lelane followed me, staring at the floor. I supposed from an onlooker's perspective, it could seem the palace had a grievance with the elf, as a guard was escorting her home. My armour and stern expression probably fed that narrative.

"Lera, relieve the cartographer of a dozen parchments. Ask for the smoothest grain and tell her they are for the queen," I instructed as a particular stall caught my eye. "Then, see if Chanree has any Okra left to sweeten your supper." Turning to Lelane I asked, "Do you have Gossum berries in your pantry?" When she shook her head, I gave Lera further instructions. "Get a pouchful of those as well, then return straight home."

Surprisingly, Lera looked to her mother for permission, and when given the slightest of nods, she departed from our company. The moment Lera was out of sight, I clutched Lelane's arm, carefully avoiding her wrist and hoping there were no other injuries that I had yet to see. I guided her quickly to her front door, opening it on her behalf and ushering her inside.

"Quin, please do not be upset with me," she began, but

I ignored her, gesturing for her to sit at the table.

"I need you to be honest with me," I told her, maintaining eye contact. "Is Terra hurting you?" I was worried I already knew the answer. Her eyes glazed as she turned her head away, and I brought a chair next to her, sitting closely.

"Terra wants us to become a family again, she gets frustrated when I refuse," she whispered.

"She hurts you." I tried to remain calm as I watched her slowly nod her head in confirmation.

"She likes to remind me how weak I am." She pulled back the sleeve of her blouse, revealing a line of bruises.

"What was wrong when I came here yesterday?"

"I had just returned from the market, and no one would trade with me. Someone even smashed a ceramic I had tendered."

"Why?"

"Peril holds great influence over the market, and Terra is her right hand. She has the power to make things difficult for us if I continue to deny her what she wants."

I drew in a slow breath to keep my anger under control. Addox had warned The Sanctum was a front for something, that Peril was using her connections and power to gain influence over food supplies. I had no idea Lelane had been suffering to this extent and I should have seen the signs. The frayed attire, reheated suppers, the dwelling they resided in scarcely fit to house a Guan. I supposed Terra believed the more she could worsen Lelane's suffering, the faster she would run back into her arms.

"She is not the only one with influence." I leaned over and took both of her hands in mine. "I want you and Lera to come stay in the palace for a few days. Do not worry over provisions, I can make arrangements."

"Really? You would do that for us?" she asked, her eyes welling with tears.

"Yes," I replied, as I formulated a plan in my mind to secure her future and rewrite the resulting wrongs from my abandonment all those years ago. It was my fault she was stuck with this life, and I planned to do everything I could to make amends.

13

The Bargain

I managed to source spare chambers large enough to accommodate both Lelane and Lera. As they settled, I lingered only long enough to ensure they had everything they needed. It was only a temporary solution, but at least for now, Lelane and her daughter were beyond the grasp of those who sought to control or harm them.

Re-filling my pouch with dried vertebrae, I had just returned from the Raven Tower, when a cloaked figure stepped out from a shadowed alcove. Delicate hands pulled down the hood to reveal Lyzaria.

"Quickly, come inside," I said, ushering her inside my chambers. I checked over her shoulder to make sure no one had seen her, before securing the door.

"I came as soon as I could," Lyzaria said, as she watched

me light a few candles.

"You bring news?" I finally turned to face her, gesturing for her to sit.

"I have done as you asked and observed Maiya's movements from a distance. For the first few days, everything seemed normal, no sign of unusual activity in her daily routine.

"However, after a few days, she took her first excursion outside of the city. They travelled by horse which made it impossible for me to follow inconspicuously. Instead, I hid nearby, taking note of the exact time of her return and subsequent departure. At times, she ventured out alone, while on other occasions, she would be accompanied by a small party of warriors. But without fail, she would always return alone, the warriors who left with her were never seen again."

"What happened to the warriors?" I asked aloud.

"I do not yet know, but there is more," she said, and my eyes met hers expectantly. "A few nights ago, she entered The Sanctum and met with Peril in her private chambers. They talked for hours, and when she finally left, it was with a gleeful expression."

It was just as Truda suspected, General Maiya had been taking warriors out of the city, doing who-knows-what with them. To make matters worse, she was meeting with Peril privately in The Sanctum, blatantly disregarding the raised concerns of the council regarding its activities. While this information was disturbing, I could not jump to conclusions. To build a case against the general, I needed further details before attempting to incriminate her.

"We need more," I said. "Proof that General Maiya is betraying her duty for her own interests."

"I will see what I can find," Lyzaria replied with a determined look, and a singular nod of her head.

"Be careful, Lyzaria, your safety matters more to me, remember that."

"I will." She offered me a quick salute, before she pulled up the hood to her cloak and snuck out of my chambers.

"Time to say goodbye, my prince," I called, as Lelane helped me clear away the discarded arrows and weaponry from another morning's training. Lera was taunting Yuki, flicking his snout, and leaping out of the way before he could nip at her ankles. Prince Felyx chuckled as he tried to grab Yuki before the fox could take a bite, which was proving fruitless, as the animal was unable to match Lera's speed and vitality.

"Lera, stop that!" Lelane tried, biting her lip while her daughter still ignored her. She was having far too much fun teasing the little canine.

"Allow me." I rested a hand briefly on Lelane's shoulder. I produced a particularly small pouch from my pocket and gave it a shake. Yuki was immediately brought to attention, scrambling to heel at my feet, his snout pointing to the hide sack containing his favourite snack. I quickly fed him before returning my attention to the prince. "Let us get you back to your parents," I said, keeping my voice stern, and he immediately nodded his head.

"See you later Lera," he said, following Yuki and me out of the hall.

"I shall stop by later to see if you need anything," I said to Lelane, but she only chuckled, rolling her eyes. Looking back, I saw her take Lera's hand and head down the corridor towards their chambers, as I escorted the prince through the palace.

To our equal surprise, as the prince and I stepped onto the open courtyard, we found the queen and her consort were not alone.

"Truda!" Prince Felyx exclaimed, running from my side straight to the picnic where Truda and Erik sat opposite his parents. Yuki bound off to greet them in equal excitement at this irregular visit. I felt Truda's intense gaze bore into mine, and I responded with a nervous smile, before retreating to stand beneath the large blossoming tree at the far end of the garden.

As I watched over the royal family, it was hard to ignore their delighted features as they talked animatedly over a picnic. Although I could not hear the topic of conversation, Truda's booming laughter seemed to carry in the garden, as though she purposely wanted me to hear it.

We still had not spoken, and although I felt ragged and drained of guilt, I could not help but measure the behaviours of our friendship, its foundation built solely on Truda's terms. I wanted to rekindle things and gain her forgiveness, but this time she would be the one to make the first move. I would settle for nothing less than the apology I was owed for the way she spoke about Lelane and Lera.

When Truda finally excused herself from the royal family, she left Erik engaged in a deep conversation with the queen's consort. My spine tingled, and I raised my chin, pretending not to notice.

"You have not returned to the Training House," she said, taking slow, measured steps towards me. "The queen tells me you have made a training arena in the palace. I hope that was not for my benefit."

"Not everything is about you," I replied, keeping my voice neutral, with a hint of defiance.

"Any news from your spy?" She flicked a piece of dirt from beneath her nail, before looking up to meet my gaze.

"No."

"Nothing at all?" she asked again, her eyes narrowing, and I felt a swooping sensation in my gut.

Was that her motive for being here? Not to visit the royal family or to make amends with a friend, but to find evidence of General Maiya's malcontent, gaining leverage she could use against her, the only thing she genuinely cared about.

The thought made me angry.

"I will inform you the moment I hear from her," I lied.

"Good. I hoped you would not be foolish enough to allow a petty disagreement to interfere with what truly matters, Acqueline," she said, meeting my eyes again, the gold in them glittering in the bright sunlight.

“Of course not,” I said, clenching my hands to hide my inner turmoil.

Something tickled my face, and I swatted it away instinctively, turning to rest on my forearms as I roused from my sleep. I quickly realised the cot was dipping to one side due to the weight of a large figure sitting beside me.

“Hey,” Addox said casually, as though this was an acceptable ornery occurrence.

“Addox, what are you doing here?” A common question I felt like I asked every time our paths crossed.

“I’ve been thinking about our kiss,” he said, and I groaned, covering my face in embarrassment.

“Please, Addox, can we not talk about that? It was a mistake, it can never happen again.”

“Wait, just hear me out,” Addox stayed at his spot on the edge of the bed. “I’ve got a bargain I’d like to make.”

I ignored him, closing my eyes. Perhaps if I remained silent and fell back to sleep, he would leave me alone and I could pretend my body was not so alert to his proximity.

“You’ll like it,” he added, a hand brushed up my arm.

“What are you doing?” I asked, sitting up abruptly, my eyes wide with surprise.

“Showing you,” he replied, coaxing his hand along my skin again, his gentle finger strokes so delicate they sent tingles across my skin. His touch travelled from my shoulder, snaking slowly down to my wrist, and finally resting in my palm. I found myself staring at his hand for a moment, marvelling at the difference between our sizes, unable to pull away.

"What kind of bargain?" I asked nervously.

"Train me how to fight," he said without hesitation, his finger tracing the edge of mine. Of all the things I had expected him to say, that was certainly not one of them. "You're clearly more skilled than Truda, and I want you to teach me instead. I'll make it worth your while."

No one truly knows what I am capable of because I purposely hold back my abilities. Demonstrating a skill that poses a challenge to your opponent is one thing, proving you are superior is an entirely different matter. I wanted to be treated as an equal, revered, and respected, but when it became clear I could surpass my mentors, I held back my skills. I did not want to attract the wrong attention for the challenge or threat I could pose to them.

"There is nothing I want from you," I said quickly, remembering myself and flinching away from him.

"That's not exactly true, is it, little elf?" He quirked a smile while outstretching a hand to reach for me again. This time, when I swatted his hand away, he stood and paced the room in two strides, before turning and facing me again. "This is my bargain, you'll train me. Teach me to be better, to fight like you," he said, his voice firmer this time. "And in exchange, I'll give you everything your body desires."

My jaw dropped in shock, unable to respond.

"It's a simple temporary arrangement," he said slowly, leaning casually against the wall, folding his arms. "You teach me your skills and I'll show you mine."

"What kind of skills?" I asked, my throat suddenly dry.

Why did I even ask that?

"The kind a decade locked in a Pleasure House awards you."

"I have seen you fight in the Training House, you do not need my help," I replied, trying to instantly forget his meaning.

"Against a human contender, sure, but it's your kind I want to match against."

"How…" I stuttered, feeling nervous at the thought of uttering the words aloud. "How do you propose this arrangement would work exactly?"

Addox's smirk intensified, obviously revelling in my temptation to agree.

"Simple, you train me after your duties, and then, I'll spend the night with you."

"The whole night?"

"If you want, or until you're satisfied." I felt my cheeks warm.

"No, I cannot jeopardise my duty. The royal family need me."

"They're not going to know, this'll be a little arrangement between us," Addox said, boldly sitting back down beside me on the bed, his hand stroking up my leg. I froze, watching his fingers trail lightly from my knee to the apex of my thigh, stopping just as our gazes locked. "Aren't you curious?"

"Maybe," I admitted. A shiver ran through me as he pressed his palm and kneaded the inside of my thigh. Slowly, he leaned forward, our lips brushing as my pulse raced.

"I want to know what you feel like," he whispered, pressing a tentative kiss to my lips. "What you sound like."

I groaned, wanting that, too.

"If I agree to this, no-one else is to know," I warned.

"I'm good at keeping secrets."

"It will be as you say, a temporary arrangement. It stops the moment I command it," I added, keeping my tone firm.

"Whatever you want," he replied with a smile.

"I mean it, Addox, if this becomes complicated in any way, I need assurance you will not return to your taunting ways."

"Don't worry, little elf, I've no plan to get attached," he said, extending his hand to me. I ignored it, not knowing what he expected me to do with the gesture. "We have a deal then?"

"Yes," I breathed, hardly able to believe I was agreeing to do this. "Meet me tomorrow, at midnight, in the training hall."

"Then I look forward to tomorrow, little elf." A firm smirk plastered across his face before he slunk out of my bedchambers.

The prince's joy grew with every session that we trained,

with Lera standing clean and groomed at his side.

"How are you today?" I asked, stepping into Lelane's path, and gesturing to her wrist, not only addressing her injury, but inquiring about her overall well-being.

"It is healing nicely; I will be able to spar against you in no time," she replied with a blushing smile.

"I have invited Brenith to train today," I said. "To give the elflings a chance to work together against an opponent." Lelane's eyebrows raised in excitement.

"Do you think they are ready for that?"

"Only one way to find out." I ushered her into the training hall, the trainees already briefed and prepped for engagement. I directed Lelane to stand beside me at the most ostentatious viewing point.

Lera and Prince Felyx took their wooden swords and raised them against Brenith. They abruptly moved in unison, but the seasoned warrior was too fast for them, dodging their attacks easily.

Realising thrusting aimlessly was not going to work, Lera pulled the prince aside and whispered something in his ear. Passing Prince Felyx her sword, Lera stepped aside, allowing him to take the lead and advance on Brenith. My guardswoman kept her focus on him, skilfully avoiding his hearty, yet ultimately futile two-handed thrusts. While Brenith was distracted, Lera crept up behind her. However, she quickly became wise to their ruse and spun to face Lera.

Prince Felyx immediately lunged forward, forcing Brenith's attention back to him but she stumbled, and in that moment, Prince Felyx tossed one of the wooden swords in the air. Lera caught it, swinging the sword hard, hitting Brenith low on the back of her leg. She lost her balance completely and fell on her back. Lera placed her boot on Brenith's chest defiantly, as Prince Felyx held his sword against her throat.

They did it. Working together they had easily beaten one of the toughest warriors in the royal guard. Lera stood tall as Prince Felyx rushed to her side. He clutched her hand and raised it in the air in triumph, both proudly posing together as one. Brenith stood, brushing herself off as she gave them a brief and entirely insincere congratulations, before spouting criticisms of how their attack could have been better.

"I never imagined they would have come so far in such a short time," Lelane said, astonished.

"I do not think you realise how much talent your daughter has. With skills of her calibre, she could reach the highest of positions within the city," I said proudly. Truly, even I had overlooked the potential Lera held. She watched other's fight, observing for weaknesses and vantage points. She had the mind of a warrior far beyond her years, even in her stubbornness.

I could not help but think of the asset she could be to the monarch, the things our future king could accomplish with such a vicious, loyal servant by his side. I realised the opportunity she presented. I could teach her and provide her with skills I would never pass on to kin of my own. Lera was still so young, an infinite number of possibilities for her future, and I wanted to help her grow into the best version of herself.

The idea of my legacy continuing in another brought a smile to my face.

"I should go," Lelane said abruptly, her face pained.

"What, why?"

"I will return to collect Lera later," she added, her voice low and sad as she walked away. I glanced at the children, thankful to find them still heavily involved in Brenith's instruction, before turning to follow her.

Feeling flustered and confused, I picked up my pace, my boots thumping against the sandstone marble. When I reached Lelane, I spun her around to face me, catching a glimpse of a tear before she wiped it away.

"What just happened?" I asked.

"This is my fault, I cannot be here."

"I thought watching Lera train brought you joy?"

"It does." She rubbed her face with her hands.

"Then why are you so upset?" Without answering me, she shook her head and turned away again, walking faster from me this time, and something constricted in my throat. I sprinted in front of her, arms spread wide, blocking her path. Lelane was forced to stop, searching for an alternative exit, her attention was everywhere but on me.

"Lelane, please talk to me," I begged in desperation. "Did I say something wrong?"

"It is too painful to bear," she cried. "Watching someone else I love be torn away from me to pursue honour and prestige." Her tone was full of agony.

I understood immediately. This was not just about her daughter, Lera. She was referring to the fact I had forsaken what could have been between us by choosing to join the royal guard. Lelane had been heartbroken the day I told her.

"Lelane—" I began, but she pulled away, clenching her fists.

"I thought I could do this," she interrupted. "I thought I could be your friend again and ignore all the reminders of what we could have meant to each other. To see you in your guard's uniform and all it represents, to watch as you are so unaffected by our nearness."

"What are you saying?"

"I have no place in your life anymore, Quin," she wailed.

Instantly, I felt the turmoil at the thought she would rescind the notion of our rekindled friendship. I selfishly needed her, to have someone to confide in when the burdens of my duty weighed too heavily on my shoulders, to laugh with, and remind me of the little wonders in life. To reminisce of childish mischief and hopeless dreams.

"I know I hurt you, Lelane—" I began, but she cut me off, becoming more hysterical as our conversation continued.

"Hurt me? You chose a life of duty over me!" she shouted, and I winced.

"It was not like that." I kept my tone gentle.

"The moment you befriended Truda, you were never the same. You spent all your time training, ignoring everyone and everything else that should have mattered more," she said, wiping the fresh tears running down her cheeks.

"You are right," I blurted, raising my hands, begging her to wait. "We were elflings and you were my best friend. I was so scared I would lose you, I figured joining the royal guard was the safer option."

"Safer than what?" She sniffled, pausing in her movements.

"Than telling you the truth."

"So, instead, you joined the royal guard, and lost me anyway."

"Yes, because I was not brave enough then. I knew how you felt about me, Lelane, and I loved you too, but like a sister, nothing more."

A pregnant silence stretched between us, only disturbed by the occasional sniffle emitted from Lelane, and the muted sounds of the Prince and Lera training in the banquet hall.

"Lera is all I have left, I cannot bear to lose her, too," she finally whimpered.

"I would never take her away, Lelane," I soothed, stepping closer towards her.

"I suppose, I never gave you a chance to explain, did I?"

"I do not blame you for that, I handled the situation poorly." I kept my voice soft. "The moment I saw you outside the Training House after all those years, I knew I wanted to make things right between us again."

"I wished for that, too."

"Then stay," I pleaded. "Let me continue to do everything in my power to make up for the last decade."

A fresh tear fell down her face, and I could no longer

stand the emotion in her eyes, stepping forwards, I pulled her into me.

"I never want to lose you again." She clutched me tightly as she wept into my chest.

"I promise you, Lelane, nothing will ever tear us apart again," I said, stroking the back of her head. "You are my best friend, I will protect you, always."

"She abandoned her post again?" I asked a member of my guardswomen.

"Yes, she was barely at the palace for more than a few moments, before, without warning, she took off," she replied.

Due to other distractions, it had been a while since I had the time to check in with my guardswomen, aside from overseeing patrolling rotations. It seemed Shanon had not heeded my warnings, and still neglected her duties regularly despite the threat of being removed from the royal guard.

I let out an exasperated sigh, knowing I could not ignore her misgivings this time. She was a liability and a weakness we could no longer afford, and though disbanding her would upset me greatly, the alternative posed a great risk to the royal family's safety.

"Acqueline!" Brenith cried, vaulting around the corner in panic. "The queen…" she stuttered, unable to finish her sentence.

I swallowed hard as I took in her terrified expression.

No, no, no!

A shudder ran through me as I thought of the worst possibilities. Before I had crossed the threshold of the gardens, a shrill scream pierced my ears, as a gust of wind assaulted my face, blowing my hair back from my shoulders.

I froze in terror as I witnessed Queen Fortuna howling in the centre of a vortex of wind, erratic gusts violently swirling shredded greenery around her. The queen's consort had wrapped Prince Felyx in his arms against the force, Yuki huddled behind them as they cowered at the edge of the stream. I saw a large oak tree creak and sway behind them, with a large branch folding too far forward, and I sensed it was on the brink of snapping. Phoenyx and the young prince were caught between the falling branch and the whirling tower of flying debris.

"Get them to safety," I shouted to Brenith, attempting to carry my voice over the deafening sounds of the wind assaulting the garden. The stream rippled as it flowed over its bank, flowers were torn from their soil beds, and everything surrounding us was forced to bend to the magic summoned by Queen Fortuna.

"Your majesty!" I called, but she could not hear me. Absorbed in the power, her neck craned back as her pitch raised impossibly higher. The wind spiralled with such force; her hair waved vertically above her head.

My thighs burned as I slowly fought forward to reach her, the strength of the wind rattling my armour with intensity. I held up my arm to shield my eyes, and I finally managed to enter the vortex, trying again to call out to her, but my voice was barely audible. With all my might, I strained forward and placed a singular hand on Queen Fortuna's shoulder. The moment she felt my touch, the vortex abruptly dissipated causing me to topple to the ground, having no force to fight against.

Resting my body breathlessly on my forearms, I gaped at our queen in disbelief. Brenith and Phoenyx ran to us and immediately the human cradled our queen in his arms, brushing the hair from her face as she cried into his chest.

"I'm sorry, I'm so sorry," she repeated, clutching onto his tunic tightly as he lifted her into his lap. Lifting her gaze, he pressed gentle kisses to her forehead, nose, and lips, all the while whispering sweet words of comfort to soothe her. His expression was full of worry and passion.

"Acqueline?" I looked up to find Prince Felyx outstretching his hand to attempt to help me up. I took it gently, while brushing off the blades of grass that had lodged into the crevices of my armour.

The prince tugged at my finger and looked at me in secret suggestion, tilting his head towards the calm stream. When we reached the bank, the watercourse having regained its peacefulness, he lowered his voice, "There's something wrong with mother, isn't there?" I took a slow breath.

"She just needs a little guidance. Your mother grew up outside the city. She never had the opportunity to train in the Mages' Temple to learn how to utilise her gifts."

"She's scared."

"I know, but your father is here to support her, we all are."

"I'm scared, too." He looked down to the floor, and kicked a stone awkwardly into the water.

"Which is only natural," I told him honestly.

"Can you teach me to be brave?"

"I do not need to teach you a characteristic you already possess." I smiled down at him. "But I will train you to conceal your feelings." After all, I had trained myself to do just that over the years; hiding the ever-constant turmoil of my own insecurities.

14

Broken Oath

I was a bundle of nerves, my brain fogged with apprehension over what was going to happen after our training. As agreed, Addox and I met in the training hall after midnight, and despite my exhaustion from everything that had happened in the last few days, the thought of allowing myself to become so vulnerable in his presence both exhilarated and terrified me in equal measure.

It was only when I heard his determined growl, that I realised he was launching at me with another mock attack. I stepped towards him in a flash, bracing his weight onto my shoulder, as I instinctively flipped him over. His body landed with a heavy thud on the mat.

"Sorry," I quickly said, shaking my head, and trying to clear away my distracting thoughts. I realised in my lack of concentration, I had haphazardly tossed him across the room for the third time since our training had started.

"Is this how you train the prince?" Addox groaned from his position on the floor, "Throw him about till he learns to be faster on his feet?"

"Of course not," I replied, leaning over with my arm extended to help him up.

"Your instructions don't make sense, the practises are backwards and I'm not learning anything new," he said, aggravated.

"I am not accustomed to training fully grown humans." I took a step back from him, desperate to create space between us. Teaching him hand-to-hand combat had huge disadvantages I had not considered before, such as regular contact and forced proximity. My body felt tense, and sweat streaked across my brow.

"Are you ill?" he asked, commenting on my appearance and somewhat erratic demeanour. I raised an eyebrow to insinuate the ridiculousness of the suggestion.

"I have not suffered sickness since I was an elfling." We were not as susceptible to ailments as humans, thanks to the advantages bestowed by the flawless genetic legacy inherited from our magical ancestors.

"Then pull yourself together," he snapped. "Because we had a deal, and right now, I don't feel like I'm getting my fair end of the bargain."

He was right, I was teaching him everything wrong. I focussed on confusing combat sequences and completely disregarded all the common practices I had used to train Prince Felyx and Lera. It was his fault I deduced. Simply being in his presence, I could not stop thinking of the impending, invisible countdown that would conclude with us moving on to other physical activities. I had spent more than one sleepless night trying to imagine what connecting with a human might feel like. I even asked Truda about it, in the past, though she withheld the details, and I had no one else whom I could openly talk to about such things.

So far, we had only kissed, but the sensations were enough for me to obsess over the memory of how my body reacted to him, how a strange tingle spread across the surface of my skin wherever he touched. I had tried to imagine it, as I used my own soft hands to replicate the scene, stroking my fingers slowly up my arms, pretending they were his rough calloused hands instead.

"You're not concentrating!" Addox barked, folding his arms across his broad chest.

"I know, just give me a moment," I replied, reaching for a decanter filled with water.

"What's wrong with you today?"

"Nothing," I lied, as I took a sip and wiped my mouth with the back of my hand, but Addox was not falling for it. Striding towards me with a determined yet irritated look on his face, he could tell I was not my usual self, and it made my skin flush watching him approach.

"What's wrong, little elf?" he asked gruffly. I really did wish he would stop calling me that, recognising it was a crude reference to my physical height, used mockingly to remind me I was a lesser being compared to my peers. I let out a deep sigh.

"You will think me foolish," I replied candidly.

"Tell me anyway."

"I am nervous," I admitted. "As any untouched elf would be." It took him a moment to grasp what I had meant, but the moment realisation dawned on his features, I felt my face blush.

"We don't have to do anything you don't want to," he said, surprising me, his voice soft as he inched closer to me.

"I do want to, I mean. I just…" I mumbled, struggling to find the right words to express what I wanted to tell him. Addox cupped his hand over my cheek and hooked his thumb under my chin, tilting my face up to meet his dark eyes.

"Okay," he said, resolute, and my mouth creased into a straight line, confused, my brow mirroring the movement. Then, tentatively, Addox reached and took my hand in his, pulling me to the door of the training hall.

"Where are we going?"

"To your chambers, I'm going to fulfil my end of the bargain tonight. Then tomorrow, you'll pay me back with a properly structured, thought out, training session. Where I'll have learnt something uniquely invaluable." He looked back over his shoulder, waiting expectantly for an answer. I merely nodded, the fluttering in my stomach somewhere between excitement and nauseating dizziness.

Too overwhelmed to speak, I let Addox guide me carefully

through the palace corridors, peering around each corner to check there were no guards nearby. I was aware of the whereabouts of each of my guardswomen, and I could have easily told Addox the areas to avoid, but I was too dumbfounded for my brain to connect with my mouth. It was happening, he was going to touch me, feel me in ways no other ever had, and my stomach flipped at the thought.

We reached my chambers unnoticed, and it occurred to me Addox navigated the palace with ease, effortlessly finding the fastest route to our destination. It was as though he knew its layout intimately, a fact that should have terrified me more than it did.

Closing the door, he released my hand, and I stumbled a few steps back. I watched him take a final glance beyond the door, before closing it and twisting the key to the locking position.

"What now?" I asked, my voice shaky and unconfident.

"You'll need to take off your armour and tunic," he said, shrugging out of his surcoat. The only layer he removed I realised, as he stood there watching me, waiting for me to follow his instruction. My hands felt clammy, and my heartbeat pounded in my chest as I shifted weight from foot to foot.

I suddenly felt very self-conscious of what he might think when he saw my unveiled skin. The elf I hid beneath ceremonially gifted armour that extenuated my important status. Once my clothing had gone, my body would be exposed, along with all the imperfections that reminded me of my inadequacies.

"It is too bright," I said quietly, glancing at the wall torches and candles illuminating every corner of my bare sleeping quarters. After curious and unamused glances, Addox defused all the sources of light, bar one. A small candle remained lit on the bedside, creating shadows that danced about the room.

It did nothing to defuse my nerves.

I could hear faint sounds from outside, the call of a creature somewhere in the darkness, the whistle of the breeze against the glass. I closed my eyes trying to focus on the task at hand, but my hands clenched, and I bit my bottom lip, unable to move.

"I cannot do this," I finally said, turning to face him.

What was I thinking?

I had made a vow, promising to not let personal desires interfere with my duty. If General Maiya knew the things I had planned to do with Addox in this room, she would disband me on the spot, and banish me from the palace forever. I would never admire the gardens again or be able to spend time with the royal family. Removed as Prince Felyx's trainer, I would miss him growing into the magnificent man I knew he would be.

Addox closed the distance between us, his thumb brushing along my bottom lip.

"Do you want me to touch you?" he asked, and I did. More than anything in this kingdom, I wanted to feel desired and treasured. I wanted to experience what it felt like to be loved.

Slowly, I nodded.

"Close your eyes," he whispered, and I followed his command. My body grew tense as I felt his hands pull at my buckles and leather bindings. It was an agonising moment I was desperate to get past. I knew I would never be comfortable in my own skin, but the apprehension of what he would think upon seeing me for the first time truly terrified me.

"I didn't think you'd be so coy," he said, standing behind me, as he carefully removed my breastplate. His touch was gentle and purposeful as he removed each piece. I kept my eyes closed, trying to hide the tremor in my hands as he unfastened the straps on the last piece of fabric concealing my skin.

My tunic fell to the floor in a heap, slipping from my shoulders, and the moment my bare skin came into view, I heard his audible gasp. Despite the dim light, I knew he could see them, the reason why I pushed myself to surpass my peers in my youth.

"What are—?" he began to ask, confused, as I hung my head low, ashamed of the marks on my body. They were mainly on my back, swollen streaks of pink and white. A few had landed on my biceps and inner thighs, the places where my skin was most sensitive but easily hidden from view.

I was covered in scars.

"What happened to you?" His tone was sincere and absent of all mockery. I turned to face him, unconcerned my chest was not covered, and my small breasts were fully on display.

"Not all elflings live up to the high expectations of their mothers," I confessed, watching as he looked torn, his eyes searching the empty space around us.

"She did this?" he asked, and I nodded.

"Certainly made it easier for me to choose a life of celibacy." I felt the water begin to well in my eyes. "For who would want to look at me?" Addox swallowed, his features tightly knit, as though equally pained to witness the evidence of my mother's cruelty inflicted upon me.

"Quin," he said, barely above a whisper, as a single tear fell down my cheek.

"I understand if you would like to leave, I will still train you and hold up to my end of…" My words were cut off as he pulled me in closer and pressed his lips against mine, consuming me in a deep, passionate kiss. His hand on my lower back while the other caressed the back of my head, he took control of my body and held me prisoner against him. I could not help the cry that escaped me, my nipples becoming sensitive as they rubbed against the hard leather of his tunic. His fingers pressed into my skin, and he continued to embrace me as though I was the most important thing to him in the kingdom.

I knew it was not real. That he was just overwhelmed by the sight of my marred skin and the suffering I had endured, but still, it felt far too good to push him away.

When my head fell back, his kisses trailed down my chin, across my jaw and spread down my neck, causing my breathing to quicken. His tongue ran across my body, unashamedly along my breastbone until he veered, purposely biting the tip of one nipple. I gasped, shocked by the sensation that seemed to heighten all my sensitivities. His firm hands scorched my skin as he explored and caressed.

"I want to look." His words vibrated along my skin as he whispered them between kisses across my body, his hands slid over my hips, as he guided us slowly back towards the bed. He lay me down, balancing his body over mine. He was still fully clothed, while I only wore boots and leg coverings, already untied at the waist. My breathing remained heavy, my chest rising and falling as my heart pounded.

His hand glided between the valley of my small breasts and settled just above my heart. His hand paused there, feeling the erupting thrumming beneath my skin. His eyes locked with mine and my throat caught as something unnamed passed between us. It was as though we both recognised our lives would be forever changed from this moment on; that perhaps our fates were entwined, whether we wanted it or not.

Wordlessly, he removed the rest of my clothing, leaving me completely naked and exposed to him. His calloused hand glided up from my ankle to the sensitive skin on my inner thigh, finding more scars and brushing his thumb tenderly over them. My body shuddered at his touch. I never imagined physical intimacy would elicit a reaction like this. I yearned for more; from him and from this sensation.

Suddenly his fingers stroked against the apex of my thighs, and I gasped, instantly feeling warm and slick as he began to rub and tease, my body trembled at the rhythm of his gentle caress. He kissed me, stealing my breath away, and at the same time, he pressed a finger inside.

"Addox," I whimpered, unsure why I had spoken his name aloud, but just knowing I had to. I felt overwhelmed and confused as the pressure in my core began to build. He pulled the finger out, only to gently slide it back in as he used his thumb to rub against my sensitive nub. I gasped.

"I know," he replied between another kiss, "I've got you." Addox continued to stroke and tease, adding a second finger and increasing the delectable pressure. I began to tremble, losing all control as my body rocked into a rhythm against his hand, seeking the friction to a climax I could no longer fight against. Just as I thought I could bear no more, my thighs clenched and quivered as I let out an explosive cry. Addox expressed words of praise as he kissed the edges of my open mouth.

For a while, I lay there, eyes closed, as the sensation slowly dissipated, and my breathing returned to normal. The bed creaked and shifted as Addox moved to lie beside me, and I instinctively rolled into him, resting an arm over his stomach as I nestled into the crook of his arm.

"How was that?" he asked.

"Unlike anything I have ever experienced."

Addox got up from the bed, reaching for a water decanter

and offering it to me. When I declined, he pulled off the cork lid and took a large gulp. I could not help but stare, taking note of his impressive frame, even with his slightest movements. He really was breathtaking to look at, and the things he had done with his fingers... I had to pull myself out of my thoughts to avoid blushing all over again. A sound echoed outside, and he glanced at my chamber door.

"Expecting company?" I shook my head with a nervous smile.

"My guards will be occupied elsewhere, namely the gates and the Queens tower."

"What about the raven tower?" he asked, a small smile forming on his lips. "You don't have any guards there."

"I would if I had enough to spare. For now, I must concentrate our efforts where they are needed most."

"Why don't you have enough guards?" He returned to sit beside me on the bed.

"General Maiya had them reassigned."

"What's more important than protecting the queen?" he asked, now running his fingers along my brow and down my cheek.

"Nothing, in my opinion, but a general outranks a commander of the royal guard," I said dozily. I looked up at him nervously, "Will you stay?"

"If that's what you want, little elf," he whispered, lying back down beside me, he brushed his hand lightly up and down my arm, soothing me into a dreamless sleep.

15

Men And Monsters

With a great thud, his body vaulted onto the mat, and I stepped forward, towering over him.

"Do you want to know how I beat you?"

"Because elves are born with advanced speed and strength?" Addox grunted, allowing me to pull him up from the floor.

"Your strategy is too aggressive. Strength and speed are not enough. You need to learn from your opponent and anticipate them. Look for weaknesses," I said, thinking of my many conquests against much larger foes.

"What if they have none?"

Everyone has a weakness.

Some are better at hiding it than others, I thought grimly, deciding to keep that to myself.

"Then you outsmart them. Here, take this blade." I threw the dagger in the air, waiting for him to catch it. "Try to assault me," I instructed.

"Can you pretend to be at least a little bit nervous?" he said dryly, pointing the sharp blade at me. "There's a chance I could hurt you."

"Then I shall keep my doubts to myself."

"But not snarky comments, obviously..." He rolled his eyes, before parting his stance and flipping the blade in his hand, preparing to lunge. He attacked, and with little effort I grabbed his wrist, twisting it until his face contorted in pain, causing him to drop the knife.

"You should have anticipated unarming you was a possibility and prepared yourself to counter the action."

"It's impossible, you're too fast," he replied, appearing worn out already from our sparring. We had started with various attack formations, and as I had promised, I was setting out to teach him something more valuable.

Neither of us spoke of what had happened the night before, of the euphoric sensations he wrought across my body until I finally fell into an exhausted sleep.

He had been gone by the time I awoke at dawn, and still I blushed at the thought of it.

"Here, I will demonstrate, disarm me the same way I disarmed you," I said, returning my focus to the task at hand, collecting the knife from the floor and mirroring his stance. Addox hesitated, mocking as though he was about to attack, but he paused to watch my response. I remained motionless, waiting with the hilt of the knife firmly in my grip. On his next lunge, he grabbed my wrist, twisting it the same as I had, and he watched as the blade began to fall from my hand. Ducking low, I scooped the blade with my other hand and immediately brought it to his throat.

"I could've done that," he said in the realisation of what just happened.

"Then next time, you will," I replied, retreating, and sheathing my dagger. He smiled as though entertained by the idea.

After our training, we returned to my chambers, and just as the night before, Addox offered me pleasure. Though I still felt somewhat nervous, I found myself becoming more excited for him to touch me again. Quickly peeling off the layers of my clothing as he watched, I rested on the bed, ready for him. Addox remained fully clothed, kissing me fervently. The urge to feel him intensified, and I began to hate the clothing I felt against my skin, wishing it was his warmth rather than the smooth cold material.

Once we were finished, he returned to lie by my side, this time pulling me to nestle against his chest.

"Why did you join the royal guard?" Addox asked, as he lightly stroked my arm.

"To protect the royal family," I replied, looking up in curiosity to his question.

"No, I mean, it's clear you could have done anything. Become general to the queen's armies even, so why this?"

I shifted, propping myself up on one elbow.

"Do you not think there is honour in my position?" I quirked an eyebrow.

"Didn't the queen nearly destroy the Coliseum with lightning? Doesn't sound like she needs much guarding."

"You sound like Shanon." I chuckled. Returning my head to rest on his broad chest. "Yes, Queen Fortuna has powerful magic, but she is also young and frightened of her own abilities."

"I guess even the most powerful need protection," he replied, kissing the top of my head and I shuddered. Addox raised the furs higher to cover my body, assuming I was cold. "Who looks out for General Maiya?"

"I think Cobal does, they have a kinship I do not understand."

"Because he's human?" Addox said, distastefully smirking.

"No," I replied quickly, "Cobal is kind and considerate. I just find it hard to understand his loyalty to General Maiya, they seem to have nothing in common."

Addox did not reply, his eyes searching as we both looked up at the ceiling. "What occupies your time during the daylight hours?" I asked, attempting to break the silence.

"I can show you," Addox said suddenly, and I craned my neck to look up at him. "If you'd like?"

"Okay." I was suddenly very eager to see how he spent his days when he was not training.

"Okay," he repeated, "sleep tight, little elf. I'll wake you at dawn."

I woke to the feeling of Addox's caress between my legs, rolling me onto my back as he kissed my neck, whilst simultaneously rubbing my sensitive nub.

"Morning," he whispered between kisses, his stubble lightly scratching across my skin. He pressed his fingers deep, and I clamped my thighs around his arm, trying to create more friction. The feeling quickly crested into an overwhelming sensation in my core that had me clutching his face with both palms, pulling him towards me so I could kiss him.

"I confess, I like waking up this way," I declared, as I began to come down from the euphoric high. "Am I to expect this every morning from now on?"

"Don't push your luck, little elf," he said, giving me another quick peck before getting up and reaching for his boots and surcoat. I looked out the window, admiring the familiar orange hue from the early light of first morning. "We should get going, it's almost breakfast time."

"For whom?" I asked, sitting up and swinging my legs over the edge. Addox watched me with a renewed intense gaze, eyeing my half-naked form.

"I'll give you some time to freshen up." He shifted uncomfortably for a second, before opening my chamber door and slipping outside. I dressed quickly, wiping my body down with a bowl of water and washcloth from the previous day, donning my coverings and light armour in haste. I was still trying to tie my hair back when I stepped outside, to find Addox leaning against the wall next to a shadowed alcove. He stepped forward, pulling at the leather band in my hand.

"I like it when you let your hair down," he said, brushing the side of my cheek and touching the still-loose strands of hair. "You ready?" he asked and I simply nodded, leaving my hair as it was and returning the leather bindings to my pocket.

We strode side by side, at an inconspicuous distance, as Addox led me out of the palace to the centre of town, until finally, we stopped outside of Tobias's House.

Without waiting for me, Addox briskly walked to the fence and greeted two humans tending to the garden outside. A man covered head to toe in dirt opened the small wooden gate, patting Addox's shoulder. The other smiled warmly, both familiar and happy to see him. I strode forward quickly, ignoring the strange looks I received as I rushed inside, only to immediately knock into Addox's large back. He held out his arm to try and steady me, but I quickly straightened myself, ignoring his extended hand.

"Hey Addox," a chirpy voice said, his eyes widening when he saw me.

"Hey, Castor, are we too late for breakfast?"

"It's okay, Naill's got that covered. But Shanon's out back if you want to give her a hand," he said, pointing his thumb over his shoulder.

Shanon was neglecting her duty again!

"No worries," Addox said casually, heading in that

direction, and leaving Castor to take another fleeting confused glance between us. I began to follow in the direction Addox left, but I paused when I heard Addox's soft timbre speaking sweetly to someone. Curious, I turned the corner to find him crouched beside the stairs, talking to a small boy in worn mismatched clothing huddled in the corner.

"Got you a new one." Addox reached inside his pocket and produced an item to give to him. I approached, allowing myself a better view of them both. The boy held a dark wooden object whittled down to resemble a horse. The young human examined it, before placing it next to another two wooden horses of different sizes and colours. "I'll have to get you your own stable at this rate, huh," Addox commented with a grin. The boy returned the smallest of smiles but flinched back again as soon as he noticed me. Addox stood, taking a protective stance between us.

"It's alright, she won't hurt you," he said, keeping the same soft tone as he reached for my hand. This time I allowed him to guide me slowly down into a crouched position beside him. "Kass, this is Quin, she's a friend of Shanon's."

I did not correct him by stating I was her superior commander. Instead, I gave the young boy a tentative smile. "It is nice to make your acquaintance," I supplied, trying to match the same calming tenor Addox had used. The boy was so small, no more than ten years of age and far too skinny.

"He doesn't speak," Addox whispered in my ear, getting so close to me, I felt my pulse rate increase. I wanted to ask what had happened to the boy, but I kept my questions to myself. It was not my place to enquire here; in a shelter and haven from my kind. In the palace, I was Head of the Royal Guard, but in this house, I was just an elf who would frighten this boy in the same manner any other elf would. I did not like the feeling that assaulted me.

"I should find Shanon." I rose to my feet slowly so as not to alarm young Kass.

"I'll be right back," Addox said, deciding to follow as I retreated out into the garden.

I spotted Shanon immediately. Standing at the far end, her arms were bare and streaked with sweat. I walked over to her, keeping to the grass and avoiding the open muddy patches. She looked up, watching me approach as her chest rose and fell rapidly.

"Knew it would only be a matter of time," she drawled sardonically. "Addox," she greeted, with a nod to the figure standing behind me.

"You should be in the palace," I said firmly.

"Had better things to do." Shanon shrugged.

"You consider digging up dirt while sweating in the blistering heat…" I stopped as I noticed freshly planted shoots peeking from the upturned soil. A few faces were staring at me cautiously, equally confused about what was going on. "What is it you are doing?"

"Planting potatoes here. We have carrots and tomatoes growing over there," she said, pointing to the far end of the garden, "And we are hoping the melon seed will take root under the pantry window," she finished.

"This is what you have neglected your duty for?" I asked. She nodded, wiping her brow, and leaning proudly on the end of the spade she had been using to dig away at the ground. The entire garden looked vastly different compared to the last time I had seen it. The people occupying the residence had worked tirelessly to transform and utilise it for cultivating purposes. This made sense, considering the known food shortages and the fact humans genuinely suffered most. The only corner of the garden untouched was a small fenced-off area with a few marked graves. I found myself briefly wondering if one of them belonged to Sole now.

"Make your threats and be done with it, Acqueline, I have a lot to accomplish today."

Despite the earliness of the morning, she already looked worn out, and for the second time, I felt all my anger dissipate in her presence. Yes, she had neglected her duty and disobeyed my orders, and continued to participate in the garish fights at The Sanctum, but she provided essential help to these humans. She was using her time to support Castor and his mission to help those left fortunate. To help malnourished boys like Kass.

"How can I help?" I asked her.

Hours had passed, and the sun began to set. Between Shanon and Addox, I could not tell who was more surprised to witness me arm myself with the selection of tools scattered around the garden. Neither of them said anything beyond offering instructions as we worked, and I would occasionally glance at Addox, discreetly admiring his flexed muscles as they contracted with his labour. We all worked together to plant various crops until dusk.

"How long will they take to sprout?" I asked Shanon, gratefully accepting a container of water Castor had filled for each of us.

"A few months, if the weather stays warm."

Months? These humans need food now. How would they sustain themselves until then?

I wiped my mud-clogged boots on the rear entrance mat, and we returned inside the house. A human had just finished lighting candles and wall torches. I glanced under the stairs as we passed, searching for a small figure, but Kass and his wooden horses were gone. Assuming he was upstairs sleeping in one of the rooms, I found myself hoping he had a safe space to return to.

"It appears you have freed up my night," Shanon snarked as we left Tobias's house. "Want me on watch in the south tower?" she asked, and I was overwhelmed with relief. She was returning to the palace for duty. It seemed she was showing gratitude for my decision not to reprimand her earlier today, opting instead to assist with her task.

"Once you have cleaned yourself up, tell Brenith she is relieved for the evening; she will relish the news," I said, and Shanon nodded. When I did not make a show of immediately following her, she passed a puzzled glance between Addox and me. "I will return shortly," I confirmed, pleasantly surprised as she gave me a respectful salute, before taking off in a light run towards the palace.

"I get the sense she doesn't take orders well," he said.

"Shanon knows her mind and speaks it often."

"You surprised me today," he said, his tenor genuine.

"Why? Because I helped? Is that not what any empathetic, abled person would do?"

"If that were true, they wouldn't be in the mess they are." Addox was right, it was one thing for humans to be freed from the bonds of their masters, but another entirely to give them the rise in status that would make them our equals. Most elves still despised humans, perceiving them as inferior beings.

"What happened to Kass? Why can the boy not speak?" I asked. Addox looked back to Tobias's House, and I kept my gaze on him, marvelling at the perfect angles of his jaw, and the smooth bridge of his nose.

"His owner cut out his tongue. Guess your friends aren't as empathetic as you think. Only a monster would do that to a child." I grimaced at the thought, completely repulsed by the idea something so horrific could happen to a boy no older than Prince Felyx.

"Things are worse here than we know," I said.

"Guess it's hard to tell from the palace towers. We must look small and insignificant from that height." I needed to do more to ensure the council worked harder to negate the unnecessary suffering of humans. Places like The Sanctum existed because of our neglect, leaving human havens like Tobias's house to fall into desperation and disrepair.

"I will see you later for training?"

"Not tonight, little elf. You've had a hard day, and I think we both need some rest. We can continue our training tomorrow," he replied. I looked over to him, trying to shake the sudden feeling of disappointment.

"Okay." I refrained from asking him to spend the night in my chambers. "See you tomorrow," I said, beginning to walk away.

"Quin!" Addox called and I stopped, turning to face him. "Sweet dreams," he added, quirking a smirk and I instantly felt my cheeks blush. I shook my head before heading back to the palace.

16

Confessions

"I noticed how much detail you put into Lera's sling," I said to Prince Felyx as we strolled through the palace to meet with Lelane and Lera. "The intricate details of Yuki's snout and whiskers were exceptional."

"I think Lera loves it too, even though she knows Yuki doesn't like her very much," he replied.

I chuckled and looked down at the little white fox as he skipped closely beside the prince, his fluffy white tail swishing from side to side.

"Do you think you could whittle other animals?"

"Like a bird?" His eyes widening with excitement at the thought.

"I was thinking of something a little bigger. You see, I met a boy who has a fondness for horses. I saw him playing with a couple of replicas, but none had the detail in which you had so cleverly depicted Yuki."

"I can make him one, it'll be easy. I can carve a whole bunch of horses," he said with confidence.

"I had hoped you might say that," I replied with a toothy grin. "Perhaps when you have it finished, you can gift them in person."

"Okay." He leapt forward to meet Lera at the gate. "Lera, Lera! I'm going to carve horses," he called excitedly.

"Good morning," Lelane said as I approached. "You must tell me what you feed the prince for breakfast to have him so animated at such an early hour," she continued, pointing over her shoulder to a very grumpy-looking Lera, who was only mildly paying attention to what Prince Felyx was talking about. Yuki growled beside me, his snout pointed at Lera, and I shooed him away with a gesturing hand.

"Honestly Yuki, you have made your protests clear. Why do you insist on coming if you dislike the girl so much?" He ignored me as usual, which was a common occurrence unless I held a treat in my hand. The fox followed closely behind Prince Felyx as we walked through the palace to the training room.

In the absence of Brenith, I was grateful to have Lelane as a training partner today. We were focussing on swordplay, with the little prince so confident he would be the greatest sword master in the kingdom. I had asked Lelane to spar with me so I could demonstrate the techniques step-by-step. We chose real swords for our demonstration, as Prince Felyx,

Yuki, and Lera stood at the side, watching intently.

It has been many years since Lelane practised so fervently, and I was impressed at her skill with a blade. Her eyes came alive when our swords clashed, her tongue peeking from her lips in concentration as she tried to anticipate my movements. I held myself back of course, as I always did against competitors.

Lelane thrust forward with a cry, and I deflected the strike, countering in quick succession. Our weapons clanged as steel connected. She blocked, the hilt of our swords locking together as she tried to push her weight forward with both hands. Suddenly, she winced, lowering her sword, and clutching her injured wrist.

"Lelane," I breathed, instantly reaching for her in a panicked state from hurting her. She swiftly jutted back, kicking the sword from my hand and pressed the end of her blade to my throat. When I met her eyes, she was smiling. "How ruthless of you," I declared, admiring her deflection.

"I could not help myself," she replied, her cheeks turning the slightest shade of pink at my compliment.

"There you have it." I addressed both the prince, and Lera. "It is not always about strength and skill. You must use your opponent's weaknesses against them. Now both of you go and practise," I instructed, watching as Prince Felyx ran to the weapon rack and retrieved two wooden swords. He raced back and gave one to Lera, which caused Yuki to emit a barrage of grumbles. "It's okay, Yuki, she's my friend," Prince Felyx offered, but the fox merely huffed and turned his back to them.

"You seemed distracted today," Lelane commented as we watched the two young ones train.

"Are you admitting that is the only reason you won?" I teased, making her chuckle, but she was right. I was distracted by a great number of things, most of which involved Addox and what we had been doing each night, the same thing that would happen tonight after we trained.

"Does it truly still trouble you?" I motioned to her wrist, noting she kept moving the steel blade from one hand to the other.

"Not that much, I just forgot how heavy these blades were," she said, re-sheathing the weapon and placing it on the table behind us. "How are your duties?" she asked, purposely changing the subject.

"Uneventful, which is a pleasant reprieve," I replied, inviting her to come and take a seat beside me.

"It still feels weird to be here." She looked around and admired the tall ceiling of the hall.

"Trust me, I am still getting used to it myself."

"Does your duty make you happy?" she asked, catching me off guard, and I was unconfident in the answer I would give. There were many aspects of my service I found joyful; training the prince and Lera for one. I was thankful it had given me the opportunity to rekindle my lost friendship and spend some time outside of the palace.

"I will be happy when this kingdom finds peace again," I replied honestly, thinking of my time in Tobais's House and the great number of things the city still had to work through.

We returned our attention to the children training in front of us. It was evident Lera had surpassed Prince Felyx. She absorbed everything I taught with a determined eagerness that was astonishing. Swift and silent, she barely paused or flinched from pain, pushing her body to limits far beyond any an elf so young should go. Prince Felyx seemed in awe and completely absent of competitiveness. He was only encouraged by her tenacity. Yuki did not share the prince's fascination with Lera. As she moved, he stared cautiously, occasionally whining softly.

Eventually, I stood, clearing my throat.

"Enough practise for today," I commanded. "The prince has other studies to attend to."

We said our goodbyes at the palace gates, and Lelane surprised me by leaning in and kissing my cheek. At first, I panicked, glancing around nervously, but then Lelane gave me an innocent smile and I realised she meant nothing by it.

"See you tomorrow," she said sweetly, taking Lera's hand before they turned and walked home.

"What if I wanted to kiss someone?" Prince Felyx suddenly asked, and I looked down exasperated while I tried to think of an answer. "Do I have to ask? Or can I just do it?"

"I think you are too young to be thinking about kissing," I replied, unsure of what else to say.

"How old do you have to be?"

"Much older."

"Ten?"

"No."

"Twelve? I don't know if I can wait that long."

"It is not a matter of age; it is a matter of knowing," I said, feeling awkward. My pace quickened to return the prince to his parents. Surely it was their duty to answer these embarrassingly difficult questions.

"Knowing what?" he asked.

"You must be mature enough to know what it is you truly want. Not to mention, you should also consider the consequences, what if the recipient does not want you to kiss them?"

"I don't need to worry about that," he replied with a confident grin.

"Oh really, why?" I smirked back at him.

"She definitely wants to kiss me."

I chuckled, shaking my head as my guards opened the garden gate, and I watched Prince Felyx hurtle toward his waiting mother and father, with Yuki chasing behind.

"That was incredible," I said, my head still a daze from the intensity of pleasure that had just run through me.

"Want me to do it again?" Addox teased, tracing his hands down my stomach as he bit at my ear lobe.

"I need a moment." I smiled, reaching for his travelling hand, and pulling it to my chest, lacing his fingers with mine, the pair of us transfixed at the sight of our entwined hands.

"If I didn't ask you to train me, who would you be in bed with now?" Addox asked.

"No one. I would have denied myself."

"What about your little elf friend?" he asked, and I looked up. Addox was avoiding my gaze as he continued to stare at our hands. I instantly knew he was referring to Lelane.

"I need you to understand something." I sat up and removed my hand from his. He too straightened, leaning back on his elbows.

"You love her," he stated, finally meeting my gaze, and I let out a deep sigh.

"Lelane and I were destined to strike a kinship from a young age, we lived next door to each other, and our mothers were close friends. I remember feeling as though we were invincible, nothing would separate us. Our mothers would talk of our future, often teasing about us moving into a home and bearing elflings together. I had no notion of how such things could be achieved back then.

"When I asked Lelane about this, she told me of a place she knew that would better explain what our mothers had meant. I remember questioning why we had to sneak out in the middle of the night to travel to this mysterious location. Lelane warned me that if we were caught, we would be in more trouble than the time we tried to hide a pair of ravens in our bedchambers."

"Where did she take you?" he asked, suddenly now very interested in my story.

"I remember the fluttering in my heart as Lelane dragged

me though back alleys, avoiding guards on patrol. The house she had brought me to had no extraordinary features, appearing a common elven home, but larger and more lavish than the dwellings where we lived at the edge of the farming fields. She led me to a side entrance, and we broke in through a partially opened window.

"The lighting was dim, and we easily kept ourselves hidden in the shadows as Lelane led me by the hand down a corridor. We stopped to peer through an open doorway, and I remember my jaw dropping at the sight inside."

"What did you see?" Addox asked, and I told him all I remembered.

"Half a dozen elves in various stages of undress. They were touching, caressing, and moaning into each other's mouths as their lips and tongues melded. Lelane seemed completely enthralled by them, so mesmerised she did not notice when I let go of her hand, retreating in disgust.

"I was about to turn and sprint from the house, when I heard a faint sound resonating from a narrow stone stairway. Initially, I did not want to go down there, it was pitch black and eery, devoid of the plushness and rich colours that seemed to drench the rest of the house. As I heard a quiet plea from its depths, I felt drawn to it, and against my better judgement, I carefully crept down the damp steps.

At the end of the stairway was a tall oak door, left slightly ajar, a faint candlelight flickering just beyond. I silently leered into the room, my hand clasping over my mouth at the sight in front of me.

"Two elves stood in the centre, both completely naked, in an intimate embrace like those who resided above. Their hands were stroking and roaming each other, kissing, and smiling as they teased. One of the elves moved her hand down between the other elf's legs, her finger slowly massaging and dipping inside. At her touch, the elf clung to the other's shoulder, her leg lifting and wrapping around her hip. As their embrace became frantic, and they moved aggressively to the other side of the room, I realised they were not alone.

"Behind them was a young, collared Guan, lying on raised stone. His arms and legs were elongated, bound in chains at either end. His torso and feet were bare, displaying the fair skin that was covered in a sheen of sweat. When his eyes locked with mine, I barely contained my gasp. I quickly shrank back in the doorway, in fear of getting caught, but the elves seemed far too lost in each other's pleasure to notice. I still remember feeling disgusted at how one elf referred to the human as their 'present' to the other. They both studied him intently, one elf running her hand down his torso. He shuddered, pulling against his restraints, but they did not seem to care. He looked close to my age, not a child, but not yet fully grown. They even acknowledged his youth in excitement, which made me feel sick. He looked frightened as our eyes met again.

"I wanted to help him, to untie his chains and to steal him away, but he was not my Guan, and it was not my place.

"Lelane had noticed my disappearance, as she quietly called to me from the top of the stairs. As the elves started tugging at the waistband of his coverings, ignoring his attempt to twist his hips away from their grasp, I panicked.

"Without thinking, I quickly pulled my bow from my back, loaded it with an arrow, and released, aiming at a candle at the far side of the room. It flew past the elves and knocked the candle onto the floor beside long drapes, causing them to catch alight.

Addox sat opposite me, his body rigid, stunned by my words.

"That…was…you?" he stuttered in disbelief.

"Yes."

"Did you get caught?"

I shook my head.

"When I realised what they were going to do, I felt nauseous and just reacted. Afterwards, I just ran, barely stopping to grab my friend as we fled. You must understand up until that point, I had not been aware of my divergence from societal norms. My friend had already developed a crush, and she did not understand why I did not reciprocate her attraction."

I did not consider I could have endangered every elf in that building if it had caught fire. All that mattered in that moment was getting them away from him, in any way I could. "Seeing you for the first time, was the day I knew I would never feel the same level of affection towards her, at least not in the way she wanted. Afterwards, I was so appalled by my reaction, I avoided all association with humans altogether. I kept my feelings hidden and buried my deepest desires under a mountain of responsibilities," I said, my heart pounding from my confession. This was the first time I had spoken the truth aloud to anyone.

"The royal guard can't have families," Addox said, realisation dawning as he nestled himself comfortably back on the furs. His arm stretched down, stroking the edge of my thigh, sensing my uncomfortableness.

"At the time, it was a simple solution to escape facing my truth, but I broke Lelane's heart in the process. She did not talk to me for over a decade."

"She never knew?" he asked, still stroking me.

"She does now. Not the human attraction part, but that I never felt the same way she did for me. Lelane has had a hard life, Addox, and it is all because I turned my back on our friendship. I want to do all I can to make it up to her."

"That's why you didn't like it when I called you Quin."

"I do not mind it so much now. I like to think it is a nickname reserved only for friends."

"Is that what we are? Friends?" he asked, leaning up and pulling my naked body to rest on his, and I let out a smile of relief. He was not mad, if anything, he seemed more attentive after my confession, and I enjoyed the feeling of his large, warm form beneath me, silently wishing his skin were as bare as mine.

"You're truly unlike any other elf I've ever met."

I liked the compliment, but not the connotation behind its meaning.

"So, was it all men that made you realise you don't fancy

women, or…?" He raised a playful eyebrow and I swatted at his chest.

"Just you," I said, still smiling, "but do not start getting cocky about it, clearly it is obvious I have bizarre tastes." He chuckled, pulling me down for a kiss, inhaling deeply and pressing his firm lips against mine. "I am truly sorry, Addox," I breathed between kisses, and he pulled back slightly, looking into my eyes.

"For what?" he whispered, his brow furrowing.

"I should have done more and found a way to get you out of there somehow. I am sorry, for the part I played in the life you led." He placed his palms on either side of my face, his thumb stroking firmly against my cheek.

"You've got nothing to be sorry for," he said slowly, his breathing heavy, gaze intense, as though he wanted to say more but was restraining himself. Still holding me, our eyes locked, he opened his mouth to continue, but quickly snapped it shut. He then removed his hands from my face, guiding me to lie back down on his chest. "I've got to leave early. I promised Castor I'd help the boys," he said, but there was something strange in his voice.

"How is Kass?" I asked, wanting to break the sudden uncomfortableness.

"He'll be better when he has a full stomach, the boy just needs a wholesome meal or two," he replied. He shifted to cradle me in our familiar sleeping position, leaving me to question the cause of his sudden mood change.

As I lay in his arms, my mind wandered to the garden at

Tobias's house. It would likely take a long time for the plants and herbs to grow, meaning little Kass would have to wait a long time to get all the nutrients he needed.

Unless… An idea suddenly sparked in my mind.

17

Early Harvest

The royal family were picnicking near the oak tree when I entered the garden. I was feeling particularly gleeful, perhaps it was because it was such a beautiful day, or maybe it was the excitement of what I had planned. The timing of it all could not be more perfect; Prince Felyx told me he had finished carving a pair of horses from redwood and oak, and I decided it was not just him I wanted to bring to Tobias's house.

I searched for Shanon this morning, hoping she would want to accompany us, but when she could not be found, I recruited Brenith who seemed delighted at the prospect of spending a few hours outside of the palace.

"Your majesty," I said, approaching the three of them, unable to hold back my smile. "I have arranged a horse and carriage and would like you to accompany us. I asked Prince

Felyx to prepare a little something ahead of our visit."

"For the boy who likes horses," he said excitedly. At the mention of a human child, Phoenyx looked less worried as Queen Fortuna began to stand.

"Yes, I would like to meet this boy that Felyx has been talking about," she said sweetly.

"The carriage awaits." I gestured for them to follow.

I knew taking the queen to see them without the council's pre-approval would likely land me in another bout of trouble. However, this was not about following the chain of command or stroking one's ego. I wanted to show the queen a glimpse of what her council were hiding from her, the true reflection of the people's suffering, and how I knew she could help them unlike anyone else.

The journey was brief and swift. As the carriage pulled up outside Tobias's house, Castor stumbled out through the entrance, appearing completely gobsmacked.

"Brenith, wait by the carriage," I instructed. I helped the queen and Phoenyx step down to the ground, while Yuki and Prince Felyx eagerly jumped down behind them.

"Acqueline?" Castor asked, looking perplexed.

"Castor, may I present Queen Fortuna and her consort, Phoenyx," I said, as the couple held each other's hand, striding forward.

"Hey, wow, it's been a long time," Castor said, awkwardly, still unsure of what was going on.

The prince poked his head around curiously from behind them. "This courageous young man is Prince Felyx. I wanted to show them all the work you have done here, and Prince Felyx has made a gift for young Kass."

"Of course, please come inside." Castor spun on his heels excitedly. "Do you like tea? I can ask Naill to make some," he added, walking backwards and almost stumbling on a stone before he righted himself.

"Tea would be lovely," I replied, and he nodded animatedly. The moment we entered the house, I noticed a large body striding down the stairs, his eyes meeting mine in surprise. Even though Addox told me he stayed at the house sometimes, I had not expected to see him here today. My skin prickled with awareness in his presence, recalling the way he stroked and caressed my skin the night before.

Pretending not to notice him, I craned my neck to see if a particular small form could be found hiding beneath the stairway. As I had hoped, I caught a glimpse of Kass and was excited as I turned to the prince.

"Prince Felyx, this is the boy I was telling you about. Did you bring your gifts?" I whispered, and he pulled out a leather wrap bound in twine, holding it up for me to see. I tipped my head to the side, indicating where the boy was hiding, and Prince Felyx gave a toothy grin as he approached. In that same moment, Castor returned, Addox walked down the remaining stairs, and we all froze. We listened intently as the prince planted himself cross-legged next to the stairs and introduced himself.

"Hi, so I carved these. I can be the red one and you can be the brown one, or we can swap if you want? I don't mind.

I'm Felyx by the way," he said, holding out the two hand-carved horses towards Kass. I had already explained the child would not talk back, but equally, I knew it would not matter to the prince. He was used to carrying a one-sided conversation from his interactions with Lera.

Slowly, a hand reached out and selected the redwood horse. Prince Felyx immediately launched into a detailed story about how the two horses became lost from the stables and were now trying to find their way home. We left them that way, to play and enjoy each other's company. Kass did not move from his spot beneath the stairs, but that was unimportant, he was interacting with another. He began showing Prince Felyx the other horses he kept clutched tightly to his chest.

Castor led us through the house, giving us a tour as he spoke about the men they had sheltered there. All had harrowing backstories, and they ended up here with nowhere else to go. I was vaguely aware Addox had decided to trail our small party, but I acted oblivious to his presence.

"Would you like to see the gardens next? Acqueline has been helping us with the crops," Castor said warmly, and both the queen and her consort nodded eagerly. We walked out into the small garden and noticed a few able-bodied humans watering outside, nurturing the various small shoots that had sprouted from the very ground I had helped to dig up.

"When I heard the crops would take weeks to yield anything, I instantly thought of you and your gifts," I said, turning to the queen.

"You could help them," Phoenyx added encouragingly, catching my meaning.

With a breathtakingly wondrous smile, she walked on the freshly irrigated earth, completely unfazed by the fact she was dragging the hem of her dress through the mud. She crouched down, placing her hands on the earth and began to whisper. None of us could hear the words of her chanting, and we watched in fascinated awe as the ground began to move and greenery began to rapidly grow. The stems split and flattened as they formed small leaves and new shoots began to sprout. Invigorated leaves curled to allow more to form, and stem's widened, turning a darker shade of green. As Queen Fortuna started to move forward, they continued to grow, until they were fully formed and ready for harvest.

She repeated the process in every corner of the garden, her fingers delicately stroking the tips of newly formed plants until they were out of her reach. We were all assaulted with a fresh earth smell in the air.

She moved to the tomato plants last, motioning her hands over the small sprout prongs of two leaves on a short celadon green stem. Immediately they grew, leaves forming on top of one another, quickly reaching the queen's waist. A few of the men gasped as small yellow flowers began to bloom, seeking the sun, or perhaps the queen's warmth. Eventually, all the plants were covered in the small yellow blossoms.

Her hands waved from side to side and as the petals began to fall and small, green bulbous shapes formed, swelling until patches began to change hue. More large, round green tomatoes began to grow, slowly morphing to different colours, before finally ripening to a perfectly bright shade of red.

"This is the least I can do," Queen Fortuna said, biting her bottom lip, as though nervous of their reaction. A great silence filled the garden as more humans came out of the house to marvel at the spectacle. Prince Felyx joined them, a very shy Kass hiding behind him, still clutching his horses tightly. At the sight of the garden, he dropped them, stepping barefoot onto the grass, heading straight for the canopy where vines had reached the top, all bearing large, round, juicy-looking tomatoes.

"Do you want one?" The prince asked Kass, as he reached up high and plucked a tomato from its stem, passing it to the timid boy. Kass's eyes lit up as he took a tentative bite, the juices dribbling down his chin. Everyone in the garden began to cheer, rushing past me and surrounding Queen Fortuna. They thanked her for sharing her gift, and many equally helped themselves to ready, and ripened fruit, taking large eager bites.

I felt a presence behind me, his large form looming over mine. Wordlessly, he reached for my hand and pulled me back inside, dragging me into the space behind the stairs near where Kass usually hid. With great urgency, Addox dug his hand into the back of my hair and pulled me into him, devouring me with a passionate kiss. I clung to him, my fingers clutching at the fabric of his clothes.

"Addox, do you know where…oh," Castor said, rushing inside, only to discover us in our embrace. We hurriedly pulled apart, both our lips swollen, and clothes dishevelled. "Never mind," Castor blurted, his cheeks turning a bright shade of red as he backed away, spinning on his heels, and heading straight back to the garden.

"Don't worry, he won't say anything," Addox said, as he straightened his tunic.

"I should get back to the queen," I declared, feeling flustered at being caught, but Addox reached for me before I could pull away.

"Quin," he said, lightly holding my arm. I paused, turning to meet his gaze. "Thank you."

With a small smile, I nodded, before slowly moving away, our fingers brushing along each other's hands as we returned to the festivities in the garden.

We stayed until mid-morning, with Castor insisting the royal family join them all for breakfast; a meal full of the freshly harvested fruits, slathered in honey from the supply in the pantry. Just as Addox said, Castor made no mention of what he witnessed between us, and I spent the rest of our visit sitting as far away from Addox as possible to avoid raising suspicion.

Upon our departure, the men filled the carriage with gifts and fresh fruit for the royal family as a gesture of gratitude, despite the queen's protests. Addox stood in the doorway of Tobias's House, little Kass positioned next to him, waving goodbye to the prince.

In that moment, as I watched the man I spent my nights with lift the small child to sit on his shoulder to improve his view, something fluttered through me. A feeling more profound than the moments of pure euphoric pleasure Addox brought my body.

It was a moment of realisation that threatened to shatter everything I thought I stood for.

I did not want our bargain to be temporary. I wanted it to be forever.

As the carriage arrived at the palace, it was met by one of General Maiya's warriors.

"General Maiya wants to speak with you," she said the moment I stepped down, and I glanced back at the royal family, who watched our exchange with curiosity. "Now," she insisted.

"Brenith, please escort the queen, I will meet with you later." She nodded, offering a salute, and returned to the carriage.

I followed the seasoned warrior to the Throne Room, only to be greeted by an enraged general.

"You better explain your actions, Acqueline, and pray to the ancestors I am in an agreeable mood," she scathed, her commanding voice echoing loudly. "Where did you take the queen?"

I should have known my actions would not go unnoticed, but I was fully prepared to stand my ground. I was right in this, and I believed so, wholeheartedly. The queen needed to see the conditions the humans had been living in since the manumission of slaves. All I had to do now, was convince General Maiya of that. Hardly an easy task I was sure, considering the opinion she had of me already. With a deep breath, I walked forward, taking my place opposite her at the council table.

"I took the royals to Tobias's House," I said clearly. "I felt it was important she meet the humans there and use her gifts to help them."

"Use her gifts how?" she asked, her eyes narrowing.

"By enhancing the growth of plants to produce food ahead of season," I declared, my chin raised high. Mentally bracing myself for General Maiya's customary brusqueness, I knew she would be furious. Enduring it seemed to be the only option, and that, hopefully, would be the end of it.

"You took the entire royal line to a human house, and encouraged the queen to use her magic publicly?" she snapped.

"Yes."

"She used magic!" she snarled again, emphasising her point.

"Nothing bad happened, she merely used her gift to hasten the growth of some vegetables."

"The city has long suffered with a depleted harvest each year; do you expect Fortuna to visit every farm and field?" General Maiya asked, waving her arms around.

"Perhaps she would want to."

"The risk is too great. She is still burdened by her part in the death of her sister and the dark mage. What if she loses control of her powers again?"

"Hiding and isolating her away is surely not the answer?" I replied boldly, and General Maiya pulled back in surprise at my answer.

"That is not for you to decide." She stepped closer to me. It was hard to not be drawn to the differences between us. Still, I stood as tall as I could, letting her know this time, I would not cower at her command. I was resolute, I accomplished something positive for those humans and I would do it again, regardless of any punishment General Maiya might bestow upon me now. "This is your final warning, Acqueline, your duty is to keep the queen watched and protected within the palace, nothing more."

"I understand," I said, bowing my head with a respectful salute, and hiding the small smile that crept on my face.

I could not help being distracted during Addox's training, my thoughts constantly revolved around how I could broach the subject of our arrangement, and how strongly I desired it to change. I wanted to feel him, all of him, naked flesh against naked flesh, and experience all the physical activities I had briefly witnessed that night in the Pleasure House.

"I have shown you a few dagger tricks, imagine all I could teach you with a sword or bow," I began, as we took a moment for rest and refreshment.

"I'm listening." He stretched his limbs, before steadily

placing one foot in front of the other, his fists raised high.

"I know you have been holding back, there is more…" I paused, unsure how to openly discuss what I was truly asking. "I want to experience it all, no clothes or barriers between us." He froze, his eyes widening as he stared at me.

"I can't do that, little elf," he replied, his voice dropping an octave.

"Why not?" I asked, hating the desperation in my voice. "We trust each other, and without a breeding potion there is no chance of conception." I took a few steps forward, hoping to reason with him.

"It's not about that."

"Then be with me, wholly and completely," I pleaded, looking up to meet his eyes.

"Don't beg me, little elf." He shook his head, and took a few frustrated steps back. "The deal we have works fine, and I don't need to learn new skills."

"What about what I want?" I asked boldly. "I have the right to renegotiate if I am unsatisfied with our arrangement."

"I've satisfied you plenty."

"That is not what I meant." I felt frustrated at his dismissal because I knew he too, was incapacitated by this constant need to be in each other's company. "Do you not also feel this connection we share?" I asked, suddenly feeling very insecure, as though I may have completely misread everything that had passed between us.

"Quin, my answer is no. So, drop it okay," he suddenly snapped, before wincing at his own words and turning around. He began to remove the leather gauntlets fastened to his forearms.

"Fine, forget I mentioned it," I said solemnly. I tried to ignore how rejected and hurt I felt, clenching my fists, and preparing to resume our training. Addox followed suit, his muscles flexing as he prepared to receive me. We fought roughly, and I blocked his blows as he tried to find an opening against my defence.

"If it's a new experience you're after," he said breathlessly between punches, "next time, I'll use my tongue instead of my fingers," he said crassly. I froze, astonished, and that momentary lapse allowed him to strike me hard in the chest, grabbing me at the waist and hurling me over his shoulder.

I bounced onto the mat, in a complete daze. An amused Addox appeared above me a moment later, extending his hand. "Guess I found my opponent's weakness," he declared with a cocky grin.

"You just surprised me, that is all," I replied, as I allowed him to haul me up. Once I was on my feet, he surprised me further by pulling me close to his body, his warmth connecting with mine.

"I'm sorry I snapped at you," he said, his hand caressing under my jaw. "I hate that I can't give you everything you want," he added, his breath fanning across my face. I met his gaze, stepping up on my tip toes so our lips would brush. "There's no future for us, you're head of the royal guard and I'm… this isn't going anywhere." He gestured between us. "It just can't."

I was speechless, my heart plummeting at his words, and I bit my lip to stop it from trembling. Although I was hurt, I could not deny those things mattered. I cared far too much about the royal family to neglect my duty completely to be with him. It was unfair of me to ask.

He was right, there was no future for us. However, I already felt as though I had surpassed the point of being able to walk away from him.

18

Innocence

I stood under the oak tree; its final blossoms falling from empty branches, leaving nothing behind but yellowing leaves. The season was beginning to shift, with colder weather preparing to set in. My body shivered lightly in response to the cool breeze.

As I watched over the royal family, I observed Pheonyx and the queen exchange frequent affectionate gestures and glances. An inner turmoil surged from within me, yearning to experience the joy they felt. The queen, Truda, every elf who had found happiness in companionship, and everything I would be denied because of my vow to the royal guard.

I suddenly became very envious of the things I could never have.

I was snapped from my thoughts when I noticed my

guardswoman, Brenith, rushing towards me with a sense of panicked urgency.

"Shanon is fighting in The Sanctum," she blurted, devoid of any formal greeting.

"This is not news to me, Brenith, I know all about Shanon's immoral use of her time off duty."

As well as on duty.

"You do not understand," she said, her voice urgent. "She is fighting the champion, and she is losing." My eyes widened. Shanon was fighting Terra, Lelane's brutish ex-partner who hurt and tormented my friend over many moons. I felt instantaneous panic, my heart rate increasing.

"Come with me," I directed, sprinting from the gardens, leaving the palace behind as we darted through the city.

"How long has the fight been going on?" I called back, anxious about the state in which I would find my second-in-command.

"I do not know; the moment I was alerted, I came to find you," Brenith replied, struggling to keep up.

When we reached The Sanctum, I pounded my fist repeatedly on the door. Without waiting for an answer, I kicked it open, finding the guard on the other side completely bewildered.

"Where is Shanon?" I barked, but the guard tried to restrain me, attempting to push the door closed.

"You are not permitted to enter," she protested, standing no chance of keeping us at bay. Both Brenith and I pushed past her, causing her to barrel down the steps three at a time.

We descended rapidly, astonished by the size of the audience surrounding the two elves still locked in combat in the ring.

At my elevated height, I saw Shanon stumbling carelessly on her feet, trying to guard. Terra swung her fist, instantly connecting with Shanon's already battered face, causing a spray of blood to scatter across the ring. The fight was long over, anyone could see that, but as Shanon refused to yield, Terra continued to pound into her, occasionally spinning with her arms raised, as the crowd chanted her name.

I pushed through the sea of people, disregarding numerous insults, as Brenith and I forcefully made our way until we reached the centre. Terra raised her massive, bulging arms with a maddening grin, as she aimed again for Shanon's already brutalised face.

I charged forward and stood directly in front of Shanon, blocking the blow and gripping Terra's oncoming wrist in my hands.

The crowd gasped and fell silent.

Terra snarled, stepping back from my grip. Brenith reached for Shanon behind me, propping her upright and supporting her under one slack arm.

"You," Terra growled. "First you take my family, and now my victory." The crowd emitted murmuring whispers. I remained silent, lifting my chin in defiance, and adjusting my stance, ready to defend Shanon. Terra snickered, wiping away a small trace of blood running from her nose. I was satisfied my second in command had at least landed one punch. "I will have what is owed," she said, pointing menacingly as she retreated into the crowd. I waited until she was completely out of sight before I turned around.

Shanon was a mess, and it was clear she was close to collapse. Her nose was crooked, both nostrils streaked with blood, her bottom lip swollen and bruised. I checked her over while she was slumped against Brenith, finding evidence of more injuries. Both hands were gashed with bleeding knuckles, the skin peeling back, leaving the wounds exposed. I lifted Shanon's spare arm carefully to assist Brenith in holding her weight.

"Can you walk?" I asked, as a voice chimed behind me.

"Such spectacular tenacity, Shanon, the crowd could not get enough of it. I look forward to the next time you compete," Peril snarked, flanked by two warriors as bestial as Terra. A human held a stack of parchments behind them.

"She will not be returning," I declared, straightening as best I could without putting too much strain on Shanon's aching body. "I will be reporting your blatant disregard for the duty of care toward those who participate to the council," I stated firmly. "General Maiya would not want her warriors injured to the point of exhaustion." Peril's eyes narrowed.

"The Sanctum does not discriminate; we invite all beings of varied skill and titles. General Maiya understands a warriors' need for a challenge," she said, smirking at me.

"The Coliseum's repair is almost complete, soon there shall be no use for this place, or you," I said, returning my focus back to Shanon, my grip tightening around her waist to help her walk.

"We shall see about that," Peril said, as we walked past her to the stairs. We carefully took one step at a time, and I ignored the glaring eyes of Peril's compatriots, as Shanon struggled to remain on her feet.

"Take me to Tobias's House, they have bandages and the salves I need," she coughed once we reached the fresh air. The sun had long set, with only a few street torches remaining unlit.

"Your injuries are beyond that Shanon; you need a healer."

"It looks worse than it is." She pulled her arms from our hold, as she stumbled to the side and leaned against a wall. "I just need to rest for a moment."

"You can barely stand, perhaps I should carry you," I offered, as Shanon's breathing became more ragged.

"Not a chance, I am fine," she spluttered, before keeling over in pain. "Okay, maybe you should take me to a healer," she agreed, begrudgingly.

Recognising she was about to fall, Brenith and I rushed forward and held her upright together.

"The palace healer will report this to the general." Brenith grunted as she took Shanon's weight.

"I have a friend who can help."

When we reached our destination, Shanon's weight finally straining my muscles, I did not bother to knock. I opened the door, thankful it was unlocked, finding a stunned Lelane frozen in the middle of her chambers.

"Quin, what are…" One look at Shanon's condition and she immediately became alert. "Place her on the bed," she instructed. Brenith and I hauled over, Lelane stepping behind holding clean rags.

Brenith leaned over as I helped Shanon climb up on the bed. She weakly protested, attempting to push me away as I gently laid her down. I stepped back, allowing Lelane to take over. Shanon hissed, stiffened, and ground her teeth in pain while Lelane examined her.

"This may take a while," Lelane said.

"Call if you need anything." I gestured for Brenith to follow me out, and gave Shanon one last look, expressing my expectation that she would remain on her best behaviour and allow Lelane to do her work. She nodded to show her understanding, and her head dropped back, her eyes fluttering closed.

"I need you to alert Council member Cobal. Tell him what happened and summon him here," I instructed Brenith. It was clear I had performed a disservice as Shanon's mentor. I had no other choice but to hope he would prevail where I had failed and knock some sense into her.

I waited for what felt like an eternity, filled with regret over how far I had let Shanon fall. Her stubbornness had shown she had never known when to concede and admit defeat or reflect upon the consequences. She could have died tonight, and I would have blamed myself for it.

A moment later, Lelane emerged from her chambers,

wiping her hands clear of blood.

"How is she?" I asked.

"She is in pain but refusing to rest, perhaps you can remind her it will speed up the healing process?"

"I will try. Thank you, Lelane, I am so grateful for your help," I said sincerely as I stepped inside.

"It is the least I can do. I will check on Lera in the gardens," she replied, giving me a tentative smile as she walked away.

With a deep breath I opened the door and stepped through. Shanon peered at me through narrowed eyes, her wounds clean and wiped away of blood, but now even more visible because of it. I grimaced.

"I do not want your pity," she barked, struggling to sit up. I rushed to her, placing my hand firmly on her chest.

"Shanon, stop!" I ordered. Feeling her tense, I immediately lightened the pressure of my hand. It was clear her injuries were more severe than I had previously thought. Lelane had changed her clothes, unseen wounds likely treated and dressed. "This reckless fighting stops now, do you hear me?" I said, feeling angry.

"You cannot tell me what to do."

"I am your mentor and Head of the Royal Guard," I replied, my tone stern.

"Like anyone actually cares, do any of your guard even follow your orders?" she gritted out.

"Enough, Shanon! I truly have tried, providing everything I thought you needed. You have support and a purpose, but nothing seems to make a difference with you. Your heart is so full of anger, you project your hatefulness towards everyone around you." She stood, shocked, her breathing short and frantic. "Despite all that, there are those who still care," I followed.

"Then you are all fools," she seethed, turning to face the wall, hiding the glistening in her eyes.

"Why Shanon? Why do you continue to ignore our guidance, persisting instead to punish yourself this way?" I asked, my tone softer.

"Because it should have been me!" she cried, finally facing me, her fists clenching.

"What?"

"She was smart, beautiful, and strong, everything I am not. I should have died, not her!"

"Shanor…" I whispered tenderly, the pieces finally clicking into place. She had been forever changed the day she had watched her twin sister die on the battlefield. They were both so young, the battle hungry age of eighteen, yet they had only just started to experience the brutality of war.

"I was the betrayer. The one whose life should have ended," Shanon said, individual tears falling down her cheeks. "If I had listened to her, and kept the location of the rebels a secret, protecting the innocent, instead of revealing everything to Queen Cassandra, she would still be alive. It is my fault!"

I reached out to sooth her, but Shanon moved her arm away from me. "It was Terra that killed my sister. I watched as her arrow pierced Shanor's throat. I saw the life drain from her eyes."

"This is why you entered The Sanctum's fights." I did not know Terra had been the one to kill her twin. Terra had become champion to the underground fighting haunt, presenting the perfect opportunity for Shanon to enact vengeance without repercussions.

"I wanted her to suffer, to be stripped of her false glory. I needed to shame her in front of everyone, and I trained hard for it, but it did not matter." She faltered for a moment as she spoke, but I did not look away, meeting her eyes as she let everything out. "I was not strong enough..." She stopped, unable to finish her sentence.

"Punishing Terra will not bring your sister back, and this is not the life she would have wanted for you."

"I know," she finally whispered, another tear slipping free. It was the first time I had seen Shanon cry and the sight of it unnerved me. I leaned towards her and took her hand.

"Are you disbanding me?" she asked, her eyes wide and full of sorrow.

"Is that what you want?"

"It is the least of what I deserve."

"True, but no," I said, taking a seat at the edge of the bed as I spoke to her. "You cannot change the past, Shanon. It is time you let go and think of your future."

"I miss her so much," she sobbed, and I gripped her hand tighter.

"I know, but she is not truly gone. You carry her with you every moment of every day. As long as your heart still beats, she will always be with you, and through you, her legacy continues."

"I do not know how to move on."

"It will take time and patience, a skill I understand you are sorely lacking," I said light heartedly, and she gave me an awkward smile. "This kingdom needs you, and you have people who only want the best for you. All you must do is start listening to them," I said, and almost on cue, knowing I was talking about him, a rapid light tapping began to knock frantically outside the door. With a smile, I walked over to open it, expecting to find Cobal. However, to my surprise, Castor barged past me, rushing over to Shanon. His jaw dropped slack at the sight of her.

"Shanon! What's happened? Were you attacked? Are you in pain, how badly are you hurt?" he said hastily, reaching over to touch her, but she swatted her hand at him.

"Stop fussing over me, boy," she replied, before giving me an irritated look.

"You should have thought of that before you allowed yourself to get pummelled to near death. You wanted to be punished, now prepare to get all the unwarranted attention your actions deserve," I said, folding my arms, as Cobal then walked into the room.

"Thanks for sending for me," he said, resting a hand on my shoulder.

"Do not let her off easy," I said, raising an amused brow as Castor tried to bundle Shanon with blankets, asking if she was cold or in need of refreshment. I slowly closed the door, leaving them to talk with her alone. I then realised the sun had already set, the beginning of an orange glow on the horizon as a herald for a new day.

I had been with Shanon throughout the whole night, missing my final patrol for the day and breaking my promise of training with Addox. I ran to the banquet hall, wishing with all my might he would still be there. I hoped after our last encounter, he had not thought I wanted to pull out of our bargain altogether. But it was too late.

The banquet hall was empty.

I made my way to my chambers, my pace languid as I thought through how I was going to make my apologies, what more could I offer him to keep his interest aligned with mine. We had already discussed training with weapons, perhaps I could offer it again, not to change our bargain but to keep it. I would teach him how to master every weapon in the entire kingdom if only to keep him in my company.

I opened the door, only to find a figure sitting on the wooden chair in the corner.

"Addox."

"I heard about Shanon," he said, standing to greet me. "Didn't think it was a good idea to loiter in the training hall."

"You waited," I breathed, overwhelmed with gratefulness.

"Of course, I did, sounds like you had a lot to deal with," he said, and instantly I felt the soothing effects of his voice.

"Is she okay?" he asked, and I nodded. Shanon would be fine; I could feel it.

"I also waited because I have something I need to tell you, too." he said, sitting back down on the bed.

"Okay." I sat beside him, nervously watching him.

"My time in the Pleasure House, it wasn't always bad. Sometimes they were nice, made me feel…" He hesitated, and I shuffled uncomfortably, not sure if I wanted to hear the full story of what it was like for him. "I know others had it worse, I was always fed and bathed. They didn't lock me in a cage or beat me, sometimes they were even kind. But I…" he paused, looking down at his hands. "They didn't care about me. I was an object, something to be toyed with, used, and then discarded."

"I am so sorry." My heart ached for everything he had endured, longing to touch him but not wanting to pull him from this moment of honesty. "I understand," I began, "It is okay that you do not want to… be with me."

"You're wrong!" he snapped, interrupting me as he looked over his shoulder. "I want you so damn much, it's all I can think about."

"You do?" I asked, feeling more confused than ever.

"Yes, that's why I can't get lost in you. It feels too real."

"It is real," I said, daring to touch him this time, brushing my hand over his, he looked at our hands, slowly watching as they linked together. "What do you want?" I reached forward tentatively with my other hand and lightly guided his chin to look at me.

"Everything, Quin, I want everything you'll give me."

At his words, I suddenly felt very bold, and with a need to comfort him, I straddled his thighs, removing my leather tunic. His hands instantly caressed my sides up to my breasts, and I stroked his hair as his warm fingers pressed into my skin.

"Show me," I whispered, brushing my nose against his, before I pressed my lips to his mouth.

We had kissed before, but this time it was different; charged with something neither one of us could explain. When his impatience grew, and he cradled the back of my neck to deepen the kiss, I let my hands roam. Stroking across the exposed skin on his arms, I ran my fingers lightly under the hem of his sleeves, reaching for places concealed. Addox only groaned, his hips flexing lightly, showing me how much he was enjoying my fingers brushing across his warm skin, it only made me want to caress more of him.

Reaching low, I tugged at the hem of his tunic, gliding it upwards as the fabric bunched in my fingers, and I felt his smooth hardened muscle underneath. His body trembled, and I broke the kiss long enough to pull the tunic completely from his shoulders, tossing it to the floor. Immediately, I shuffled up his thighs, straightening my knees to gain more leverage and press my bare chest against his. My hands wrapped around his neck, my fingers running through his hair, as I momentarily basked in the feeling of us touching.

"You have no idea how long I have wanted to feel your bare skin against mine," I breathed, trying to pull myself closer to him, but it was not enough. I wanted to feel more of him, to crawl inside him and somehow merge my body with his. Addox tugged at my hair, pulling my head back so he could kiss me again. He held my thighs as he lifted me and twisted our bodies until I was lying on my back, his heavy weight pushing me deeper into the furs. I wrapped my legs around his waist, feeling something build again as his leather-covered hardness pressed against my centre.

"You're so beautiful." His hands glided up my torso and caressed my breasts, and my body trembled with excitement. I took advantage of the freedom of my wandering hands and cupped my palm over his hardness. His body shook as he rocked into my hand, allowing my fingers to explore the shape and length of him, marvelling at his size. Suddenly Addox moved his hips away from my touch, and using one hand, he untied the fastenings of his trousers. He made an irritated sound as he struggled, and I quickly reached down with both hands, matching his urgency as I tugged the bindings free. As I removed my leg coverings, he pulled his trousers past his thighs, and kicked them the rest of the way off.

He straightened back over me, his finger curling a lock of hair over my ear, as his other hand brushed my thigh before stroking between my legs. I moaned as he moved his hand through my sensitive slickness, dipping a finger gently inside. I parted my thighs wider, concentrating on the sensations as his hand moved deeper in and out. I moaned when he increased his speed, and again when he added another finger, his thumb brushing upwards, bringing my body to a sudden shuddering release. The pleasure spread like fire from my centre, causing my lower abdomen to tighten.

Addox kissed me as he rested his hips over mine, and I felt his hardness tease where his fingers had just been. When I felt the tip of him press inside, I gasped, unprepared for how thick it was compared to his hand. He froze, lifting my chin so our eyes met.

"I don't want to hurt you," he said, cupping my face, his expression thoughtful and sincere.

"Do not stop," I said, stroking my hands down the smooth of his back, brushing my fingers along his hips and travelling further to where our bodies were connected. I could feel he was already partially seated inside me as my fingers brushed across the rest of his length, before wrapping my hand around his shaft, and gently guiding him deeper.

Slowly he rocked forward, and I gripped his arms tightly. I winced at the slight pinch as Addox kissed me through it, holding still as his hips rested against my thighs.

"Are you okay?" he asked breathlessly, as if he was only just holding himself together, and I nodded. The pain had subsided, leaving me with an incredibly satisfying feeling of fullness. Addox watched me intently, his eyebrows furrowing and breathing heavy.

"We are connected," I said with a smile, as I glided my hands up again, cradling the back of his neck and bringing our lips together. His tongue swept inside as he moaned into our kiss, beginning to move his body against mine. His hips ground, making way for a new sensation beginning to build.

When he pulled out slightly and rocked back inside, a deep moan escaped me, my hips now moving desperately to try and increase the friction. As he moved, he buried his face in my neck, his moans matching my erratic breathing. I wrapped my legs tighter around his waist, my hands clawing at his skin, leaving light scratch marks as I suddenly froze, a wave of something so intense building in me and as clenched around him, I felt his body shudder.

"Quin!" he cried, his body trembling above mine, until he finally let his entire weight fall upon me. I could feel his heart thumping against my bare chest, and his trembling breath against my skin.

"Now I get it," I whispered, feeling his frantic breaths fan across my face.

"What?" Addox asked, his sweat-stricken forehead resting against mine.

"Why Truda would fight against an entire Kingdom to save the life of one man," I continued, unable to hide my bashful smile. Addox chuckled, kissing me as he ground his hips further still, rolling our bodies until I was lying on top of him. Still joined at the hip, I felt his length hardening again, as he moved upwards, making me groan as he nestled deeper inside.

"Acqueline," a voice whispered in my ear, and I jolted awake to find two brown eyes leering over me.

"Lyzaria?" I asked, stretching my arms, bringing myself out of my sleep-deprived haze. Sunlight beamed through from the small window, and I clutched at the furs to cover my nakedness as my head snapped to the other side of me, thankful to find Addox gone.

"My apologies for this disturbance, but I think I found the evidence you asked for."

"What did you find?" I asked, sitting up. When Lyzaria noticed my state of undress, she turned around sharply. I quickly rose from the bed, donning my clothes and armour as she spoke.

"There is a map," she said, her back still turned to me. "General Maiya keeps it in her war room at her private residence. I managed to examine it while she retired for rest, leaving everything untouched so she would be oblivious to my presence."

"What is so significant about this map?" I asked, and Lyzaria glanced over her shoulder to check I was decent before turning around to face me again.

"There were markings not depicted on any other map. I watched her hidden in the shadows as she altered one of the symbols. She moved counters to mark their exact location, as you would in battle strategy," she said, her eyes wild with the discovery. "I am certain, all you will need to do is retrieve that map and dispatch a party of warriors to investigate those locations for yourself."

"Then we will learn the truth of what General Maiya is doing with our warriors."

"Exactly."

"Thank you, Lyzaria, your efforts will not go unrewarded," I said, and she gave a salute. "Take the rest of the day to recoup, I will have you return to guard rotation on the morrow." Lyzaria nodded gracefully, retreating from my chambers as I thought over everything I had learned.

We were on the verge of revealing the truth of General Maiya's betrayal. Now, all that remained, was deciding who I would tell, and the course of action we would take.

19

From The Ashes

As I waited outside of the Throne room for today's council meeting, I could not help but think about our most recent midnight rendezvous.

"You have no scars," I said, my hands tracing the smooth skin of his chest, a few dark curls in the centre of his pectorals.

"Mine are all internal," he replied, his arms behind his head as he watched me study him with hooded eyes. I liked how he gazed at me; the way his eyes captured mine before flicking to my mouth as though distracted by my lips. "I know it's not a common thing, to find a slave with no scars. There are some elves that enjoy making their mark," he said with a crooked smile, referring to the scratches I had just made down his back.

"I cannot be blamed, perhaps next time you should be gentle," I said, distracted as I tracked a thin hairline down his torso with

my fingertip.

"Has anyone seen your scars?" he asked, his baritone voice sultry and soothing. "Besides me, I mean."

"Just Lelane. Sometimes after my mother had struck me, I would go to her for healing aid." I recalled the times I had crawled from my bedchamber window to hers, failing miserably at treating the weeping wounds myself.

"What happened to your mother?"

"Always so full of questions," I teased, running both my hands up his chest as I straddled his thighs, my latest favourite position.

"Can't help but be curious, there's so much I don't know about you." He gave me a heated look as he shifted slightly beneath me. "Was she in the rebellion war?"

"No," I said, rolling my eyes, finding amusement in his persistence. "She died before, in an accident."

"I'm sorry."

"Several times I had wished to be free from her cruelty, but still, I mourned her after she died. Do you find that strange?"

"Everything about you is strange." I smacked at his chest, a smile tugging at my lips, and he reached for me, pulling my body over his. "Luckily for you I like strange."

"Careful, you are getting rather close to complimenting me."

"Must be in a giving mood," he said, breathing in deep as he kissed me.

"So am I," I replied, pushing back slowly as I lowered myself down his body, not stopping until my face became level between his legs. I watched him shudder as I boldly licked him from base

to tip.

"Good morning, Acqueline," a male voice greeted, pulling me out of my reverie, I turned to see Cobal walking towards me.

"Good morning," I smiled back, still feeling flustered from my thoughts.

"You look well rested." I barely managed to refrain from blushing. My nights had been filled with anything but rest, and I felt my cheeks warming at the thought.

"How is Shanon?" I asked, redirecting the topic of conversation.

"She's still very frail, but now able to walk. Castor is having a hard time keeping her bedbound." Cobal chuckled and I found the gesture infectious, glad Shanon was on the path to recovery.

I extended my arm to respectfully offer him entry into the Throne Room. We both shared surprised glances as raised voices echoed from inside. Upon entering, we discovered General Maiya, Truda and Erik already engaged in a heated argument. We hurried to our seats, instantly identifying the familiar topic of discussion.

"Since the curfew, we have had no further human deaths," General Maiya argued.

"Or they're being abused behind closed doors," Erik argued.

"Something is going on in The Sanctum, Maiya, that place should still be investigated," Truda added.

"You would have me waste my resources on a fool's

errand?"

"I just simply do not understand," Truda continued, "You say you cannot further your investigations against The Sanctum because you do not have the resources, yet you will not accept the support of my human elite."

"I thought I made my view on this subject clear," General Maiya exhaled.

"Explain it again."

"Do you truly expect me to weaken my defences to appease the will of men?" General Maiya drawled.

"We can be more than how you perceive us," Erik said.

"Just as my warriors can do much more than wield a blade, but you will not find them picking grain in the fields."

"But you expect us to? We're supposed to be making a difference," Erik replied.

"Notice how you are no longer bound in chains." Truda's lips formed into a snarl as her fists clenched.

"You will speak to him with respect." Maiya rolled her eyes, disinterested. "We vowed to ensure men would have the same rights as us," Truda reaffirmed.

"And pray tell, Truda, when we have sent all our men to fight our battles, and we solidify our premeditated extinction, who will be left to defend us then?"

"You keep talking like we're about to go to war," Erik countered.

"With the lack of warriors, we have left to defend our kingdom, I can say with certainty it would not be much of a war."

“Then let me ask you once again, why humans cannot ascend in the warrior’s ranks?”

“Humans have weaknesses we do not, they are fragile and far too few. No amount of training will change that truth,” General Maiya replied. She was wrong of course, Addox was proof of that. There was still much for him to learn, but now, after everything he had learnt, I was certain he would be a formidable opponent against even a well-seasoned elven warrior.

“So, your method of protecting humans is to strip them of their rights?” Truda asked, but before General Maiya had a chance to answer, the Throne Room door burst open, and Shanon hobbled in.

“Acqueline,” she said in a rush, clutching her side, still recovering from her severe injuries. “Tobias’s House is on fire.”

I shot up from my chair, my heart hammering as everyone around me launched into action. Truda and Erik left hastily, while Cobal rushed to help steady Shanon as she turned to follow.

“We have to help them,” I blurted, turning to General Maiya.

“Where is the queen?” she asked, rounding the table.

“In the gardens, Brenith is on duty.”

“Join them now, ensure she is within your sight at all times.”

"No, I can help," I said frantically, and General Maiya studied me with intense eyes.

"Sometimes, I truly believe I am the only clear-thinking elf in this kingdom," General Maiya said, holding the bridge of her nose before peering at me. "This could be a planned distraction, someone looking to take advantage while all of our attentions are elsewhere."

"Brenith can protect them if anything…"

"Your duty is to the palace," General Maiya said firmly, becoming increasingly frustrated. Still, I hesitated, thinking only of Addox. I needed to know he was okay, and not now trapped or crushed beneath wooden beams, crying out for help as the building was engulfed in flames. "Acqueline!" General Maiya snapped, and I turned to see her staring at me harshly.

"I will go to the gardens," I reluctantly resigned, trying to conceal my shaking hands, and offering her a salute. General Maiya sneered down at me before storming out, her heavy boots reverberating as she rushed to join the others.

The family were playing a game when I arrived in the gardens, blissfully unaware of the events in the city. Their laughter carried in the subtle breeze. Prince Felyx squealed when his father splashed him with water from the stream, fleeing to the other end of the garden and burrowing himself in Yuki's fur.

"It was kind of her majesty to allow Lera to join them," a voice sounded behind me. I turned, surprised to find Lelane walking on the grass, Lera leaving her side to join the prince.

The moment she saw my expression, she gasped, taking an urgent step forward. “Quin, what is wrong?” she asked, and I brushed my hands to my face, realising it was wet with tears.

“Nothing, all is fine,” I replied, wiping away at my cheeks. “A fire has broken out in the city, but it is under control.”

“Is there anything I can do to help?” I shook my head, smiling reservedly at her thoughtfulness.

“They will call for us if needed,” I replied, my stomach recoiling, knowing that was a lie. Lera stood with Prince Felyx by the stream, snarling at Yuki as he growled and bared his teeth to her. The young prince found it all amusing, crouching to splash a huge wave of water over them both, bursting into laughter. The queen’s consort took advantage of their distraction by pulling the queen behind a tree to shower her with sweet and affectionate kisses, and I felt fresh tears fall.

“Quin, please tell me what is wrong? Lelane pressed, and I turned to face her.

“The fire,” I began, trying to steady my emotions as I spoke. “I am fearful someone may be hurt, but I cannot leave, my duty is here.” Lelane looked past me, to the royal family and her daughter that was playing beside them.

“Go,” she said urgently. “I can stay and watch over them.” My eyes widened in surprise.

“Are you sure? What if the family need me?” I whimpered, still hesitant at betraying orders.

“You have trained Lera and me, along with my healing skill, what more could the family need?” she said, already pushing me towards the door. "Go, Quin! Help your friends, return when you can."

I ran.

The moment I stepped out of the palace I saw great plumes of black smoke billowing towards the sky, and I took off into a sprint, picking up speed as I ran through the cool night air. I followed the fastest sandstone path to Tobias's House, hearing multiple raised voices as I approached, and I skidded to a halt when I rounded the corner.

It was chaos. Dozens of humans were scattered on the ground, suffering with twisted limbs and severe burns. Castor and Cobal were helping amongst them, as they treated those with the greatest need. Shanon led another small party of humans hauling buckets of water, as they focused on extinguishing the last of the embers. Half of the building was gone, the remains a black, charred pile of rubble where it had collapsed.

I spotted Truda and Erik lifting heavy beams and stones, as they called in desperation for assistance.

Addox was nowhere in sight, and my stomach churned with a nauseating feeling. Without question, he would be here in a time of such crisis, and I worried my fear of his entrapment was true. In rapid steps, I reached Truda.

"How can I help?" I called, her head snapping to mine, surprised to see me.

"We need to move that beam, without the far wall collapsing. Can you brace it?" she asked, and I nodded. I climbed steadily up the debris until I stood at the head of the mound, with a clear view of the other side, and that is when I saw him.

Addox.

He looked up, our eyes locking. He was covered in black smudges, his brow streaked from sweat, as he helped remove more rubble from the lower side. Overwhelmed with relief, I wanted to fall to my knees as I saw him, whole and uninjured. Aware of our audience, I merely gave him a small nod, before moving towards the wall Truda wanted me to support.

"Slowly," she called once my hands were spread wide against the stone. Truda, Erik, and a few others began to move. The beam was blocking access to the inner doorway leading to the part of the building that had not yet collapsed. Desperate murmurs of those trapped inside could be heard.

Something vibrated within, and dust drifted onto my face as a stone seemed to shift beneath my hand. The wall was on the brink of collapse, endangering the stability of the rest of the building. I had to keep it supported for as long as possible, the lives of those trapped inside depended on it. "Truda," I shouted, as I pushed harder against the weight, hoping I could give them enough time, when I felt a warm body stand next to mine. It was Addox, his back was leaning against the wall, as he used leverage against another beam to push.

"No, Addox, it could fall at any moment," I said, unable to hide my panic.

"If you're staying, then so am I," he grunted, putting all his strength into holding back the wall. I did the same, refusing to give up, determined to push for as long as I could. Truda and her team removed the beam and rushed to open the door, two humans immediately fleeing from inside.

"Is there anyone else?" Truda called, and a man covered in ash shook his head, guiding his injured friend to sit with the others. Another wisp of dust swelled from the depths as the wall felt heavier. Addox and I looked at each other with a unified nod, realising what we had to do. We leapt forward simultaneously, falling on the grass in the nearby verge. We looked back breathlessly, and watched in horror as the wall fell, the ruined building creaking before finally toppling into itself.

Briefly, Addox reached for my hand, our fingers intertwining as we lay on the grass, gazing at what was once a safe refuge for humans, now reduced to a heap of scorched stones.

"Are you hurt?" Truda asked, coming to stand beside us. I quickly pulled my hand from Addox's before she noticed.

"I am fine, I need to return to the palace before General Maiya notices my absence," I said.

"Then go, we can handle this." I nodded, taking a final glance at Addox before straightening. A piercing cry suddenly ran through the air, and all of us rushed towards its source. We found Castor crying out in horror, as Shanon removed a large stone from the ground, revealing a small, mangled figure beneath the rubble.

It was Kass, the young boy who liked horses. He was dead.

"Shanon, get Castor out of here," Truda instructed,

turning him away from the sight of the crushed boy's body. Cobal and Shanon approached immediately, grimacing before guiding a weeping Castor away.

"They'll pay for this," Addox said, his anger rippling through him as he clenched his fists.

"Not now, Addox," Truda replied.

"Then when? We know who did this. It's time we act," he shouted. Erik stepped forward and his gaze flicked to me, which caused Addox to tense, as though remembering I was here. An untrained elf would likely consider the gesture insignificant, but I detected the momentary awkwardness. It was clear they had a better understanding of what transpired here than I did.

"The priority right now is providing these humans with healing aid and shelter," Truda said,

"We should take them to the Training House," Erik said, looking over the rubble sorrowfully. I remembered Tobias's House had been his first project as a free and independent man, endorsed by the queen and council, at a time when the vision of a unified people seemed possible.

"Agreed." Truda wiped her hands as she assessed the scene in front of her, determining how to proceed. They left in the same direction Shanon had taken Castor, who was no longer crying but still ghostly pale, with Cobal still trying to console him.

Addox and I faced each other, mere inches apart, my fingers flexing as I wanted to comfort him. I had seen that he cared for Kass, and I knew him well enough now to know these signs of anger were mere masks to hide his pain.

"Addox!" Truda called, and he shifted his eyes to mine, as though he too had something he wanted to say but was holding back.

"Find me later," I whispered, and Addox gave a small nod before jogging to catch up with the others. I hated watching him go, I wanted to comfort him and offer my help. Never had I felt more like an outsider than in that moment.

Many questions ran through my mind as I returned to the palace. I wanted to know how the fire had started. Addox said they knew who was responsible, Truda and Erik were hiding something and General Maiya was nowhere to be seen.

An innocent life had been claimed this night, and I was beginning to understand the prejudices between our people more than ever. Through ambitions of equality, we had encouraged a greater divide between us, making declarations of freedom without understanding the full implications. Expecting men to persist in menial tasks, we dismissed the idea of them aspiring to better themselves or learning the skills of a warrior. None had considered who would aggregate our fields, or sweep our streets when elves believed themselves too important to undertake such tasks. To make matters worse, we had given elves more reason to resent humans. With food shortages, and lack of servants to do their bidding, there was certainly a motive to lash out in protest, or at least indirectly condone the actions of those who would hurt the innocent.

I returned to protect the royal family as they slumbered, patrolling in the darkness until morning. When they rose, two of my guardswomen escorted the royals to the gardens for breakfast, offering me relief. I returned to my chambers, my breath catching when I found it already occupied.

Addox sat on the edge of my bed, looking as withered and exhausted as I felt, his body covered in dust and soot with patches of blood running up his arms.

"It's not mine," he said, noticing my look of worry, and I nodded, not feeling all that comforted.

"Wait here," I instructed, returning a moment later with a bowl and wash cloth. He watched as I knelt in front of him, gently wiping away the dirt from his skin.

"I guess I shouldn't have been surprised you'd come," he said.

"I had to know you were not hurt," I admitted, pausing only when he slowly placed his hand over mine. I dropped the washcloth, twining my fingers with his.

"Three died, including Kass," he said quietly, with an edge of indignation in his voice. His eyes followed my movements as I worked to remove the layers of grime on his arms. "Just another boy I failed," he added, his eyes glazing over. Something caught in my throat at the sight of him like this.

"I should have been there sooner," I said, wrapping my arms around him, cradling his head to the crook of my neck as I stroked his hair. He took a deep breath, holding me tighter as he pressed his body into mine. We remained in that position for a while, and when I shifted uncomfortably from my kneeling stance, Addox lifted me, cradling my waist as we tumbled back onto the bed. There were things to be said, questions that needed answers, but neither of us spoke, as we desperately clung to one another. Addox occasionally breathed deep sighs of comfort as he inhaled my scent, his large hand holding my thigh while the other caressed my back. I did not know how long we stayed this way, but I knew Addox had awoken first when my eyes fluttered open to find him staring at me.

"I've got to go." His face showed deep sadness as he brushed a lock of hair from my face. "I'm sorry," he added, leaning forward to press a gentle kiss to my lips.

"Where?" I asked, confused as I watched him stand and reach for his surcoat.

"I won't be coming back," Addox said suddenly, his back to me as he stood in the centre of my chambers. Immediately alert, I sat up, slinging my legs over the bed. "Don't bother arguing about it, you knew this had to end," he added, still refusing to face me.

My heart raced, a pit forming in my stomach.

"You are going to do something stupid," I said, realisation suddenly dawning. "That is why you are acting like this?" I snapped.

"I don't know what you mean," he said, avoiding eye contact, "This was a bargain between us, nothing more."

"I do not believe you." I stomped my foot. I suddenly

felt a surge of anger as I frowned and moved in front of him, blocking the door. "You know more than you let on. The human deaths, Tobias's house, all of it!" I shouted. The words carried my rage and left me desolate all at once. Addox's features fell from anguish to shock at my outburst, but despite his avoidance, he could not hide the truth.

"They deserve everything that's coming to them!"

"Who?" I asked, my pulse still thumping.

"The Sanctum! They burned Tobias's house to the ground to destroy the food they were growing. They hated that humans could receive shelter there."

"Why? For what benefit?"

"Those who own all sources of food in the city can easily exploit starving humans. They'd gain absolute control. The two dead men were a message, made an example of. Join The Sanctum or face the consequences." The pieces fell together, and I internally kicked myself for not seeing it sooner.

"You knew this was my goal, why I had asked you to train me." He gestured for me to move away from the door. "I used you to get the skill I needed. Now I'm finally putting that training to good use."

"No wait." I was desperate, pleading with my eyes. "I need you. Please, stay with me."

"It's over, little elf. I'm sorry."

"I love you," I blurted, just as he reached past me for the door handle. His eyes closed, and I raised a hand to caress his face, trying to angle it down to look at me, but Addox fought against my hold, his jaw clenching as he suddenly shoved me out of the way, pulling the door open and slamming it firmly closed behind him.

As I watched him leave, I felt hollow, as though he was taking half of me with him.

20

Betrayer

My chamber was deftly quiet.

No sound from outside broke the silence within, as though the whole city was in a state of mourning after the fire. I sat on my bed, waiting in complete darkness, imagining he would return and beg for my forgiveness, uttering those three words I would sacrifice almost anything to hear. Instead, his hurtful truths haunted my thoughts.

You knew this was my goal.

I used you.

I questioned if I was merely a means to an end, wondering even if I had known, would I have made the bargain at all? Perhaps I would have agreed, if only to feel a slice of pure happiness.

When morning arrived, I numbly went through the

motions of adorning my armour and heading towards the gardens for duty. I stepped out into the fresh air, feeling the warmth of the sun across my skin and closed my eyes. I breathed deeply to try and calm my sorrow, and for a fleeting moment, I felt mildly better.

As I entered the garden, I was puzzled to find three of my guardswomen and Cobal huddled on the grass, their grave expressions meeting mine as I approached.

"Has something happened?" I asked.

"The Sanctum has been attacked," Cobal said.

I felt the colour drain from my face.

"Attacked? Do you know who..." I began but could not finish my sentence, a rancid nauseating feeling churned through my stomach. I already knew the answer.

Brenith shrugged nonchalantly, "Some humans have been caught, General Maiya and her guard have gone to retrieve them." I swallowed, my throat suddenly feeling very dry.

A fresh wave of panic prickled across my skin. I hoped, with every fabric of my being, that Addox was not amongst them, but in my heart, I knew to imagine the worst.

"I should guard the gate, to see if General Maiya needs assistance upon arrival," I said stoically. I was desperate to see if Addox was amongst those Maiya was collecting. Brenith saluted and I turned, my heart pounding heavily in my chest, as I made my way through the palace.

Pacing constantly, I waited for their arrival.

A momentary glimmer of optimism flashed across my mind. The incident may have had nothing to do with Addox.

Another random faction of humans could have had a grudge against The Sanctum. He would be safe, occupying himself with mundane things to distract him from reverent longing, but the realist in me knew better.

When General Maiya and her warriors could be seen approaching, I straightened, trying not to appear too eager or uncharacteristically helpful. I raised my fist and offered a salute, opening the gate for her.

"I heard of the skirmish," I said, under her watchful eye. I recognised the two warriors that followed her, but I did not know their names. A shackled line of chained humans shuffled slowly behind them, pulled by a chain wrapped around one of the women's arms like a leash. The men's wrists were clutched in manacles, connecting them by the singular chain, with thick brown fabric draped over their heads.

"It was already over by the time I arrived," General Maiya said, mildly irritated. "Not very intellectual of them to attack an establishment full of highly skilled elven warriors."

"We're not afraid of you. We'd do it again if..." one of them began, before being interrupted by a kick in the back of the knee from one of the elf warriors. He stumbled and pulled at the unified chains, making the others unsteady on their feet. The voice did not belong to Addox, and I waited for more outbursts of defiance to listen for him, but the rest of the captives remained silent.

"Yes, and what a glorious waste of effort that was," General Maiya drawled, sounding more inconvenienced than troubled.

"Who are they?" I asked, attempting to discreetly look past her and her warriors to study the humans, trying to find any distinguishing mark that would help me identify Addox from the rest.

"General Maiya!" bellowed a familiar voice, our attentions snapping beyond the gate to see Truda and Erik running towards us.

"Here we shall get our answers," the general replied smugly, but only loud enough for myself and our guard to hear. General Maiya quickly ripped each hood from the prisoners' heads one by one. Apart from the man who had spoken, the humans were all gagged.

My eyes locked on Addox the moment his hood was pulled away. I quickly scanned his face and body, feeling relief there were no signs of injuries. He saw my worried expression and looked away guiltily.

"I trust you recognise them," General Maiya stated, gesturing to Truda. There was no denying it, they were her elite. The same humans I had seen sparring with Addox in the training house several times.

"Where are you taking these men?" Truda demanded.

"To the prison, where they shall be detained for their crimes."

"They committed no crime. They were only following the orders I gave them."

"Your orders?" General Maiya asked, incredulous.

"Yes, we know it was Peril and her warriors who attacked Tobias's House."

"How do you know this?" General Maiya asked, full of scepticism.

"My elite and I continued the investigation you abandoned. We gathered intel by any means, searching for evidence of who may have been responsible for the human deaths, spying on any elf of interest," she said, and then glanced at me briefly, her expression strangely regretful.

Spied?

Then it hit me, my surroundings seeming to dull, my head spinning as I glanced from Truda's renewed stern expression to Addox, whose wide eyes were locked on mine.

Addox knew.

He worked for Truda.

It all made perfect sense now.

She asked me to assign someone to find the truth of what General Maiya was doing with her warriors, and I reported nothing back to her. I was so angry towards her after how she treated Lelane, I pretended I had no news to share. Of course, Truda had suspected I was lying.

So, she sent Addox. That was why he suddenly seemed to take in interest in bargaining with me, Truda had ordered him to gather intel, by any means. He was always so full of questions, searching through my chambers, and I had been fooled into believing he wanted to know the true me. It was all a lie, everything he said and done only measured now with Truda's betrayal. Instantly, my face felt cold and clammy, I thought I was going to be sick.

"You ordered them to attack The Sanctum?" General

Maiya accused.

"Truda, don't," Erik said, reaching for her, but she ignored him.

"Yes. Everything they have done this day, has been under my instruction," she said, her chin raised high.

"You have taken things too far this time, Truda," General Maiya said, with a snide tone. "You are both forbidden from attending the next council meeting, I will summon you when a decision has been made of your punishment," she followed, addressing both Truda and Erik. She slowly turned to me, "Do not let them enter. I must speak with the queen."

"What about them?" I asked, gesturing casually to the humans.

"They shall be locked away in the prison," she said decidedly. "My warriors and I will take them." I nodded numbly, watching as her warriors dragged the humans inside, Addox fighting against his restraints as he tried to hold my gaze. I ignored his stares but felt as though I had just walked through a window, a blunt impact, followed by shattering glass slicing into my skin.

Then, stepping forward, I closed the gate on Truda and Erik, their faces partially obscured between the wide slats.

"Maiya! You cannot do this," Truda snapped.

"I can and I will," General Maiya said over her shoulder, her voice filled with confidence. "You broke our laws, Truda, allowing humans under your command to arm themselves and attack our own. You no longer have the right to argue or challenge my authority," she finished, and then retreated, her warriors and prisoners being pulled behind them.

"You saw what happened to Tobias's House, we had to stop them," Truda said, now addressing me.

I said nothing, as I pulled the lever shut, only looking at her once the gate was secured and firmly locked in place. I blinked slowly, feeling the water glistening in my eyes, clenching my jaw tightly to prevent my lip from trembling.

"By any means?" I asked, and her jaw dropped, unable to meet my hardened stare. At the sight of my unwavering resolve, she and Erik slowly stepped back.

"Acqueline, lives were at stake. They still are."

"You could have told me, trusted in our friendship, but instead you used Addox as a weapon to seduce and manipulate me."

In silence, Truda's jaw visibly tensed. Her expression toughened and absent of any sign of regret.

"I knew your spy had made her reports, but you decided to withhold the information. You left me no choice."

"There was a choice, and you made it," I argued.

"We're sorry, Acqueline," Erik offered, his eyes sorrowful and sincere.

"You should go," I instructed, standing firm.

Holding my ground, I watched the elf, whom I had considered a close friend, and her companion slowly fade from my sight. Once they were gone, I felt my composure crack. Overwhelmed and alone, my first instinct was to find Addox, wanting to take comfort in him. I then remembered where he was and the reason for it. Pressing my eyelids closed, I slowly sank to my knees in despair.

My mother was right all along, empathy was a weakness. A warrior could not afford a bleeding heart in a kingdom so cruel; I should have paid more attention to her lessons.

I hated that it hurt so much. I allowed myself to get attached to someone like Addox, who had made it known from the beginning I could never mean anything to him. But in my foolish desperation to find someone who could know and love me for everything I was, I dared to hope, to feel, to love. Now, I must face the consequences of my actions.

For the days that followed, I was a useless walking shell. When I was not on duty, I hid in my chambers, focusing on discarding anything that would remind me of him. The furs had been replaced, the positioning of my room switched, I lit spicy aromatic candles to mask and help me forget what he smelt like. I sat on the floor in a position not suited for comfort, moving only when I felt the tingling that usually accompanied numbness. I missed Addox terribly, I wanted to go to him, to tell him I abhorred the notion of living the rest of forever without him, that we could find a way to work things out between us. General Maiya was certainly uncompromising, but perhaps if we explained our situation to Queen Fortuna, she would surely be understanding.

The knock at the door was so quiet, I would not have heard it if I were asleep. My heart dared to hope, despite knowing Addox was locked away elsewhere in the city. Slumping back down where I sat, I called for whoever had knocked to enter.

"I just dropped Lera off for training, is it a bad time?" Lelane said as she poked her head around the door.

"No, I was just..."

Doing nothing but sitting solemnly as I tried to meditate the man of my desires from my mind.

"Please, how can I assist?" I asked, inviting her to enter.

Lelane entered, surveying my chambers, and curiously reaching to touch a few surface items, much like Addox had. My stomach knotted at the haunting memory.

"I have not seen you since the night of the fire," Lelane said, turning to address me.

"I have been busy."

"It feels as though you have been avoiding me," She replied quietly.

"Of course not."

Which was a partial truth because I had been avoiding everyone. Ensuring my nights were occupied with duty, so I would have less interaction with those whose hearts had not been wrenched from their chests.

"I had unavoidable late-night duties," I offered, by way of explanation. It also made a good enough excuse for why I was unable to attend council meetings and have Brenith train the prince in my absence.

"Quin, are we truly friends?" Lelane asked, taking a seat at the foot of my bed.

"Of course."

"Then you should know I am here to talk, or listen, or whatever else it is you need." She reached forward and took one of my hands in hers. "I care about you, and it pains me to think I have made you unhappy."

"It is nothing you have done."

"You do not need to protect my feelings, I need to know if I have—"

"I am attracted to humans," I blurted. Her head shot up and watched me as I fumbled with the next set of words, instantly embarrassed. "Specifically, one human."

"Oh," she said, getting to her feet as the true extent of my truth sunk in. beginning to pace the small room.

"I should not have said anything," I said, causing her to stop and face me.

"No, Quin, I am really glad you told me, I was just..."

"Surprised," I finished, and she agreed. "Trust me, I was, too. It was one of the reasons I wanted to join the royal guard, believing it would be easier to conceal that part of myself."

"You should have told me sooner," she said, her smile returning as she came to sit beside me on the bed.

"I did not know how to; I was so ashamed." Lelane did not hesitate as she sat opposite me again, taking my hand and clutching it tightly in hers. "None of it seemed normal then, there were no permanent elf and human pairings, and I did not see him again for years."

"I should have been a better friend instead of leaving you alone in this."

"You were the greatest of friends," I said, thinking of the times she took care of me after episodes of my mother's cruelty. "My only regret is that we lost touch for so long," I said, stroking her fingers.

"Well, I am here now, and I have no plans to go anywhere." She wrapped her arm around my shoulder.

"I was so worried you would think badly of me."

"This changes nothing, so you find humans…" She paused trying to find the right word. "Likable. So what? Many elves share the same affliction."

Of course, I knew that, and it made it much harder to deal with my secret. I watched as Truda fell in love with her human, hiding the truth from me for the same reason. I resented her the moment she confessed, for being brave enough to admit what she wanted and going after it. I could never imagine myself doing something so brazen. Until now, with Lelane.

"Does this human know of your affections?" Lelane asked.

"Yes, but it ended."

"Why?" she asked, sounding genuinely disappointed for me.

"He was using me to get information, I do not know if I could forgive him for deceiving me, in truth, I am heartbroken." I felt myself becoming emotional again. Lelane squeezed my shoulder lightly in comfort.

"Does he feel the same way for you?" she asked, and I blinked, considering her words for a moment.

"He never admitted to it, and now that I am aware of his

deceit, I can only think the worst."

"But you have not spoken to him since?" I shook my head.

"No, and now he is trapped in the prison. There is no chance I will be able to see him without raising suspicion. Even if I did, and by some miracle, he felt something for me, there is nothing to be done. My path is already chosen."

"You are Head of the Royal Guard," Lelane proclaimed. "Demand to see him and find the full extent of the truth for yourself," she said, and I found myself nodding instinctively. "Then you will know what to do."

"What if it is all true, that everything was a lie, and nothing was real between us?"

"Then I will be here when you return, to help you grieve and move on," she finished with a sincere smile.

I stood outside the large prison for a long while, my steps faltering as I stared up at the unembellished exterior, my blood pumping wildly through my veins. Composing myself, I walked up the stairs and opened the large heavy door, coming face to face with one of General Maiya's warriors guarding the entranceway.

"State your purpose!"

"I must speak to one of the prisoners, he has information regarding a plot against General Maiya," I said, my tone emanating confidence.

"Of course, Acqueline," she said, acknowledging my

rank and offering a respectful salute, as she took a step to the side. "Proceed."

The prison was dark, with a dank and unpleasant smell. Cast iron sconces held torches in place along either side of the wall, the light dimming as some of the flames turned to a low ember. As I walked, I could see the cells ahead, spaced evenly along the narrow corridor, each probably occupied by a prisoner. The sound of my boots reverberated against the stone, despite my conscious effort to step lightly.

As I strode past the first cell, a human stepped forward, his hands gripping the metal bars. Ignoring him, I raised my chin, keeping my feet moving, until at last, in the final prison cell, I found Addox.

There was a ceramic bowl of untouched soup and a piece of bread just inside the door, along with a small cot covered by a single blanket in one corner that, judging by its appearance, had also not been slept in. He sat in the opposite corner, his legs bent, arms resting on his knees, his face turned down.

"You shouldn't be here," Addox said, briefly glancing up before returning to his defeated posture.

"I just need to hear the truth." I took one step forward, encouraging him to look at me. "You owe me as much, and then I will leave you to your fate."

"Quin," he whispered, his eyes closed.

"Was any of it real?" I asked, my voice already trembling.

"You wouldn't believe me, even if I told you." He flinched when I abruptly gripped the bars, the action startling him.

"You were spying for Truda. Was that why you made

the bargain?"

"It wasn't like that..."

"Then what was it like?"

"You knew I was one of Truda's elite, I was just following her orders."

"I trusted you," I said, looking up at him. "I told you I loved you," I shrieked, feeling the metal bend slightly beneath my grip.

"Fine," he said, suddenly standing and walking over to face me behind the bars. "You want to know the truth?" he asked, his face contorting in anger.

"That is all I want," I replied adamantly.

"Truda ordered me to follow you, watch your movements and search your chambers. When I couldn't find anything, she asked me to get closer, to use other skills if necessary to get you to talk."

"An assignment you took very seriously," I said distastefully.

"I warned you, told you, I didn't want..." he began but stopped himself.

"So, this is my fault?" I asked incredulously, but Addox just shook his head.

"That's not what I meant."

"I put my duty at risk because I thought we were in this together, but you played me the fool," I said, staring at him intensely.

"I wanted to tell you the truth, but Truda was convinced you were keeping secrets."

"How ironic." I laughed. "Everything I thought I knew

about the people I cared for most has been a lie."

"Not everything," Addox argued, and I desperately wanted to believe him. However, as I looked at him, all I could see were the number of times he had carefully examined my room or deceitfully interrogated me, all so he could report them back to Truda.

"How could you do this to me?" I asked, as the pain in my chest intensified.

"You didn't know how hard it was to walk away from you the other night. How much I wanted to stay, and tell you that..." He paused, his head bowed. "I made a promise to protect them, it's what I have spent the last few years training myself for."

"I would have helped you," I said, my eyes glistening with unshed tears.

"I know," he whispered, "It's all I've been able to think about. I know I screwed up, Quin, and I don't expect your forgiveness because I know I don't deserve it," he added, gripping the bars more tightly. "But please know, that I'm sorry."

I could not bear to hear any more. As tears welled up in my eyes, I retreated, hastily retracing my steps back down the corridor, ignoring his final call to catch my attention.

"Did you get everything you needed?" The guard asked once I returned to the entrance.

I nodded, "Yes, I got what I came for."

"Good, General Maiya has plans to execute these men before the week is out. Best you finish your interrogations before they are disposed of."

21

Defiance

Two guards were stationed either side of General Maiya's house entrance, neither of whom halted my approach or provided any gesture of greeting. Ignoring them, full of trepidation for what I was about to do, I knocked on the iron cast door. My nerves increased as I heard the great thudding of heavy boots and the door being briskly yanked open.

"I am busy," she said the moment she saw me. She was about to slam the door in my face when I stepped forward, lodging my foot in the doorway. General Maiya raised a singular questioning eyebrow, clearly surprised by my lack of cowardice.

"I will be but a moment."

"Fine," she drawled, stepping back, and allowing the door to widen enough for me to step inside. I gave her a small smile as I entered, taking stock of my surroundings. It was the exact opposite of how I imagined her home to be. Bright, with large windows, the walls decorated with lavish tapestries and exquisite paintings, and small side tables adorned with trinkets and ornamentals.

"You have a nice home," I said candidly.

General Maiya ignored me, and I followed her casually from the bright colourful hallway into the adjacent room. The room was well-lit and warm, the flames flickering high in the open fireplace. It was cosy and inviting, much like I imagined Lelane's home might have been, if she were presented with such luxuries. General Maiya sat on a scooped saddle chair, lounging lazily with one leg stretched and draped over the armrest.

"What do you want?" she asked, her voice dry and unimpressed.

"How did your talks with the queen go?"

"Let us not waste time, Acqueline, you do not need to bargain on Truda's behalf, Fortuna has already forbidden me from casting her out."

"That is not why I came," I said plainly. "Truda acted independently from the council's orders, there should be repercussions for her actions."

General Maiya narrowed her eyes, assessing me.

"What would you have done?" she challenged, and I took the opportunity to step further into the room, noticing the shelves of maps beside the fireplace.

"Truda's skills are undeniably an asset to this kingdom; she is an exceptional instructor and the responsibilities within the Training House suit her well," I said, taking a seat opposite General Maiya. "But she makes a poor council member, and I would have had her stripped of that title long ago. Erik too, if you were so inclined."

"I am surprised you think so."

"You should not be, it is well known Truda is stubborn and subordinate. She leads well enough, but you may have noticed, she is not all that great at following orders. Truda lacks all the necessary diplomacy skills, and although we are not currently on speaking terms, my opinion on the matter would not change either way."

"Why are you not on speaking terms?" General Maiya asked, easily playing into my hands.

"We had a disagreement when we spoke of the old breeding laws." Her interest was piqued at that, leaning forward.

"I confess, I did not think you were capable of a differing opinion," she said. I could not find insult in that. If anything, I was pleased I had not drawn unwarranted attention, moulding myself to be a dull comparison to the imposing form of others. "So, if it is not Truda you have come to discuss?" she asked, turning serious again.

"I was more concerned over the humans," I said, my eyes flickering away, unable to hold her smug inquisitiveness. "Are they to be punished for being led astray?"

"I do not see how I have another choice. We cannot afford more humans to adopt their rebellious mentality."

"Surely you do not mean to execute them?" I exclaimed.

"Truthfully, the thought brings me no joy. Perhaps if Truda had not trained them to be so dangerous, I would reconsider..."

"We could help them, build a new sanctuary and rehabilitate the humans," I suggested. General Maiya stared at me strangely. "I understand it is not common practice to feel compassionate about preserving a human life, but I cannot help but think any misstep of theirs is only a reflection of how we have failed to protect and guide them."

"I have not seen this side of you before," she said, studying me with new interest. She slowly stood to walk towards me, filling two goblets with water and offering me one. "What is this opposing opinion on the old breeding laws you have?"

"I understand why Truda was defensive in our argument. The nature in which a human's service was demanded, was immoral. But her anger stems from her protectiveness over Erik and his experiences. What about the number of elves that were chosen to deliver human offspring? Were they not equally and immorally directed? The only difference I see, is we celebrated the birth of elves, and appropriated humans, but the duty is the same."

"But who would willingly birth a human, if given the choice?" she scoffed.

"I would," I replied honestly. "If I was dedicated to a different duty. Raising a child like Prince Felyx would be a joy. He is a wondrous person, kind-hearted and a skilled archer. In another life perhaps..." I began but stopped, feeling overwhelmed at the sudden thought of a young boy, mirrored in Addox's image.

"Refreshing," she said, taking a slow sip from her goblet, giving nothing away of her thoughts. "I find I may have misjudged you, Acqueline."

"Of course, it is just an opinion, I am no expert on the matter," I stated, sipping my water.

"You remind me of a friend I knew long ago." She walked over to a small side table where a silver frame lay flat, picking it up and examining it. "She would often speak passionately about such matters."

"Where is this friend?" I asked, and General Maiya outstretched her arm, handing me the silver frame. I turned it over and saw a portrait of a large farmhouse and its surrounding valley painted on a creased and worn material, the detail of the image was exquisite.

"She was murdered, two days after she gifted me that painting."

My head snapped up in surprise, my brow furrowing at her anguished expression.

"I am sorry."

"If our breeding laws had been different, she would have lived." I looked back at the painting, further admiring its beauty. Despite the age of the parchment, the brush strokes were incredibly intricate, only a person of refined skill and patience could have painted it.

Everything else in General Maiya's house appeared shiny and new, nothing like the wrinkled, slightly faded image now protected behind glass and silver. She must consider the painting very precious.

As I placed my goblet on the centre table, I stumbled, purposely letting go of the frame and watching it topple to the floor. It bounced once and cracked, before landing face down, the glass shattering completely.

"I am so sorry," I said, rushing to collect it and slicing my palm after hastily grasping a shard of glass. "Ah…" I hissed, holding my hand up as a small pool of blood formed beneath my curled fingers.

"It is fine. Wait here, I shall get you a bandage," General Maiya said, reviewing the mess on the floor before leaving. The moment she was out of sight, I rushed over to the bookshelf and unfolded the maps layered at the top, finding nothing spectacular about them.

"I would appreciate some healing balm, if you have any," I called, trying to stall for time as I desperately continued to search through the pile of parchments, my heart pounding. In the distance I could hear General Maiya moving around on the floor above, passing from one room to another. Roaming over the last shelf, I caught a glimpse of chalk marks at the edge of a well-used map, just as General Maiya's heavy footsteps could be heard coming down the stairs. I folded the map into a compact square and stuffed it down the front of my breastplate. Rushing to the broken frame, I safely extracted the painting, holding it ready as General Maiya returned.

"I made sure not to bleed on it," I said with a warm smile, holding the parchment out to her.

"Thank you," she replied, exchanging the painting for medical supplies. I rubbed paste into my palm and bound my hand, General Maiya's eyes on me the entire time. "Your words have moved me today. We shall build a new sanctuary for the humans, and I will pay closer attention to their care."

"Thank you," I said, shuffling on my feet as I discreetly looked down to ensure the map was concealed securely.

"However, my decision on the humans in the dungeon, cannot be so easily swayed. I will have to think on it."

"That is all I would ask," I said, slowly making my way to the hallway. "Thank you for your time General Maiya," I added, offering a salute before fleeing from her home and hastily heading back to the palace.

"Quin, what is wrong?" Lelane asked, puzzled as I hurriedly cleared the table in her chambers, causing its contents to scatter to the floor. I pulled out the map from my breastplate as I showed her my blood-soaked bandages.

"You would think after all this time I would be better at covering wounds."

"What happened?" Lelane asked, watching as I unfolded the parchment, spreading it flat and smoothing the creases.

"Lyzaria spoke of a map containing strange markings. She witnessed the general modify said map after she had returned from venturing outside of the city, I took this from General Maiya's house."

“Wait, Quin, slow down,” she said, reaching for my hand and inspecting the poorly fastened bandage. “I thought you were going to speak to the human?”

“I did,” I said, pausing and looking into her bright green eyes. “Lelane, General Maiya is going to have him killed.”

She froze in place, her eyes widening in surprise.

“Why?”

“She believes the humans to be dangerous, that their rebellious nature is infectious and would encourage others.” I felt like every action I had taken from learning of Addox’s execution was completely emotive, as though my body was making independent choices before my mind had caught up. I knew despite everything that had happened between us, allowing Addox to be killed was not an option. “I will not let him die.”

“What will you do?” Lelane asked, returning her focus to the wound on my hand.

“General Maiya is keeping secrets from the council, and I fully intend to find out the truth for myself,” I said. If I could discover the truth of her betrayal, I could give Truda the evidence she was so desperate to obtain and have General Maiya removed from her position of power. “I need more light.”

Lelane reached over to retrieve a mounted candle and leaned closer to me, angling the flame over the map, being careful not to let any wax spill from the brass candleholder. At first glance, it appeared to be no different from any other map I had studied with Truda. Then, my eyes narrowed as

I noticed strange markings drawn in multiple locations.

"What is that? The location of the old rebellion base?" Lelane asked, pointing to a marking in the south, at the edge of the desert. I shook my head.

"The rebels lived in the woodland, beyond the catacombs," I replied, pointing slightly higher from where the symbol was placed, remembering what Truda had shown me.

"What do the markings mean?"

"Only one way to find out," I replied, as I stood and gathered food and healing provisions for my journey.

"How long will you be?" Lelane asked, as she gently rubbed healing paste on my shallow wound, causing me to slightly wince.

"Hopefully, no longer than a day."

"Horseback would be quicker," she commented, and it would, but aside from my dislike of the creatures, a steed suddenly missing from the stables would make my absence more noticeable.

"No one must know I have left."

"I still do not understand why you cannot hand the map over to Truda and let her uncover the General's secrets."

"I cannot trust she would take the right course of action, it has to be me." I would find the leverage I needed to sway General Maiya into sparing Addox's life. "Can you watch over Addox?" I asked, hopeful.

"What if General Maiya…" She trailed off and I turned to look at her, silently completing her sentence.

What if she sought to have the humans killed in my absence?

"Delay it."

"How?"

"Poison them if you must, fabricate an illness, anything to slow General Maiya down."

"Okay," she said, wrapping her arms around herself uncomfortably, "I will do what I can."

"Thank you, Lelane, I shall find a way to make this up to you."

"Do you want me to tell your human anything?"

"No," I said quickly. A realisation suddenly dawned on me that I may never return. If I found the truth of what was happening to General Maiya's warriors, it may be so gruesome, that even I could not come back from it. "Tell him…" I paused, carefully considering the words I would want to relay, "I forgive him." Lelane nodded, pulling me into a tight hug before allowing me to leave.

"Come back quickly."

"If you need anything, Brenith will attend you."

"We shall be fine, Quin, I am more worried about you."

"I shall return as soon as I can," I promised, before slipping out and discreetly leaving the palace.

22

Radiant Death

Dusk had fully nestled over the city, covering it in a blanket of cold shadows, which made it easier to navigate my way unseen. The large black gate was not so simple to get past concealed, with guards patrolling the top of the wall holding bright torches. I crouched low, waiting at the side of the nearest building until the opportunity to slip past presented itself. Eventually, two guards crossed each other's paths and struck up a conversation. I pulled the hood up on my cloak to cover my face and climbed up a ladder, vaulting over and lowering my body to hang on the other side of the wall. As I dangled for a moment, I hissed at the sharp pain in my bandaged palm and gauged the distance below, dropping to a soundless crouch outside of the city.

Discreetly, I looked back up to see the guards continue

their steady patrol along the wall, monitoring multiple directions, and searching for danger. Viewing beyond the darkened horizon, I quickly recognised a flaw in my plan. There was no way I would make good headway over the grasslands with sentries keeping a watchful eye for any movement.

I removed my bow carefully, gripping it with my injured hand while I searched for something of use on the ground, two smooth pebbles catching my eye. Thinking of Lera and her sling, I readied the first stone between my fingers, nocked it, and took aim at the closest patrolling warrior. Exhaling a steady breath, I pulled back and released, with enough force to stun. The pebble ricocheted off her temple, causing her body to slump in a heap. The moment she was down, I nocked back the other stone, shooting it before my next target could notice.

When the second guard had fallen, I slung my bow over my back and sprinted off into the darkness, only the peak of the mountains visible above. I was not entirely confident in the direction I was headed, but I knew I could correct myself once I was concealed from the view of the city. I did not slow until my feet touched sand and the city was small enough to hold in the palm of my hand.

I had been an elfling the last time I had left the city, remembering how delighted I was at the first sight of the endless yellow landscape. That was, until I had touched it for the first time, and I became instantly irritated at how it seemed to want to cling to me. Now I felt nothing but trepidation for the unknown, fearing the discovery of what General Maiya was doing with our warriors. Taking a deep breath and one final glance at the city, I hoped Lelane would be able to hold to her promise and watch over Addox in my absence.

Despite the distance between us, I felt an uncontrollable urge pulling me back to him. Apparently, my traitorous heart did not understand our relationship had been fabricated by his motivation to serve Truda, and loving someone who would never love you back brought nothing but misery.

My thighs burned from repeatedly scaling the small vertical mounds of sand, reminding me I was long overdue for an arduous training schedule of my own, which I planned to implement when I returned to the city.

If I returned to the city.

I jogged to the peak of the next dune and pulled out General Maiya's map to get my bearings, attempting to lay it flat on the uneven surface. I still had a way to go before I reached the closest mark, so I shook off the sand, and returned the map to my satchel, taking off into another sprint. If I was away from the city for too long, Lelane would be forced to implement a secondary scheme of distraction.

By the time my pace slowed, the sun was beaming high, and I could see strange shimmering shapes in the distance. I thought it could be the heat playing a trick on me, but as I crawled closer, I realised what it was.

Beyond, just in front of the catacomb pass, tents were erected, with heavily armed warriors busying themselves as they walked through the small camp.

Some were recognisable as General Maiya's warriors by their city armour, but others seemed to be dressed strangely. I was too far away to determine the differences between them. Feeling confused and unsettled, I checked behind me before urging myself forward, keeping my body as low as possible. I hoped the remaining dunes would keep me hidden from the scouts up ahead. I crawled until I was close enough to hear the faint murmuring of chatter between the warriors, all oblivious to my approach as they continued with their mundane tasks.

Aside from the fact they were camped in the middle of the desert, and the strange attire some of the warriors wore, nothing seemed out of the ordinary. It was just a camp, no different than any other in the days of the rebellion.

What is the purpose of them being here?

I ducked low instantly as a warrior moved out of formation and headed in my direction.

Tall and lean, she had long brown hair plaited into two tails, concealing everything but the tips of her ears. She was dressed in mismatched leather and silver armour, with daggers filling her waistband. Holding a blade casually in her hand, she seemed to gaze across the desert with a solemn expression. I did not know who she was, her face as unfamiliar as the armour she wore, she was not part of General Maiya's army.

"Shea! The captain summons you," another guard called.

Captain?

I wondered, watching as Shea nodded, turning from my location to follow the guard. Checking my surroundings, I sprung to my feet and charged towards the closest tent, hugging my body as closely to it as possible without creating a dent or shadow in the fabric.

I peered carefully underneath the canvas and discovered crates of supplies, including various chest pieces and leathers. I stashed my cloak, bow, and satchel between them, as I dressed in armour that resembled General Maiya's warriors' attire and stepped fully into the camp.

I kept my head low, avoiding eye contact with anyone as I rushed forward to catch up with Shea, catching sight of her again just as she entered a large tent. I moved discreetly to the rear, away from view. Hearing voices coming from within, I pulled out a dagger, steadily cutting a small slice in the cotton canvas. Slowly and carefully, I pulled the fabric apart and peeked through the gap, shocked at the sight of who was inside.

Wearing stained and dented metal armour, with her palms planted at either end of a table, stood Imelda, Truda's old captain in the days of the rebellion.

The same elf that had been exiled for betraying Truda, and almost becoming her executioner.

"General Maiya wants us to send more warriors to the crag mountain," Imelda told Shea as she approached. "I just received the message by raven."

"I can go, I am getting sick at the sight of sand anyway."

"No, I want you here," Imelda replied.

"Did she mention when she plans on taking full command over the city?"

My heart began to pound at her words.

"It will be soon. She will be held to her promise," Imelda said.

"And you can finally get your revenge on Truda," Shea replied, rounding the table, and reaching for her.

"I just want what was taken from me."

"It was unfair what they did, branding you a traitor while giving her the freedom to live a comfortable life with her Guan."

"I cannot live like this for one day longer, Shea. I do not understand how you have endured it for so long."

"We deserve better, my darling," Shea replied, placing her hand under Imelda's jaw, stroking it gently. "So, play your part, appease General Maiya's orders. Send more warriors to the crag mountain. You will be in the city again before long."

"I do not know how I would have coped through all this without you," Imelda breathed, and Shea smiled before leaning down and pressing her lips to the crown of her head.

Appalled, I stumbled back, my breath shallow and hurried as my mind ran frantic, digesting all I had just heard. Truda had been right to worry, General Maiya was deceiving us, working with Imelda, and scheming to use their combined forces to invade and take over. All the while she depleted our ability to oppose her, gradually reducing my guard and refusing to allow Truda's loyal elite humans to join her ranks.

However, I struggled to comprehend the strategic

advantage of General Maiya scattering her warriors across every corner of the kingdom. It made no sense. If she planned to ally with Imelda, commanding them to storm the city and overthrow the queen and council, why would she deplete her own forces this way?

There was more to their plan, yet to be uncovered, and I would not return to the city until I had enough leverage to save Addox. Imelda had mentioned another encampment based at the crag mountain not too far from here, a place of importance to General Maiya, perhaps there I would find my answers.

As I turned to retrieve my belongings, I halted, suddenly finding I was surrounded by a line of warriors, their blades pointed directly at me.

I reached behind my back for my bow, wincing when I remembered I had left it behind. Frantic, I looked past them, planning my route of escape. If I could only reach my weapon, my golden arrows would give them enough cause to be cautious.

I could not be captured, Addox's life depended on it.

I leapt forward, tackling the first elf, twisting her arm, and wrenching the sword from her hands. I kicked at her ankle and pushed as she fell forward, ploughing her into another elf. Sword in hand, I extended my arm, pointing the blade out to them.

“Stand back, I do not wish to spill blood,” I commanded, but someone grabbed me from behind, alarming me enough for the other warriors to advance at once.

“Who is this?” Shea asked. The elf restraining me tightened her grip, and I narrowed my eyes at them all.

“Acqueline?” Imelda said, puzzled and in shock. “Was she alone?” she asked the group of warriors, a hint of panic in her voice.

“Worried I may have Truda in my company?” I mocked, watching Imelda’s face pale.

“What are you doing here?” Shea asked, stepping protectively in front of Imelda.

I remained silent, pulling in resistance to the arms continuing to hold me.

“So, this is Truda’s loyal little lacky,” Shea said amused, as she looked over my petite frame.

“She has earned my loyalty and is well deserving of it,” I spat.

“It must take a loyal friend indeed to look past her egotistical introversions and manipulations, to believe Truda cares about anyone but herself,” added Imelda.

“You are the last elf who should speak of loyalty,” I replied, feeling angered by her description.

“I was loyal!” she shouted. “To the queen and council. I would have fallen on my own sword if they asked me to, and how was I rewarded?” She took a step closer to me, her expression hard and full of anger. “Exile,” she scathed.

“You tried to kill Truda.”

"Has not everyone?" Shea added, finding the exchange amusing.

"Because she was the enemy!" Imelda screamed. I stared her down, desperately tugging against the force of the elf behind me.

"Let us slow down with the dramatics," Shea said, rolling her eyes. "So, you came here, for what? To spy for Truda?"

"I came to discover the truth."

"Then allow us to enlighten you," she replied, so confident it verged on the edge of arrogance. "Witness what General Maiya and Imelda are doing to protect your precious kingdom. Then we shall revisit this discussion of traitors."

I frowned, unsure of what she meant.

"That is of course, if as you say, you come to seek the truth."

I looked around, taking stock of the number of elven faces watching me intently. I recognised and had trained or sparred against some of them. They were virtuous and loyal women, and I felt confused to judge them so harshly, their actions not matching the personalities I knew for them to possess.

"Then show me," I agreed.

"Excellent. Tie her hands, and saddle up the horses, we head to the crag mountain," Shea instructed, and Imelda was the first to barge past me.

Horses?

Without another word to me, Imelda instructed a peculiarly armoured warrior nearby, who tied my hands together tightly with rope. Moments later, half a dozen saddled horses appeared, ready for travel. A peppered speckled white mare was brought to me, and I shuffled back, feeling disorientated as I struggled to mount the horse.

"Help her up," someone said, as another picked me up by the waist like an elfling, guiding one foot into the first stirrup. My other leg came over as she guided my bound hands to the front, allowing me to hold onto the horn at the top of the saddle. My possessions were retrieved from the supply tent and placed into the saddlebag, just out of reach. Imelda and Shea mounted two stallions in the front, providing quick instructions to another warrior tending to them.

"Send a raven to inform General Maiya we are headed to the pass. Make sure to add the detail of our unexpected visitor," Imelda said, glancing back at me, amused. With that, she kicked in her heel and her steed began to trot forward, our horses following behind.

The ride was hard. At full speed for half the day, my hair was swept back and falling loose from its ties, as my eyes filled with water from the assault of the wind. Darkness had fallen, and relief washed over me when the horses began to slow and come to a halt before the mountain. The colossal crag that marked the end of our kingdom's borders. Reaching its vertical edge, I looked up, witnessing a few pieces become loose, jutting over the edge, and shattering before my horse's hooves, causing him to rear back.

"We go on foot from here," Shea called back, dismounting her horse, the warriors behind her following suit. Not waiting for assistance, I swung my leg over and jumped down, glad to create some distance between myself and the beast. I craned back to look at the sheer, haggard, sharp cliff, that stood taller than the highest palace tower. There were no visible passageways or tunnels, no caverns or passes that would indicate an easy route through.

"This way," Imelda said coldly, and I followed. Two of her warriors flanked me, while the last stayed behind with the horses. A sense of dread swept through me, the hairs on my arms standing on end as I felt the colour drain from my face. I had not been hesitant enough in my decision to be led here alone, with only Imelda and her loyal warriors as company. I had given her more cause than ever to find a way to be rid of me, perhaps here is where she would see to my end.

"The way through is narrow, and the edges sharp," Imelda warned, bringing me out of my disturbing reverie, and I followed her gaze. Just ahead of us, disguised by the sharp bouldering slate edge, was the beginning of a pass. It was so narrow, I did not think it possible for a grown elf to fit through. A warrior to my side approached the opening, stepping sideways before entering. The second warrior followed closely behind.

"After you," Shea invited, with her arm extended and ever-present smugness marring her features. I took another hesitant step forward, peering through the gap where her two companions had just disappeared. I could not see the direct route through, as the mountain's edges warped, adding twists and turns to the other side. Taking a deep breath, I turned sideways and began to carefully step through, thankful of my small build. The cold and sharp stone pressed against my skin, the surface scratching against my armour as I squeezed through the narrowest spaces. As I shuffled, the atmosphere shifted, the temperature dropping, and the scent and taste of salt permeated the air.

When the end drew near, I shimmied through the final space, stumbling and slipping on a green rock that brought me to my knees, palms pressing into grey sand.

I looked up, and gasped.

My mother had never been interested in myths or legends, but they always fascinated me as an elfling. Lelane would repeat the tales her mother told her at night, stories of legendary swords, mythical creatures, and lands that were flooded by our ancestors, drowning all life with endless saltwater.

Once, the rain had assaulted our city for a seemingly endless number of days. As a result, some of our banks filled with water, creating great puddles we elflings spent hours playing in.

It was the most water I had ever seen.

Depictions of vast oceans stretching beyond the eye could see were merely elements of another legendary tale in one of Lelane's childish stories. Yet here I was, struggling to stand, boots digging into wet sand, looking out at the unimaginable and unfathomable expanse of endless waters, just as described in one of those stories.

"This cannot be real," I muttered, my eyes gazing across the watery vastness.

"Have there been any further sightings?" Imelda asked an unknown elf who approached us.

"Two earlier this day, the same times as always," she responded, and I looked between her and the water's surface shimmering in the light.

What are they talking about?

I was confused and overwhelmed, unable to fathom the connection between the endless rippling waters and General Maiya's decision to spread our armies so thinly across the kingdom.

"I do not understand," I said, my voice trembling slightly, still shocked. Everyone paused and stared at me. "What are they doing here?" I asked, noticing several of General Maiya's warriors had set up a camp on the beach. Some were sharpening arrowheads beside crates full of weapons. Provisions lined the base of the cliff, and other warriors were using makeshift ladders to scale the mountainside, perching themselves in various vantage points overlooking the ocean.

"Welcome to the line of defence," Shea whispered in my ear as she shrugged past me to greet an elf signalling in her direction. I stood there confused, my hands still bound in front of me, while I took in my surroundings, utterly vexed.

What is this place?

How had we never known such a great sea could be found

so close to the edge of our borders? None of our cartographers had recorded such a thing.

"Captain," a hurried and hushed voice called from behind. I turned to find an alert young elf, her tone unsettling. "There is another one approaching."

"Everyone take your positions," Imelda instructed, grabbing my arm as she pulled me to a rope ladder, and shoved me to urgently climb up.

"My hands," I muttered, and with an irritated look, she reached for a knife and swiftly cut through my bindings. Elves frantically moved in all directions, swiftly clearing the beach of any item or person, scrambling to conceal themselves along the edge of the cavern. "What is going on?"

"Climb and see for yourself," Imelda hissed, waving her hands at the ladder. When we reached the top of the platform, Imelda clutched the back of my neck, pushing me down to a crouched position.

"You only have to ask," I hissed back, shrugging off her firm grip.

"Stay low," she whispered, maintaining her cowered stance as we stealthily crept across the mountain top, my gaze drawn to the mesmerising waters below.

"There," she whispered, pointing to the sea. I crawled to the edge and cautiously peered over, witnessing the last movements of the warriors below. Their forms became one with the mountain edge, cloaked in shadow.

"I do not see…" I began, but Imelda clutched the bottom of my chin, forcing me to look up. I was about to dramatically jerk my face away, when a strange object floating on the water caught my attention.

"What is that?" I asked.

"A vessel," Imelda said simply, as though such a thing were not of myth and legend. "Aboard it, are foreign travellers, this is a route they frequent." She crouched lower, her eyes narrowing as she focussed on the horizon. "It seems our ancestors were not as thorough in the execution of our enemies."

She turned to me, her piercing brown eyes holding mine, transfixed.

"We are not alone in this kingdom, Acqueline." Suddenly, shouts could be heard from below as we realised the vessel was getting larger and heading towards us. As the object grew closer, I gawked at the dark wood oval, with tall beams of fabric making its way to the shore. Strange sounds of creaking wood, the chiming of metal, and loud shouts of life alerted my senses.

There were dozens of them. Creatures scurried across the structure's surface, pulling rope and barrels, and tossing things in the water. The monstrous floating shape suddenly changed, with something protruding from its side, the large vessel now birthing a smaller version of itself. More figures appeared, climbing over and into the smaller wooden object, as others helped lower it to the water's surface.

"They are coming to shore," someone whispered from beside us, just as more of General Maiya's warriors appeared from the cavern's edge, armed, and readying themselves for battle.

"I have to find Shea," Imelda said suddenly, getting up to move past me.

"Where is my bow?" I asked, grabbing her arm. She hesitated, looking between me and the approaching vessel. "If they are hostile, you will need my aim," I added, and she tersely agreed. At her instruction, a warrior emerged with my redwood winged bow in hand, tossing it up for me to catch, while Imelda left in the opposite direction.

I crossed the uneven slate of the crag until I found a flat surface that allowed me to maintain a steady stance, offering a better vantage point of the entire waterfront.

Figures hopped out of the small vessel and trudged through the water. They appeared to be human, though varying much in height and size. Each wore heavily protective clothing, their metal weapons gleaming in the moonlight. I readied my bow, pulling the string taught and taking aim, the wisps of gold appearing at the end of my fingertips.

A signal was called, and suddenly our warriors revealed themselves, charging forward and vanquishing the first few invaders with ease. Caught off guard, but now alerted to the pre-emptive strike, the adversaries began to fight back, more of them advancing on the few warriors within reach.

I could see Imelda fighting on the beach, taking command of a small myriad of warriors as they advanced ahead of the rest. My heart was racing, and I noticed Shea singled out on the other side, crowded by three hulking figures. Her boots etched a circle in the sand as she guarded, they had her trapped in. I aimed and released my first golden arrow, piercing the first human straight through the chest. Equally swift, I brought down the second with a shot to the head. Shea vanquished the last, waving to me in thanks before she ran to join the others.

My attention was drawn back to the larger watercraft, which was once again evolving and changing shape. A moving silver cylinder, levied on a wooden frame, appeared at its edge. Another emerged, then another, until the structure had four strange new limbs, each shrouded by moving silhouettes.

Suddenly, a great boom thundered, the vessel breathed fire, and shortly after, the mountain quaked beneath my feet, as part of the stone cliff tore away. I calmed my breathing as much as possible and focused my attention on the figures on top of the floating atrocity. This was not a mythical creature, but a preternatural weapon, controlled by the humans coming from and residing within it. Another blast sounded, this time the fire assaulted the beach, the sand mounding in all directions as our warriors began to retreat.

The humans controlled this floating weapon of fire, if my arrows could reach, I could kill the enemy and vanquish their ability to wield its magic.

I assessed my surroundings until I spotted an overhang curving into a thin verge overlooking the sea, its position much closer to the open water edge. Without hesitation, I sprinted to it, leaping over cracks and loosened stone, trying to ignore the vast vertical drop below. I heard the stone crack beneath my weight as I carefully crept across the ledge, going as far as I dared, while praying to the ancestors it would hold. I knelt on my shins, keeping my back straight, as I stretched my arms and aimed, the figures on the vessel now easily within my sights. As the first golden arrow materialised, my battle instinct took over. They would taste fear at the hand of our magic and think twice about approaching our borders again.

I shot, hitting my first target with ease, the body slumping and falling overboard. Immediately, I rained radiant death upon them, until the human creatures took notice and shouts of confusion rippled in the wind. They moved to the silver cylinders, tilting them back and turning to my location. My cover was blown, they were preparing to fire their magic upon me in retaliation.

Still, I did not stop, launching arrow after arrow, ignoring the tension in my aching arm.

Another explosion sounded, the mountain shook, and the stone cracked beneath my feet, as the ridge below me began to crumble. I felt a sudden dip in my stomach, and I closed my eyes, picturing Addox's face as I gripped my bow tightly, my body falling into the abyss.

23

Second Chances

I could hear the crackling of kindling and feel the warmth of fire, as a familiar stench filled my nostrils. A scent my mother had been particularly fond of.

"I hate green tea," I managed to grumble in revulsion, rolling over in the strange cot, my throat feeling coarse and dry.

"I think you should be thankful you live to drink anything at all," an irritated voice answered, and I opened my eyes to find Imelda standing next to the healer's cot.

"How did I get here?" I asked, quickly scanning my surroundings, and realising we were back in General Maiya's temporary desert camp. As I tried to sit up, a sharp pain stabbed through my abdomen and chest, enough to make my eyes blur as I slumped back into the soft furs.

"Make no sudden movements, you were buried in rubble from your fall." Imelda reached over for some Gossum berry paste. "You are lucky to be alive," she added softly.

"What of the attack? The strange vessel…" I asked, remembering the onslaught of golden arrows I had unleashed upon the invaders.

"Gone. They left their dead on the beach. A few managed to return to the vessel and steer it away."

"Will they come back?"

"This was not the first time they have scoured our shores," she replied, rinsing her hands in a bowl of water. "I was surprised of your assistance."

"Why would I not help?" I asked, recalling an old phrase my mother used to say. "After all, an enemy of my enemy is my—"

"Friend?" she asked, eyebrow raised.

"I was thinking more along the lines of ally," I replied, and she chuckled.

"Lay still, I need to check over your injuries."

"I thought you nothing more than a sword hand," I commented inquisitively. She attended to me as a healer would, inspecting my wounds and applying a soothing paste to my sensitive skin. "Truda spoke indignantly of your faithless ambition to rise above her."

"Do you make all of Truda's villains your own?"

"Only those who try to kill my friends," I retorted. Imelda gave me a small smile that did not reach her eyes.

"I have guards posted at the entrance, so do not waste

your energy and injure yourself further by trying to escape," Imelda said, as she stood and began to clear the healing items away.

"I need to get back," I said, thinking of how Addox and Lelane needed me.

"General Maiya will decide what to do with you when she arrives."

"She is coming here?" Imelda nodded.

"I would take advantage of the respite, Acqueline, you will need it."

I tried to relax, dreading the inevitable outcome, but I found comfort knowing that, at the very least, it meant Addox would be safe in the short term, as the general would not be in the city to carry out the order of his execution.

"You saved many lives this day, including Shea's," Imelda said, preparing to leave. "I know General Maiya is not one to express gratitude, so allow me." I nodded slowly, feeling confused and surprised at the change in her demeanour. Truda had not spoken kindly of her at all in past conversations, and our paths had not crossed enough in the city for me to know better. This was not the Imelda I had come to know in my mind.

"It was nothing another warrior would not have done in my stead."

"Except I know of no other warrior capable of using their skill against a fire-wielding vessel the way you did," she said, with amusement and admiration in her tone. "If General Maiya is smart, she will rally you to our cause," she added, before finally leaving me alone in the tent.

Though there was still much I did not understand about what was going on here, it was clear it was anything but what I originally thought. General Maiya was keeping secrets and preparing to make a move against the council, but the question is whether her motivations were malicious or if she was trying to protect us from a threat, of which we still knew very little. Despite the constant uncomfortable pain, I tried to rest as much as possible, until voices woke me from outside the tent, one I recognised all too well.

"It seems your bow is as surprisingly unbreakable as you are," General Maiya said, parting the canvas and walking to me, leaning my bow against the end of my cot. "We have much to discuss," she said, taking a seat opposite me.

"You are not angry at me?"

"I was, when I learned of your foolishness, but I have had time to reflect."

"And to speak to Imelda," I concluded, pushing on my elbows to sit up slightly. "Why did you hide all of this from the council?"

"Because you would not agree with what needs to be done." I noted the way she had phrased her sentence, as though she was still trying to determine if I could be trusted.

"We cannot help, if you do not let us."

"I do not need council's opinions, I need warriors. Thus, why I do not have time for Truda's petty melancholy, not with threats of unknown origins at our border."

"Is that why you're working with Imelda, because she

can provide you more warriors?"

"You should not be so quick to judge, it was she who first discovered the outsiders. Her warriors vanquished trespassers on the outskirts of Fortuna's Forest, now we have warriors stationed at every corner of the kingdom to keep them at bay. Imelda offered to help in exchange for a pardon."

"So, she attacked first?"

"Do not be so naïve, Acqueline, our ancestors sought to irradicate mankind for good reason. Only now, it seems they failed, and while our numbers have dwindled, they have thrived."

"Then why not accept Truda's human elite? Perhaps if you had allowed them to join your armies, then they would not have had the misguided opportunity to attack The Sanctum." Not that I relished the idea of Addox going into battle, but I hated the thought of him forever being locked in that dungeon more.

"And what happens when all the men are dead? Taking with them all chances of repopulation," she asked.

Breeding? Is that why General Maiya was against the humans joining our ranks?

"You mean to enslave them again?"

"I mean to change the laws to encourage the unity between our people." Again, an image of a young boy unwilfully shot into my mind, a replica of Addox, his father. "Our people are dying, Acqueline, slowly fading into extinction, if our new enemy does not eradicate us first."

"You know the queen and council will not agree," I said.

General Maiya remained silent. "You mean to overthrow us?"

"Yes," she replied honestly.

"Then what are you waiting for? Why have you not implemented your plan? Oust the council and make your demands."

"I have one issue left to resolve, a last deal to strike," she said, her arms crossed.

"Then you will need my cooperation, and silence."

General Maiya leaned in close to me, "Do you mean to blackmail me, Acqueline?"

"I mean to make a bargain of my own."

"I am listening," she said, staring at me intensely.

"If human life is so precious, then you will spare those who are captive in the prison."

"I do not think—"

"They will be freed, and no punishment shall be inflicted upon them," I interrupted, and after a pause she nodded. "I have a friend who needs a new dwelling, she is to be gifted a lavish house, somewhere close to the palace for her and her daughter Lera to live the rest of their days, provided for in comfort."

"Anything else?" she asked dryly.

"Just one more thing," I said. My voice lowered and I felt uneasy at my last request. "The royal guard are not permitted to have attachments; we are forbidden to engage romantically or have families. I want these things for myself, without losing my title or duty to the royal family."

"Does this have something to do with this friend you

want me to gift a house?"

"Do we have a deal?" I replied, purposely not responding to her last question.

"There will be conditions," she replied, standing so she could tower over me. "I will free the humans, grant you this house, and even abolish the rule that forbids you to have a family." Her tone suggested she considered her offer was generous. "In exchange, you and your guardswomen will align your loyalty to me. When the time comes and I need your bow, you will use it at my command. No matter who your opponent may be."

I did not like the thought of that, but I had no other choice. "You have my word."

"The humans stay in the dungeon. Consider them my leverage until my plan has been fulfilled. If you go back on your word, or inform anyone, especially Truda, of what you have learned, I shall have them killed."

"I understand," I said, my body slumping with exhaustion.

"A horse will be readied when you are well enough to travel. I look forward to seeing you at the next council meeting, Acqueline. It is sure to be an interesting one."

The return ride was pure torture, the galloping horse rocking my wounds to the point of agony, leaving me struggling for breath by the time the city gate came into view. I let the beast canter itself through the open gate, catching sight of the guards approaching from my periphery, as my grip relaxed on the reins, unable to hold on any longer. I slumped from the saddle, falling to the ground, and once again slipped into unconsciousness.

There was a clattering noise around me, and I groaned as my eyelids fluttered open to find Lelane by my side.

"This feels like a habit," I grumbled.

"Quin, thank the ancestors, are you alright?"

"Never better," I said, wincing as I tried to sit up, the pain in my ribs feeling less excruciating than before. "How long was I asleep?"

"A whole day and night."

"Addox?" I asked with urgency.

"He is fine, has been asking after you relentlessly."

"I need to go and see him," I said, preparing to get out of my bed.

Lelane pushed me down gently. "You need to heal. Whoever treated your wounds did a terrible job."

"Likely on purpose," I replied with a small smile.

"What happened to you, Quin, where did you go?" I looked at her, my expression serious.

"If I tell you, I need you to promise me you will not say a word. Lives are at stake; people will die if anything is discussed outside of these walls."

"You are scaring me," Lelane replied. I kept my features continually stern. "I promise," she followed.

"I found out what General Maiya has been hiding," I said, before I told her everything. I described the camps filled with both exiled elves and General Maiya's warriors, and the pardoning she had promised Imelda in exchange for protecting our borders. She had gasped at my description of the ancestor's sea, then fell completely silent when I spoke of the battle against the watercraft and the foreign humans that controlled it.

"Surely it will not return, if it was defeated as you say?" Lelane said, her arms wrapping around herself.

"General Maiya believes it will, especially now we have alerted them to our presence."

"Does she have a plan?"

"She does, though I am ignorant of the exact details," I replied, forcing myself into a seated position.

"What do you think you are doing?" she asked, as I started to stand once again.

"I have a duty to attend."

"You mean to see Addox." she said sternly, placing her hands on her hips.

"No," I lied, "I should check in on the royal family."

"They are fine, Quin, and Addox is not going anywhere," she replied, not believing my lie. "You can rest for one more day at least. Go and see them in the morning." I nodded.

Lelane smiled and offered to prepare me some food after she had checked on Lera. I agreed once more, making a show of getting myself comfortable and settled in my bed, pulling the furs up to my chin, as I closed my eyes.

I waited until the door was closed and listened as her steps became quieter before I climbed out of my cot. I was instantly hit with a rush of dizziness, causing me to stumble as I slowly got dressed and walked over to the door. The hall was empty when I peered past it, and I quickly crept out of the palace and headed to the prison, thankful no one noticed me on route.

As I approached, one of General Maiya's warriors stood guard at the entrance, and she greeted me.

"General Maiya has summoned you," I said, and she looked past me, confused. "Go, I will stand watch until you return." She offered me a salute, then hurried past me, as eager to comply with General Maiya's command as I had hoped she would be.

I took a deep breath and leaned against the wall for a moment, before righting myself and walking down the prison row. Despite my shaking legs, I tried my best to carry myself high and appear strong the moment I came into his view. At the sound of me stumbling the last few steps, and with my hitched breathing, Addox shot to attention, his eyes widening at the sight of me.

"Quin!" he said, rushing to the bars, his eyes frantic as he shook against his cage. "What's happened? Did someone attack you?"

I kept my distance, leaning against the damp brickwork opposite his cell.

"I have negotiated freedom for you and your companions," I told him, still slightly winded and out of breath.

"What did you say?" he asked, sounding desperate as he looked me over.

"A bargain was struck; you will be released after I have fulfilled my end of the deal."

"What kind of deal?"

"It is done, Addox. You have been given a second chance at life."

"I didn't ask you to do that!" he snapped and I flinched.

"Why are you so angry?" I argued, outraged at his reaction. I had gone to extreme lengths to find the truth of General Maiya's plan, to find a way to save his life, and I had not expected this kind of reaction from him. Gratitude yes, indifference even, but not his anger. He took a step back, running his hands through his hair, as he began to pace back and forth.

"You want to know why?" He spun to face me. "For days your friend has been coming here, telling me nothing except you forgave me, like some kind of cryptic goodbye," he said, his head dropping low.

"You were worried about me," I said, realisation dawning as he rubbed his face with both hands.

"Of course I was." Despite feeling dizzy as soon as I pushed myself off the wall to walk closer to his cell, I continued anyway, driven by the need to be near him, to feel his warmth even with steel bars between us.

"Why?" I asked.

"You know why," he said, pressing his forehead against the cold metal. I reached through, placing my hand under his chin and lifting it to make him look at me. He winced immediately, instantly affected by my painful expression.

“Tell me,” I said, my eyes locked with his.

“It was all real, Quin, all of it.” His chest rose and fell as his gaze locked with mine. “Every kiss, every touch, every heartbeat. I started falling for you from the first smile.” My lip began to tremble as I laced my fingers with his. “Then I went ahead and screwed everything up by lying to you and pushing you away. I should have told you the truth, but I was so scared you would hate me and never want to see me again.”

“I could never hate you,” I confessed.

“I love…” he began, but before he could finish his sentence, I pushed forward, pressing my lips against his. It was awkward and difficult with the limited access through the space between the bars. Nevertheless, I reached to hold as much of him as I could, tasting the salt of my tears as I kissed him deeply.

“Finish that sentence when you are free of this place,” I said the moment our lips parted. He nodded, resting his forehead against mine. “I must go, but I promise to return soon.” I slowly kissed the tips of his fingers, before turning to head back to my chambers, hoping Lelane had not found my empty room.

“Quin!”

“Yes,” I replied, looking back over my shoulder.

“Please, be careful,” he said.

“You do not need to worry, Addox, I have everything under control.”

24

Manumission

For the next two weeks, all seemed quiet. Minus a few aches and pains, I was feeling much better, so I had returned to my normal duties of patrolling the palace and training the prince.

I snuck into the Prison to check on Addox as frequently as I could, and each time he would try to ascertain the details of the bargain I had made with General Maiya, but I kept everything to myself. I did not know the details of the last part of General Maiya's plan, but I hoped she would see it through soon. I hated the apprehension and worry I would feel every time I saw her, as she gazed upon me all knowing.

One night, I returned to my chambers to find a silver key with a small scroll attached to it. Wrapped in blue ribbon, I opened it to reveal an address, and my face instantly lit up the moment I realised what it was. I rushed from my chambers to Lelane's, finding her reading to Lera.

"You need to come with me now," I said, barely able to contain my excitement.

"Is everything all right?"

"More than," I said. "And I know its late, but you both need to follow me this instant!"

"Okay," she said with a chuckle. Lera curiously watched my elated demeanour with interest, as she too donned her heavy boots and cloak to follow me outside. When we were on the street, I held the ribbon from the parchment in my hand and held it up to Lelane.

"Can I cover your eyes? I want this to be a surprise."

"You are acting very strangely," she said, laughing, "more than usual." She turned around so I could fasten the ribbon over her eyes. Then, holding her hand, I guided her behind me, taking it slow to avoid causing her to trip or fall.

Soon after, we stopped outside the correct house, and I nodded to Lera to open the door. I was standing behind Lelane to guide her forward, and I did not let go until we were in the centre of the hall.

"Quin," Lelane breathed, becoming impatient and desperate to be able to see.

"Just a moment longer." I lit some candles, handing one to Lera. I pulled the ribbon slowly free from her eyes and stood back to gauge her reaction. She looked around the room, confused as her gaze travelled from Lera to me.

"Where are we?"

"Home."

"What?" she asked, bemused.

"Well, your new home to be exact," I beamed, and Lelane's jaw dropped.

"This is incredible, thank you so much, Quin, I cannot believe you did this for us."

"You deserve it."

"Can we look around?" she asked, still uncertain.

"Lelane, this is your home. Do with it what you like," I said, smiling brightly.

With that, she took off into an excited run and I followed her as she skipped from room to room, chattering loudly of all the things she would do with the space. She happily listed the stock she would use to fill the pantry, excited about the number of pastries she would bake in the kitchenette, which was at least three times larger than her entire old house. She then dragged me to the small fenced off garden, where she talked of growing herbs, and planting her own Gossum berries she would use for a new healing recipe she had been working on.

We explored the living room next, with its high beamed ceiling and sandstone walls, adorned with paintings and golden woven tapestries. A grand fireplace was prominent as the room's main feature, surrounded by ornately designed furnishings, where Lelane said she would read Lera her stories.

Her face beamed with happiness as she led me from room to room, hurrying me upstairs, eager to look over the rest of her new house.

"I have never been inside a house so luxurious before," Lelane breathed.

"Do you like it?" I asked, sweeping past the room Lera had claimed as her own, as she silently lay face-up on the bed frame in the centre.

"Quin, this is more than I ever would have hoped for." She spun to face me.

"Now you can give Lera the life we should have had," I said, feeling elated at her reaction.

"You truly are the greatest friend."

"I shall remind you of that when I come to scavenge a bowl of your vegetable stew after duty."

"You are always welcome," she smiled radiantly. "Addox too, if you wanted to bring him," she offered and my heart swelled, feeling hopeful for the future.

General Maiya called an urgent council meeting.

After receiving her summons, I promptly checked in with my guard, ignoring the temptation to see Addox, before setting off to meet with the rest of the council. My heart fluttered with anxiety, wondering if the sudden meeting was related to the number of secrets I had promised to keep. When I approached the Throne Room, I heard murmuring voices. I entered to find everyone present, and to my surprise, even Truda and Erik were there. As I neared, Cobal was the only one who smiled at me warmly.

"Good morning," I said, as I took my seat, ignoring Truda and Erik. The Throne Room doors swung open dramatically, and General Maiya, adorned in her customary golden armour, purposely approached, taking her place at the head of the table.

"There is no easy way to address this matter, so I shall just come out with it," General Maiya said, her gaze flicking from one council member to the next. "Our kingdom is under attack."

Silence filled the Throne Room; the memory of the human invaders came rushing back to me.

"The exiles?" Erik asked, looking worriedly towards Truda. General Maiya shook her head.

"No, Imelda and the woodland elves have allied with us against this enemy. As we speak, our combined forces protect our borders."

"What kind of nonsense is this?" Truda snapped, standing to match General Maiya's height. "You speak of conforming with traitors over some imaginary enemy and you expect us to believe you?"

As the council argued, I remained silent, conflicted as to whether I should join in to support Maiya's truth, my pact of secrecy keeping me hushed. General Mayia seemed to sense this, as she looked at me and discreetly nodded.

"General Maiya speaks the truth," I shouted, silencing them as I stood. "There were strange adversaries at our borders. They came by endless water beyond the crag mountain. They wield a magical vessel that breathes fire and fractures rock. I saw this with my own eyes." The council's faces contorted with disbelief, Truda and Erik looked at each other as though they were grappling to make sense of my words.

"This cannot be true," Cobal whispered, shaking his head.

"I was sceptical at first," General Maiya added, retaining her serious demeanour. "When Imelda initially wrote to me with warnings of hostile explorers, I thought it was a ploy of some kind. That was, until she brought evidence of the creatures she had vanquished at the edge of the forest. They appear to be human, but of a different nature than we know."

"Different how?" Erik asked.

"Differing skin tones, and their armour appears nothing alike," she said, sharing a fact I did not know.

"They were not of the same people?" Cobal suggested.

"No. Which means the world has evolved greatly since our ancestors used their magic to eradicate the enemy from our lands."

"They'll come back?" Cobal asked, and General Maiya nodded in confirmation.

"Our ancestors had shaped our land with dangerous mountains and natural defences, in reality, they kept us isolated, enabling our naivety, to believe that a world did not exist beyond our borders," General Maiya said.

"So that's why you're enlisting additional warriors," Erik stated.

"I have a myriad of warrior sentries stationed in all corners of the kingdom, to monitor the land and call for aid if there are sightings. Believe me when I say, we still do not have enough."

"What do we do?" Cobal's question hung in the air, his perplexity evident.

"I have a strategy I would propose, but you will not likely find it agreeable," General Maiya said, watching Truda closely.

"What is it?" Erik asked.

"This." General Maiya placed a small red vial of liquid at the centre of the table and the room fell silent. "We rescind the manumission of humans." The moment the words left her lips, Truda vaulted in front of Erik, her sword raised, ready for a fight. "Lower your weapon, Truda, before I order my guard to disarm you."

"I will destroy you all, and the invaders, before I allow you to lay a finger on Erik!" she shouted, pointing her broadsword around the room. I avoided her wild stare and remained silent, guilt rising within me.

"Calm your temper, Truda," General Maiya snapped. "I have no intention of separating you, or any others who have formed…" she paused, waving her hand in the air as though searching for the right word "…attachments to humans."

"You can't be serious? After everything we've been fighting for?" Erik held out his hands, attempting to appeal to Maiya.

"Do you not see, Erik? This was her plan all along," Truda said, her sword still drawn.

"You just cannot help yourself, can you?" Maiya snapped,

rubbing her face with her palm.

"Some of us care about what goes on in this kingdom," replied Truda, not looking at me.

"I care more than you will ever understand!" General Maiya snapped. "Unlike you, I am also willing to make the necessary sacrifices to ensure our survival."

"At the expense of humans," Erik added.

"There is a world beyond our borders, full of unknown threats. Our Kingdom will only remain hidden for so long. If we continue as we are, we will simply lack the numbers to adequately defend these lands," Maiya said.

"You mean to turn us back into breeders?" Erik asked, trying to step forward, but Truda continued to shield him.

"We can't go back to how it was before," Cobal said, his voice soft and alarmingly calm.

"I know." She softened for a moment while something passed between them. She straightened, addressing the rest of us again. "The rules shall be simple; each elf may claim a human for their own."

"You would force them to—" Truda began, but General Maiya raised a hand to silence her.

"Let me finish, Truda," she asked, lowering her arm. A profound silence filled the room, and Maiya refrained from speaking until she was certain there would be no interruptions. "An elf may lay claim to a human, yet, given our greater numbers, the stipulation shall be, the human must, in turn, choose her. Each pairing will be assigned the duty to produce at least one offspring."

“You cannot possibly think we would ever agree to this,” Truda snapped, “Threat notwithstanding, we do not force people to conceive against their will.”

“Is this how the council truly feels?” General Maiya asked, crossing her arms, and looking between us, her gaze lingered over mine for a fraction longer than the others.

“It is,” Truda firmly replied on our behalf, no one else speaking up in protest.

“Have it your way,” General Maiya said, her eyes narrowing before she stormed from the Throne Room, leaving us to digest what just happened.

I could feel Truda’s eyes on me as I prepared to leave, and I did not blame her.

When Queen Cassandra was in power, she assigned Truda to Erik for breeding, an order Truda had secretly fought against. She would certainly protest strongly against this proposed proclamation.

I could not understand why General Maiya would ask this of the council. She had already told me she expected us to oppose her plan, and therefore, we could not be trusted. Unless, of course, she knew our rejection was inevitable, affording her the chance to take her final, unknown step.

25

THE NOTE

"I brought you more furs," I said, passing the thick material through the bars.

"What excuse did you give the guard this time?" Addox asked, gladly accepting my gifts.

"None, I imagine by now General Maiya is aware of my visits, considering the number of times I have come," I replied, taking a seat opposite him.

"Aren't you going to get in trouble?"

"I think our general is far too busy working up schemes to repopulate the city."

"Single handedly or…?"

I laughed, despite myself. "She wants to encourage the pairings between human and elves."

"Why?"

"To prevent our extinction, and she needs warriors."

"How much have I missed since I've been locked up in here?"

"I will catch you up on everything once it is all over with," I said. Much to Addox's disappointment, I had refrained from telling him of the bargain I made, or the secrets I had discovered.

"How long will that be?"

"Soon," I said, the same way I had the day prior. "Can I bring you anything tomorrow?" I asked.

"A key to get out?" he joked, and I smiled, shaking my head lightly, "No? Okay, just you then." I chuckled as I stood, wincing from my bruised ribs. "You're still in pain?"

"Just a minor ache, I am sure it will be gone in a few days."

"Maybe get Lelane to check you over? Just in case," he suggested, concern lining his features.

"Oh, she is Lelane now? Not my friend?"

"Whatever," he said, smiling and pretending to turn from me.

"You know, I am looking forward to when you get out of this cell and we can spar again, I think you need a little humility."

"That's not all I need," he added, casting me a hot glare, and I blushed.

"Goodnight, Addox."

"Say hi to your friend for me," he called as I left the prison, reminding me how much I had wanted to catch up with Lelane after my last visit. When I had last collected

Lera, the entire house smelt of freshly baked pastries, warm and sweet, I might have snuck a few in my satchel, were it not for Lera, who seemed to notice everything.

Perhaps Addox was right, it seemed I was healing quite slowly, and Lelane may have finished perfecting one of her healing recipes. Providing they did not share the same ingredients as green tea; I was willing to try anything.

As I approached Lelane's front door, I noticed it seemed quiet, and absent of any light. It was not that late, but certainly beyond the time they would be out. Lelane usually had a few candles lit, even after Lera had gone to bed. I carefully opened the door with my spare key, and as I stepped inside the cold hall, I instantly realised something was wrong.

"Lelane!" I called, but no answer came.

"Lera!" I tried instead. It was eerie and dark inside, the silence enveloping me as my heart pounded in my chest whilst I looked for signs of them. Finding nothing in the kitchen or living room, I rushed up the stairs to continue my search. Lera's large glass window was wide open, her curtains blowing in the gentle breeze, the room stone cold. My concern grew as I quickly reached for the handle and pulled it closed.

It was obvious the house had been empty for hours, and I had no idea where they could be. There were no signs of forced entry, nor any items missing that I could tell. I noticed a slight glow emanating from under Lelane's bedchamber door, and I darted across the hall, entering the room, but it was empty.

A small singular candle had been lit on the bedside table, the melted wax reformed as a pool at the base of the brass, its glow barely offering enough light for the room. Next to it, resting on the edge of the furs, was a lone parchment, neatly folded and secured with twine. I tore it open and read the words etched into the material. The writing was scratched so deeply, it left angry and jagged indents in the paper.

"I will have what I am owed."

My hand instantly covered my mouth as I gasped. Turning and vaulting down the stairs, I yanked open the front door, not bothering to close it, and I ran. I felt the spots of rain the moment I stepped outside, the sky overhead covered by dark clouds. I almost lost my footing on numerous corners, but I did not stop, as my lungs gasped for air, ignoring the heavy downpour assaulting my skin.

The rain turned into hail, and I raised my forearm high, attempting to shield myself. A fork of lightning flashed across the sky, causing me to jump, as a strong gust of wind accompanied the frozen onslaught from above. There was no time to question why the storm had suddenly appeared as I reached the crossroads, my thighs burning as I gathered my bearings for the fastest route to The Sanctum. I knew Terra had taken them, and I did not know where else to look. Another fork of lightning struck and the rumble that followed bellowed, vibrating beneath my feet. I looked down to see the crumpled parchment soaked in my hand, the ink smudged beyond recognition, and I shook my head vehemently in disbelief.

This cannot be. The rain, hail, and lightning as I ran to the crossroads, the torn parchment in my hand, its ink running. How was it possible I dreamt of this very moment moons before it happened?

A deafening explosion roared from behind me, not of thunder, but the sound of sandstone colliding with the ground below. I turned to face the palace, as glass erupted out from the queen's tower, half of its roof already fallen away. Shouts echoed from the steps of the gate, while warriors rushed into the palace. My vision blurred, and I trembled as I screamed to the dark clouds, overwhelmed by a desperate rage at the choice I must now make.

I faced the impossible decision between fulfilling my duty to the royal family, and saving my best friend.

More of the roof from the queen's tower crumbled away, stones continuing to crash to the floor. In that moment, my mind was flooded with unbidden images of the frightened prince calling out for help. Another crash sounded from the palace, and I looked to the cracking stone walls, the tower now tilting, the spire descending and smashing on the steps below. I did not falter.

Dropping the paper, I took off in another sprint, my lungs pulling tight in my chest, as I charged through the gate.

I had made my choice.

"The queen's tower!" I shouted to my guard, who had

already gathered inside the palace. We reached the Throne Room, and I leapt over a large crack that had split the corridor in two. I rushed up the tower stairs, taking three at a time as violent vibrations unsettled the stone beneath my feet. While clutching the window ledge for support, I felt the bite of glass cutting through my previously injured palm. Despite the pain, I pressed on. I reached for the queen's bedchamber door and tried to push it open, but it did not budge, as though locked from the inside.

"My queen!" I called, hammering on the door, but there was no answer. I could hear the familiar deafening whirl of wind as it shuddered through the foundation of stone. "Phoenyx!" I called instead, but still no one answered. I took a step back and kicked at the door with all my strength. My boots repeatedly struck the wood, causing it to open slightly before slamming shut again.

Although it was not locked, the pressure of the wind kept the door closed. I turned to my guards, ordering them to assist. They positioned themselves around me, and between the four of us, we pushed. When it opened a fraction, I squeezed my arm through, positioning my bow in front of me so I could slide my body further into the gap, holding it partially open. I glimpsed the blurred figure of Queen Fortuna, trapped within the vortex of wind, lightning crashing down on the tower as if guided by her will.

"Alert General Maiya, at once," I shouted to one of my guards. She nodded hesitantly, and upon seeing the queen's condition, she began to back away slowly. "Go!" I screamed, turning my focus back to gaining entry to the room. The pressure of the door painfully crushed me to the doorframe. I knew the instant my body no longer blocked the door, it would slam shut.

Gritting my teeth, I pushed with all my strength. I managed to make it through, the door crashing behind me, while my guard pounded on the other side. My hair whirled up around my face as I was pushed against the wall.

My attention immediately fell to Queen Fortuna, her body shimmering against the whirls of the cyclone. Her mouth hung open, as if emitting a scream, but any sound was engulfed by the powerful force of the wind. Debris flew all around us, the silk curtains torn from their hinges, ceramics smashed across the floor. The roof of the tower was cracked, with parts of the ceiling broken and spinning inside the room. I shifted my focus beyond her, glancing at the bed to find Phoenyx sprawled across it, partially clothed and motionless. A deep sense of dread filled me as I realised something was terribly wrong with him.

"Send for a healer!" I called back to the door, desperately hoping my guard could hear me. I edged towards the bed, struggling with each step as my body was continually forced against the wall.

"Phoenyx!" I called, as I grabbed the wooden post of the bedframe, pulling myself forward, but he did not respond. His eyes were open and unblinking, his skin far too pale.

I recoiled as something grabbed my ankle, and I looked down to see a small hand clutching the top of my boot. Using the bed frame as leverage, I lowered myself into a crouch, to see Prince Felyx and little Yuki taking shelter underneath, their eyes staring up at me in fear.

"Prince Felyx" I gasped, reaching for him. I pulled from underneath and gripped him to my body. "Are you hurt?" He shook his head, yet my hands still swept across him in search of any injuries.

The door vibrated erratically as my guard tried to get in, but the wind was stronger now, the floor shifting all around us. The tower swayed and I felt unsteadiness beneath my feet. I looked to Prince Felyx who clung to my leg with both arms, tears streaming down his face.

The chamber door opened slightly, and a guard slipped through, her arm extended as she gestured for us to reach her. The tower shook again violently, as the ceiling cracked and crumbled away, large shards landing paces from my guardswoman. Her position faltered, and she lost her footing, falling into the swirling cyclone that surrounded the queen. My guard was thrown around the room as though she weighed nothing, colliding with debris and crashing against the walls, until her disfigured body was left pinned in the corner of the room. There was no time, we would not make it out of this tower alive.

"Queen Fortuna!" I screamed, clutching Prince Felyx tighter with his head buried in my thigh. She did not respond, seeming too absorbed in the overpowering emotions that now wielded the magic around her. I looked at the prince, fear rising in my throat as I tried to think of what to do. I could not let him get hurt, I promised to protect him with my life, and I would not fail in that duty. She had to be stopped, no matter the cost.

I looked down and stroked the prince's soft hair, leaning as close as I could to him, "Keep your head down," I stuttered, as I pulled my bow from my front, terrified at what I knew I had to do.

I gripped the centre of my bow and willed a golden arrow in my fingertips, taking aim but hesitating as my emotions overwhelmed me. Tears flowed from my eyes as I looked from Prince Felyx to the queen, images of their loving family moments flashing through my mind.

I shouted to Queen Fortuna once more, praying to the ancestors with every ounce of my being that she would relent, but my efforts were futile. Her magic had consumed her.

I was utterly decimated in that moment, but the prince deserved a future, and I was the only one who could ensure it. I focused my aim and released an arrow, watching the streak of shimmering gold fly, penetrating the vortex and piercing Queen Fortuna.

Her body jerked back until she stumbled and began to fall, her hand moving to clutch the golden rod that had penetrated her. The wind dissipated, and the hurling objects dropped steadily to the floor as the storm calmed outside.

The door burst open and General Maiya charged through, quickly followed by Truda and Erik, pushing past them to approach the bed where Phoenyx lay.

"Nyx," Erik muttered, looking down in disbelief at the

queen consort's body, as Truda came to his side, a hand resting on his shoulder. Other elves poured into the room, respectfully removing the body of my poor guardswoman.

"We must get them out," I said, feeling un-confident the tower would hold against all our weight in its fragile state. As I spoke, a crack travelled beneath my feet and the tower began to shudder. Something broke loose from above, plummeting towards us. Swiftly, I shielded the prince's body with mine, releasing a guttural cry as a heavy object collided with my shoulder.

"The queen!" I heard General Maiya bellow.

I picked up Prince Felyx with my good arm, Yuki weaving between my feet as we ran from the room, not stopping until we were out of the tower and safe in the Throne Room.

Truda came after, Queen Fortuna was unconscious and draped in her arms, blood dripping from her wound. The rest quickly followed; Phoenyx's limp body carried over Erik's shoulder.

A sound from above boomed, and the palace shuddered. I watched in horror as the tower above us toppled, falling into view from the large windows in the Throne Room, before smashing to the ground below, the whole palace vibrating on impact. We all stood there, frozen in disbelief at the events that had just transpired. If we had been in that tower for just a moment longer, we all would have been crushed or fallen to our deaths. I pulled Prince Felyx gently away from me and guided him towards General Maiya.

"Have a healer check him over," I said, breathless as I

started to turn and move away, wincing from the pain in my limp arm. Truda and Erik both just gaped at me in confusion. I ignored them as I made my way to the door.

"Where are you going?" General Maiya barked, but I paid no attention to her either, my bow still clutched in my bleeding hand. "Acqueline!" she shouted, expecting me to stay and explain, but there was nothing more I could do for them, my stomach was tight, and I felt sick. I could only focus on my need to leave.

"I have to go," I muttered as I pushed past the guards, and despite being overwhelmed with exhaustion and pain, I broke off into another sprint.

The rain had subsided, but it made no difference to me. I returned to the crossroads and this time, I did not stop, moving as fast as my legs would allow, pushing the muscles to work harder than ever before, until finally, I stopped outside a familiar door. My breathing was too heavy, as though my lungs would not fill with the air they needed, my ears still ringing from the previous vortex of wind.

Shaking, I kicked open the door and entered The Sanctum, descending the staircase within.

"Lelane!" I breathed, immediately spotting her. She was in the centre of the empty fighting ring, her arms tied behind her back, her clothes torn, with tears streaking her face. Terra stood behind her, clutching the back of her neck, as my friend whimpered and tried to break free.

Lera was sitting alone quietly in the corner, her eyes meeting mine the moment I came into view at the bottom of the stairs.

"It will all be okay, Lera," I assured her, taking the last few steps slowly.

"Now, why would you tell her such lies, Acqueline?" Terra said, her tone cruel and menacing, as she pulled Lelane up to stand beside her.

"Let them go, Terra," I ordered, taking another small step forward.

"Not until I get what I want," she seethed through gritted teeth, pressing her cheek roughly against Lelane. Her hand travelled down Lelane's neck, past her collar bone and below her breasts, wrapping one arm around her midriff as she pulled closer into her body.

Lelane's panicked eyes met mine for a moment.

"Hurting them is not the way," I said, taking another timid step towards her.

"I am not going to hurt them!" she shouted, as though insulted by the insinuation she would. I took another glance at Lelane, the bruise marks already appearing around her neck and arms. Her hair had been ruffled, perhaps pulled by a strong hand, her eyes swollen and red from too many tears. I had to get her away from Terra. "I left that note to lure you here."

"What do you want?" I asked, remaining calm.

"You owe me a victory, and I want to show them how

weak and unworthy you are," she sneered, removing one hand from Lelane to point at me.

"You want to fight me?" I crouched low and slid my bow across the stone floor away from us. I made a show of removing my weapon, knowing I still had a knife concealed within my boot. "Then let us fight." She let out a maddening laugh and pushed Lelane harshly to the corner where Lera sat, causing my friend to stumble and fall to the floor beside her daughter.

"I am going to enjoy breaking you," Terra said, clasping and tightening her fists until they clicked.

My arm dangled limply by my side as it throbbed, and I was now certain it was dislocated. I squinted as further pain shot through my other hand, the open wound seeping blood as I stretched it.

Lelane's eyes widened at my obvious injuries, and I knew I had no chance of winning against Terra in my current condition. My only hope was I could compromise her enough to pull out my hidden blade and strike her down.

She circled me, her eyes narrowing as she smirked, raising her fists just below her chin, preparing to strike. I sidestepped cautiously, keeping my back straight as I searched around the room for anything I could use as an advantage over her. My eyes met Lelane again, her chin trembling as she whimpered for me.

The first blow was struck so fast my vision blurred, my head snapping to the side. The second crashed my body into the wall, and I let out a scream as pain tore through my injured shoulder.

"What is this?" Terra said, pulling up my bloody hand into hers. I winced as she stretched my palm wide, the skin splitting open. "So fragile," she teased, pressing a finger between the parted skin, and I cried out, trying to pull my hand away but she clutched my wrist tighter. "No wonder you absconded my healer," she mused and I wrenched my hand away.

"I did not steal her, I protected her from you," I gritted back, head-butting her square in the jaw. She stumbled, a spray of blood bursting from her nose. I stepped forward, spun around, and kicked her in the chest. However, she barely moved, casually wiping away the blood with the back of her hand. I rushed to kick her again, but she grabbed my leg, lifting and launching my body through the air. I closed my eyes and braced for impact, but nothing could have prepared me for the agony that rippled through my body, my ribs seemingly cracking on impact.

"Quin!" Lelane screamed.

I rolled over to face her, trying to blink the dust from my eyes. As I watched her wriggling, trying to remove her restraints, I shook my head. I wanted to tell her it was going to be okay and I would find a way to break her free, but Terra kicked me in the gut before I could speak.

"You see how pathetic she is." Terra laughed, looking over her shoulder to address Lelane, and I took the moment to stretch my arm and reach for the blade concealed in my boot. I felt the hilt around my blood-soaked hand, but struggled to keep a grip on it, as I tried to stand. Swaying, I got to my feet and swung the blade towards her, stumbling with each step. She easily caught my arm and pulled the knife from me, tossing it away.

"At least I will grant you the honour of dying by my hand," she whispered, gripping me by the throat as I sagged in her hold, my feet giving way. As I collapsed to the floor, Terra cried out abruptly, staggering to the side and revealing Lelane holding a heavy wall torch in her hand.

"Leave her alone!" she cried, raising the still-burning torch in her hands, holding her ground.

"You still choose this pathetic creature over me!" Terra bellowed, thumping her closed fists against her chest.

"I said, stay away from her!" She came to stand protectively in front of me. Terra's fists clenched as she slowly approached her.

"Lelane…run!" I grunted, trying to sit up, but the pain was immobilising.

With lightning speed, Terra disarmed Lelane and backed her into the wall. Desperate, she looked around for an escape, but Terra had boxed her in. She tightened a firm grip around Lelane's throat, lifting her from the floor. Lelane's legs attempted to kick out, her hands clawing at the strong hold around her neck. I dragged myself forward, urging my feet to support me, but a sharp pain shot up my leg when I tried to stand.

Terra angled her head, looking at me. "If I cannot have her," she said, maintaining a tight grip around Lelane's throat while the other hand stroked her hair, Lelane's eyes falling to me, "then no-one shall."

"Noooo!" I screamed weakly, unable to drown out the sound of her neck being crushed. Lelane's hands and legs fell limp as her head sagged and Terra released her hold, discarding her body to the floor.

"No, no, no. Lelane! Noooo…" I shrieked, trying to drag myself closer, but Terra stood on my hand with her heavy boot, the pain unbearable.

"This is all your fault," she said, but I did not look up at her, my focus only on Lelane and my struggle to reach her. Terra's boot found me again, kicking me in the chest and rolling me onto my back. She then came down on me, both of her hands wrapping around my neck.

"You took her away from me," Terra spat in my face, and this time I did look at her. Veins protruded from her throat, spit gathered in the corner of her mouth, her face red and seething. I had tried to protect Lelane from Terra's madness, but I failed, and now she was going to kill us both. I felt the struggle within me wane as I teetered on the edge of losing consciousness, gasping for breath while waiting for the inevitable end.

Instead, the grip around my neck loosened and I felt warmth trickle down my face. I opened my eyes to witness Terra fumbling at a neat, straight line forming around her neck, blood streaming down between her fingers. Her enraged expression shifted to one of pure shock, and after a few blinks, she toppled over, landing beside me, blood spreading onto the floor.

Silently, behind her, Lera stood with a knife clasped in her hands.

Then, everything went black.

26

Fate And Future

I woke to the trickle of cold water dripping across my lips. I tried to move but merely groaned from the pain, as a small hand landed on my chest. I opened my eyes to see Lera crouched beside me, a wet cloth in her other hand.

It was dark, the torchlight long extinguished, while the moon cast a thin beam through the solitary window. We were still in The Sanctum.

"Lelane," I cried, fresh tears swelling in my eyes as I recalled all that had happened before I lost consciousness. Only silence lingered now. "Lera," I whispered, aware of the elfing's presence beside me. "Help me sit up," I asked, and I felt her reach for me and pull, while I breathed heavily, slumping forward.

I noticed Terra's lifeless body, laying in a pool of her own blood, and as I turned my head, I caught a glimpse of Lelane's unmoving form, her blonde hair cascading across her face. My body shook as tears poured from me, and I lost track of how long I sat there, wailing, and crying in absolute agony. She was gone, my best friend, I had failed to protect her.

I felt Lera's hand clasp mine and I pulled her into my lap, her head falling on my shoulder.

"I am so sorry, Lera," I managed to choke out, stroking her head. "I am sorry for everything." She did not move, or a shared a tear, but I felt the moment she clutched onto me tighter, as I cradled her, rocking back and forth.

"We need to get out of here," I finally rasped, now desperate to get Lera away from her deceased mothers. Slowly, I managed to get to my feet, hopping up one stair at a time, with my good arm draped around Lera for support. We made it halfway through the city, before I was finally recognised, and an elf ran off to get help. I could not speak, my mouth was dry and sore, I felt completely numb. When I eventually collapsed on the sandstone path, Lera sat by my side, and we waited for help.

When the guards arrived, they carried us back to the palace. Amongst them was Brenith, her brow knitted in concern.

"You will find their bodies in The Sanctum," I rasped, a fresh tear tracing down my face. Brenith nodded, watching the guards carry us away, before instructing two others to follow her. I remained wordless, reaching for Lera's hand, and clutching it tightly as we were taken to the healer's chamber in the palace. At some point during the healer's examinations, I drifted into sleep, only to be awakened by hushed whispers that grew louder as they argued in hissed tones. I tried to open my eyes, but I was exhausted, my body feeling incredibly heavy and weak.

"My champion is dead because of her, and yet you tell me you will do nothing?"

"Enough lives have been lost this night, Peril," replied General Maiya.

"We made a bargain."

"Yes, and that bargain was not to poison the queen's consort," she seethed, keeping her voice low.

"You said you wanted the queen frightened enough to abdicate."

"By threatening or hurting Phoenyx. Not killing him."

"Still, you got what you wanted."

"At what cost?" I heard General Maiya ask, as I slipped back into the darkness.

When I woke again, it was to the sound of birds chirping and the smell of a warm summer morning; of blossoms and warm fresh air. Hearing a light thumping sound, I sat up slowly and found Lera, silently playing with a wooden horse in the corner of the room. She appeared clean and freshly groomed, dressed in fresh clothing with neatly plaited hair. A streak of sunlight spilt onto her from the open shutters.

"Where are we?" I finally asked, her eyes snapping to mine as I spoke. She did not reply, but quickly ran from the room, leaving the door open. A moment later, Addox stepped through, and my mouth fell open at the sight of him.

He rushed over and cradled me into his arms, and I clutched against him tightly, pulling myself into him, as tears streaked down my cheeks. Everything that had transpired felt like a crushing weight on my lungs. I stayed like that for a long while; Addox stroking my back as he let me sob into his broad chest as I wallowed in his musky scent.

"How do you feel?" he asked as my breathing regulated.

"I do not know how to answer that," I replied honestly, pulling back from his chest so I could look at him. His eyes were tired, but everything about him appeared radiant. His overgrown facial hair had been trimmed back to stubble, and his hair was cut short again, the ends curling. "Physically, a little sore, but better than I probably deserve," I followed.

He kissed my forehead, stroking my cheek as he breathed me in.

"What is this place?" I asked, taking stock of the small one-story building. Its humble furnishings were chipped, but freshly painted as though someone had cared to repurpose them.

"Castor's cottage. This is as far from the palace as I could get you."

"I thought Castor lived in Tobias's House?" I asked, bringing my legs up to my chest as Addox moved about the room to provide me with water.

"He did for a while, then he gave up his room for Kass before he…" he paused, his forehead creasing. I closed my eyes, running a hand down my face.

"How long did I sleep?"

"Four very long days," he said, his tone laced with relief, and I could not deny it felt good to be held by him again, to feel wanted and warm without bars between us.

"General Maiya let you out?"

"Yep, right after she took over as regent and disbanded the council, making her proclamation over the humans known. She made a whole speech about it. Truda detested every moment of it, of course. Erik had to hold her back to stop her from doing something stupid." I closed my eyes, the heaviness still in my heart. It was difficult to take a breath without remembering all I had enabled General Maiya to do by keeping her secrets. There was no denying I was an accomplice to her plan, even if I was naive to all the details. "General Maiya extended a claiming offer to Cobal, and he accepted."

"She did?" I asked, puzzled by that revelation.

Addox nodded. "Then reluctantly, to make a point, Truda claimed Erik in front of everyone, declaring loudly in graphic detail what would happen to anyone that went near him."

"I did not mean for all of this to happen," I said, my head falling in my hands.

"None of this is your fault, Quin, it was all down to a bigger plan that would have happened regardless of your choices."

"Except Lelane would still be alive if it were not for me."

"That's not your fault, you couldn't have known Terra was going to hurt her."

"I suspected it. That was why I made my bargain with General Maiya. To save you, and award her the better life she deserved."

"Because that's who you are, you think of everyone else before yourself, and feel responsible when others suffer."

"You are wrong, I did not uphold my vow to the royal family. I allowed myself to get distracted and they have suffered because of my actions."

"Quin, look at me." I shook my head, trying to hide away. Taking a deep breath, Addox cupped my face with both hands, gently forcing my neck to crane back. "Look at me," he repeated, and my watery eyes looked up at his perfect face. "I'm alive because of you, so is Prince Felyx and Lera, as well as the boys that were trapped in Tobias's House, not to mention the warriors you helped on the beach."

"You knew about that?"

"Truda told me, though she didn't seem all that happy about you sneaking off into battle without her," he confirmed. "You can't save everyone on your own, you're going to need some help."

"What do you mean?"

"It's not over, Quin, we're going to fight back, and we want you with us," he said, his eyes full of hope and longing.

"With you?"

"Truda's started a revolution against Maiya's rule, and

this time I'm not keeping anything from you. We do this together."

"Truda will not want my help, after everything I have done, she must truly hate me."

"Not quite," a voice spoke from the doorway, and I saw Truda stood on the threshold, her arms crossed. She pulled a chair closer, took a seat and leaned forward, resting her arms across her thighs. "I am sorry for the loss of your friend. I was harsh with my words about her before," she said, and I swiped my eyes, trying to prevent new tears from forming.

"She was more than just a friend to me," I whispered.

"I gathered as much when your fist collided with my jaw," she teased, and I gave her a weak apologetic smile. "Luckily for you, I do not break easily."

"You should have hit me back," I said, but she shook her head.

"The thought had crossed my mind."

"I am sorry, Truda."

"I know, and Addox is right. You cannot control the actions of others; it was our fault for excluding you from our plans. Perhaps if we had told you, you would have felt compelled to come to us rather than face trouble alone."

"What do you plan to do about General Maiya?"

"She is right to worry over the threat at our borders, but forcing pairings is one step away from returning men into servitude, and I simply cannot allow that to happen. By disbanding the council, she has removed the obstacles that would prevent her from making new proclamations, and without Queen Fortuna—" she said, but I interrupted her.

"I think General Maiya made a bargain to have something happen to Phoenyx, enough to scare the queen into abdicating."

"She had him killed?" Addox asked, but I shook my head.

"I am not sure that was what she intended, but those she had bargained with made their assumptions."

"Then the prince could be in more danger than I feared," Truda replied, her brow knitting intensely.

"The prince, why?" I asked, full of worry.

"Do you think Maiya will let him grow and become our next monarch? Or will he suffer a similar fate to his father?" Truda asked, her question rhetorical.

"We have to protect him." I clenched my fists and ignored the dull ache of my healing wound.

"Getting to him is difficult, but that's where you can help," Addox suggested, reaching for my hand.

"You and your royal guard can protect and watch over him on our behalf, as well as share any information that may be deemed as valuable." Truda said.

"You want me to spy for you?"

"General Maiya trusts you now, believing you are dedicated to her. She will not assume anything less than your loyalty and honour."

"If I do not agree?"

"That would be a conversation between you and Addox, but if you both choose to stay out of it, I will not hold it against you."

"Can I think about it?" I asked her, undecided on my next course of action.

"Of course. Ensure she gets plenty of rest, Addox," she said with a pointed look. "We have much to do tomorrow." I watched her leave, closing the door behind her.

"You hungry?" Addox asked. I shook my head.

"I do not think I can eat anything right now."

"I know it's a lot to think about, and I won't ask you to do anything you're not comfortable with."

"How you can say that, after everything?"

"I already told you I'm not lying anymore, and I'm not leaving either. Not unless you ask me to," he replied, pulling me closer to him again.

"It seems selfish of me to experience the happiness I do not deserve while the rest of the kingdom suffers because of something I helped come to pass."

"Then join Truda's revolution, or don't, and just watch over Prince Felyx. You don't have to spy for Truda. You can teach and train the boy and let him make his choices when he's ready to rule."

"What will you do?"

"You mean if I'm not involved in Truda's plan? I'll spend my time watching out for you, maybe even help to train the prince. Whatever we do, we'll figure it out together."

"You would really turn your back on them for me?" I asked, my brow knitted together. Addox smiled, tilting his head slightly as he leaned down and pressed his lips to mine.

"Isn't that what people do for the ones they love," he

whispered against my mouth. He pulled me closer again and kissed me passionately until I felt dizzy with lust, his fingers sliding to the back of my neck as he devoured me.

We suddenly ripped our mouths apart as the door opened, and Lera walked through.

"Oh yeah, I forgot," he drawled, creating some space between us. "Lera also sleeps here; I could ask Shanon if maybe—"

"No, it is fine, I am glad she is here. I would rather keep her close."

"Then it's a good thing you're still healing, otherwise I would've had her ushered away," Addox chuckled, wiggling his eyebrows. "Come on, lie down, the little elfling and I will sort some supper," he said, patting Lera on the head, failing to notice her eyes narrow at him distastefully.

I took a deep breath as the guards opened the large double doors, allowing me entry into the throne room. It was crowded, with many warriors lining the walls. It seemed Maiya had fortified herself inside until the new proclamations had settled across the city. I recognised some of the elves; those who previously wore mis-matched armour were now equipped with uniformed metal plating, reflective and shining. They all held weapons.

General Maiya sat in the queen's chair on the dais, staring down at the table. Imelda and Shea were engaged in deep discussion as they animatedly pointed at the maps laid out.

"Acqueline, it is good to see you have recovered," General Maiya said, looking up as I approached. I spent days healing and mourning Lelane in Castor's cottage, which provided plenty of time to consider Truda's offer to join her revolution. Although General Maiya's actions had been for the greater good of our people, Truda was right to fear the lengths she may go to see her plans through. Her bargain had seen the queens consort murdered in his bedchamber; I would not allow the same fate to fall upon Prince Felyx.

"Thank you general." I bowed my head slightly as I respectfully placed a closed fist over my heart. "I am thankful to be fit enough to return to duty."

"Did you not hear? The royal guard have been disbanded," a voice crooned. Peril quirked a smile and stepped forward, standing in front of the council table. "Which means our general has no further use for you,"

"The prince will still need guardianship, there is much I still have to teach him." I raised my chin high, focussing solely on General Maiya. The negative, hostile atmosphere pulsing within the throne room made me feel uncomfortable, but I did not show it. "I promised his mother I would always protect him. With permission of our new leader, I would like to keep that vow."

"Then go. Keep your promises, Acqueline. You will find the prince in the gardens."

"Thank you." I saluted once again, as I began to slowly retreat.

"And, Acqueline!" General Maiya called. "I trust you have also not forgotten other vows made."

With a nod, I quickly slipped out of the Throne Room and headed towards the palace gardens.

I found the prince sat by the stream, with Yuki as his only companion, lying on the bank beside him. Neither of them stirred as I approached. Kneeling, I rested my hand on the boy's shoulder.

"I am so sorry, my prince," I whispered, and his neck twisted to the side to look at me. A vacant expression on his face, his eyes were red-rimmed. It was as though he had cried so much, he no longer had the energy, nor tears left to shed. It had been my arrow that had killed his mother, my action had left him an orphaned boy. "Can I get you anything?" I asked. His eyes welled with fresh tears, his bottom lip quivering, as he suddenly launched into my arms. His cries were muffled as he bunched the fabric of my tunic in his small hands.

I cradled him in my arms, my own tears falling as I held onto him tightly, the pain in my still-healing body unable to compare to the pain in my heart. For a long while, I simply rocked him in our embrace, begging for his forgiveness and whispering words of promise. When he quietened, I realised he had finally fallen asleep in my arms. I gently walked him over to where Brenith stood, carefully handing him over to her strong arms.

"Ensure he is comfortable and has everything he needs," I said, watching as she carried him inside. Yuki followed close behind with his tail tucked between his legs.

"I will protect him," I whispered into the wind. "By any means, I will keep him safe."

⋙⋘

The next day, after breakfast, Addox brought me to the outskirts of the city, stopping outside an old familiar farmhouse, Truda and Erik were waiting outside.

"We want you with us, Acqueline," Truda said.

"And to prove it, we're going to show you something General Maiya doesn't know," Erik added.

"What is it?" I asked, looking to Addox for reassurance, and he smiled, giving me a small nod.

"You will need to come inside." Truda gestured to the slightly opened door. For a moment I hesitated, taking Addox's hand before walking inside the small wooden building. My eyes quickly adjusted to the dimmed light, and inside stood Kayla, a friend of Truda's. A cloaked figure was beside her, hiding their face from view. I looked around in confusion.

"I do not understand."

"Acqueline?" came a soft voice, and I redirected my attention just as the concealed figure lowered their hood. Blonde hair cascaded over her pointed ears, and her cloudy white eyes were fixed on me.

"Queen Fortuna!" I gasped.

"In the madness of the tower, General Maiya did not

double-check when her warriors declared the queen dead. It was only as I held her in my arms that I felt her faint breath on my skin," Truda said. I broke down immediately, rushing to take her hand and dropping to one knee, sobbing.

"I am so sorry my queen, I failed you and your family."

Her voice was quiet when she responded, "I'm the one who should apologise. I knew something was coming, and yet, I could not control my magic when Phoenyx..." she began, tears trickling from her eyes, and I stood, wrapping my arms around her.

"Your nightmares?" I asked.

"Our nightmares," she softly corrected, tears streaming down her face as she spoke into my ear.

Our nightmares? Did she mean hers and Phoenyx's, or...

Then my stomach dropped as realisation dawned. The nights I had woken after my dreams of the storm, only for my guardswomen to summon me regarding Queen Fortuna's state of distress. They were her nightmares, and she had shared them with me. She must have known Lelane was going to die, and I would have to choose between my friend's life or theirs. It was why she had chosen me to train Prince Felyx, she wanted me to be close to him, to care and worry for him like any mother would.

"No one else would have made the sacrifice for my son as you did," she said, as though hearing my thoughts. My legs shook as I stepped back and lost my balance. Addox quickly came up behind me, holding me steady.

"You knew," I whispered, closing my eyes, envisioning

Lelane's smile as she accepted an apple from my hand, blushing and nervously twirling the ends of her hair.

"I knew there would be a choice, and that I was going to lose Phoenyx. If I didn't find the right elf to protect my son, I knew I would lose him, too. But I didn't know what fate would take from you, or the price of your decision," she replied, her tone compassionate and remorseful.

"What's going on?" Addox asked, wrapping a protective arm around me, concerned about my reaction.

"Fortuna has visions, and sometimes they show her the future. She has no control of how or when they will appear," Truda explained, quickly following the truth of what was happening.

"And this is how you wanted her to find out? Has she not suffered enough?" Addox shouted in her face, defending me.

"I did not know until now; we did not mean for this to happen to you, Acqueline," Truda said.

I turned, nodding slowly, unable to speak as I straightened, remaining close to Addox.

"We are hiding her far away, somewhere General Maiya cannot hurt her, or abuse her power," Truda added. "She will return when the time is right."

"When will that be?" I asked, finding my voice again.

"It may not be for several years, but we have promised to keep Fortuna's son protected. We will do all that is—" she began, but I cut her off, stepping away from Addox as I approached Fortuna.

"I will uphold my vow and keep him safe." I had never

been more sincere in my entire existence.

"Thank you," she replied, clutching both of my hands in hers. "I know I don't deserve it, but I am grateful for everything."

"We should go," Truda said, reaching for a cloak of her own, as she nodded to Kayla. I watched as she stepped aside and pulled back a small rug, lifting open a hatch door, which revealed a ladder and vertical tunnel. "I will be back in a few days," she told Erik, as she helped to guide Queen Fortuna down the ladder.

"Truda," I said, just before she descended completely. "I want to be a part of your revolution."

"You already are," she said with her typical smug smile, dropping to the ground as Kayla closed the secret hatch.

We left Kayla's farm and collected Lera to visit her mother. Lelane had been buried beneath the large oak where we used to play as elflings; the same fruit tree I found Lera and the prince playing in after he had run away. The pink blossoms were in full bloom, preparing to fruit for the autumn harvest. At the sight of the tiny pink flowers, I pictured Lelane making a small crown from them, saving the most beautiful blossom to tuck behind my ear.

"I miss her," I said aloud as Addox came to my side, his arm wrapped around my waist. Lera disappeared, climbing up and finding a quiet hiding spot in the branches.

"We must take care of her, Addox."

"We will," he replied, kissing the top of my head.

"I will train her. I will push Lera to develop all the skills necessary to survive this life and ensure she can protect the prince," I said, loud enough for her to hear. I wanted her to know my plans for her. Lera would be the fiercest of warriors, becoming the shadow I knew the prince would need. She would always be there to protect him against any adversary, even our own people, if necessary.

The branches rustled as Lera shifted, her small, expressionless features and piercing blue eyes gazed down at me. Slowly, she nodded, curling her thin fingers into a fist, raising it just above her heart. Then, just as quickly as she made herself visible, she disappeared, climbing higher and out of sight.

"What do we do now?" I asked, turning to face him.

"Well, you must ask to claim me," he said, and I widened my eyes, my mouth falling open. "I'll make a fuss about it at first though, pretend I don't want you to," he continued, pressing a palm against my cheek. "Eventually, I'll say yes, if you're lucky." I pushed his hand away gently.

"Addox, General Maiya is not vying for our happiness, she wants warriors."

"I know," he said, remaining in his spot.

"We would have to take a potion and conceive."

"Quin, I know what it means. So, just claim me already and let's plan our future."

"I do not deserve you."

"Yes, you do," he said, looking at me intently. "No matter what comes next, we'll fight through it together," he followed.

"I love you," I said, nuzzling into him, as his arms wrapped tightly around me.

"I love you more, little elf." He stroked my hair, tugging lightly to prompt me to kiss him. "Can I take that as a claim?" he asked, a singular eyebrow raised, and I shook my head.

"No," I said with a sly smile, "You can claim me."

Thank you so much for purchasing this book I hope you enjoyed reading it. I would like to say a huge thank to family and friends for your enthusiasm and support. Without you, this sequel may not have happened.

Also a special thanks to my writing friends, beta readers and my wonderful editor Natalie, who has helped bring out the best of my creativity.

It doesn't end with Incandescent, the next installment is already well underway and I can't wait to share the next chapter with you. For the latest news, follow me on my social media pages. @rahattonfantasy

Follow General Truda's story, as she unveils the kingdom's secrets while risking everything for the human she is forbidden to love.

Manumission - Kingdom of Slaves (Book 1)
Paperback available now
on Amazon.co.uk & Amazon.com

R. A. HATTON

MANUMISSION

1

Sacrifice Eternal

Today I was confident my sword would run red with the blood of our enemies. My finger trailed across the works of Nysa's finest cartographer, lingering my touch over the depiction of the great white city at the heart of the map. The place that gave me my name and rank.

The city of Kven.

I craved the comfort of a soft bed and a real bath. However, for now, I had to be content with a bowl of water and washcloth. At least my Guan always heated the water on a campfire before bringing it to my tent.

I appreciated this, not that I ever told him so.

"Tobias?" I called, glancing toward the tent entrance. Shortly after I had called, the young human in his early twenties walked in. Dressed in a plain untanned cloth tunic and trousers, he bowed his head in greeting. He was average in height and was of a medium toned build, but still much shorter than I.

I was tall for an elf.

His strong muscular arms were visible with his sleeveless, loosely stitched tunic. He had a round face with hazel brown eyes and small lips. His copper hair usually hung just past his shoulders, but today it was wrapped back in a bun.

He was a Guan of few words. Others of his kind often asked questions or replied with answers like, 'yes my master' which became tedious after a while. Tobias took direction well, and I never had to ask or explain things twice. He had been my Guan since he was just fourteen years old.

"Bring me some nuts and fruit, then fetch me a bowl of water, a clean cloth and a towel," I instructed. He gently closed his eyes whilst bowing his head, and then retreated from my tent.

With a deep sigh, my focus returned to the map. Further analysing the valleys and desert domes we had already scouted. We were tracking a band of rebels that had been spotted from the city wall. The queen had sent me to lead a few dozen of our strongest warriors to track them down and eradicate them. I was in charge. My soldiers referred to me by my title, 'General'.

Queen Cassandra relied on me; trusted me to bring an end to the idiocracy, the lingering remnants of conflict. I would do anything to bring that reality to fruition.

Turning away from my table, I looked to see a plate of food

placed on a chair near the entrance of the tent. Tobias must have left it there and then retreated to fetch my hot water.

I grabbed the plate with one hand, and with the other, I parted the cotton canvas to peer out. The light of the rising morning caused my eyes to squint for a moment as they adjusted to the glow emanating from the sun.

By the time I had finished my food, Tobias walked back through the tent and placed the ceramic bowl of water on the rug in the centre of my pitch, and then placed the clean cloth and towel on a stool next to it.

"Tend to my horse and saddle him up. I want to be ready to ride out early this morning," I told him. Tobias gave me a courteous nod and left.

I touched the surface of the water with my index finger. Vapours of lavender oil wafted over my face; it was my favourite scent. The temperature was perfect; not hot enough to burn, but warm enough to turn the skin on my finger a pink hue. I removed my soft cotton pants and cropped top I had slept in and stood naked in the centre of the tent. I submerged a clean cloth in the fragrant water and ran it along my body.

Once I was clean, I patted myself dry with a towel. After rubbing soothing oils laced with peach nectar on my skin, I walked over to my armour stand and started dressing.

First, I wrapped myself in clean cotton undergarments and a blouse, then donned my azure painted chest piece, which had a floral pattern engraved into the body of its hard leather. The same uniform that my predecessor wore before me; my mother. Her responsibilities fell to me after her honourable death.

I pulled on my dark leather pants and placed my cotton wrapped feet inside black knee-high boots.

Using stretched leather, I tied my thick, long brown hair back into a high ponytail, scraping the strands past my pointed ears, ensuring it was tight enough to stop it from falling down my face.

Then I fastened the buckle of the black belt that holds two daggers, one either side, around my waist. I picked up my sheathed sword attached to the thick strap and wrapped it around my shoulder, allowing the large weapon to sit comfortably against my upper back.

Closing my fingers around the sword's handle and pulling it from its casing. I opened the lid to my pot of woad dye, using my sword to reflect the image of my face. Dipping two fingers into the paste, I smeared rough lines diagonally over from my forehead, across the lid of my left eye, stopping just at the ridge of my cheekbone.

I looked at my reflection, the blue markings conflicting with the colour of my bright green eyes. Taking one final look, satisfied that I was ready, I walked out of my dimly candlelit tent, into the natural light of dawn.

Outside mingled a few other warriors already awake, beginning to emerge from their partnered tents. I closed my eyes for a second, taking a long slow inhale, smelling the morning fresh air. I felt strong and energised, ready to take on the challenges of the day.

My current focus was to find the rebel base and destroy it. I wanted legendary stories to be told of the great warrior that finally brought an end to all the fighting and restored peace to the Kingdom of Nysa.

"Good morning, General," Captain Imelda said, slamming a closed fist against her heart, showing respect for my rank. It was something we all did to those who were a higher rank than ourselves. I only had to use this gesture for one person: Queen Cassandra.

"And what a good morning it will be, Captain," I replied with positive assertiveness.

"Shall I round up the camp to get ready to move?"

She was already dressed in full armour, her sword sheathed to her side. She was always up early and ready for my instruction. Imelda was almost as tall as me, though much leaner. Our bodies were incomparable as she had not yet put hers through the rigorous training that would give her the defined muscle and core strength that I had. She had a thin face with blue eyes and long brown hair. Despite the beauty of our race, Imelda was plainer than most.

"Yes, fetch the twins and some of the others, we shall take a small group and head out earlier today." With that, she signalled the salute of respect and walked away. I liked including the twins in our excursions. Although young and inexperienced, Shanor and Shanon were at the battle-hungry age of eighteen, both recently becoming my shadows, eager to learn. Shanor was especially keen, confiding that she aspired to be a great leader herself one day, upholding peace for the kingdom; I held great affection for them both.

As Captain Imelda hastened the readiness of my warriors, I took a moment for myself. Looking towards the rising sun and feeling the slight warmth on my face. It had not yet reached over the hills, and darkness still cast shadows over the camp.

Tobias led my saddled horse towards me. Thio was a large black stallion, the mount I favoured for any journey beyond the city walls. Tobias patted the side of his neck, his hand half-covering his mouth as he said something in his ear whilst walking along the mud track. I found myself curious as to what he whispered into the animal's ear. My eyes softened as I watched them, gratified with the attention and care as he tended my horse. Thio seemed agitated and Tobias was trying to calm him.

My focus sharpened as my peripheral vision caught a blurred image running between the tents to my right. I grabbed my sword handle, pulling it from its sheath.

Shouts of 'ambush' rang throughout the camp.

"We are under attack. Stay back," I commanded Tobias, whose eyes were darting around frantically.

Ahead of us, figures dressed in old, battered armour appeared from the shadows between the tents.

Shanor was confronted by a rebel elf holding a short sword and broken shield. As they swung their sword towards her, I watched as she took a quick step back just in time, allowing the blade to only slice a shallow cut through the side of her arm.

I charged towards Shanor to come to her aid, but a scream of rage sounded close behind me. As I turned, I saw a ragged elf in shredded clothes run towards me with a dagger in her dirty hands.

I raised my sword, ready to step forward and strike my blow, when another figure stepped directly in front of me, blocking my body from the attacker like a shield made of flesh.

It was Tobias.

I could only watch as the elf's blade pierced straight through his chest. Immediately, with a frustrated growl, she pulled the dagger from Tobias. As he started to fall to the ground, she came at me again, blood dripping from her knife, with determination to strike.

Without hesitation, I thrust my sword through her. A scream of rage escaped my lips as I yanked out my blade, wet with her blood, and rammed it through her neck. With one booted foot, I pushed her lifeless corpse off my blade and watched it crumple onto the mud.

Behind me, my warriors had finished off the other attackers with ease. They searched around the tents for anyone hidden and began checking the fallen bodies, to make sure none were left alive.

On the ground by my feet, facing away from me was Tobias, looking towards his now dead attacker lying on her back in the mud.

"Stupid boy, why did you do that?" I crouched to one knee, gently rolling Tobias onto his back. Blood soaked through his clothes as his hand feebly pressed on the gaping wound in his chest. I knew there was nothing that could be done. There was too much blood, and no way he would survive.

I looked down at his face, he was looking directly at me, his breathing sharp and erratic. He looked into my eyes, his lips moving as if to speak, his bottom lip beginning to quiver.

"I… I'm… I… Truda." He struggled to get the words out as he fought for breath.

"It is okay, Tobias." I gently placed my hand over his. He gripped my hand, holding it tightly to him as he again tried to form words, my name being the last coherent sound to come from his lips.

"You may rest now," I told him, and he closed his eyes. I kept my hand rested on his until his grip loosened, and he let go.

I watched as his arm slumped back and dropped to the ground. My muscles vibrated as I looked at Tobias's lifeless body, a wave of unexpected anger bubbling up inside me. I stood and swiftly turned to grab my horse's reins. Pulling myself up onto his back I cantered closer to my warriors and shouted my instructions.

"Captain Imelda, you and half a dozen others mount your horses now and follow me immediately, we will scout the area for any retreating rebels."

"Yes, General." She looked towards the twins and signalled to a few others who quickly dashed off towards their steeds.

We searched in all directions, at least half a mile around the camp, but found no others. I steadied my fury and considered the events that had transpired this morning. They must have tracked our camp, knowing we were nearby, hunting for them.

They were clever to attack at dawn when they could linger in the shadows of the night not yet passed. They knew we would be at a disadvantage, less prepared for an attack.

We trotted back and I saw a great fire blazing a few metres away from the camp.

"Report," I commanded one of the warriors as we passed the first tent.

"There were no survivors. We searched their bodies before we burnt them but did not find anything informative."

"Good. Pack up the camp; we are leaving to return to the city." I nodded at Imelda, signalling her to oversee the preparations and disassemble the camp.

I dismounted my horse and walked him towards my tent. The bodies had indeed been removed, and all that was left behind were a few bloodied patches where our enemies had fallen. The blood-stained ground was still damp from where Tobias had been slain; his body would no doubt be burning in the large smoke-filled pyre along with the rest of the deceased.

There would be no burial or funeral for the death of a Guan, even one who had sacrificed himself for his master.

My eyes averted from the red dirt, I hitched my horse to a post outside my tent and entered. For a moment, I just stood there, listening to the sound of my deep breaths.

I looked down at the dried blood that covered my hands; it was Tobias's blood. In all the years he had been my slave, I had never touched him. I had never yelled at him or punished him, but I had also never been kind. I had never said thank you or given him a gift of gratitude. It was not our way. Men were beneath us, they were our slaves, born into our race of female elf warriors as servants.

The histories told us that a long time ago we had been human, in a world of constant war because of men, with their natural inclination and tendencies towards violence, until a group of women discovered they could use magic. They rose together and killed all but a few of the men. As the knowledge and power of magic grew, so did we, evolving into something stronger, faster, smarter and more gifted, with longer life.

Men, however, stayed the same, never evolving and remaining insentient and imbecilic, the lowest of beings.

We used them now for construction, agriculture, and breeding. Higher ranking elves, like myself, were granted a Guan to assist with all the daily mundane tasks.

Tobias was my Guan. He had been a farmer as a young boy assigned to me soon after, and now he was dead.

I rushed over to the pot of water that was still in the centre of my tent and dropped to my knees in front of it. Using a cloth, I scrubbed the blood from my hands until all traces had gone. I stood slowly and reached for a towel.

Why had Tobias sacrificed himself? I could have easily fought off the elf, there was no need for him to die; he still had many years left. Why did his death trouble me so?

Just then, Imelda walked into my tent, distracting me from my conflicting thoughts.

"General, we counted six rebels. We had no casualties, nor severe injuries, except for a graze on Shanor's arm."

"Good," I replied. With my hands now dry, I threw the towel on the floor. "Ensure the camp is ready to leave. Send word to the city of what has happened here and that we are returning."

"I will have our Raven Keeper send a message," said Imelda, and before leaving she placed her closed fist over her chest.

Now standing alone, I scanned my clothes, armour and weapons, thinking about how I would have to pack all these things myself. Yes, that was it; I did miss Tobias, but only because of the inconvenience of it all, having to make do without a Guan's service until he could be replaced.

2

Reflections

After riding for most of the day, we finally left the desert and reached the grassland. In the distance the beautiful sandstone city of Kven came into view. It was still light but soon would become dusk; we might make it home just in time for supper. I guided my horse into a quick trot towards the city, with my warriors following behind me, also on horseback, some pulling carts full of our camping supplies.

The white palace was truly magnificent with its great needle-like towers, the tallest hidden in the clouds. The enormous decadent structure sat animated in the centre of the city. There were other large buildings, such as the Battle Coliseum, Mages Temple, Training House, and some larger households belonging to wealthier elves.

From here, all the larger buildings looked like they

were connected to the palace, making its size appear more impressive; perhaps that was the intent with the layout design. Most people who lived inside the city had substantial sized homes. The queen, princess, and royal guard all lived in the Grand Palace.

Thoughts of Tobias not returning with me clouded my mind. His presence in the house had never offered me any real comfort, as being alone never bothered me, but returning to an empty and unusually quiet home unnerved me now.

Looking on towards the city of Kven, I saw the large wooden gates laced with silver that defined the main entrance in and out of the city. As we approached, I saw the gates open and a single rider galloped on her horse towards us, stopping directly in front of me.

"General. Welcome home, for we are pleased of your safe return." She signalled the salute of respect.

"Thank you," I said, wondering why this young warrior had saddled her horse and passed the city's stone walls just to welcome me home. Of course, I did not have to wait long before this was explained.

"Queen Cassandra has sent me to fetch for you, my general. She has asked that you urgently present yourself upon your return in the Great Throne Room."

I nodded, and she steered her horse to gallop back towards the main gates. A hot bath and some proper rest sounded more appealing; however, it was a small price to pay for being the general, and duty to my queen always came first.

The palace was quiet, guards posted in the usual spots as I passed them, the sounds of my heavy boots reverberated against the marbled floor.

"Tru, you are back!" Acqueline exclaimed, dashing towards me with a beaming smile.

"Acqueline, it is good to see you," I said, and I meant it. She was my lifelong friend and sparring partner, and despite her being a few years younger than me, we had always been close. Where I would describe Imelda as plain, Acqueline was far from that. She had long chestnut coloured hair, lighter than mine, half tied up, half left loose with its natural waves covering her shoulders. She had a soft oval face, with a pointed jaw that matched the symmetry of her petite pointed nose. Her lips were a natural rose in colour, her bottom lip larger than her top. She had small hazel brown eyes and lids covered in full lashes. She was shorter than I and had retained much of her childlike figure.

"I heard you got into a bit of trouble, let some rebels catch you off guard?" said Acqueline with a playful smirk.

"Hardly a surprise attack, just half a dozen lucky few that managed to get past my scouts; they were dealt with quickly," I replied curtly. I knew Acqueline did not mean to insult me, but the morning attack was still fresh in my thoughts. I was not in the right frame of mind to talk about it as though it was a game or a laughing matter.

Acqueline must have detected my mood as she quickly

added, "Were there any casualties?"

"Shanor got a nasty scrape on her arm. It looked deep enough to get a scar, so that will please her."

"Oh yes, the young ones do like their battle scars," Acqueline sniggered. I did not tell her that I had lost Tobias. The loss of a Guan did not mean much to us in the higher ranks, and she would not understand my feelings on the matter. I would be granted a new one, but it would not be the same. Tobias and I had built up an understanding, he knew how things needed to be, and I was content with him in my service.

"The queen has requested your presence, she seems agitated. I think she was worried for you after hearing about the ambush."

"Well, the Throne Room is where I am headed now, so I will be able to put her mind at ease." She nodded, placed her closed fist over her chest and continued forward. Just as she was about to walk past me, I turned towards her. "We should have a sparring session soon. I am keen to see if your new duties have made you careless and slack." Acqueline had recently been titled head of the royal guard, a position earned through unfaltering loyalty, dedication, and sacrifice. Patrolling the halls and guarding the royal chambers, she rarely ventured outside of the palace.

My invitation lifted her spirits as she almost jumped in excitement at the challenge. "Ha! You wish. I look forward to proving you wrong," she finished with a bigger grin, making me chuckle at her eagerness. After Acqueline showed the signal of respect, I turned to continue my walk down the long corridor towards the Throne Room. Her light and pleasant character always managed to put a smile on my face.

Unfortunately, my amused mood was not to last, as a figure appeared from the shadow of an unlit doorway.

“And so, the queen’s favourite warrior has returned.” Her voice croaked as if someone had left scratches at the base of her throat.

“Freyja,” I said with a frustrated sigh, knowing the sound of that voice only too well. The elder from the Mages Temple whom I had never trusted. The distasteful feeling was mutual.

“I am so pleased you have returned safely. When I heard about the ambush, I was worried that something awful may have happened.” She moved closer towards me from the shadows and spoke in a dry and sarcastic tone.

There was no doubt in my mind that she would get pleasure if I were injured or did not return at all. If an elf’s appearance could match a personality, then Freyja should have been so unsightly that her image would haunt the nightmares of children. In reality, she was very beautiful.

She had much paler skin than most, probably attained by the fact that she spent most of her time hidden from the sun, as most of the temple’s acolytes did. The contrast between her skin and mid-length black hair was striking. She also had perfectly small symmetrical facial features and a perfectly shaped body. She was wearing a black leather fur-lined tunic, with a hood covering most of her face. The material fell just below her knees and underneath I could see her black leather pants and boots.

On her shoulder was her pet raven. It was an ugly-looking deformed creature, large for a bird of its type, with great sharp talons and a razor tapered beak that curved slightly at the end. It glared at me with its garnet eyes that matched Freyja's red face paint that she used to decorate her eyelids and lips. She called the creature Jetta.

Choosing not to reply, I stepped to walk around her.

"I am very much looking forward to our next council meeting," Freyja muttered. Our eyes momentarily met as I reached her side. She grinned at me, enjoying my silence, then saluted half-heartedly as I walked past. I did not have time for Freyja's nonsense. Right now, I had more important places to be. As I continued, I imagined two sets of eyes burning into my back.

Guards flanked the large arched double doors that were the entrance to the Great Throne Room. They both nodded their heads in unison to let me know I was free to enter, gesturing the salute as I passed.

Inside the stone hall, large hand-threaded tapestries covered the walls, some laced with silver cotton which shimmered in the sunlight. The large windows encased in metal frames held the stained enamelled glass of painted flowers and vines, sun rays illuminating every corner of the monumental room.

Prominently placed upon a raised surface sat the throne of dignitary itself; an enormous wooden chair painted entirely in silver. Chiselled into the armrests were patterns of trailing vines and blossoms with a single red cushion on the flat centre. Next to the Throne was another impressive silver-painted chair with a single pink cushion.

Behind the two prestigious chairs on the floor lay smooth stone slabs that worked as steps leading to a small door, which I knew was the royal entrance for the queen and princess, leading to their private chambers. This door was guarded by an elf warrior of the royal guard.

As I walked towards the throne, the small door opened, and my queen entered. As soon as I saw her, I knelt on one knee and placed my clenched fist up to my chest, just above my heart.

Queen Cassandra was tall and beautiful, her hair was champagne blonde and cascaded down past her waist. Flowing freely except for a few small plaits that were randomly weaved in through her hair and tied at the ends by silver silk strands.

Upon her head, she wore a gold tiara that was embellished with sapphire gemstones. She wore a floor-length ivory silk dress, with thick straps over her shoulders. On her feet were golden flat sandals that made no sound as she gracefully walked from the royal chamber door to the throne in the centre, which was where she sat when being approached by her subjects.

The smaller chair that mimicked the throne in design, was for her daughter, Princess Callidice, who was very rarely present for council meetings. Today was no exception as Queen Cassandra entered the hall and took her place in her seat, without her daughter by her side.

"You may rise my dear Truda, let me look upon you," she said in a gentle tone. As I rose, she smiled at me with endearment.

"My queen, I bring good news. We found some rebels, they were vanquished quickly and easily," I reported proudly, with my head held high; I wanted her approval and respect. I always wanted her to see me as a strong warrior that would defend her kingdom and her life with my own.

"Truda, it brings me great joy to hear of your victory. It brings me even greater joy that you are here before me, telling me the news yourself."

She tilted her head towards me, making me smile. She had always been so kind to me, even more so after we lost my mother. I had lost my parent, but she had lost her best friend, and because of that we had formed a bond, finding comfort in each other.

Queen Cassandra asked me more questions about what had happened in the days of my absence, asking if I had discovered any information of the rumours behind a rebel base hidden beyond the deserts. I told her my soldiers had searched the bodies of the rebels we came across but found nothing. Thinking of the bodies brought me back to thoughts of the pyre where Tobias had burned.

I must have frowned, for Queen Cassandra looked at me with concern.

"Was anyone badly injured?"

"No, my queen." My gaze dropped to the floor, and when

I looked back at her she was watching me as though waiting for me to finish my sentence.

"One of the twins, Shanor, was badly cut on her arm and..." I paused for a moment. "And I lost my house Guan. He was stabbed in the chest by one of the assailants."

I looked directly at the queen when I spoke, hoping that she did not see my hesitation, as my conflicted emotions regarding Tobias's death began to resurface. I was relieved when Queen Cassandra smiled at me sweetly and nodded her head as though she understood.

"I will send for a healer to visit Shanor, ensuring she gets all the care she may need, and I will have a new Guan delivered to your home."

She did not seem phased by me talking about Tobias. I assumed she thought my hesitance and concern was for Shanor as she knew I was close with the twins, recognising their great potential as warriors.

"If you please, my queen, if I am not needed for anything else, I am weary from travel and would like to retire for the evening." I also longed for that hot bath, and a night's sleep in the comfort and luxury of my bed covered in soft furs.

"Of course, Truda, I understand you must be exhausted. I have called for a council meeting first thing tomorrow. I would like you to report your recent events to the council and..." She paused before she continued. "We have some other important matters to discuss."

"Of course, my queen. I will see you then." I saluted towards her and headed home.

The leaves crunched beneath my feet, as I walked through the unfamiliar forest, with trees so tall you could not see the tops. Only a few stray beams of light made it through the thick branches full of green leaves.

My skin shivered as though an icy wind caressed the surface of my body, but not from the breeze, as it was a warm day. With each step, fallen twigs snapped under my toggle boots, which forced me to tread as lightly as I could. The forest was unnaturally quiet. No birds chirping, no whistling of the wind or the creaking of branches as they swayed.

I crept forward, carefully weaving through the trunks, conscious of each step.

I froze as a strange creature came into view.

Ahead of me in the distance, surrounded by a sea of natural greenery, sat a pure white fox; its narrow muzzle turned as it looked towards me. Although visually out of place, it was comfortable with my presence. The fox stretched and slowly crossed its front legs as if demonstrating how confidently relaxed it remained. I slowly approached to investigate. The fox did not move as it lazily basked in the soft green thicket.

A tree rustled behind me, and my hand darted to grab the hilt of my sword whilst I instinctively swivelled to check my surroundings. My breathing was slow and shallow as I listened carefully. I was an intruder here, a prisoner to my surroundings, and the trees were my jailors.

I glanced back to where the fox had been relaxing only to find it was gone. I scanned the forest, my eyes searching for tracks or a sign of a white shape, but there was nothing.

I walked forward once again, with more haste this time. The noise of my steps was no longer a concern as a sense of unease built within me.

A streak of white flashed in front of me, as I pushed forward.

The fox had returned, this time with its back to me. It glanced over its shoulder as if inviting me to follow. I decided to humour the creature and comply with its suggestion, maintaining a safe distance.

The fox took off in a sprint, and for a while, I matched its speed until eventually losing the animal once again. The flick of its shiny tail was my final sight as it disappeared through a small gap within the dense foliage. The ferns and brambles in my path thickened, wrapping around the trunks, blocking my way forward.

I pulled my sword from its sheath on my back, swinging the steel blade in all directions to clear a path. Once my route was open, the end of the treeline came into view, a grass field bathed with sunshine in the distance. My heart skipped a beat, and I sprinted towards the light.

A figure stepped from beside a tree at least a metre in front of me, with their back turned.

I halted.

My body tensed, I held my sword forward with both hands, creating a steel barrier of protection between me and this potential threat. The stranger turned, I gasped in shock when my eyes landed on her face.

She looked nearly identical to me, yet there were some differences between us. We could easily pass as the same person if it were not for her softer features. While my body was well covered with thick leather clothes and plated armour, hers was on display. She wore a sage green cotton dress that fell just above her knees—a beautiful match to the shade of our eyes. The thin, loosely stitched material showed off the attributes of our body that I always hid. She had a narrow waist that was supported by long, strong legs, a toned stomach, and an ample sized chest, the shape of her breasts more visible in this poor excuse for a garment. With thin hide slippers on her feet, and no weapon or sword, she clutched a basket full of wild mushrooms.

Her long russet hair, the colour of autumn, was left loose, hanging beyond her shoulders. In the spring and summer months, my auburn hair would be full of flecks of gold, lightened by the sun's rays as I spent hours in the daylight—just as her hair did now, shining in the sun's beams of light between the trees.

"Who are you?" I asked. She did not respond or react to my presence as she gazed in the distance beyond where I stood, as though I was invisible. A branch snapped loudly as someone or something was approaching me from behind. I recoiled and sharply inhaled.

Turning to find two cloudy white eyes staring at me from underneath a dark hooded cloak, they whispered my name... "Truda."

I jolted awake, my heart pounding, sweat beads rolling down my forehead. A dream so vivid, I could still smell the damp shrubbery with the hint of a sweet floral scent coming from the flowers. The mysterious cloaked figure with white eyes, and the one who looked like me.

Who were those people? I had experienced strange dreams before, but nothing so intense.

"Tobias!" I called instinctively. Grunting to myself when I allowed a moment to pass, and my surroundings again became familiar.

I was home. Alone.

The images of blood and the sound of my name spoken with his last breath resurfacing. Running a hand through my hair I sat up, dangling my legs over the side of the bed.

Silently I rose, ignoring the grumblings of my stomach as I donned my armour. I was fully composed by the time I reached the palace.

Inside the Throne Room, it was the same as before except for one difference; the usual large rectangle table now sat in front of the queen's throne and around it were four other chairs.

One meant for me, as general, the second for Acqueline, my closest friend and head of the royal guard. The third chair belonged to Peril, she was Master of Guans and operated the Breeding House, amongst other things. Finally, in the last seat was Freyja, ambassador of the Mages Temple.

Acqueline and Peril were already there, just about to take their seats. Hearing me enter, they both looked towards me and smiled.

As I got to my seat, we struck up a conversation while waiting for the others. We did not have to wait long before Freyja entered. She quickly grimaced at me before taking her seat. Then the queen appeared from her private entrance and walked towards our table. We stopped our conversation and respectfully looked towards her, watching as she took her seat.

"I would like to make this meeting brief," said Queen Cassandra. "We have two things on the agenda this morning," she said, scanning across the table to all of us. I nodded in respect when her eyes reached mine. I could see her serious gaze soften for a moment, although she did not smile.

"General Truda, please can you report to the council on yesterday's events." She gestured her hand for me to speak. I stood from my chair and looked around the table as I reported on my scouting efforts and the ambush.

"Did you find out anything about the rumoured secret rebel base?" Peril asked.

"I am afraid not, but I believe I am getting closer." That was not exactly true, but I had certainly searched out enough lands in the kingdom to rule out many places, meaning I must be closer to finding it. If it even existed.

With that, I nodded my head to the council members and sat back in my seat. As Queen Cassandra prepared herself to speak again, I glanced towards Freyja who, to my surprise, was glaring at me with a huge grin. Why was she staring at me like that? Had I said something amusing?

"In light of this news, I think we can agree that the rebels are not currently much of a concern, or threat to the city. Despite not knowing the location of this rumoured base, their numbers are low, attacks are infrequent, and after taking advice from other members of the council, I think now is as good a time as we shall have."

She then looked directly at me. What was she talking about? I glanced over to Acqueline, who was looking at the queen puzzlingly; she did not know what was going on either.

"General Truda, we have assigned you a breeder. You are to report the Guan Master's House, where your schedule for conception shall be supplied." My mouth dropped open. I blinked and gasped in shock.

Printed in Great Britain
by Amazon

62720946R00241